The twin trails led down into the wilderness. After the first two hundred meters, the people who had taken the meteorite hadn't bothered to sweep their tracks. Trailing them became easier. Hella could almost jog and track at the same time.

"Some kind of sled?" Riley paced Stampede, both of them to the left of Daisy.

Stampede kept his head moving, tracking motion all around them. Shadows danced constantly across the ground, and the moving grasses made spotting anyone lying in wait along the impromptu trail difficult.

Hella pushed her fear aside and concentrated on her tracking skills. That was one area where her abilities transcended Stampede's.

"Yeah. A sled." Stampede kept his voice low.

"Why didn't they use a vehicle?"

"Because the 'Chine don't frequent trade camps and they're too mobile to set up stills to make their own fuel."

"They're primitives?"

Stampede snorted derisively. "Not like anything you've ever seen before."

"Then what are they?"

"Machine people. 'Chines."

Riley glanced at Hella. "You mean with nanobots?"

"No. I mean cyborgs. The way the story goes, there was a group of military survivors here or in Texas that tried to hide out after the collider self-destructed. They remained in lockdown for a few generations, till all their stockpiles were gone, before coming back out into the world. By that time they were inbred and physically deformed. They fixed what they could with military prosthetics. One of the military detachments was a medical unit working on next-gen bionics and neural mapping. So maybe things turned out better than they would have otherwise. But the way things turned out was pretty horrifying."

ALSO BY
MEL ODOM

SOONER DEAD

MEL ODOM

A

GAMMA WORLD

NOVEL

Dungeons & Dragons
Sooner Dead

©2011 Wizards of the Coast LLC

Published by Wizards of the Coast LLC

Printed in the U.S.A.

Cover art by Jason Chan

First Printing: February 2011

9 8 7 6 5 4 3 2 1

ISBN: 978-0-7869-5736-1
ISBN: 978-0-7869-5886-3 (e-book)
620-28053000-001-EN

U.S., CANADA, ASIA, PACIFIC,	EUROPEAN HEADQUARTERS
& LATIN AMERICA	Hasbro UK Ltd
Wizards of the Coast LLC	Caswell Way
P.O. Box 707	Newport, Gwent NP9 0YH
Renton, WA 98057-0707	GREAT BRITAIN
+1-800-324-6496	Save this address for your records.

Visit our web site at www.wizards.com

IN THE FALL OF 2012, scientists at the Large Hadron Collider in Geneva, Switzerland, embarked on a new series of high-energy experiments. No one knows exactly what they were attempting to do, but a little after 3 p.m. on a Thursday afternoon came the Big Mistake, and in the blink of an eye, many possible universes all condensed into a single reality.

In some of these universes, little had changed; it didn't make a big difference, for example, which team won the 2011 World Series. In other universes, there were more important divergences: The Gray Emissary, who was carrying gifts of advanced technology, wasn't shot down at Roswell in 1947; the Black Death didn't devastate Europe in the fourteenth century; the dinosaurs didn't die out; Nikola Tesla conquered the world with a robot army, and so on. The Cold War went nuclear in eighty-three percent of the possible universes, and in three percent the French unloaded their entire nuclear arsenal on the town of Peshtigo, Wisconsin, because it had to be done. When reality stabilized again, an instant after the Big Mistake, the familiar Earth of the twenty-first century was replaced by one formed from many different realities.

The year is now 2162 (or 151, or 32,173, or Six Monkey Slap-Slap, depending on your point of view). It's been a hundred and fifty years since the Big Mistake, and the ruins of the Ancients (that's you and me) litter a landscape of radioactive deserts, mutated jungles, and vast, unexplored wildernesses. Strange new creatures roam a world populated by beetles the size of cars and super evolved badgers with Napoleonic complexes. The survivors of humanity gather in primitive tribes or huddle in trade towns that rarely rise above the technology of the Dark Ages. Even the nature of humanity is now different, because generations of exposure to radiation, mutagens, and the debris of other realities have transformed humans into a race of mutants who have major physical alterations and potent mental abilities.

Fluctuating time lines, lingering radiation and toxins, and strange creatures and technology transposed from alternate dimensions have combined to create a world the Ancients would think of as the height of fantasy. But to the inhabitants of Gamma Terra, fantasy is the reality.

GAMMA WORLD™

Welcome to the post-apocalyptic world of Gamma Terra

SOONER DEAD

CHAPTER 1

Thunder rolled across the night sky and shivered through Hella as she leaned against the trees on the hillside. Rainwater gurgled as it raced along the ground beside her and joined the swift-moving creek fifty meters down. A hundred meters farther up the hill, in the cold camp in the Buckled Mountains where Hella and Stampede had bedded down the expedition, Daisy snuffled mournfully. The mountain boomer didn't like storms. She would be tired and miserable in the morning.

Hella smiled as she turned her face up to the sky, though. The thunder and lightning, the pouring rain, all of it combined to make her feel truly alive. She wondered if the storm made the creature stalking them feel the same way. She ran her fingers through her long, red hair and pulled it back.

The thing certainly wasn't afraid. It hadn't holed up during the rainstorm as a lot of predators would have.

For three days, the beast had trailed them through the Redblight in what had been western Oklahoma before the collider melted down nearly two hundred years before and changed the world. A creature that big—and it was big, Hella knew from the occasional glimpses she'd gotten of its movements during the night—was dangerous. Only predators stayed focused so long. Nonthreatening creatures would have gotten bored and wandered off. The rain would have been a natural deterrent.

Lightning blazed across the sky, searing the wine-dark clouds that scudded across the quarter moon. For a moment the earth stood out from the shadows, the rocks bare and white like broken bones pushing free from the dark flesh of the earth. The running water looked like streams of silver threading across the uneven landscape.

A flicker of movement below caught Hella's eyes. Instinctively she shoved her hands away from her sides. Almost instantly her hands morphed, changing from flesh-and-blood into tribarreled pistols at her command. Her body metabolism shifted the nano-bots within her to high production, prepared to absorb the lead and chemicals from her backpack and turn it into rounds for her pistols.

When the lightning cut the sky again, she caught a brief glimpse of the creature less than a hundred meters away. The fur was dark and matted, maybe a mottled gray and black, but the beast looked powerful and not timid. Festering, yellow eyes reflected the lightning; then with a blink, they disappeared.

Quietly as she could, Hella shifted beneath the microweave camouflage blanket she'd taken with her to keep watch. Daisy snuffled again then bleated mournfully. Hella wondered if the predator thought of Daisy as prey or if the big lizard had been part of the reason the thing had hung back for so long. Daisy was intimidating to many things, including several that were larger than she. The lizard hunted her meals too, and she was deadly in the wilderness.

Breathing rhythmically, Hella tapped the comm in her ear to wake Stampede. "Wakey, wakey."

Stampede answered almost immediately. He always came up out of sleep and into full wakefulness in a heartbeat. Despite the fact that she and Stampede had been friends and partners for several years, Hella still had a hard time accepting how quickly he could shift from sleep.

Lightning blazed across the sky again, and the peal of thunder that followed sounded like a cannon shot. Hella's ears rang.

"We have company?" Stampede kept his voice low, but it rumbled like the thunder as well.

"Yeah. And it's getting more curious."

Stampede snorted and that sound wasn't human at all. "Or hungry."

"Maybe." Hella let her gaze go loose and didn't focus on anything. Trying to focus in the dark, even without the barrage of light and noise, was foolish. Human eyesight was limited at night, and peripheral vision was strongest. Not looking at something allowed her to see it better.

"Don't know why it couldn't have waited till a decent hour to fill its belly."

If the situation hadn't been so tense, Hella would have grinned at that. Stampede groused about everything. And he hated getting out in the rain.

"Any idea what it is?"

"Something furry."

"So am I."

Hella grinned at that. Stampede took a *lot* longer to dry than she did, and he stank when he was wet. Even he admitted that. "I don't know if it's people-smart, but it's clever enough. And definitely patient."

"If I'm going to get out in the rain, I'm ready to hunt it." Stampede growled a curse. "I'm tired of playing cat and mouse with this thing."

"The night will work against us."

"It's never around in the day." Stampede blew out a breath.

"That we can see."

"I know." Gear clanked as Stampede pulled it on. "I'm going to wake Poole and Smothers. Set them up to watch the camp."

"All right." Hella agreed with the choice. They'd been in-country with the expedition for five days. During that time she, like Stampede, had taken stock of the security team the New Mexico scientists had brought with them. None of the guards were used to the Redblight, or the harshness of the wilderness for that matter, but those were the two people Hella would have picked.

"I'll be there in a few. Don't get killed."

SOONER DEAD

3

Hella hunkered down as another lightning bolt seared the night. Then the creature exploded out of the darkness to her right.

. . . . .

The soundless approach caught Hella completely off guard. She'd never faced anything that big that could move so quickly. The appearance was almost like a magician's trick—first she saw it, then she didn't—only in reverse.

She pulled her head down and threw her arms over her face to protect her eyes because there was no time for her to take aim and fire. She had an immediate impression of bulk and wet fur and ferocity as the thing snapped at her with gleaming jaws made even more fiercely white by the lightning flashes.

Driven by the predator's mass, Hella flew backward. Desperately she tried to keep her feet under her, but the muddy ground made that impossible. Her boots tore through the loose earth and slipped. She caught herself on one knee and one gun hand. She felt the mud pack the barrels of that weapon and knew it would take the nanobots in her body a short time to clear the blockage.

Twisting, she aimed her other hand at the darkness and the creature. She couldn't see it, so she aimed by instinct. She willed her gun hand to fire, and rounds cycled through her transformed fingers with rapid-fire barks. Muzzle flashes tore holes in the night, but they also played havoc with her night vision.

Bullets peppered the leaves and branches, causing a flurry of motion. Hella's heart trip-hammered inside her chest when she ceased firing. Another streak of lightning revealed that the creature had ripped away the front of her blouse. The abbreviated chain mail half shirt she wore next to her skin showed fresh scratch marks, and she dimly remembered the bruising second effort the creature had made during the attack. Thin streamers of blood flowed from three scratches beneath the edge of the chain mail. She didn't know if the marks were from teeth or claws. She was certain her attacker had both.

"Hella!" Stampede's bellow rang in Hella's head.

"I'm fine." Hella concentrated briefly, focusing on her gun hands and re-forming them into larger-caliber weapons. If she could have willed them into bazookas, she would have done that. As it was, she'd configured her hands into .50-caliber weapons, the largest she could manage. The new rounds offered sheer knockdown power, but they also took away some of her control and recovery, and they'd deplete her ammo backpack faster.

"Did you get it?"

"No. It nearly got me. Come ahead slow and make sure I know where you are." Hella stood with her knees bent slightly, her weight low and spread so she could manage the slippery earth better. She tried to listen, but the drumming rain and the aftereffects of the loud detonations ringing in her ears ruined her hearing.

Branches jerked into motion to her left.

Immediately Hella pointed her hand at the brush and fired. The heavy recoil jerked her arm and knocked her off balance again as her feet shifted in the mud. She cursed and tried to stare through the rain and the leftover blind spots from the muzzle flashes.

"Hella!" Stampede sounded hoarse. His voice was so loud that the comm nearly ruptured her eardrum, and she heard the echo of his voice—delayed by the distance—coming from farther up the hillside.

"I'm all right." Hella swiveled and kept breathing, making herself use her peripheral vision instead of her direct sight. The creature was still out there. She felt certain about that. It wouldn't die quietly, not something that big and that fierce.

She moved quickly through the brush, dodging behind trees as she went but still maintaining a small area. Standing still did her no go. The creature had found her. At least motion meant her hunter had to move as well.

A branch cracked behind and to her left. Hella swiveled and brought up both hands. The barrels were once more open. A huge form vaulted at her, raking at her with its claws. The chain-mail shirt took another hit, but the claws slid down far enough to slice into her flesh as well. She bit back a cry of pain, thinking that it would be her luck that the creature carried poison on its talons.

She threw herself to one side and fired again, cycling rounds through her hand. No cartridges spilled out. Her body manufactured caseless ammo. There was only the repeated detonations as she unleashed a cascade of death.

A pained yelp rewarded her attention. The predator crashed through the brush without its usual surefooted grace. When she thought back over the image her mind had conjured, she knew the creature stood almost up to her hip.

"The thing's big." Hella stayed in motion, depending on that sixth sense she'd honed in the Redblight and the wilderness to keep her safe. With increasing frequency, the lightning flashes lifted the darkness again and again. Everything looked surreal, and the falling rain painted jagged edges on the world.

"How big?"

"Not as big as a bear, but it reminded me of a coyote. Doglike. Only a lot thicker."

"The coyotes in the Redblight don't grow that big."

"I know." Hella sank in to a large elm tree. She liked the sense of protection the massive tree gave her, but she knew it was false. The thickness of the tree and the density of the brush blinded her as well. She pushed away and kept moving. If it were light, she was certain she could have found the blood trail the creature left.

"Something new, you think?"

"If it was, we'd have heard about it at the trade camps." News and gossip flew like quail at the trade camps. "Something like this, everybody would have been talking about it."

"Maybe it's too new."

Hella considered that. Genetic abominations still cropped up all around the world after the collider exploded. Strange animal life—new creatures as well as hybridized old ones—were the norm. Plant life and climatic conditions had lists of their own. She'd seen examples of all of them.

Something large stepped in behind her, and the presence washed over her. She whirled and brought her gun hands up, aiming for the center mass.

"Don't shoot." Stampede spoke softly but his voice filled the space around them. He stood almost eight feet tall, dwarfing Hella's five foot three. Massive shoulders and a thick neck supported a huge, bovine head. Like his forebears, the buffalo, Stampede had short, curved horns. A gold nose ring gleamed against his muzzle, and gold studs gleamed in his short, tufted ears.

His body was humanoid, but the trace of the animal his ancestors had been remained. His arms and legs were thick as tree trunks, his hands and feet massive. Short brown fur covered his entire body except for his muzzle, palms, and the hooves of his feet. A short, shaggy tail hung out of his leather pants.

He didn't wear a shirt, but he did sport a specially made Kevlar vest with an ammo rack for the huge machine gun/rocket launcher he carried as his main weapon. Twin revolvers, tooled in matte black to fit his hands and fitted with ivory grips, rode his hips in an Old West gunfighter style. He went barefoot, and his shaggy hooves dug into the ground.

"You shouldn't come up behind me like that." Hella drew her hands back but held them out a little from her sides.

"If you heard me, it would hear me." Stampede shifted his rifle and tilted his head. "Is it still here?"

"Has to be." Hella glanced around the woods. Up the hill, Daisy chirped in agitation.

"That stupid dinosaur's not making the situation any better." Stampede stepped in beside Hella. "Let's find that thing and get in out of the rain."

Hella nodded and took point, leaving Stampede to guard her rear. Before she'd gone a dozen careful steps, Stampede grunted in surprise, and his machine gun shattered the night.

Instinctively Hella went to ground then swiveled to face Stampede. He stood out in the open, covered with a stringy layer that closed around him. The sight froze Hella because the stringy mass looked like a huge sprawl of spider's webbing. As she watched, another bundle of the webbing sailed through the air and smacked into Stampede.

The bisonoid growled in rage and tried to move his weapon, but the sticky strands bound it to him. He released the long gun and palmed one of the revolvers then the long knife holstered near his ankle. He pointed the pistol up into the trees and sawed at the webbing with the blade.

Following her partner's line of sight, Hella peered upward. The possibility that the coyote-thing could climb had never entered her mind. She lifted her hands to take aim.

The mutie-coyote scuttled out of the darkness along a branch twenty feet from the ground. For the first time, Hella saw that it had six legs, not four. Mottled in gray and brown, the creature definitely had lupine genes, but—like many things in the world these days—it was much more.

The mutie-coyote paused and opened its long jaws. Instead of a triumphant bay, the creature vomited another ball of webbing that crashed down onto Stampede. The additional strands caused Stampede to topple over as his hooves got tangled in the webbing. He fired the huge revolver. The tracer rounds smacked into the tree near his attacker and left smoldering miniature craters.

Silently the mutie-coyote launched itself from the branch and dropped gracefully onto Stampede. The thing's jaws opened wide to expose the serrated fangs. Then a proboscis extended from its throat. Saliva dripped from the end and spattered Stampede's broad face as he struggled with his bonds.

Hella heaved herself into motion, both hands pointed before her. She was a gun sight, totally locked in on her target and knowing where every bullet would hit. She yelled to startle the mutie-coyote, to let Stampede know she had his back, and to burn off the excess adrenaline that suddenly drenched her system.

The bullets struck the mutie-coyote and tore through flesh. Blood spurted from the wounds, and the creature staggered back under the onslaught, but it turned to Hella and snarled. In the next instant, it vomited a strand of webbing into the trees and swung away.

Hella swung her guns overhead and fired, but the beast was a slithering shadow among the branches.

Beside her, Stampede sliced through the webbing and grabbed his rifle. On his knees, he lifted the big weapon with practiced ease, sighted, breathed out, and fired. A rocket screamed from the muzzle, flashing in and out of sight as the lightning flickered around them.

A heartbeat later a yellow and white explosion burst in the forest and set several trees on fire. Concerned voices mixed in with Daisy's frantic yowling. If they'd been there before, Hella hadn't noticed them. The detonation echoed in her ears.

For a moment Hella thought Stampede had missed his target. Then chunks of mutie-coyote, the fur matted and black and burned off in places, plopped to the ground around them. A leg bounced off Hella's chain-mail shirt and left a greasy blood smear.

Hella kicked the leg away from her. "That was nasty."

"Yeah."

High up on the hill, someone cut loose with an automatic weapon. Then laser blasts illuminated the campsite.

Stampede cursed and reloaded as he kicked free of the webbing. Hella already had the point.

CHAPTER 2

"You were supposed to be here! We're paying you to protect us! You can't do that if you leave us in the middle of the night and go haring about in the dark!" Klein Pardot, the head of the New Mexico expedition, frothed at the mouth as he declared his displeasure.

Hella stared at the man and kept her jaw cranked shut. Everything in her screamed to punch him in the face. Maybe she would have too, except Stampede stepped between them and pushed her back. Grudgingly Hella allowed her partner to take over. Despite outward appearances, the bisonoid was the better peacekeeper and more levelheaded in times of stress.

"Mr. Pardot—" Stampede looked down at the little man.

"It's not *Mr.* Pardot." The scientist's voice was shrill and quite possibly the most annoying sound Hella had ever heard, even worse than the mating call of a rabid Arkansas razorback. Over the past few days, she'd grown sick of hearing the man speak. "It's *Dr.* Pardot."

"My apologies, *Dr.* Pardot."

Despite the more than half a meter difference in their heights, Pardot didn't seem intimidated in the slightest by Stampede. The bisonoid stood his ground with arms folded like he got yelled at in the middle of the night under pouring rain every night. Anything less than a paying client would have gotten pounded.

The expedition security men looked uncomfortable and even a little embarrassed. A couple of them wore fearful expressions, as if they were afraid they would have to try to subdue Stampede when he'd gotten a belly full. All eight of them had their black hardshells on. The formfitting, protective gear included boots, gloves, and helmets, and all of that contributed to make them look like beetles.

The hardshells provided a lot of protection from guns, knives, and lasers, even some strength and speed enhancement, but they didn't work well out in the wilderness. Inside cities, Hella thought the security guards could have claimed some advantages. But that wasn't true when all movement in the suits looked artificial. Stronger and faster counted when a firefight was going on, but a hunter/predator's ability depended on being able to flow without a misstep and to vanish in a moment if the chance presented itself. The hardshells stood out.

The camp weathered the storm fairly well. Microweave tents kept the rain out and the warmth in. When keyed properly, the tents also turned opaque and kept light trapped inside. One of the guards used a small flamethrower to reignite the fire in the center of the camp area. The microweave canopy covered a four-meter-square area and kept it mostly dry.

Hella held her tongue. Normally after lights-out she wouldn't have allowed any kind of light in camp. Fires kept a lot of animal predators away, but they drew the two-legged kind. The Redblight was rife with brigands and nomadic gangs that preyed on whomever fell in their sights. That night, though, the expedition's anonymity had already been shredded by the gunshots.

The scientists thought they were roughing it, and the idea—when it didn't irritate Hella immensely due to the chronic complaining—amused her. They had no idea of what hardship in the Redblight was. They'd come with tents, sleeping cots, and supplies, and even had engine-powered ATVs to pull small wagons to carry them in.

To Hella, roughing it was cutting back to a bedroll and Daisy. Luxury was a spare set of clothing. Everything else she and

Stampede could get from the wilderness. Of course, the Redblight remained ready to take back everything from the unwary.

"When we procured your services, we were assured you and your partner were two of the best." Pardot was wound up. Based on previous experience with the man, Hella knew the scientist could continue in that vein for a while. Pardot didn't sleep like other people. If he took two or three hours of sleep at a stretch, one of his party would go check to see if he was still alive.

Pardot was one of the oldest men Hella had ever seen. She guessed that the scientist was in his seventies. That age might not be so remarkable in civilized areas, but the Redblight wasn't kind—or even fair—to the young or the old. Pardot had a bulbous, bald head; a thin, pinched face; and thick glasses that made his eyes appear too large. He wore a skeletal support exo that moved him along in a hurried, jerking fashion. Every move seemed to be a twitch and lacked all fluidity. He could never quite manage to stand still while wearing it. As long as the exo was powered, though, he could walk everyone into the ground. The security men had a hard time keeping up with him because of the disparity between the power usage levels required.

"We are the best." Stampede spoke matter-of-factly, without any hint of pride or arrogance. "We were being tracked by an animal, Dr. Pardot. A predator that was determined to hunt us down. My partner risked her life to make sure that stopped tonight. *Before* any of you got hurt."

"You let the *other* one get through when you abandoned us." Pardot gestured back toward the second mutie-coyote sprawled over the collapsed remains of a tent.

The scientist had a point. Scouting for one predator had left the camp open to the second. Hella gritted her teeth. Two of the things hadn't been expected. Large predators usually hunted alone.

"Your men were prepared." Stampede spoke in a level, reasonable voice. "I made sure they were in place. They killed this thing before it could harm anyone."

"The point is, we shouldn't have to protect ourselves. You people were hired to get us across country without anything like this happening. Either you should have killed it before it reached us, or we should have avoided it entirely."

"This is the Redblight, Dr. Pardot." Stampede's words held an edge. Even he wasn't without his limits when it came to a scouting contract. "What you saw tonight, it could be a whole lot worse. The protection you're used to, the *civilization*, you're used to, it all ended days ago. You're in a new world now, and you'd better recognize that. And the decision to settle for just Hella and me was yours. You were the one that wanted a small group."

Hella shook her head at that. Pardot's idea of a "small" group left a lot to be desired. The expedition was heavy with security people. They were a small army. Stampede had pointed that out, and he'd suggested Pardot let him hire more local bodyguards, people Hella and Stampede had worked with. The scientist had refused. Pardot obviously had trust issues. Hella had to admit that was the most understandable quality about the man. The only person she trusted outside of her own skin was Stampede.

"Dr. Pardot." The lean scientist walked up to join them. She had mouse brown hair and a severe face. Her pallor and the resulting sunburn over the past few days suggested she rarely, if ever, got out of a lab. She wore thick rain boots, man's pants that didn't fit her properly, and a shapeless sweater. She had on bloodstained surgical gloves. Spots of blood showed on the sweater as well. "If I may."

Pardot swiveled quickly in his exo, almost looking as though he *hopped* around to face her. "Dr. Trammell, must I remind you that I am not to be interrupted? *Ever*?" He somehow made that sound like doing so was tantamount to a death sentence.

Colleen Trammell stood her ground, though the hesitant expression she wore suggested she'd rather be anywhere else at the moment. "I wanted to point out the possibility that this—*these*—encounters might not have been something our guides could have foreseen."

"Dr. Trammell, the last thing I need is for you to manufacture excuses for these people."

"I wouldn't do that, sir." The woman's expression blanched only slightly in the light from the campfire. "I would like to direct your

SOONER DEAD
13

attention to the nature of the dead beast. I don't believe you've examined it thoroughly."

Pardot waved the suggestion away. "It's a coyote. Genus *Canis*. Species *Canis latrans*. Barking dog. How interesting could something like that possibly be?"

As always, Hella stood in awe of what their charges knew about the world yet didn't really know about living in it.

"When is the last time you've heard of *Canis latrans* having six legs?"

Without a word, Pardot twitch-walked over to the dead animal. Mud splashed with every step. He switched on a mini lamp attached to the exo's head support, and bright light bathed the bloody corpse. "Six legs. There *are* six legs."

"Yes."

Pardot spun back around without switching off the lamp. The bright beam stabbed into Hella's eyes before she covered them with a hand and looked away. "The other creature had six legs as well?"

Hella didn't know how that could possibly mean anything to the scientists.

Stampede nodded. He didn't look into the scientist's light either. "It did."

"This is unusual?"

"Very."

"I've heard that the Redblight is home to all manner of strange creatures." Pardot rubbed his weak chin. "Surely something like this isn't all that uncommon."

"I've lived here all my life. I've never seen anything like these animals. Now and again, you expect a mutation. Every so often, the genetic soup of something gets rattled and you see something like you've never seen before." Stampede held up two huge fingers. "But this is *two* creatures. Exactly the same. Six legs. The ability to spin webs. More like a species than aberrations."

The word rolled off Stampede's tongue. Normally he and Hella didn't keep company where words like that would be exchanged.

Stampede read a lot, though, and he shared a lot of what he read with Hella.

Pardot glanced back at Colleen. "You have a theory?"

"I do. I think they're from a *ripple*."

A chill skated down Hella's back. She didn't know what the event was called anywhere else in the world, but in that part of the world, such occurrences were called ripples. They were a disturbance in the world that opened up brief windows into other worlds of past, present, future, and might-have-beens.

Several creatures that had been extinct in the world before the collider self-destructed had managed to slip into the real-world present as well. Some of them were flourishing again, and they were threatening the food chains in different areas because they had no natural predators. The Redblight's ecosystems were constantly at war with each other, seeking some kind of balance.

"Nonsense." Pardot waved the thought away with a twitch. "If there had been a *ripple*, you'd have noticed it."

"Perhaps I did." Colleen shrugged and looked perturbed. "It's this world, Dr. Pardot. Things just aren't the same as they were back at the lab."

Back at the lab. Not *home.* Those were distinctive word choices—revealing more insight into the tall, angular woman. As a general rule, Colleen Trammel was a closed-mouth person and not at all inclined to gossip. The security men gave her a wide berth as well, but it wasn't out of fear, as their dealings with Pardot were. Rather, her personality was either vacuous or filled with ordinary snobbery for the hired help.

"Nonsense." Pardot adjusted his glasses and pinned the woman with his harsh gaze. "You're sensitive to these things, Dr. Trammell. You would have known. You would have *felt* them. That's what you do."

"There was . . . *something*. I felt it three days ago."

Stampede stepped closer to them. "That was when Hella discovered the predator on our trail."

Pardot didn't look at the bisonoid. "And you didn't think to mention this?"

Trammell shook her head. "That wasn't the ripple we were waiting for, Dr. Pardot. Also, I couldn't tell how far away this ripple was."

"She's a precog." Hella whispered into the comm, low enough that no one around her could hear.

Stampede gave a slight nod to let her know he'd received the message.

A shiver passed through Hella. She didn't care for precogs. Anyone with near-mystical ability to sense things or do things with forces of nature bothered her. Stampede had powers of his own that came from the same weird genetic cocktail that spread throughout the world. Hella's nanobots were pure, definable science. They were quantifiable and she could depend on them.

Precog and psi powers tended to be somewhat unpredictable even in the hands of a master. Stampede struggled with his control at times as well.

Despite everything she'd seen, Hella had never met anyone in tune with the ripples. A skill like that could be worth a lot. Most people avoided the ripples because there was no telling what the time/world holes would vomit out. But she understood why Pardot didn't lash out at the woman.

"Not telling me was a mistake, Dr. Trammell." Pardot grimaced. "You know how I feel about mistakes."

"Yes, Dr. Pardot."

"Don't let this happen again." Pardot spun in a perfect half circle and left Colleen standing there.

Hella blew out a long, slow breath and spoke into the comm. "Tell me again why we need this job."

"Because we're no good lying around. We lose our edge."

Hella snorted. If someone lost his edge in the Redblight, he was dead.

"And I'm interested."

"One of these days, your curiosity is going to get us killed."

Stampede smiled in the rain and the campfire glinted from his golden nose ring. "Maybe."

· · · · ·

Hella tended her wounds in her tent then, unable to sleep because the tent smelled of wet bisonoid fur and maybe because she was still irked at Klein Pardot, took a feedbag to Daisy.

The mountain boomer slept curled around a tree and was relatively dry. The lizard's multicolored skin still gleamed wetly, though. That was how her hide always looked. She was four meters long, including her prehensile tail, which was half her length. When she stood on four legs, she came almost up to Hella's shoulder. Her scales were mottled gray and green and brown, but black bands surrounded her neck and shoulders. Those distinctive patterns gave her species its name: collared lizard.

Daisy slept with her head propped on her forelimbs and looked almost childlike to Hella. When Daisy had first hatched, Hella had been able to hold her in one hand. But that was before the wild card mutation gene had kicked in.

"I know you're not sleeping." Hella ducked under a low-hanging limb to get to Daisy. "You breathe differently when you're really sleeping."

With obvious irritation, the lizard popped open one black eye and gazed at Hella.

"Be mad if you want to, but I'll just take this feedbag back to the tent."

Daisy stirred then, lifting her head and turning it toward Hella. The lizard chirped disconsolately. That was another trait that set her off from her lesser cousins: Daisy was vocal and she had a high intelligence that made her trainable to the sound of a human voice and hand signals. Her tongue slithered out to taste the aroma reeking from the feedbag. She chirped again, more excitedly.

Daisy wasn't leashed to the tree, nor was she hobbled. She stayed with Stampede and Hella because she wanted to. She rose to her full height, and her head towered above Hella's, crashing through the lower tree limbs. Daisy trotted in place eagerly.

"Happy dance." Despite how the night had gone, Hella's spirits lifted at the sight of the lizard acting so childlike.

Lowering slightly, Daisy rubbed her rough head against Hella's shoulder. Hella staggered back for an instant then wrapped an arm around the lizard's big head. As Daisy chirped excitedly, Hella secured the feedbag around the creature's head with Velcro straps.

"How do you know that thing's not going to eat you?"

Hella spun, both of her hands already morphing into weapons.

CHAPTER 3

The man standing three meters away from Hella raised both hands to show that he offered no harm. He wore a hardshell with a machine pistol slung around his neck. His face shield popped open with a liquid hiss and revealed a handsome face and a shock of blond hair so pale it was almost white.

"Easy. Didn't mean to startle you."

Hella flushed, irritated at herself for not knowing the man had walked over to her and equally bothered by the fact that she was pleased to see him.

"Did Riley sneak up on you again, Red?" Stampede's mirth vibrated over the comm. The fact that he'd called her by his nickname for her served to underscore his enjoyment. "I saw him walking over in your direction."

"You might have warned me."

"I don't think he has anything sinister in mind."

"Not used to guys walking up on me, Stampede."

"Not guys that you'd like to have walk up on you, I agree. Riley, though, he's something else, isn't he?"

"A little privacy here?"

"Sure."

Hella knew that Stampede would still monitor the comm, but he wouldn't say anything. When they were in-country, which was nearly all of the time, they never cut the comm link. Staying almost inside the other's head was hard, but it helped them watch over each other. On more than one occasion, the practice had saved their lives.

"Friends?" Riley wore a confused look because she hadn't responded directly to him. "Or maybe I should head back to camp."

Hella turned her hands back into hands again and relaxed. "Something you wanted, Captain Riley?"

Riley put his hands on his equipment belt and smiled at her. "You're a hard person to get to know, Hella."

"You know enough." Hella turned back to Daisy and scratched the lizard under the jaw.

"Probably. But that doesn't make me any less curious. I haven't met many women like you."

Women. The term startled Hella. She was twenty, so she was a woman by most standards. She just didn't think of herself as that. Captain Riley looked at least thirty, and was probably older. In her mind, she was just a scout, just Stampede's partner.

"I'm sure you've met your share of them."

Riley chuckled. "Is that a question?"

"No." But Hella did wonder. Over the past few days, she'd grown more curious about the handsome captain than she was comfortable with. She'd learned early to stay away from men.

"Sounded kind of like a question."

Hella concentrated on her anger. At least that part of the emotions darting around inside her was something she understood. She wheeled on Riley. "If I have a question, I come right out and ask it."

"Then maybe I should too."

Hella didn't say anything. She stayed focused on the man and wished he'd go away. She wanted to be by herself.

"Dr. Pardot hired you. I didn't get much of a chance to interview you. The last few days, we've both been busy with our respective responsibilities."

The way he spoke sounded soothing to Hella.

"Normally I like to do my own investigating when it comes to people I'm going to work with."

"Do you work with a lot of people, Captain Riley?" Hella wanted the answers to questions of her own, and she knew how to barter.

Surprise flashed in the man's eyes. "Sometimes. Depending on what I'm doing for Dr. Pardot."

"Have you always worked for him?"

"No. There have been other scientists at the lab that I've handled security for before."

"But you haven't been to the Redblight before?"

"No."

Hella studied the man and regretted the fact that so little of Riley's face was visible through the face shield and that the hard-shell masked his true body language. A person's body language gave away a lot. "Then why come now?"

"Because I work with Dr. Pardot, and this is where he wanted to go."

"Why?"

Riley hesitated. "I seem to be giving more answers than I'm getting."

Hella stroked Daisy's muzzle. The lizard chomped in noisy satisfaction. "Ask."

"How long have you and Stampede been together?"

"Nine years." Hella had barely been surviving on her own and been old enough to start pinging men's radar as female. She'd learned to cut and run, and she'd learned to hunt in the wilderness. Stampede had taught her the rest.

"You don't look that old."

"I was eleven."

"Kind of young."

"Not for the Redblight. A lot of kids grow up without their parents. Or they don't grow up at all. I got lucky. Stampede had just lost his partner."

"Then why didn't he take on another partner?"

Hella arched a challenging brow. "Not a kid?"

Riley looked uncomfortable. "That's not what I meant."

"I think it is. Anyway, to answer your question, you'd have to ask him."

"I was trying to figure out the relationship."

Stampede laughed in Hella's ear.

Hella made her voice cold. Riley seemed to understand that from Dr. Pardot just fine. "We're partners."

"All right. I just didn't want to be stepping on any toes."

"How would you do that?" Hella put on an innocent face, as if she didn't have a clue what he was talking about.

"In case your partner was . . . *interested* in you."

"He is interested in me." Hella adjusted the feedbag so Daisy could get to the bottom. "If I'm alive, he's got a better chance of staying alive too. That's about as interested as you can get, Captain Riley."

Riley rubbed the back of his neck. His armored glove clanked against his helmet. "I just haven't ever seen a bisonoid before."

"And you didn't know if Stampede was interested in human women?"

"You do get straight to the point, don't you?"

"Saves time. You save time out in the Redblight, you're likely saving your own skin. Or someone whose skin you've been hired to protect." Hella shook the feedbag again. "As to Stampede's sexual preferences, you'll have to ask him. I do know for a fact that a lot of women like Stampede." The bisonoid had women in all the trade camps they visited, and he had no problem connecting with women on expeditions.

"But not you?"

"No. Not me. You're getting personal."

Riley shrugged. "I like knowing how people work together. That's part of my job."

"We won't be working together long." Hella unfastened the feedbag. "Hopefully Dr. Pardot will find whatever it is he's looking for soon. Then you won't have to learn one more thing about me." She paused. "I would like to know what this expedition is looking for."

"Even if I could tell you, I wouldn't."

"Then I suppose we're through exchanging pleasantries, Captain Riley. Good night." Hella tossed the feedbag over her shoulder and walked back to camp. Riley followed her, and she knew he watched her every step of the way.

. . . . .

Hella stood outside the canopied area where Dr. Colleen Trammell performed an autopsy on the dead mutie-coyote. She'd even had some of Riley's men search the forest for the bits and pieces of the one Stampede had killed. Those pieces lay arranged on a silica skein, a piece of fabric so thin that stains couldn't take hold. Hella knew she could have bartered the fabric dearly at a trade camp. And Colleen treated it like a kitchen utensil.

Colleen worked like a machine, slicing and removing organs and musculature with a surgeon's skill. Blood splattered her clothing, her mask, and her goggles. A robotic assistant spread thin arms around her, recording audible and visual input as Colleen worked.

The mutie-coyote lay husked out on the collapsible table. One of the ATVs carried a generator that hummed quietly as it supplied power to Colleen's tools.

After a moment, Colleen put one of the laser knives down and looked up at Hella. "Would you like to come closer?"

"Not really."

"You may never get a chance to see something like this again."

Curiosity finally pulled Hella under the canopy. She gazed at the corpse and almost felt sorry for the creature. Killing it while fighting for her life was one thing, and field dressing it to eat was another, but what Colleen Trammell was doing was almost obscene.

"You really do think this thing is from another time line?" Despite herself, Hella was interested.

"Not from another time line." Colleen picked up an instrument that offered numerical readouts. "Another world. I've never seen genomes like this."

"Another planet?"

Colleen shook her head and absently pulled hair back from her face. As a result she tracked blood through her hair. "No. I think this animal came from another version of our world."

Hella was familiar with the concept. Some of the people Stampede talked science stuff with brought up ideas such as "string theory."

"You're familiar with the idea of multiple earths?"

"Sure. String theory. Dozens of different worlds just one second or genetic breakthrough out of step with the world we know."

"A layman's point of view, but it will suffice." Colleen removed a mass from the dead animal.

"Why are you taking it apart?"

That stopped the woman for a moment. "To study it, of course."

"Why?"

"Because that's what I do to learn things. You've learned to take animals apart too. I've watched you do it."

Hella and Stampede tended to their own meals. They'd guided expeditions in the past that had charged them for food they'd thought was free. And once they'd even been poisoned by a client. They didn't trust anyone if they didn't have to. They also took half the payment up front and hid it before they left.

"I take animals apart to eat them." Hella gazed disdainfully at the hollowed corpse. "There's not anything on that thing I would eat. Unless I was really hungry. And I haven't been that hungry in a long time."

"Didn't you ever take an animal apart to see how it worked? How the legs functioned? Where the heart, liver, and lungs were?"

"No." Hella shivered at the thought. Watching Colleen do an autopsy the first time a few days earlier had almost unnerved her and made her sick. She didn't get sick easily, especially not when fighting.

"Do you know how your hands become weapons?"

Thinking Colleen might have been interested in cutting up her hand since the day Hella had first revealed why she didn't carry pistols made her a bit anxious. She thrust her hands in her pockets. "Sure. I think them into guns. The nanobots do the rest."

"Where did you get those nanobots?"

"I don't know."

Interest lifted one of Colleen's eyebrows. "What do you mean?"

"I never knew my parents. Since the earliest I can remember, I was on my own. Till Stampede made me his partner."

"Then how did you learn you possessed the ability to transform your hands and process materials through your body."

"The first time was an accident." Hella still remembered the old man's wrinkled face as he'd pawed at her in the trade camp. He'd caught Hella raiding the trash bins out back of the tavern, and he'd put a knife to her throat, telling her he would kill her if she didn't stay quiet. Fear had filled her mind with screaming insanity, and she could remember wishing she had a pistol to defend herself. Then she had and she'd killed the man. She still remembered his hot blood raining down on her. But she'd retained enough composure to steal everything of value from him before fleeing. "After that, Stampede took me to a man he knew—a professor of science, like you—and he told me I had nanobots inside me."

"Couldn't he identify them?"

The uncomfortable feeling inside Hella multiplied. She'd made a mistake accepting Colleen's invitation. "No. When he tried to take a blood sample, the nanobots made me leave."

"They can control you?"

"Not really. But they can make me afraid enough that leaving isn't an option."

"What about when you're asleep?"

"They watch over me. If someone sneaks up on me, they'll shoot him—or her—at the first sign of trouble."

Colleen frowned. "That's unpleasant."

"I just think of it as a security system."

"You could be drugged."

"No, I can't. The nanobots process drugs and poisons and render them ineffective almost immediately."

"Amazing."

Hella shrugged. She was what she was. She didn't question the way her body worked any more than she questioned Stampede's ability to manipulate the earth with his power.

"You've been wounded before?"

"Sure."

"What about that blood?"

Hella shook her head. "The nanobots don't leave my body. Stampede had a friend examine bandages from when I'd been shot. When he looked, there weren't any nanobots in the blood."

"They stayed in your body."

"Maybe. Stampede thinks maybe they deconstruct themselves when they're outside of me. Don't leave anything behind."

"Interesting." Colleen rubbed a knuckle against her chin as she thought about what she'd been told. Blood streaked her thin face. "What about the lizard?"

"Daisy? I found her when she was a baby and kept her."

Colleen smiled and she looked more human than Hella had ever imagined she would. "That sounds like something my daughter would do."

"You have a daughter?"

"Yes." Colleen stripped off her gloves and took a PDA from her pocket. She punched a couple of buttons then showed the summoned image to Hella. The PDA screen showed a little girl, maybe eight or nine, with mouse brown hair like her mother. The girl clutched a pink pig to her cheek and smiled happily.

"Nice kid." Hella didn't know anything else to say. Most of the kids she met in the trade camps or on the roads were thieves and con artists in the making. None of them would have held a stuffed pig like that unless they were trying to make someone else think it was worth something.

"She is a wonderful child." Colleen smiled tenderly at the image.

"Why didn't you bring her with you?"

The smile slipped and almost gave way to sadness. Then Colleen put away the PDA. "She's safer at home. I couldn't bring her to this place." She cleared her throat. "So you found Daisy. Did you know that she was going to grow so large?"

"No."

"But you're not afraid of her? She seems awfully fierce."

"She is fierce. Daisy will defend me or Stampede to the death."

"How do you know that?"

Hella shrugged. "Because she told me."

That seemed to surprise Colleen. "The lizard can speak to you?"

"No. But she thinks things. Something like that, I know what she's thinking."

"I see."

Though the professor said that, Hella didn't really think the woman did. Then she changed her mind. "You're psi sensitive, aren't you?"

For a moment Colleen looked as if she wouldn't answer. Then she let out a long breath. "I am, though Dr. Pardot would think me remiss for giving out such information."

"There wasn't much to give out. Stampede and I already had that figured."

"You're very observant."

"Keeps us alive. So what can you do?"

"Every now and again, I can see glimpses of the future. Sometimes those glimpses just surround an event. Other times they focus on an individual." Colleen grimaced. "Unfortunately most of those glimpses are tainted with darkness and evil."

"You can also track ripples."

Colleen pressed her lips firmly together and looked even more stressed. "It might be a good idea not to let Dr. Pardot know you're in possession of such knowledge."

"All right. But you can sense the ripples?" It was a lot for the woman to admit to. Such an ability would be highly prized by many people. Not for the first time, Hella wondered what the lab where the scientists came from was like.

"Yes."

"Is that why you're here in the Redblight? To track ripples?"

"I'm afraid you're way past anything I feel comfortable answering at this point." Colleen glanced around at the security guards. "Dr. Pardot keeps a tight rein on things."

Stampede whispered into Hella's mind. "Back off, Red. You're not going to get anything more from her, and you don't want her retreating to Pardot's side after she's been at least a little forthcoming with us."

Hella knew that was true, but she wished she could learn more.

Everything they didn't know threatened Stampede and her. "I understand. Thank you for telling me what you have."

Colleen hesitated. "I want you to know, Hella, that the reason we're here is important. And not just to Dr. Pardot. Your efforts, and those of your partner, are deeply appreciated."

Hella glanced meaningfully at the eastern sky. "Not much time left before dawn. The morning's going to come early. I'm going to try to get some sleep. You should probably do the same."

"I will. It's been interesting talking to you, Hella."

"Thanks. I enjoyed it too." Hella walked away and thought about Colleen having a daughter. That had truly surprised her. As cold and driven as the woman acted, Hella hadn't expected that. The knowledge gave Colleen a more human aspect that Hella didn't know if she was prepared to acknowledge.

"Everybody's hiding something." Stampede snuffled, sounding on the edge of sleep.

"I know but their secrets are dangerous to us too."

"Me and you, we've always lived on the edge, Red. Do you really want to change that now?"

Hella smiled sourly. Even if there were a way, she couldn't imagine any other life she'd want to live.

CHAPTER 4

Hold up." Hella reined in Daisy, and the mountain boomer stopped immediately and went low to the ground. While astride her, Hella knew she was a tall target for enemy gunners. The tradeoff was that she could see a long distance and the lizard was incredibly fast.

"What's wrong?" Stampede spoke over the comm link. He'd have already pulled the expedition into safe positions.

"There's a smudge to the east." Hella shaded her eyes with a hand and squinted against the misty brightness. Her eyes felt grainy and irritable from lack of sleep, and she hated the continued soaked feeling from the rain. "Do you see it?"

More heavy rain still threatened from the low, gray clouds that scudded slowly across the sky. The air was thick and moist, and she felt the cycling heat and cold flashing through the air. With the way the weather was behaving, they could be in for a tornado. She'd heard that before the collider had exploded the Redblight had suffered seasonal storms that left great tracts of ruination. At least during that time the tornadoes were somewhat predictable. The weather in her time permitted tornadoes to form at nearly any time, even in the chill of winter.

"I see it. Thought it was just a dust cloud."

"Too wet to have dust."

Stampede growled unhappily. "Wasn't thinking."

"Deener's Crossing lies out that way. This time of year, there'll be a lot of caravanning, getting crops in and trying to turn a profit. That always draws the brigands."

Stampede heaved a curse. "Agreed. We can go around Deener's Crossing."

"After that rain last night?" Hella studied the dark smudge threading through the sky. "Flatbottom Creek will be washed out and running white. It'll be more like a river. We can't cross that unless we travel ten miles north. I don't think Pardot would be happy about that since he's so dead set about going in this direction. Brigands will travel the creek too."

"All right. Let's get these people situated; then you and I will ride up and take a look."

Despite the wind she saw bending the trees, the smudge remained consistent against the sky. Hella turned Daisy back toward the expedition.

· · · · ·

Klein Pardot was in another foul mood when Hella reached the expedition. Or maybe he was still in the same mood from the previous night. The little man slogged through the mud and struggled to keep his exo under control. "I don't see why we're supposed to stay here."

"Because you'll be safe if something goes wrong." Stampede talked slowly, as he would to a child.

"I question your logic. We'd be just as safe if we rode with you."

Stampede gripped his big rifle and glared down at the professor. "You hired me because I'm good at what I do, Dr. Pardot. If I say that riding on without checking out that smoke is dangerous, then it's dangerous. The last thing you want to do is get too sudden into a situation that can get you killed. Now if you don't want to take my advice, you're welcome to ride on ahead. But my partner and I won't be riding with you."

Hella sat atop Daisy and watched the security men. If any of them tried to push on ahead, she'd let them go. But if any of them attempted to draw a weapon on Stampede, she would drop them.

"Sir." Riley's voice was calm as he rode his ATV beside Pardot. "I don't think that smudge is from a dust storm either. It looks like smoke."

"According to the maps—"

Hella snorted in disgust at that. Maps were almost useless in the Redblight. Maps showed where things *might* be, where they *should* be, if they hadn't been destroyed, but they didn't keep up with all the things that could get a person killed.

Pardot glared at Hella for interrupting him. "There's a village ahead of us." He sounded like a petulant child.

"Not exactly a village, sir. It's a trade camp. Deener's Crossing. They've got supplies and goods to barter for there. That was one of our scheduled stops. But the place is also a target for roving marauders." Riley looked at Stampede. "I think we need to do what he says."

Pardot grimaced as he swallowed a sharp retort. "Get it done quickly, Captain."

"Yes, sir." Riley touched two fingers to his headgear in a small salute. The face shield winked shut. "We'll be back soon as we can."

Or you won't be back at all. Hella thought that but she stopped herself before she said it because she didn't want to jinx them.

. . . . .

Hella took the lead, riding low on Daisy as they followed the trade track worn through the thick trees and brush. Animal hooves as well as tire treads had left impressions on the soft ground, and the trail was concave from years of wear and tear.

Instead of riding on the trail, though, Hella kept Daisy ten meters off to the left, following in tandem. Stampede and the security men followed a hundred meters back, and the silenced drives of the ATVs never reached her.

She listened to the birds chirping around her, to the scurry of lizards, rabbits, and ground fowl cutting through the brush. If those noises hadn't taken place around her, she would have known someone else was nearby. Riley and his men probably wouldn't have known that. They were used to relying on night vision and thermal imaging systems built into the hardshells. Those were useful crutches for someone not born to the wilderness, but anyone not used to the forest was a cripple. Technology didn't help a neophyte understand the language of the feral world around them.

When she'd been younger, Hella had been fascinated by tech, mostly because her body was full of nanobots that she didn't understand. She'd fallen in love with the gadgets and gizmos hucksters had brought out for barter. Stampede had pointed out the inherent weaknesses in the systems, that circuitry could fail, power supplies could drain, and that she would lose the natural sense she had of the world. Reluctantly, then, Hella had bypassed the devices that had so amazed her.

She sniffed the air too. Much of what happened in an area could be sensed on the breezes for someone who'd trained to notice such things. The odor of burned wood and fuel pinched her nostrils.

Another eighty meters on, she urged Daisy up the incline toward the trail. A bridge spanned Flatbottom Creek there, one of those steel-and-concrete remnants from the old world that had somehow survived the past one hundred fifty years of strangeness. Bits and pieces of the old highway that had once led to the bridge shoved up through the earth in places.

Hunkered in the lee side of a massive oak tree, Hella peered down the length of the bridge. It was almost a quarter-klick long. In a few places, holes gaped in the expanse. Still, it was navigable on horseback or by groundcrawlers such as the ATVs Riley and his men rode. Surplus steel had been taken by scavengers, and only the flat surface of the bridge remained.

Hella took a pair of binocs from her chest pouch and held them to her eyes. The binocs whirred as the servos automatically adjusted the magnification and focus. Stampede wasn't against all tech. Binocs and cutting-edge weapons were adopted with relish, but he haggled for them fiercely.

Two corpses littered the bridge. Both men had been shot in the back, evidently while trying to flee, and had been picked over. No gear or firepower remained on them, and one man's boots had been taken.

On the other side of the creek, Deener's Crossing sat in ruins. The whole trade camp had consisted of three permanent buildings. Two hundred years earlier, the place had been a farmhouse, barn, and an outbuilding, all made of cinderblock against the tornadoes. Transitory shelters, mostly tents, had filled in some of the empty places around those buildings, all of them paying rent to the merchant who ran the trade camp.

The tents sat in pools of tattered ash, and the three buildings had all suffered severe damage. All of the structures had broken walls that had tumbled inward, and the barn lay in devastation like two halves of a broken egg.

More bodies littered the cracked hardpan road that lay between the buildings. The road continued beyond Deener's Crossing, but the forest had already reclaimed most of it. A larger city had once lain in that direction, but large cities had been the first to die when the food shortages and transportation problems started after the effects of the collider kicked in.

Sickness twisted through Hella's stomach as she put away the binocs. She'd known some of the people who had lived in Deener's Crossing. Most had been good people, and even the worst among them hadn't deserved what she saw.

"Stampede."

"Yeah."

"I don't think there's anyone left alive there."

Stampede didn't answer right away. "Before we bring the others in, we need to know for certain. I don't want to walk into an ambush."

"Okay." Hella urged Daisy up onto the trail then across the bridge. The lizard's claws scraped and skittered against the concrete.

When they passed the first of the dead bodies, Hella glanced down at the corpse, wondering if she'd recognize the man. Thankfully she didn't. The second was unknown to her as well.

She hated crossing the bridge. It had been a long time since she'd felt that exposed. Constant awareness of what a sniper could do left a permanent chill threading through her spine.

. . . . .

"Whoever it was slaughtered the whole trade camp." Stampede pulled a dead man into the pile they'd made in the center of the area between the buildings. "With this much firepower backing them, I'd bet it's a brigand gang that's trying to stay together instead of splitting up." He snarled in disgust and spit. "Idiots."

"What are you talking about?" Riley pushed a dead woman onto the pile.

"The vermin that did this got too big." Stampede glared at the collection of bodies. "As harsh as the world is these days, it's hard for a city to survive. Gangs like this are better off staying to smaller numbers. They're not farmers; they're predators. A predator has to have a hunting ground that will support it. Otherwise it overhunts an area and runs out of prey, eventually starving out or cannibalizing itself. Brigand groups aren't much above hunter-gatherer clans. If they get too large, they have to separate, find separate hunting territories."

"In order to survive, this group has to kill more people?"

Hella dragged over the body she'd found. She tried not to look too closely at the face in case she recognized the woman. "They don't have to kill more people. They have to take more supplies, more food and trade goods, clothing and ammunition. In order to do that, they generally take those things from people not willing to give them up. Killing people is just part of the process."

"Why didn't the trade camp just give up their goods?"

Anger stirred inside Hella. She wanted to know what Riley's life in the lab had been like because he certainly had no clue what things were like in the Redblight. "Because out here the things these people had are hard to come by." She knew her anger was audible in her tone, but she just didn't care. They were burning children too. "Giving up those things meant they might not eat either. No one lives in the land of plenty out here. I don't know how things are back where you came from."

Riley looked somber. "Where are the people that did this?"

"Where are the monsters, you mean. People didn't do this." Hella turned her face up into the light rain and let it cleanse her. She shook her head. "They're holed up somewhere. They'll eat and drink what they've taken then stake out their next target and repeat this."

"Unless they're stopped." Stampede brought over a new body and heaved it onto the ground at Riley's feet. "Not all of them got away."

The body on the ground looked humanoid, but genetically its ancestry could be tracked back to an armadillo. The creature had two arms and two legs, but it also had an abbreviated tail and a shell that shielded it from shoulders to mid thigh. Lizardlike hide, crusty and dense, covered the male from head to toe. The hide was dark brown and ochre, and the shell was slightly lighter and had a greenish cast. The broad face was too wide, and the mouth curved cruelly. Ill-fitting leather clothing covered it, pants, a vest, and wide boots.

"What is that?" Riley unconsciously lifted his machine pistol in both hands.

"Dead now." Stampede kicked the corpse, which rolled loosely. "It's a Sheldon."

"I don't understand the reference." The face shield hid Riley's lack of understanding, but Hella heard the confusion in his amplified voice.

"Maybe they were armadillos before the collider broke down and mutated them into something near human." Stampede grabbed a fistful of the black leather vest and yanked the dead creature over onto its back. "Or maybe they stepped out of a ripple a hundred years ago and set up shop here. They're strong-arms, sometimes hiring out to protect caravans, and they're brigands, stealing from anyone weaker than themselves. They're crafty and canny but not really intelligent. And they're not loyal to anyone that isn't one of them."

Hella knelt and went through the dead thing's clothing. "They're known locally as Sheldons."

"Because of the shell?" Riley leaned in for a closer look.

"I don't know." Hella looked up at Stampede. "His clanmates took time to strip him before they left."

"Figured as much." Stampede rolled the body over to expose the image on the back of the leather vest.

Whoever had made the marking had spent time with it. The image of a rearing dragon had been burned into the leather; then purple coloring had been rubbed into it. Scarlet trimmed the image, making it stand out in bold relief.

"He was a Purple Dragon." Stampede growled. "I've heard of them."

"I thought they were south of the Red River." Hella stood.

"Evidently they aren't anymore." Frowning, Stampede grabbed the dead Sheldon and heaved it on top of the pile of dead despite its bulk.

· · · · ·

Two more armadillos turned up in the woods outside the three buildings. One of Riley's men also found three motorcycles in a ditch farther out.

Hella surveyed the mishmash of tracks that tore up the ground. "Can't make out how many riders there are."

Stampede nodded. "A lot." He frowned at the surrounding woods. "We'll do our best to stay away from them."

Taking Daisy's reins, Hella stepped back into the stirrup and remounted. The mountain boomer was twitchy. Being around that much food—that was how she viewed the bodies of the slain—made her harder to control. Despite her above-average lizard intelligence, Hella hadn't been able to convince Daisy that eating dead people was not all right. The tendency had put off a lot of clients in the past.

"The clients needed the supplies they could have gotten here." Swiveling in the saddle, Hella looked at the burned-out trade camp. Smoke from the pyre they'd made of the bodies to prevent a spread of sickness rose to stain the sky again.

"We'll head to Blossom Heat." Stampede started back toward the bridge. "Riley, tell your people they can come on ahead."

Riley radioed his team and gave the instructions then powered his ATV to catch up to Stampede. "What's Blossom Heat?"

"Another trade camp. Bigger. They'll have fuel for your vehicles. With an outlaw gang of Sheldons on the loose in the Redblight, I don't want to take a chance on running out of fuel."

CHAPTER 5

Klein Pardot stabbed an angry finger at the map image on his PDA. "Blossom Heat is ten miles out of our way. A half day's travel. I don't want to lose that kind of time. Perhaps I haven't made myself clear." He stood under the canopy in the center of the camp as darkness closed in around them.

Hella soaked up heat near the cook fire and thought dry thoughts as she spooned rabbit stew from her bowl. The rainy season remained upon them. Stampede had made the stew even though it had been her turn to cook for them. She was grateful because his cooking was always better than hers and she'd wanted something hot and filling.

"Blossom Heat has fuel." Stampede didn't back down from the twitchy, little man.

"We took fuel into account when we mapped this route."

"You took the distance into account. I'm sure you did that. But did you take the rain into account?" Stampede thrust his big head into Pardot's face. Electric light glinted from his horns. He'd argued against the use of electrical lighting, stating that it was visible and might draw the Sheldon biker gang like bloodmoths to a flame. Pardot had disagreed and said that Riley and his men were equal to any threat the marauders might offer. It also kept the defense bots fully charged and at the ready in case there was an attack.

The confrontation between the two would come to a head,

and that realization left Hella with mixed feelings. She was sick of Pardot and his pushy manner, but she knew Stampede and she could use the profit. Having funds meant being able to hole up in a safe spot for a while without the necessity of immediately finding another guide job. Resting between expeditions meant better health and continued alertness, a greater chance to stay alive out in the Redblight. Traveling by themselves was easy, but traveling with others was risky.

Stampede pointed a big finger toward the pool of ATVs and groundcrawlers in the shelter of the trees. "Ask your quartermaster or clerk to take stock of your supplies now. I guarantee that the extra strain of getting through the mud has exhausted more of them than you'd planned on."

Reluctantly Pardot punched keys on his PDA then studied the results. After a moment he looked around and singled out one of his men. "Is this correct?"

The man checked the figures on his own device then nodded defensively. "As you can see, we're still within the established parameters, Dr. Pardot. I'm confident we can make—"

Stampede remained focused on Pardot and drew the little man's attention through sheer force of will. "Do those parameters include possibly being flushed off your trail into the brush by a gang of scavengers? Because if it doesn't, your escape at some point is going to be on foot and will mean jettisoning everything you've brought with you."

"Captain Riley and his men are well equipped enough to—"

"Enough to be a major attraction for those Sheldons when they find out about you. The weapons your security men carry and those groundcrawlers are going to be necessary additions to an outlaw gang trying to survive its own numbers. If anything, they're more reason to attack. Once they find out about you, they may well come after you just for raiding privileges. Can you enter those facts into your little machine, Dr. Pardot? Let me know how that ciphers out for you."

For a moment Pardot was silent. He shook with rage, which made his exo twitch even more.

Hella didn't know how the argument would go. Mentally she was already packing her gear. She knew Stampede well enough to recognize a make-or-break call. And she thought she knew Pardot well enough too.

Pardot put his PDA away. "All right. We'll do this your way." Without another word, the man turned and stomped away.

Stampede continued to stand there. Then Riley's men grew self-conscious and wandered away. Growling under his breath, Stampede joined Hella at the fire.

"That was surprising." Hella handed the bisonoid his bowl.

Stampede sat cross-legged and held his stew in one shaggy hand. "Wasn't sure how that was going to go."

"So why did he knuckle under?"

"Because I'm right. I think he was maddest because this was something he would have thought of if he'd given the situation any consideration." Stampede shook his head and snorted. "Kills that sawed-off little runt for anyone else to be right before he is."

Hella glanced around at the encroaching darkness. "We're lit up like a glowbug."

"I know. I'll be surprised if the Sheldons don't attack tonight."

"I'll take first watch."

Stampede shook his head. "Not us, Red. Me and you are going to get a good night's sleep for a change. Lit up like this, there's not much you or I could do except offer an early warning. And out there, the Sheldons might take us before we knew it."

"Not on their best day."

"We've been pushing ourselves. The rain isn't helping. We need to rest."

"What if the Sheldons attack tonight?"

Stampede didn't hesitate before answering, and he didn't look guilty either. "We run. Even with those stupid defense bots, we're not set up to hold this place. We signed on to deliver experience and maybe to die protecting these people, Red, but we're not sticking our necks out if they insist on committing suicide. We sell our experience, our expertise, but we don't sell our lives. I've told you that since Day One."

Hella chewed her food. Truthfully she looked forward to resting. Just the thought of her bedroll was almost enough to make her happy.

Stampede blew on his stew. "So how did your talk with Dr. Trammell go?"

Hella shrugged. "You were listening over the comm."

"Thought maybe you had some insights you wanted to offer."

Hella thought about everything she'd sensed about the woman. Stampede remained convinced that Hella could read humans, especially women, better than he could. "She doesn't like being here."

"Why?"

"She has a daughter back home; I got that. Doesn't want to be away from her. The only reason Colleen seems to be here is because she's sensitive to the ripples." Hella glanced at Stampede and studied his long, shaggy face. "You ever heard of anything like that before?"

"No."

"Do you believe it?"

"Maybe. I've seen weirder things." Stampede smiled but the effort was joyless. "You have too. Some people that haven't gotten out much think I'm one of those weirder things."

Hella didn't disagree. Bisonoids were few and far between. In all her years, she'd met only four. Some believed they were from another reality, not a strain of creatures that had mutated from local stock. Even Stampede didn't know. "There are people that hunt the ripples."

"Fools."

"Sometimes good stuff comes through them."

"And sometimes whatever comes through kills you in a heartbeat." Stampede shook his head. "I'd rather face an enemy I know any day. You don't know what's getting hold of you till after it's crawled through a ripple. The people that go chasing after ripples have zero life expectancy."

"Yet here we are."

"Me and you are different, Red. We're not looking for what comes through those ripples. We're just here to guide these people through the 'Blight. The minute it gets any more dangerous than that, we fade back into the forest and leave them with whatever they've found."

Hella spooned more stew into her mouth and gazed around the tent. She chewed thoughtfully, thinking about Riley and his men and the careful way they treated Pardot and Colleen. "What do you think they're after?"

Stampede sighed. "I don't know and if you really start caring, you're stepping into a bear trap. Curiosity kills more people than stupidity. I've told you that from Day One too."

* * * * *

Hella woke curled in her blankets inside the dome tent she shared with Stampede. Her hands were still hands, so she knew whatever had woken her wasn't immediately threatening. Stampede slept on his back only a short distance away. He held his big pistols in his fists, and the tent air was filled with the thick, animal stink of his fur. If the land had been more dry and the possibility of rain less strong, Hella would have slept outside. As it was, she'd been tempted to curl up with Daisy.

She turned back over and willed herself to go to sleep. She could tell from the blackness on the other side of the tent walls that it was still dark outside. Getting so much sleep was pampering herself, but she didn't feel guilty. Her dreams had been disturbed by images of the dead people at Deener's Corner. They weren't any worse than a lot of dreams she'd had before but more fresh. The mutie-coyote things had been in there as well.

After a few minutes, Hella discovered that her bladder had awakened her because she couldn't get comfortable. She hated to get up in the middle of the night for that, but she knew she wouldn't get to sleep any more if she didn't. Reluctantly she grabbed her pack, pushed herself out of her bedroll, unsealed the electrostatic door, and stepped out.

The camp lay quiet around her. Riley had guards posted at all four points of the compass around the camp. Hella picked them out easily and knew that anyone with any kind of wilderness experience would be able to do the same. It didn't make her feel protected, but at least the hardshells would make them difficult to kill. That would provide her and Stampede a warning.

"Red?" Stampede's voice sounded over the comm link.

"Nature break. Go back to sleep." Hella sealed the tent flap behind herself and headed for the south end of camp. Riley's men had dug a latrine there. Normally on an expedition, she and Stampede didn't bother with niceties like that. Travel wasn't about comfort; it was about getting from Point A to Point B.

One of the guards inside the camp stared at her. His direct gaze reminded her that Dr. Pardot had surrounded himself with men who were afraid of him, but they weren't necessarily good men. Stampede had pointed that out as well, and maybe that was why he was so watchful of Riley.

■ ■ ■ ■ ■

After putting herself back together, Hella gazed up at the sky. Clouds still blocked out the stars, and the promise of more rain left her feeling dismayed. She was tired of the precipitation, but at least it wasn't toxic. Sometimes acid rain drifted up from Texas and burned holes into the forest. That was what gave the Redblight its name. Occasionally unprepared expeditions were caught unprotected and ended up dying before they could get to shelter.

That was a hard way to go. Hella had seen the bodies. Even fresh dead, the flesh had sloughed away from the bone.

A shadow drifted through the forest a few meters away. Out of habit, Hella froze. Movement drew the eye in darkness. Until she took a step or shifted a hand, she knew she had a good chance of remaining invisible.

Using her peripheral vision, Hella spotted Colleen Trammell walking through the forest. The woman moved slowly, almost gliding across the wet ground. She was dressed in sleeping pants and a sleeveless shirt that left her cleavage exposed. It wasn't the kind of outfit Hella thought a woman such as Colleen would wear around a camp full of men even if some members of the security team were women.

Also, Colleen didn't move right.

At first Hella thought the woman was drugged. Hella almost immediately discarded that notion, though, because she'd never smelled any kind of swampweed or dream 'shrooms on the woman. Nor had she noticed any usage of orchid beetle or night leech, both of which secreted toxins that released opiates in the bloodstream.

Of course, there was the possibility that Colleen had brought something with her from New Mexico that Hella had never encountered. There were always new things in the world. She'd known that even before Stampede had given her an earful about that.

Curious, Hella trailed the woman through the forest. Even though morning was still hours away, fog rose from the ground and softened the edges of everything. The world was mostly grays and blacks, and Colleen Trammel was just a pale shadow drifting through it.

Unease prickled at the back of Hella's neck as the woman continued away from camp. A few meters farther on and she'd be out from under the protection of the defense bots.

The possibility that the woman might be making an escape from the expedition crossed Hella's mind, but she didn't believe that either. Colleen was too careful about things, too organized, to simply walk away from safety in the middle of the night, especially without any kind of supplies. She was too clever and intelligent to think she could make it back to New Mexico on her own. And Pardot's wrath would certainly follow her back home.

Hella convinced herself from the woman's jerky movements that she was sleepwalking. Just before she overtook Colleen and attempted to wake her, the woman stopped in a small clearing.

In the next breath, Colleen started speaking in a tongue Hella didn't recognize. With all her years of expedition work, Hella knew smatterings of a dozen different languages. Even if she couldn't write them, she could at least speak them passably well.

Colleen held her arms wide, as if she were calling to something.

Hella took cover beside a thick oak tree and kept watch. The wind stirred the branches around her, and damp leaves tickled her cheeks. A droplet of cold water hit the back of her neck and ran down between her shoulder blades.

A moment later, while Colleen was still speaking, a pale blue nimbus of light appeared in front of the woman. The light held steady for a few seconds then flickered and grew brighter like a cat opening its eye to stare curiously at whatever disturbed it.

The blue cat's eye grew larger, from something only a few centimeters apart to something more than a meter wide, and it still grew. In the next instant, pink tentacles covered with suction pods flashed out of the ripple.

Colleen stood before them as if mesmerized. The tentacles approached her slowly then the slid over her body and caressed her. A moment later a bulbous body slithered free of the ripple.

The thing was a mass of tentacles that writhed around a body that looked like a fat, gray plum. It reminded Hella of an inverted jellyfish, but usually those invertebrates had no control over their extremities. The thing moved a dozen or so tentacles to the ground and held itself up. The rotund mass of its central body rose to head height less than a meter from Colleen.

A trio of slick, black eyes formed a triangle on the body. It had no true defined features, but Hella couldn't help thinking of the eyes as part of the thing's face. Below the eyes was a ragged *X*. Hella didn't know what it was until the creature opened its mouth and four fanged flaps peeled back as it prepared to bite.

At least Hella assumed the thing was going to bite. By then she was in motion. Her left hand formed into a gun while her right closed around the haft of the machete sticking up from her backpack. The steel sang as it pulled free of the scabbard.

She was less than three meters from the creature when it turned toward her. Since it didn't have ears, she wasn't sure what had alerted the thing to her. Maybe the tentacles were sensitive to changes in air pressure.

The thing wrapped four tentacles around Colleen, who still wasn't moving, and lifted the woman from her feet. Afraid the creature might scurry off into the dark with its prize, Hella ran faster and opened fire.

CHAPTER 6

H ella!" Stampede's voice exploded into Hella's mind over the comm link.

"Busy!" Hella fired at the creature's center mass, realized she'd forgotten to add tracers to the mix, and reshuffled the ingredients pulsing through her body. The nanobots reacted immediately, and within a dozen rounds, green tracers sped from her barrel fingers. "South of camp!"

The tentacled thing swayed from its appendages, going violently from side to side and up and down so fast, Hella had trouble following it. Her rounds ripped through the air and exploded mushy purple foam from the tentacles, but she hadn't hit the bulbous mass yet. Most of her rounds ended up shredding trees and brush.

Whether it was caused by the sudden movement or the thunder of gunfire, Colleen came to her senses and fought against her inhuman captor. Then she screamed.

The gunfire and screams activated the defense bots, and harsh light suddenly exploded through the forest. Orange and yellow eyes of night creatures caught in the beams reflected, looking eerie. The illumination washed away what little color there was and rendered the immediate area in lights and darks.

More tentacle things poured through the ripple, and Hella quickly lost count of them. There might have been a dozen, but there were so many legs and the things moved so quickly that she didn't know for certain. She wished she knew how to close the ripple. Some lasted for only seconds, long enough for something to come through or get sucked away, but others were reputed to stay open for days. Hella didn't know if that was true, but she hoped it wasn't.

The thing that held Colleen darted behind a tree, ducked into the shadows, then swung back around toward Hella. Caught by surprise, Hella threw herself backward, flipping neatly to avoid a couple of tentacles that shot at her like harpoons. The tentacles snapped as they buried in trees behind her.

On her feet again, Hella moved at once to the attack. Even before she'd started training to fight with Stampede, she'd known that trying to run only made her vulnerable to attack. She aimed at the thing's body again, but it swung away, which was what she expected it to do. Never breaking stride, Hella swept her machete through three of her foe's support tentacles and felt a cold surge of joy as the creature listed to the side.

Taking advantage of the thing's being off balance, Hella continued on to Colleen and leaped up to slash the tentacles that held the woman. The purple, frothing stumps drew back in pain as their prisoner dropped to the ground.

Hella reached Colleen's side. The woman appeared able to move under her own power except for the fear locking her up. Grabbing one of Colleen's arms, Hella yanked her into motion. "Move! Back to camp!"

Confused, Colleen started to run the wrong way.

Hella grabbed the back of the woman's shirt, bumped her with her body, and got her going in the right direction. "Toward the lights! Go toward the lights!" Hella hoped that the defense bots didn't mow them down as they charged across the uneven terrain.

Ditches, rocks, and exposed roots tripped Colleen. Every time the woman went down, Hella grabbed her by the arm and got her up again, yelling at her to keep running.

The tentacled thing boiled around the tree and came after them. Despite the missing limbs, the creature learned quickly how to move at speed on what it had left. It came on with inexorable speed, gaining quickly. Hella knew it was too far for the woman to reach, and Riley's guards were caught up in fighting the new onslaught of creatures that had poured from the ripple.

Muzzle flashes lit up the night, warring with the sporadic blasts of the defense bots as they locked on to anything that hadn't been scanned into their Identify Friend/Foe programming. Even Daisy had been scanned in. Hella had made certain of that. The lizard was too large for the security systems to miss.

"Hella!"

"I'm here! I got Colleen!" Hella sheathed her machete, formed her right hand into a weapon, and locked on to the charging tentacled thing.

The creature tried the swaying maneuver again, but Hella adjusted to it. She opened fire, unloading full auto and depleting the stores her body could generate in that short amount of time.

Bright blossoms of purple froth erupted across the bulbous mass, and one of the eyes disappeared into ruin. But it came on.

Too stupid to die! Knowing her body didn't have any more ammo to give at the moment, Hella turned and fled back toward camp. She pumped her arms and legs, latching on to the adrenaline drenching her systems and letting it push her into overdrive.

When she spotted one of the squat defense bots, looking like a meter-tall can bristling with weapon muzzles, Hella headed straight for it. A targeting laser tracked over her eyes, and she knew she was blocking the bot's field of fire.

"Warning. You are endangering this unit's ability to respond properly." The mechanical voice piped into Hella's head over the comm link. The verbal equivalent was just a heartbeat later in front of her. "You are advised to break off your approach."

Hella managed another stride then another.

"Warning. This unit's parameters are established. Outside losses of friendly units are acceptable when camp integrity is threatened."

Hella silently cursed the mechanical thing. A flesh-and-blood defender would have moved, not held position the way the bot did.

If camp security were threatened, a flesh-and-blood defender—especially someone like Stampede—would kill her just as dead to take out an enemy.

The bot cycled its weapons, lifting slightly to alter the angle. Hella leaped into the air awkwardly. She flailed for balance then heard the defense bot open fire beneath her. Tracer fire drummed through the space she'd occupied only a heartbeat earlier.

Unable to find her balance, Hella came down hard but managed to land on her back. She slapped her arms out to her sides at the moment of contact with the ground to lessen some of impact. The wind went out of her in a rush, and she thought she might have fractured her ribs.

Groaning with effort and pain, Hella rolled over onto her elbow and folded her legs beneath herself. Then she stood, lit by the lightning given off by the defense bot's auto fire. Her guns were once more ready, but there was no need. The bot's heavy-caliber gunfire tore the tentacled thing to pieces, bursting it like a grape and leaving the tentacles hanging empty.

"Hella!"

"I'm fine. Back at camp." Hella stared through the darkness and saw one of the tentacled things explode as a rocket slammed into it. "These things are hard to kill."

"Stubborn, that's all. Definitely doable."

Smiling, Hella turned to look for Colleen.

The woman knelt next to a defense bot, hair in her face, features ironed by terror, and tears in her eyes.

Hella went to her, feeling bad for what happened to her. She turned one of her guns into a hand and gently laid it on Colleen's shoulder. "Hey. You're safe."

Colleen clung to Hella's hand with both of hers. "I don't know what happened."

Gunfire out in the brush slowed, and Hella thought the creatures were either all dead or they'd run deeper into the forest. "It's okay. We'll work it out."

·　·　·　·　·

"Colleen Trammell doesn't remember anything?" Stampede sounded as if he didn't believe that as he walked through the battlefield outside camp the next morning.

"Until she realized that thing was holding her, no." Hella flanked the bisonoid and searched the other side of the swath they cut through the forest.

"Do you believe her?"

Hella hesitated, knowing that was a loaded question. It wasn't just about her believing Colleen's story. It was also about whether he thought Hella was compromised by her belief in the woman.

"I believe her."

Stampede kicked one of the bodies over so he could peer into the hideous face. He didn't say anything, but Hella knew what he was thinking.

"I like her. She seems real."

Like a curious child, Stampede gripped the thing's face and forced the misshapen X mouth open. Fangs on all four flaps glistened. "You like her because she wants to be with her daughter instead of out here."

"I do." Hella knew better than to try to hide the respect she held for the woman.

"You can't trust people out here, Red. Not even me."

"Can I trust you on that?"

Stampede glanced up at her and smiled. His horns glistened with morning mist.

"She didn't know what she was doing." Hella focused on remembering how Colleen Trammell had acted. "It was like she was hypnotized or something. The way she was dressed—"

"Not like we've seen her before. And not something she'd wear out in the open around men. Other women might. But not that one."

Hella felt a little better then. Stampede had noticed a lot. He was only pretending to be a hard sell.

"I don't think she got up on her own." Hella slipped her sunglasses on. Even with the mist, the day was going to be bright. She hoped it meant the rain was abating.

"You think these things called out to her?"

"Not the creatures. The ripple."

Stampede pulled at his chin whiskers and flicked his nose ring. He did that a lot when he was thinking deep thoughts, especially if those thoughts were also troubling. "It's one thing to believe that Colleen Trammell is a precog tracking these ripples, but it's another if we flip that possibility and think maybe they're tracking her."

"You think she can call them to her?" Hella hadn't considered that.

"Got to admit it's a possibility."

"Then why didn't she stay back in New Mexico and call them to her there?"

"That's something I'd like to ask her. And it's why I want to know if they're following her."

Asking Colleen Trammell anything wasn't possible. Since the attack, Klein Pardot had kept Colleen sequestered and under guard. Stampede hadn't liked that either.

"I really don't like what we've gotten ourselves into, Red." Without warning, the tentacled thing spun on Stampede and lurched up to bite him. So quickly that Hella could barely see him move, the bisonoid slammed his other palm against the creature's forehead and drove the body into the ground.

Then Hella felt Stampede's power send a tremor through the ground. Although neither of them knew where the elemental power came from, they knew he had it. If pressed, he could open fissures in the ground. For the moment, he settled for driving a wave of pure seismic force through the tentacled thing.

Whatever made up the creature's insides shattered and burst. Purple froth cascaded from the ruined mouth. The body collapsed in on itself, shriveling up like a grape turning into a raisin. The thing made no sound as it died for sure.

Stampede drew his hand back and looked around at the haze that filled the tree line in the distance. "None of this, not Klein Pardot and not Colleen Trammell, is what we think it is."

"You think maybe we should cut our losses?" Hella hated asking the question in case the idea hadn't already been lurking inside

Stampede's head. She wasn't ready to walk away, but she wanted to know if that was what they would do.

The bisonoid drew in a deep breath and let it out. He wasn't happy. "Not yet."

Hella wanted to tease him, to get him back into a good mood because she didn't like it when he got all broody. She wanted to ask him if he was curious. But she didn't dare. When Stampede got in a snit, he didn't like anyone—not even Hella—asking questions.

"Wherever Pardot is going, whatever he's got in mind, I want to see it. If they let us. And not because I'm curious. Because I think someone should know what the stakes are in this. This feels big enough that I think someone should know."

"Okay."

Stampede stood and looked at her. "If you get the chance, get close to Colleen. She's here under duress. Maybe she'll open up to you."

"Sure."

"Especially since Pardot and Riley are going to be keeping a closer eye on her."

■ ■ ■ ■ ■

Colleen finally put in an appearance at midmorning. Klein Pardot had given orders that they were going to stay for a while to make sure nothing else untoward caught them off guard. Although she wasn't certain, Hella was convinced that Pardot wanted Colleen rested. Otherwise he'd have ordered them into movement.

For an hour or more, Colleen took tissue samples from the tentacled things. Every now and again, she shuddered as she touched one, and Hella knew that memory of the attack was playing havoc with her.

Hella joined her under the watchful eyes of the guard. "Can I help?"

Looking up at her, Colleen smiled and shook her head. "You don't know what to do."

"Maybe not but I'm a fast learner."

"I'd believe that. After seeing you in action last night, I know you're a capable young woman." Colleen excised a slice of tissue from the inside of one of the creatures, probably the brain judging from the looks of everything, and slid it onto a prepared slide. "I hope my Alice grows up to be like you. This world is no longer welcoming to those that can't take care of themselves."

"Alice?"

"My daughter." A smile flirted with Colleen's lips, but in the end fear won out and she dropped her gaze. "I just hope we both live long enough to see each other again."

"You will."

Tears fell down the woman's cheeks then, and Hella was surprised at how embarrassed she felt for Colleen. "I hope you're right. Truly I do." Colleen wiped at her tears. "I want to thank you for what you did last night. For saving me."

"All part of the service." That was something Stampede would say, but Hella felt awkward parroting it to Colleen. Bravado was another skill set the bisonoid had taught her, and she'd learned it well, but it didn't feel right dealing with Colleen that way. Hella was getting weak.

"No. Please don't denigrate risking your life for me." Colleen's blue eyes regarded her with desperation. "What you did was a fine thing, a good thing. I don't know anyone else that would have done something like that."

"Riley and his men—"

"Perform guard duty because they're afraid of Dr. Pardot and what he can do to their lives when we get back to the complex." Colleen lowered her voice. "Don't make them out to be heroes, and don't depend on them. They're mercenaries, nothing more."

Hella nodded because there seemed to be nothing for her to say. She waited a moment before she spoke again. "You weren't awake when you went out into the forest last night, Dr. Trammell. I saw you. You were sleepwalking."

Colleen looked away. "I don't remember."

"Has this ever happened to you before?"

"Dr. Pardot won't allow me to talk about this."

"I understand, but I need to know. Stampede needs to know. If we're going to take care of you, we need to know what to look for. It's important to know if it will happen again. Do you understand?"

The desperate look returned. "Yes. I'm not a fool." Colleen sighed. "I'm sorry. I'm not mad at you. It's just—"

"Dr. Pardot."

"Yes."

"Pardot has an armed guard around him that's taking care of him. He's protected." Hella reached out and took Colleen's hand. "I want to make sure *you're* safe. So you can go back to Alice." She felt guilty using the little girl against the woman, but she did it anyway. Her life and Stampede's were at risk.

Colleen looked up at her, and the tears were back. "Bless you." She took a breath. "What happened last night has *never* happened before. But I'm afraid it will, you know?"

Hella nodded and felt guilty about gaining the woman's trust. At the same time, though, she knew she meant what she said.

"I've dreamed about the ripples since I was a child." Colleen smiled briefly but it was forced. "Maybe I'm not exactly genetically pure either."

"I promise not to hold it against you."

"Dr. Pardot brought me out here because some of my recent dreams have interested him. There's something out here that we're going to discover that has the potential to change our world. *All* our worlds." Colleen paused. "I just don't know if it's going to be for the better."

"Can you tell me what it is?"

Colleen shook her head. "I've told you too much already. Even telling you that much may put you and your partner more at risk. But I had to tell someone." She gave Hella's hand a final squeeze and released it. "I'm sorry you got mixed up in this. You're too young to see the things you may have to see."

Hella sat there stunned, not knowing what to say. Silently she watched Colleen walk away. Two of Riley's men gazed at them. Getting to her feet, Hella walked back to Daisy. "Well?"

Stampede spoke flatly over the comm link. "From here on out, Red, we both sleep with one eye open."

CHAPTER 7

Hella hand-fed Daisy from a string of rats she'd caught that morning. All the rats were freshly killed, and it was the next best thing to the mountain boomer's running them down herself. Hella wasn't willing to let the lizard run free into the wilderness, especially not when they weren't certain all the tentacled things were dead. She was certain the mountain boomer could hold her own against two or three of them, but they still had no way of knowing how many of the creatures had slipped through the ripple.

Daisy ate greedily, gulping her meal and getting blood on her face. She cawed for more before Hella could free another rat.

Even before the shadow fell on the ground, Hella knew she had company. She heard Riley approach and knew him from the sound of the way he moved. Daisy's body language shifted, and the man's reflection showed in the lizard's eyes.

"You need to be careful there, or you're going to lose an arm."

Hella didn't bother to turn around. "Only if I get surprised."

"Maybe I should have waited." Riley paused a moment. "That was a joke, right? I guess you already knew I was coming."

"I knew you were here." Hella freed the last rat then made Daisy sit and wait for it, just to remind the lizard who was in control of the appetite.

Daisy waited expectantly. The lizard never took her eyes from the prize, but she watched Riley as well. Obviously she wasn't relaxed around him either. With a flourish, Hella tossed the dead rat into the air. The lizard rose up onto her haunches, towering over Hella and Riley as she gulped down the rat.

Hella turned while Daisy dropped back to all fours. Riley had stepped back out of fear, and his hand had dropped to his holstered weapon. Hella braced herself, determined to knock the man on his butt before he could clear leather.

With visible effort, Riley stopped moving and took his hand from his weapon. His face inside the hardshell helmet had paled. "I didn't know that thing could move like that."

"Daisy's full of surprises." Hella cleaned the bloody stringer on the grass. "Is there anything I can do for you, Captain Riley?"

"We don't have to be so formal."

"All right."

He frowned, obviously not satisfied with her answer. "Dr. Pardot wanted me to thank you for saving Dr. Trammell."

Took him long enough to get around to that. Hella nodded. "All part of the service."

Riley hesitated. "I noticed you talking to Dr. Trammell a little while ago."

Hella knew that was a lie. Riley had been nowhere near when she'd talked to Colleen. She waited.

"I was wondering what she had to say to you."

"She thanked me for saving her."

Stampede chuckled coldly in Hella's ear. "Isn't he the busy little bee?"

"Did she happen to say anything else?"

Hella lied glibly. That was also one of the first things Stampede had taught her. "She just told me how terrible it was, how she thought she was going to die, and how she didn't want to leave Alice alone in the world." She paused. "Alice is her daughter."

Riley's eyes narrowed, almost disappearing in the shadows of his helmet. "I'm quite aware of who Alice is."

"Okay. Now, if there's not anything else, I've got some gear that needs attention. Hopefully we're moving out soon. Sitting here makes me feel like a target."

"We'll be moving on soon enough."

Not soon enough for me. Hella started to pass him.

Riley put a hand on her shoulder. Daisy cawed in warning and lumbered over. The lizard really didn't like Riley, and Hella had learned to trust Daisy's instincts. On numerous occasions they had kept them both alive.

Riley jerked his hand back. "It's okay to talk to Dr. Trammell, but don't believe everything she says."

Stampede's voice turned colder, harder. "Pardot sent Riley to do damage control. That doesn't make me happy. Step carefully here, Red."

"She said she was scared and she thought she was going to die." Hella met the Riley's gaze full measure. "I don't see anything that I shouldn't believe about that."

"Of course not." Riley smiled flawlessly. However, his eyes never lost their bleak hardness. "But for future reference, Dr. Trammell suffers from a mental disorder. A near breakdown. Some days she's a walking basket case. Paranoid. You saw what she was like last night."

"Frightened?"

"Don't play with him too much, Red. Riley's not the kind of guy to take much without snapping."

Hella knew that but she couldn't just stand there and take his condescending attitude without striking back in some way. She considered her behavior on its best terms since she wasn't calling him a liar to his face.

"When she went out into the woods, Trammell was out of her mind."

"I wouldn't know. I didn't know she was out there till I heard her scream. I'd say she was out of her mind then. Anyone would be under the circumstances."

Riley tried the smile again. "That's funny. Parker said Trammell didn't scream till after you fired on the creature that had her."

"Things happened pretty quickly last night. Parker's wrong."

"He's not a guy usually wrong about things."

"He is about this. Are we done here?"

Riley stepped back and nodded. "Sure. Just wanted to give you a little friendly advice."

"Don't believe everything Dr. Trammell says. Got it." Hella retraced her steps and walked back into the camp.

Stampede growled in her ear. "They're getting all spun up about last night, Red."

"You think?"

"Hey, no need to be mad at me."

"Then you should have let me hit him."

"Maybe. We'll see. You may still get your shot."

· · · · ·

As usual, Hella rode point on Daisy, but she was aware of the wingmen Riley had assigned to her. Both guards, one man and one woman, moved awkwardly through the forest. She was certain both of them thought they were being stealthy, but the forest animals cleared out ahead of the hardshelled invaders. Anyone looking for signs of intruders would have spotted them easily.

Klein Pardot hadn't gotten the expedition up and moving till after lunch. By then, they'd wasted half the day and all the cool of the morning. With the rain gone for the moment, the Redblight turned into a sauna filled with the sound of running water as the land tried to drain the excess precipitation.

While she rode, Hella's thoughts turned often to Dr. Trammell. She couldn't help picturing the woman with her little girl, both of them tucked away in some small home in New Mexico. Hella didn't know enough about the country there to guess what the home would look like, but she thought she knew what it *felt* like. The home would be warm and safe, and only soft voices would be used there.

Everything would smell like baking bread. That was one of the luxuries she and Stampede didn't get while they were guiding expeditions. Even Pardot's group didn't have a way of baking bread.

Don't do that. Don't think about things like that. Stay focused or you're going to get Stampede killed. Hella got angry with herself, and Daisy sensed it. The lizard trilled anxiously beneath her and cocked her head to look up at Hella.

"It's all right." Hella patted Daisy on the forehead and smiled. The smile was a habit. Daisy probably didn't really register facial expressions. The lizard interpreted the world through smells, sounds, and touch. She rubbed her head up at Hella's hand.

The fact that she couldn't remember her own childhood tormented Hella. She wondered if it were possible that she still had parents and siblings out in the world somewhere. But she didn't know. Her earliest memories were of being alone and of Stampede. Sometimes she felt guilty for wanting to know more. The bisonoid had been a good provider for her until she'd been able to become a full-fledged partner.

She pushed Colleen Trammell out of her mind; then Riley jumped right in there. The man had been interested in her as a woman, and that had been . . . intriguing. A lot of the men Hella encountered were all about lust. She knew what that felt like, and she'd isolated herself from the way their looks had made her feel alternately unclean and vulnerable. In their eyes, she was just a prize to be won.

She hadn't thought that was the case with Riley. Or maybe she didn't want it to be the case with Riley. She had to admit, and it was easier doing that with herself than with Stampede, that idea was pretty stupid. Riley saw her differently than anyone else had. She saw that in his eyes.

■ ■ ■ ■ ■

To make up for some of the time he'd lost them, Pardot also insisted on traveling into the night. According to Pardot, Riley and the guards could use night-vision gear to keep watch for potential pitfalls.

"Back out of there, Red. Let them have point."

Reluctantly Hella had done that even though she felt confident about her and Daisy's ability to keep them safe. But she understood Stampede's logic.

"Maybe they think no one can see them in those hardshells,

but anyone carrying tech themselves can." Stampede had spoken over the comm link. "If they're going to be bear bait, let them run by themselves. You and I need to stay clear."

Hella knew it was true, but she didn't like hanging back with the others.

Nearly two hours into the dark march, one of the convoy trailers mired in a mud pit, and Klein angrily shut them down. They made camp on the lee side of a hill festooned with birch and blackjack. As before, Pardot insisted on setting the defense bots along the perimeter.

 ▪ ▪ ▪ ▪ ▪

"Looks like we get another night's sleep." Stampede turned the spit over their fire. The quail Hella had collected during the last hour of light roasted over their private campfire. Fat dripped off the birds' bodies and sizzled on the open flames.

"I'm not feeling very restful." Hella fed small twigs to the fire to keep it burning evenly.

"Change your mind about pulling up stakes on this one?"

Surprised, Hella glanced at Stampede. She was conflicted and she knew it. She didn't want to leave Colleen Trammell or Riley. The former she understood but not the latter. "Is that what you want to do?"

"Things have gotten decidedly more tense since this morning. Me and you are getting frozen out of Riley's security debriefs, and Pardot is making sure to drive a wall between you and Colleen Trammell." Stampede bared his teeth in a grimace and snorted. "Good sense says that what we should do is pick up our marbles and go, but that's not what I want to do."

"Because of Colleen?"

"No, not because of Colleen. She's not my problem, and she's not your problem. You need to remember that. Colleen is part of these people. Whatever problems she has, these people are more set up to handle them than we are."

"I don't believe she's mentally deficient. Pardot's lying about that."

"Maybe so but the lady's definitely got something wrong with her head. Even if it's just the precog ability messing with her. We're not set up to deal with that either, especially if she can call these ripples to her."

"So why do you want to stay?"

"Whatever they're after, it's got to be worth a lot. Otherwise they wouldn't have come out here with so many people."

A cold feeling stirred in Hella's stomach. She'd been with Stampede for years, and she felt certain she knew him well. During that time he'd never given in to any temptation to steal from their clients. Other scouts sometimes killed an expedition to the last man and took everything those people had. That was one reason outsiders were cautious about hiring scouts and never allowed their numbers to get larger than the party's.

"You're not talking about hijacking whatever they're after?"

"No." Stampede didn't take offense at the question. "I'm thinking that whatever they're after is big. Maybe big enough that we can walk away with a score of our own with what slips through their fingers."

Hella hadn't thought about that, but it made sense. "What do you think they're after?"

Stampede shook his head and flicked an ear at a buzzing insect hovering around him. "I don't know but I think we'll find out soon enough."

• • • • •

After the quail were gone and the fire had died down, Riley joined Hella and Stampede at their campsite. "Dr. Pardot says his PDA shows we've got about three more miles to Blossom Heat. I wanted to make sure that was right."

Hella worked on the rabbit hides. The furs were trade goods she could barter at the camp. She had a few others in Daisy's packs. She ignored Riley because she didn't want Stampede there when she talked to the man. Having Stampede listening in over the comm link all the time was bad enough. It would have been better if she'd known how to treat Riley.

"If we get an early start, we can reach Blossom Heat before midday. You can tell Dr. Pardot that the trade camp has generators there that pump water. By this time tomorrow night, he can enjoy a shower in a room. If he has the money to pay for it."

The room didn't interest Hella. She didn't like sleeping indoors. Inside was too noisy with the sounds of everyone around her. Outdoors had more room, and the noises weren't packed in on top of each other. But she was looking forward to a hot bath. Grabbing a quick soak in the early morning hours before the rest of the camp was up had gotten old.

"I'll let him know." Riley paused. "Get a good night's sleep, Hella."

"Sure." Hella's cheeks flamed and she didn't dare look at Riley or Stampede. "Thanks."

After a brief hesitation, Riley walked away.

"You'll want to watch yourself around that one, Red." Stampede's voice was slow and measured.

"Because he's interested in me as something more than a scout?" Hella fixed Stampede with a defiant glare.

Stampede twitched an ear in irritation, and his nostrils flared. "No. Because I don't like the way he looks at you."

"He looks at me like I'm a woman. And whether you like it or not, I am a woman. I'm not a little kid anymore."

"You're also not as experienced as you think you are. Somebody like Riley will turn you inside out."

Hella pushed herself to her feet. "I'm going to go check on Daisy."

Stampede nodded but didn't say anything.

Angry, Hella took her pack and walked over to the tree where she'd left the mountain boomer. She didn't want to be mad at Stampede but she was. There were things she needed to learn, and she didn't need Stampede blowing over her shoulder while she learned them. It was frustrating.

She also didn't want to be so interested in Riley, but she was that too. She knew she didn't trust the man completely, but that was all right too. Making a choice between Stampede and someone else wasn't anything she wanted to do soon. She was certain that Riley would be nothing more than a diversion, and a diversion wasn't a commitment. In fact, someone such as Riley—someone who would be gone soon—might be the best diversion to have.

At least having him around made her feel different.

CHAPTER 8

Blossom Heat lay at the bottom of a small valley. Hella reined in Daisy and gazed down the hill. Even with her sunglasses, the bright, noonday sun hurt her eyes a little. She was soaked in her own clothing from baking in the heat. The chain-mail shirt chafed against her skin. And it stank.

Hella stood up in the stirrups and stretched her legs. Daisy shifted beneath her, anxious to be off again. The lizard's keen olfactory senses had picked up the scent of cured meat coming from the trade camp. Carnegie, the trade camp's owner, kept a couple of hunters on permanent retainer to track feral pigs in the surrounding area. There were always fresh hams and barbecue for sale at Blossom Heat.

At Riley's command, two of the hardshells on ATVs sped down the wide trade trail toward the camp. Hella fell in behind them. She knew even a klick away that she already wore gun sights on her chest. Snipers manned the towers on the four corners of the camp. Riley's men were more confident than they had any reason to be.

From her present vantage point, she could see over the five-meter-high metal walls that surrounded the trade camp. Before the Darkness, when the collider had unleashed unholy hell to rewrite the world, the trade camp had been a supply station along the superhighways that had crossed the old world. Carnegie had books with pictures that showed the camp as it had been. Of course, nearly all of that had changed, and Hella wasn't certain that the pictures in the book were even anywhere around the Redblight.

■ ■ ■ ■ ■

The burly gorilloid stared Riley in the eyes and didn't flinch. "Not all of you are coming inside the camp." His voice was a raspy growl that sounded more animal than human, but he could be easily understood.

"That's absurd." Klein Pardot strode up to the gorilloid and looked him over.

Faust was impressive too look at. Standing two meters tall, he was broad and heavy with slabs of muscle, and he was armed to the teeth. Bandoliers of .50-caliber rounds for his assault rifle crisscrossed his thick chest. Four grenades hung like fruit. The two handguns in shoulder leather were matched by two more at his hips. The gorilloid had four hands and he used them all in a firefight. Gray and white scars showed through his matting of black hair. His close-set eyes were buried deep under a low shelf of brow.

"That's how it's gonna be, puppet man." Faust curled a lip over his canines and fixed Pardot with a glare. "Now why don't you haul your tin butt over there out of the way before I pound you one and they have to get a can opener just so you can see daylight again?"

Outraged, Pardot stood as tall as he could and barely came to Faust's shoulder, and only then because the gorilloid wasn't tall, just broad. "Take me to your master."

Faust leaned down to Pardot, causing the man to lean back. "I don't have a master, bub. I have an employer. And you'd best not make that mistake again."

Pardot stepped back. "Stampede."

Making his way forward, Stampede reached the gorilloid and shoved out a hand. Stampede stood a head taller than Faust.

Faust took the proffered hand and nodded. His black, rubbery lips twitched up in a smile that would have drained the hearts of most men. "Thought I recognized you back there. Been a long time since you were out this way." The gorilloid rolled an eye over Pardot, Riley, and the security men. "You with these guys, Stampede?"

"My expedition, yeah." Stampede's hand had disappeared in Faust's grip.

"Got some real greeners here."

"They haven't been in-country before. First time in the Redblight."

"They gotta get smarter faster." Faust shook his head and released Stampede's hand. "And if they don't, they're going to get you dead too."

Hella smiled at the look of sour annoyance on Pardot's thin lips. No one was impressed by his entourage.

"I'm working on it. For the moment, though, how many people can we bring inside the camp at one time? They've got money and aren't shy about spending it."

"Carnegie'll be happy to see them, then. I'll spot you ten." Faust pulled a PDA from his pocket. "If you're going to vouch for them."

"I will."

Hella smiled at little at that, knowing then that Pardot would have to recognize they might not have gotten inside at all if not for Stampede and his connections.

Faust gazed at the security team in their hardshells. "I get ten inside. No one else goes in until someone comes out."

"Does that include Hella and me?"

"You still got that little imp with you?" Faust looked over the crowd.

"Know anybody else that rides a dinosaur?" Stampede jerked a thumb over his shoulder at Daisy. The mountain boomer slurped from one of the watering troughs out front. Carnegie kept fresh water out front for free because people would fight and die over water if they needed it.

Faust grinned and stepped toward Hella. He wrapped her up in his powerful arms and hugged her tightly. "How ya doin', imp?"

Hella hugged the gorilloid back fiercely. His fur was smooth and soft, but the bandoliers bit into her skin. "I'm still alive."

Gently Faust put her back on the ground and looked at her. "You're growing, imp. Gonna be breaking hearts any day. But if any of them break yours, you come see Uncle Faust and we'll dig the grave together."

Even though she smiled, she knew the gorilloid meant it. In his own way, Faust was just as protective of her as Stampede was. In the end Faust wanted more of the civilized life than Stampede had, and they'd gone their separate ways four years earlier.

"And if you see something inside the camp that you like and old hornhead there won't spring for it, come see me."

"I will." Hella hugged him again and stepped back. "I'll come see you even if I don't find anything I like well enough to carry out of here. I seem to recall somebody being a stickler for extra weight when we traveled together."

"That's my imp." Faust returned to his position at the door. "Ten inside. Your scouts don't count, puppet man, because I think of them as part of our own. The rest of you pick a shady spot and settle in."

. . . . .

Hella walked through the open gate and crossed the worn, cracked concrete skirting that made up most of Blossom Heat's inner courtyard. The original building remained at the center, but it had been rebuilt several times over the intervening years. Some of the work had come as a result of time and decay, but other work had been required after attacks. Firebombs had gutted all the other buildings, but they'd been rebuilt as well. Most of the buildings were small stores with bars across the windows. None of the windows held glass because shattered fragments turned into deadly weapons during a rocket or grenade blast.

"Hella."

Recognizing Colleen Trammell's voice, Hella stopped and looked back.

Standing between two security people who had obviously been assigned to her, Colleen looked pasty and worn. Sweat glistened across her cheeks, and dark circles hollowed her eyes. She walked a little unsteadily.

"Are you all right?" Hella felt certain the woman was on the verge of collapse.

"I'm fine." Then, as if recognizing that Hella saw through her lies, Colleen swallowed and lifted her chin. "I'll be fine. Dr. Pardot gave me something so I could function better."

Or be more manageable? Hella thought that was more likely the truth.

"It's a necessary evil if I'm going to function. The senses that I have that tie me to the ripples have never been stronger." Colleen fingered a simple, silver chain at her neck. A small oval containing a picture of Alice hung there. She recognized the girl from the photo on the PDA. As in the previous photo, Hella recognized the sense of joy and wonder about her that she had never before seen in a child.

"Maybe you should sit down."

"I'll be all right. If you don't mind, I'd like you to show me around."

"I'd be happy to."

The security guard on the left shifted. "Dr. Pardot gave us strict orders that we were to stay with you."

"Stay with us." Hella didn't look at the guard. She looked at Colleen. "You don't know your way around this place either."

"Careful, Red." Down the small street, Stampede stood in front of the armorer's shop and spoke over the comm link. "You're flirting with the edge."

"Do you know any other way to find out what's going on?" Hella whispered under her breath.

Stampede's silence was the only acknowledgment she needed.

Colleen smiled weakly. "That sounds fabulous." She held out her hand. "Perhaps you wouldn't mind steadying me."

Hella wrapped the woman's arm inside her own and took some of her weight. Colleen was slight and helping her was easy, but the tremors that ran through her almost unnerved Hella. To a person who lived out in the Redblight, sickness was one of the most fearful things to encounter. That was why they burned the dead instead of burying them.

. . . . .

"The security chief knew you."

"Faust? Yeah." Hella guided Colleen through the main building of Carnegie's trade camp. They walked along a line of clothing that scavengers had discovered and brought in to sell. Some of them had bright colors, were in styles that would never work in the wilderness, and had sayings that Hella didn't understand, including *DO THE DEW*. What could that have possibly meant? And why would someone need to be told to do something if it were necessary? And if it weren't necessary, why put it on a shirt to remind yourself? "He used to ride with us. He was with Stampede when they found me. He was Stampede's partner back in those days and helped take care of me."

Raised by animals? That explains a lot.

Hella started to turn in the direction of the guard who stood behind her, certain that was where the voice had come from.

Inside his open-faced helmet, the man looked back at her guilelessly.

"Did you say something?" Hella stood her ground.

"No."

Hella. The voice was different. She recognized it as Colleen's, but it wasn't like any other time she'd heard the woman speak. She looked at Colleen and noticed the sheen of perspiration had gotten wetter, dripping from her chin. *I'm sorry. That wasn't meant to get through. Don't let them know I'm talking to you this way.*

You're an espee? Hella tried to let go of the woman's hand, but Colleen held on with fierce determination.

Don't. Please. Even Dr. Pardot doesn't know I can do this. And it's very, very hard. I have to be in physical contact with someone in order for it to work best. That thought wasn't mine. It was the guard's. One of the guards'. I don't know which. I don't have a lot of control over what gets through once I start doing this.

Hella forced herself to relax. In all of her travels with Stampede, she'd never encountered an espee. She was familiar with psi talents, those that could be controlled and those that were wild. But the thought of someone able to invade her mind was horrifying.

Even worse than the tentacle-things? Though Colleen wasn't smiling, Hella *felt* that in the woman's thoughts.

Yeah. Even worse.

I'm sorry. Truly I am. But I had to be certain that we could communicate this way. It doesn't always work.

Hella took a deep breath and realized a headache was dawning at the base of her skull.

I'm sorry about the pain. It's not any easier for me.

That wasn't a consolation but Hella nodded.

As you may have guessed, Dr. Pardot has insisted on "medicating" me. He says it's to keep me from losing control the way I did the other night, but really it's to keep me docile and helpless.

Hella stopped in front of an aisle containing footwear. Some of the shoes and boots were manufactured things turned up by scavengers, but much of it was handmade. Only some ancient goods had stood the test of time, and not all of that was good out in the rough country.

What do you want from me? Hella found it hard to think one conversation while having another.

I don't know yet. I don't know what's going to happen, but whatever it is will be soon.

The next ripple?

Yes. I believe that's the one we're looking for.

Are you looking for it too? Or is it just Pardot?

Colleen hesitated. *This ripple needs to be found, Hella. I need what it will bring into our world. So does Alice. My daughter needs it most.*

For a moment primal pain and a feeling of impending loss ricocheted through Hella's mind. She almost lost herself in the enormity of it. She was suddenly struck blind and dumb. She didn't know Colleen had released her until she found herself with her hands braced against the shoe display. Her stomach rolled and she thought she was going to be sick.

"Are you okay?" One of the guards stepped forward and reached out.

Hella brushed his hand away. "Don't touch me."

Animal girl. His voice rang in her head, not her ears. Hella hoped that whatever espee powers Colleen had didn't turn on some latent ability inside her that she wouldn't be able to control. That happened sometimes. Genetic malfunctions lay in wait inside a lot of people, and eventually most of them got triggered at one time or another. The moon had an effect on several species.

"Hella." Colleen leaned toward her but made no move to touch her.

Hella flinched and drew back. "I'm all right." Her head pounded but the blindness receded.

"I'm sorry."

The guards closed in on Colleen. "We're going to take Dr. Trammell back out to the camp."

Colleen tried to pull back from them but didn't have the strength. They gathered her easily and headed toward the door. One of them called in a report to Riley.

Guilt kicked holes in Hella's stomach as she watched them walk the woman out of the building.

. . . . .

"Hey, I know you don't like the room, but it's not a cage."

Hella tossed her saddlebags onto one of the beds and gazed around at the four walls. The room was a lot larger than their tent, and she knew she should have felt thankful Stampede had chosen to spend the money to get it. At least the headache had passed.

She ran her fingers through her hair and thought about the bath. That was the one good thing about staying in for the night. She could soak, scrub her hair with clean shampoo, and get totally dry before getting back into clothes. Not only that, but the clothes would be clean of trail dust and insects that lived on them because Stampede was also paying to have them laundered.

"I'm not going to leave Daisy out there. As soon as I've showered and cleaned up, I'm going to take care of her."

"You don't have to do that." Stampede dropped his gear on the floor with a loud thump.

"She's my responsibility, and I'm not going to just—"

"Faust has made room for her in the camp bay. She's going to be inside these walls, same as us. With those Sheldons running around out there, I don't want Daisy to be any less protected than we are."

That surprised Hella. "Faust agreed?" The gorilloid wasn't a big fan of the mountain boomer even though Daisy tolerated him. Hella had sometimes wondered if adopting Daisy was one of the things that had split up the relationship between Stampede and Faust.

"Yeah. I told him if he didn't let Daisy sleep inside the camp, you'd be out there sleeping with her."

That was true.

"With the Sheldons in the area, he didn't want you outside the walls." Stampede grinned. "He even cut me a deal on the room. As long as you agree to sleep inside."

"I don't have to stay the whole night, right?"

Stampede sighed. "Your choice, Red, but if I was you, I'd take advantage of a quiet night, the bath, and a chance to get a warm meal that's something other than whatever you just killed."

"Daisy's not going to like being penned up any more than I do."

"She'll be happy tonight. Faust also arranged for someone to haul all the butcher's remnants to that lizard's stall. She's going to be eating good tonight. She'll probably sink into a food coma and not wake up till morning."

Hella looked out the window. From the height, she could see over the metal wall. Snipers manned the armored towers, and other camp guards strode the catwalks. "Have you ever been around anyone with espee abilities?"

"Sure." Stampede started unpacking his bags. When things quieted down, he'd clean all his weapons. And he'd insist that she do the same with hers. Bottles of gun cleaner and oil sat on the small table in the room.

"Somebody that could talk into your mind?"

Stampede swiveled his full attention on her then. "Colleen?"

"Yeah."

"Maybe you should tell me how this happened."

Hella opened the window and sat on the ledge, partly out of the room so the wind could reach her. In terse sentences, she told Stampede what had happened.

Stampede rubbed his hairy chin when she finished. He frowned and his left ear twitched, a sure sign that he was uneasy. "Pardot doesn't know she can do this?"

"She says no."

"Pardot has a way of knowing things. She may think she has a way to talking to you—"

"I think she's more interested in talking to *us*."

Stampede grunted. "That may be but she's mistaken if she thinks I'll put her safety ahead of yours."

"You're not responsible for my safety." Hella felt a little angry at that.

"You saying if I was outgunned, you wouldn't help, Red?"

"That's not what I'm saying."

"Let me ask you this: If you had to choose between saving me and saving her, which way would it go?"

"I'd save you." Hella answered without hesitation. "But I know that you can also save yourself."

"Thanks for the vote of confidence. Let's say that we come to a fork in the trail. One way is safe and the other way is dangerous. Maybe I wouldn't survive. Would you let me go down that dangerous path if I wanted to?"

"You'd have me. I wouldn't let you go alone."

Stampede laughed. "And that would make all the difference."

"It always has before."

"Some days it just means both of you get killed. You've still got a lot to learn about the world, Red." Stampede was silent for a moment. "The thing I'm trying to get at is that we both have lost a little of our perspective here. You're looking out for the woman, never mind Riley floating around—"

Hella started to object, but Stampede lifted a big hand and silenced her.

"And I'm interested in Pardot's prize—whatever it is. Neither one of us is completely pure here. Our decision-making capabilities are compromised. Do you understand?"

"I'm not an idiot."

"This talk is as much for me to hear as you. I just want it said. That's all."

"Okay."

A ponderous knock sounded on the door. By the time Stampede had one of his pistols in his fist, Hella already had her right hand morphed and ready to fire.

"Who is it?" Stampede stood to one side of the door.

"Me." The voice belonged to Faust.

When Stampede opened the door, the gorilloid stood in the hallway.

"Thought I'd come up and invite you to lunch, maybe wash some of the trail dust out of your throat."

Hella relaxed her hand. "You two can go ahead. I want to take a bath and get cleaned up."

"I figured that, imp, but I may need you to help keep Stampede in check. Trazall's downstairs trying to poach your expedition."

CHAPTER 9

Stampede's hooves clicked harshly against the wooden stairs as he went down. He opened first one revolver to check the loads then the other. Hella had to hurry to keep up.

"You gotta go easy with this." Faust walked beside Hella and tried to calm Stampede. "I can't have you shooting up the place. Carnegie wouldn't like it, and anything he doesn't like, I'm supposed to deal with."

"How many guys does Trazall have?" Stampede swung the pistol cylinder closed with a snap.

"Counting Trazall? Eight. All of 'em mercenaries." Faust loosened his weapons in their holsters.

"Anybody I know?" Stampede reached the first-floor landing and turned to plunge down the final length of stairs into the common room.

"Silence is with him. So is Jack Hart."

A chill ghosted through Hella when she heard the names. Both the men were hired guns and didn't mind stand-up fights.

"Silence has got that fire thing going." Faust followed Stampede as he stepped onto the main floor and looked around. "You know about that, right?"

"Ever since the brigand group burned his tongue out a couple years ago. Set off his mutation. They say sometimes stress will do that." Stampede swiveled his head and looked around the room.

With dusk coming on and everyone in the area aware of the murderous Sheldons on the rampage, Blossom Heat had swelled with travelers. No one who could reach the camp had bedded down anywhere else. Most of them would sleep outside the walls, but they'd be under the sniper guns and within range of the defense sensors.

"You've met Silence?" Faust pointed to the left. "Back of the room. Pardot commandeered a table for dinner. I guess he didn't invite you guys."

"We're the hired help. Not exactly people Pardot would have asked to the table even if we hadn't gotten sideways with him on a couple things."

"Glad to know you've got that worked out. Trazall's hitting your guy pretty hard. Silence is sitting at his right hand."

Stampede cut across the floor. "I've crossed trails with Silence and that greedy roach before."

Faust pulled a revolver and held it in his right hand behind his thigh so it was out of sight. "Jack Hart can play with gravity."

"He's new to me, but I've been around people that could do that before." Stampede focused on the big table at the back. "Split wide, Red."

Silently Hella went to Stampede's left, flanking his progress on the table. The move was a familiar one. They never stayed together when things started to turn dangerous. Separated, they both had to be considered, and they split an enemy's attention.

"When this goes down, Faust, I need to know which way you're going to bounce."

The gorilloid smiled and showed his huge fangs. "I covered your butt way too long to change that habit now. But if you break the peace in Blossom Heat, I'm gonna have to kick you out right after we deal with this."

"Good thing I haven't unpacked all the way."

"The imp's not gonna be happy. She didn't get her bath."

Hella ignored most of the snappy patter. That was how Stampede and Faust were with each other. She could function around it, but she didn't join in. She knew how Stampede would handle the situation as well and that he'd go for the throat. No one poached one of their clients. A guide couldn't stay in business with a reputation as a pushover.

Evidently people in the room sensed the presence of danger, or maybe it was because Stampede and Faust were big together. The crowd broke in front of the two like waves around a boat.

Pardot sat at the back of the table. Riley sat immediately to his right. Another guard sat to Pardot's left. Colleen Trammell sat between two guards as well and had a heavy, drugged look in her eyes. She glanced at Stampede only briefly then looked around the room. Hella felt certain the woman was looking for her, but she wouldn't be seen until she was ready to be seen. She stopped behind a fat man strapped with weapons and peered at Trazall.

Although the expedition guide looked exotic in current company, Hella knew he wasn't. Generations earlier, or maybe only a short time after the collider went boom, Trazall's species had been locusts or something like them. An event had happened—possibly due to the collider—and they'd become, or perhaps on their original world they'd always been, humanoid.

Trazall's hard exoskeleton was moss green on his head and shoulders and darker green on his abdomen. The two bottom limbs of his six had thickened and gotten stronger, turning into his primary means of locomotion. His middle two limbs ended in grippers that could double as hands without the opposable thumbs, or they could be used as another set of feet if he was in a hurry or wanted to cling to a rough surface.

The expressionless face gave nothing away, but there was a telltale flicker in the multifaceted eyes, and his antennae curled for just a moment. He wore clothing but there was no need because nothing about his naked body was immodest. Hella hadn't known he was a male of his species without being told. He chose tailored pants and a shirt, an obscene imitation of humanity because he looked so alien. But looking at him, no one would forget that he had human-level intelligence.

When the table fell silent, and Pardot looked over Trazall's shoulder at Stampede, Trazall rolled his head around in a way a creature with vertebrae couldn't have.

"Ah, Stampede." Trazall's voice had an irritating habit of buzzing on the consonants and created an undercurrent of noise in his speech. "We were just talking about you." He gestured to a chair, and one of his men quickly left it. "Perhaps you'd like to sit down."

"I'll stand." Stampede remained loose and ready. "It's easier to squash a cockroach as it scurries away when you're standing."

Trazall buzzed and Hella knew from past meetings that the insectoid was laughing. "Have I done anything to offend you?"

"Depends on whether or not you've poached my client, roach. Actually, you've already offended me by trying."

A small man seated to Trazall's right opened his mouth and breathed out a small jet of flame. He was of medium height, had a shaved head, and was covered in dragon tattoos.

Trazall put his hand on the man's shoulder as if restraining him. "Be careful. You know how offended Silence gets if he feels my honor is being impugned."

"Really?" Stampede's right leg trembled slightly, and a tremor ran through the floor as he manifested his seismic power. "How does he feel about earthquakes?"

The man on Trazall's left smirked. He wore jeweled rings on all his fingers and plucked at a carefully trimmed goatee. His hair and the beard were tinted green. "How do you think you'd feel about suddenly weighing so much, your knees snap?"

Stampede lifted his massive handgun in an eye blink and had it trained on the man's forehead. "Twitch funny, and you're going to be breathing out of your forehead." He turned his attention to Trazall. "Then I'm going to blow your head off, roach. Or maybe I'll blow your head off and let sunlight in through Greenie's skull."

Trazall carefully put his four hands on the table. "Nobody moves until I say you can move." He spoke calmly and harshly.

None of his crew moved even to acknowledge the command.

"Are you backing him, Faust?" Trazall glanced at the gorilloid.

"On this?" Faust nodded. "Yeah. One of the rules at Blossom Heat is that there's no theft. From anybody. And especially not from one of my friends."

"This?" The insectoid almost sounded surprised. "This is nothing. Just a casual conversation."

"He's lying." Colleen's voice cut through the tension in the room. "This—*thing*—"

"Dear lady, you wound me."

"—has been telling Dr. Pardot that he could guide us more safely than you can." Colleen didn't sound entirely together, as if struggling to speak.

Trazall shifted slightly in his chair, obviously knowing the statement wouldn't bode well for his immediate future.

Stampede pointed his other pistol at the insectoid. "However this goes down, they're going to be burning your corpse, roach."

Trazall made a show of looking around. "The two of you? Against eight of us?"

"Seven of you. I pull the trigger, you're already off the board. And I'll take your gravity kinetic with me. And if, by some thin chance, you manage to survive, Hella will ventilate that ugly head of yours after she takes out Sparky."

"Ah yes. The girl." Trazall glanced around. "I've heard of her, but I've never seen her. So where is she?"

As graceful as a shadow, Hella slipped through the crowd and stood in front of the fat man so she could be seen. Her hands, pistol barrels, hung at her sides. The fat man at her side immediately vacated the area. The gunmen around Trazall shifted, trying to decide which way they needed to face. That was exactly the mindset Stampede wanted them in.

"There she is." Trazall buzzed. "And look at those hands. I'd heard about that, but I've never seen anyone like her." Then he glanced back at Stampede. "If it helps, I didn't know these people were with you until Dr. Pardot informed me of that."

"It doesn't."

"Dr. Pardot said no." Colleen looked adamant and maybe a little relieved.

"That's good, Dr. Pardot." Stampede spoke casually. "Because I'll bet the roach didn't give you his full sales pitch. He leads people through the Redblight, but when they're on their own and he knows what they're looking for, he hikes up the price of his services."

"Only when things turn disastrous and I'm as fully invested as my client. When they can't get something on their own, I've discovered that most people will agree to an *adjusted* profit."

Pardot grimaced. "You rob them, you mean."

"Such harsh words from an obviously learned man. I am disappointed." Trazall looked back at Stampede. "Since my business here will obviously not bear fruit, I'd like to leave." He nodded at Stampede. "If you agree."

"Sure." Stampede gestured with his pistol. "But we're going to do this slowly."

One at a time, Trazall's men moved away from the table and went through the door. Silence and Jack Hart went last. Silence didn't seem to care, but Hart carried a load of resentment in his dark eyes.

Trazall stopped at the bar and ordered a bottle of whiskey to go. He paused at the door and looked at Stampede. "Another time, when the deck isn't stacked in your favor, and this will end differently."

For a moment Hella was certain Stampede was going to shoot the insectoid anyway. Stampede didn't believe in threats, and he wouldn't let anyone he felt certain would try to act against him later walk away. She'd seen him kill men who had threatened her. He'd always told her it wasn't the guns facing her that were dangerous; it was the ones she didn't see coming. But he'd never shot a man—or an insectoid—in the back.

"Stampede." Faust spoke in a low voice, and the only reason Hella heard him was because Stampede's comm link picked up the conversation. "I got a job here. You pull that trigger, I gotta put you and the imp out for the night or Carnegie will have a new chief of security in the morning. With those Sheldons running around, maybe sleeping outside wouldn't be such a good idea."

In the next instant, as if he'd suddenly realized he'd overstayed his safety margin, Trazall stepped sideways and disappeared into the night.

Hella readied herself to follow, already mentally mapping a route through the window of the adjoining room.

Stampede took a deep breath and put away his weapons. Hella slowly let her hands become human again.

Riley waved one of his men into motion, and the guard went toward the door.

Stampede's ear twitched as he addressed Riley. "If you have your man tail Trazall too close, you'll have to burn him come sun up. If you can find the body."

"Since Trazall took an interest in us, he seems like someone to watch." Riley placed a thin slice of ham on toasted bread and took a bite.

Hella's stomach gurgled happily at the thought of homemade bread. She was suddenly torn between the bath and the meal Faust had promised.

Lacing his fingers together in front of himself with his elbows on the table, Pardot glared at Stampede. "Your insistence on insinuating yourself into this matter only seems to have made things more incendiary. I had already dealt with things."

"I'm sure you had. But when I came down here, Trazall was still seated at this table. Now he's not. Maybe you don't recognize it now, but later you'll realize that having Trazall gone is the best thing that could have happened." Stampede shifted his attention back to Riley. "You should keep that in mind. In case you see him again."

"I will."

Stampede excused himself and left. Hella waited a moment, making sure they kept some distance between themselves in case Trazall left someone they didn't know about in place inside the room. Then she went up the stairs.

· · · · ·

"That went well, I think." Hella closed the door behind herself and double-locked it. She expected Stampede to react to her sarcasm, but he didn't. "Don't you think that went well?" She couldn't stop herself from trying to goad him into at least an argument. Adrenaline still pumped through her system.

The bed creaked under Stampede's weight when he sat on it. He looked tired. Dust filmed his shaggy coat. "One thing we didn't need, Red, was Trazall sniffing around."

"Maybe he'll go away."

"After getting a look at all the security guards and ATVs Pardot has running with him?" Stampede shook his head. "Not likely. The question is: Do we deal with the roach here, or do we do it out on the trail?"

"If we fight with Trazall inside the trade center, Faust is going to take some heat for everything. He stuck his neck out for us tonight."

Stampede smiled wryly. "And Faust doesn't have much neck to offer."

Hella grinned but the tension she felt didn't entirely go away.

Stampede rolled his neck, and the vertebrae cracked. "Go soak, Red. Lemme think about it. Then we'll take Faust up on his dinner offer. No reason for us to lose the whole evening."

Not needing a second invitation, Hella grabbed a clean change of clothing and headed for the bathroom. In minutes she was immersed in hot, scented water, and the past few days leached out of her.

. . . . .

"Hey, the guard?" Hella adjusted her sunglasses as she looked at the guards on the catwalk. The cool morning was still gray-pink in the western sky.

One of the guards looked down. "Aren't you that girl that has the big lizard in the barn?"

Hella grinned. Despite the standoff in the main building the previous night, she'd slept well after her bath and the big meal Faust had promised. If she'd dreamed, she didn't know it.

"Yeah."

"The girl with the buffalo-guy?"

"Yeah."

"Interesting company you keep." The guard was an older man in his late forties or early fifties. Hella could never tell when they got to be that age. "What do you want?"

"The name's Hella and I'd like to come up, take a look around if I can."

The guard conferred with his companion then turned and nodded. "Faust gave you guys free run of the camp yesterday when he let you in. That's good enough for me. Come ahead." He kicked a device, and a steel ladder spooled down in a series of clanks.

Hella climbed the ladder easily and quickly gained the catwalk. She stamped her foot experimentally. The steel surface clanged beneath her combat boots.

The guard grinned at her. "When I first got up here, I felt the same way. Just didn't trust it. The fall's not that bad, but I didn't want to take a tumble just the same."

"I've fallen out of taller trees. Just not onto pavement." Hella walked to the wall and peered over, the edge tucked neatly under her chin.

"They say you and the buffalo-guy—"

"His name's Stampede. If you call him buffalo-guy to his face, he might stomp you."

"Well, we wouldn't want that." The guard grinned then fumbled in his pocket and brought out a packet of jerky. He offered the packet to Hella.

Even though Hella had just enjoyed one of the biggest breakfasts she'd ever had, she accepted the jerky. Food was a prized possession, and a person never took or shared food lightly.

"Thank you." Hella bit off a chunk. The salty flavor spread across her tongue and filled her senses. When she breathed out, she exhaled jerky fumes. She didn't like staying in camp towns, but the prevalence of food—and so many flavors—made a good argument for regular visits. Plus, seeing Faust again reminded her how much she missed him.

"Not a problem." The guard put the jerky away. "Right here in Blossom Heat, we stay hip deep in wild pigs. If we didn't eat them as often as we do, they'd overrun us and eat us."

The other guard chuckled, but the line was obviously an old joke.

"I heard there was a face-off in the main building last night." The first guard chewed his jerky and watched her.

"Gossip gets around."

The man grinned. "It's a trade center. That's what folks do here in between haggling, selling, and buying. Is anything going to come of the bad blood?"

"I don't know. Did Trazall leave last night?"

"Nope." The guard pointed to a collection of tents and a handful of wagons and ATVs on the north side of the wall. "They're still there."

Only three men tended the cook fire in the camp area. Hella knew the men were guards posted by Trazall. She recognized one of them from the confrontation. "How many men?"

The guards exchanged looks and smiled. "That what you come up here for? Get a headcount?"

Hella smiled back at them, as if letting them in on a secret. "I don't think knowing how many are out there would hurt. Do you?"

"I counted twenty-six riders. Including Trazall."

"Trazall stayed down there last night?"

The man shook his head. "Nope. He stayed inside the walls. Got himself a room."

Hella nibbled at the jerky and thought about that. So far she and Stampede hadn't seen the insectoid. That bothered her. Trazall was someone she wanted to keep an eye on.

"We'll see Trazall coming if he decides to brace us, Red. Don't worry." Stampede's voice was calm.

"Not worried. Just like to know."

"We'll know. Faust has got people on Trazall."

"Trazall doesn't have to be the one that makes the move."

"You're getting to be a real pessimist. You know that?"

"You should be proud." Hella smiled. She looked out over the countryside and at the creek that meandered through the forest less than a klick away. Boats traveled the creek, and a lot of them stopped to trade at Blossom Heat. She wondered what it had been like in the ancient days, when the world had been filled with buildings and traffic. The idea was hard to imagine. She loved the open places and didn't want to think of them being filled in by structures and humans thick as ants. Trade camps were bad enough.

"Primo." The second guy reached into his chest packet and took out a pair of binocs.

"Yeah?"

"I thought I saw something in the tree line to the east."

Curious, Hella looked in that direction down the row of guards lining the catwalk. One hundred fifty meters away, the guards in the sniper tower talked among themselves.

"Clancy." The first man's voice was tight.

Hella didn't hear the answer because Clancy was at the other end of a radio connection.

"Yeah, I think there's movement out at the eastern perimeter."

Beyond the guard tower, a half klick away across the barren expanse of land shorn of trees, Hella tracked the landscape. The morning sun made it hard to look in that direction because the light slanted in at just the right angle to be near blinding.

The first guard, Primo, dropped his assault rifle from his shoulder into his waiting hands. "Clancy says he sees guys out in the bush. Must be three or four dozen. All of 'em just waiting. Go sound the alarm."

The second guard hurried down the catwalk to a crank-driven air horn.

Primo turned to Hella. "Gonna need to you clear the catwalk, kid."

The guard tower exploded into flaming pieces that rained down over the camp. A deafening boom battered the inside of Hella's skull, and the catwalk shivered, making her stomach clench.

Before the second guard reached the air horn, the back of his head evaporated in a spray of blood.

CHAPTER 10

Primo lurched across the catwalk and made it two steps before a bullet ripped through his left thigh. As he crumpled, at least one more round struck his body armor. He cried out in pain and reached for his dropped rifle.

Crouching, Hella morphed her hands into pistols and took up a position with her back to the wall. Stretching out her right leg, she kicked Primo's assault rifle over to him. He grabbed it and pulled it to him gratefully.

"Hella!" Fear underscored Stampede's voice.

"I'm fine."

"Get down from there."

"We're under attack. I can't see what's going on down there." Hella edged up and peered over the top of the wall. Bullets continued to rip along the catwalk, picking off slow guardsmen and creating a hellish racket as the rounds drummed against the sheet metal before ricocheting off.

A pack of Sheldons aboard motorcycles broke from the tree line. A few of the armadillo bikers flew small flags with snarling, purple dragons. For the most part, they rode two to a motorcycle, and a few of them were in sidecars that jerked and sailed over the uneven landscape.

"It's the Purple Dragons."

"Kid." Primo tried to lever himself up. His eyes locked on hers.

"Gotta sound that air horn. There's guards in their racks that aren't gonna know what's going on."

Hella didn't know how anyone could miss the fact that the trade camp was under attack.

"The guard's right." Stampede sounded calm but Hella knew he would be moving into a position to return fire. "If you can sound that alarm without getting killed, do it." His voice rose. "Faust! Hey, Faust! We have to open the gates, get those people outside inside before those Sheldons massacre them!"

Thinking about the people trapped outside the trade camp made Hella more angry. She morphed the guns away and took back her hands then scuttled down the catwalk to the air horn.

"I know the Sheldons are counting on the gates being opened!" Stampede sounded rushed but he was calm at the same time. His urgency was tangible. "We're going to have to get the gates closed again before the Sheldons get in here. Move it."

Hella reached the air horn, grabbed the crank, and turned it swiftly. Instantly the eerie wail rose over the trade camp. Down in the streets, the stunned guards shook off their paralysis and immediately raced into positions.

When everything went south, rely on training. That had been one of the first lessons Stampede had taught Hella. She released the crank on the air horn and raced along the catwalk toward the flaming guard post. The biker army had targeted those emplacements because they had heavy artillery there, but Hella hoped that not all of it had been destroyed.

Bullets hammered the catwalk and whined off around her. A round glanced off her left shoulder, turned away by the chain mail. She cried out at the pain, stumbled, but kept moving.

"Hella!"

"Chain mail caught a stray round. I'm fine."

Flames twisted inside the guard post and reached for the sky. Evidently the rocket that had struck it had carried an incendiary secondary payload. Dead men inside the ruined structure tightened up as the heat caused the ligaments to contract. Hella had seen a lot of bodies left by a fire. The ones that weren't totally burned up were always left looking like people getting ready to box, their clenched fists raised before them.

She had some luck, though. Thrown free by the blast or lost by someone standing outside the guard post, an XM25 grenade rifle lay on the catwalk. The rifle was squat and ugly, designed with a bullpup configuration that placed the six-round magazine behind the trigger to help provide better balance. The weapon weighed fourteen pounds but felt like an anchor as Hella tried to stay behind cover and lift the XM25 at the same time.

With the grenade rifle settled over her shoulder, Hella took a quick breath then popped up and swiveled so she faced over the wall. She squeezed the trigger slightly and activated the laser rangefinder.

Stampede had taught her to use weapons, all kinds of weapons, and she knew more information about weapons she still had yet to see. Weapons were important for survival, but they were even more important to use for barter. Rifles and pistols, things that could be easily carried by travelers, were constantly in demand. Gunsmith knowledge, which she also had, was highly prized.

The Sheldons were still seventy meters out but closing fast. The trade camp's gates were open, and getting all the people to safety was going to be a near thing.

With the rangefinder locked in, Hella squeezed the trigger at the onrushing armadillo bikers, shifted targets immediately five meters to the left, and fired again without waiting to see what the first round did. She moved to the third target and kept going till she'd launched all six grenades.

Once the laser rangefinder had the distance locked in, the twenty-five-millimeter grenade measured the flight through the number of turns it made then exploded in midair. Judging from the flames that covered the six different groups of Sheldons, the rounds had been thermobaric. The fuel-air mixture had spread more than five meters and dropped a layer of fire onto everything it touched.

Armadillo bikers dumped their rides and screamed in fear and rage as they beat at the flames covering them. Their hides and shells were proof against a lot of bullets and edged weapons, but fire burned them. When they pulled their heads or feet into their shells for additional protection, they only pulled the flames in after them. Several of them stewed inside their shells, and their burned corpses relaxed out of hiding as they hit the ground.

A wave of bullets drove Hella back behind the wall, but by then other guards along the catwalk had regrouped. Heavy sniper rifles cracked all around her; then mortars thumped as they hurled shells into the advancing ranks of bikers.

Crawling on her stomach while dragging the XM25 after her, Hella searched the dead bodies on the catwalk. The second guard had five spare magazines for the grenade launcher in a messenger bag. All of the magazines had colored tape on them, evidently shorthand code for the man using the weapon, but the only one she knew for sure was red because that matched the one inside the weapon.

She dumped the empty magazine and inserted a fresh one, also marked with red, though it was the last one, shoving it home with a click. She scrabbled on hands and knees, got to her feet, and sprinted twenty meters down from where she'd been.

One of the guards flipped around and dropped to grab another magazine from his chest rack. Blood, some his and some from someone else, judging from the amount of it, stained his face and clothing. He nodded at her and smiled. "Great shooting, kid."

"Thanks." Hella stood just tall enough to reach over the wall again.

The battlefield had changed drastically. Before it had looked as if nothing could stop the Purple Dragons, but holes had opened up in their lines. The fallen motorcycles became hazards for the motorcycles following too closely, and most of them were.

The motorcycles were within forty meters of the trade camp.

Hella emptied her borrowed weapon into the center mass of the biker gang. Three gas tanks on motorcycles blew up, launching the bikes, riders, and passengers into the air. Only scorched earth, exploded motorcycles, and corpses remained.

Hella dumped the empty magazine and popped in a fresh one, noting the blue tape. At the tents maintained by Pardot's expedition, two hardshelled security guards held on to Colleen Trammell and tried to get her to safety.

"Stampede! Colleen's in the open!"

"I see her, Red. Got my hands full."

At the gate, a small group of Sheldons engaged the security team. Stampede and Faust fought shoulder to shoulder, just as they had in the past. Hella guessed the Purple Dragons had sent a crew in at night and set them up in tents to blend in with the other campers. They'd lain in wait till the gates were open.

An explosion suddenly blew a gap in the security force. From the limited but certain devastation, Hella thought one of the Sheldons had triggered an antipersonnel device. Shell-shocked, the security people fell back, and the Sheldons surged forward again.

One of the security guards aiding Colleen went down suddenly, keeping his grip on her and bringing her down with him. She threw her arms over her head, lay there for a moment, then tried to get up. The surviving guard attempted to aid her, but one of the armadillo bikers who had gotten into the camps threw himself off the machine and tackled him. Both of them went down.

Hella didn't think twice, though she thought about it a lot later. She gathered herself and jumped over the wall. At the bottom of the five-meter drop, she landed on relaxed legs, sank to the ground, and rolled to her feet with the XM25 up in front of her. She ran for Colleen, leaping over the bodies of camp visitors who hadn't been prepared for the onslaught.

"Fire in the hole!" The yell didn't belong to Stampede, but it came over his comm link.

On the heels of the warning, the ground around the campsite erupted into a ring of explosions that threw Sheldons high into the air and left smoking craters.

Faust shouted curses that came over the comm link. "You like that? Electronic mine field. My idea and Carnegie went along with it. Figured it would be a last-ditch effort for us if we ever got attacked en masse like this."

Smoke and dust burned Hella's lungs by the time she reached Colleen. The woman looked dazed, and Hella was sure that was as much from the drugs Pardot was giving her as the attack.

"Colleen!" Hella started to help the woman up, but a motorcycle closed on them fast. She lifted the XM25 in both hands and aimed point-blank, hoping that they wouldn't get caught in a backlash of whatever the blue tape meant. She squeezed the trigger as the rear rider pointed a shotgun at her.

The grenade exploded just as Hella turned and dived on top of Colleen, burying them both in the ground. A swarm of fléchettes turned the two Sheldons into chopped meat, wrecked the motorcycle, and took out three more riding teams.

With the sound of the explosion still ringing in her ears, Hella grabbed Colleen's arm and yanked her up.

They're going to kill us! We're going to die!

"No, we're not." Hella didn't know if she'd spoken or not because the near explosion had left her almost deaf, but Colleen seemed to calm down a little and became more pliant. She held on to the woman's arm and pulled her toward the gates.

A trio of Sheldons raced at her. The armadillo bikers were smoking from the minefield. Embers flamed in their clothing and on their leathery skin. Hella lifted the XM25 but didn't fire because the Sheldons were too close to her. She dropped the grenade launcher and morphed her free fist into a .50-caliber weapon, but it would be too late.

"Hella, get down!"

Recognizing Stampede's voice, Hella wrapped her arms around Colleen and took them to the ground again. The rough earth tore at her skin, leaving bruises and abrasions. Helplessly she stared back at the approaching riders.

Then, out of the whirling chaos at the gate, from the mire of frightened people struggling to get in at the last minute and the guards trying to shut the doors, Stampede stepped into the open. He held his rifle loosely in his arms and didn't try to bring it around. Instead he lifted his left foot and brought it down—hard.

A seismic shock ran through the ground, jarring Hella as she held on to Colleen.

They're going to kill us!

Hella watched as the quake bowed the earth in front of the armadillo bikers. The tremor leaped from the ground and into the bikers, scattering them like leaves in a stiff breeze. One of the motorcycles shot by Hella and took down a small dome tent before crashing onto its side.

The Purple Dragons struggled to get to their feet, but by that time Stampede was on them. His fists, aided by his seismic power, smashed into his enemies and broke their bones, killing them with sheer concussive force.

One of the bikers tried to blindside him. Hella raised her hand, but before she could fire, a gout of flame turned the Sheldon into a fireball.

Eyes burning, body covered in flames, Silence took the battle-field and gazed at Stampede.

Stampede gripped his rifle. "Not bad, Sparky."

Silence grinned, flexed his arms, and shot upward on a pillar of fire. Then he spit another fireball that engulfed a second group of bikers.

Stampede raced over to Hella and Colleen. He hoisted the woman up into his arms as though she were a child and ran back toward the closing camp gates. Hella followed, providing cover fire from both blazing hands.

"Hold those gates!" Faust leaped to one door above the heads of the struggling crowd, gripped the door's edge in both left hands, and fired into the arriving mass of armadillo bikers with guns gripped in both right fists. His bullets tore through the front line of the Purple Dragons, and he kept firing despite the fact that bullets drummed the heavy, metal doors.

Hella stayed close to Stampede, no more than an arm's reach away, and he bulled through the mass of frightened people.

"Close the gates!" Faust flung himself through the air, flipped over the heads of the people, transferred his pistol to his left hand, and dropped onto his two feet. He reloaded his weapons, and a bullet ricocheted from his Kevlar helmet while two others thudded into his vest and drove him backward two steps. "Close the gates! Now!"

Hella fought clear of the crowd, found a nearby ladder, morphed her hands back, and practically ran up to the catwalk. As soon as she hauled herself onto the catwalk, she morphed her hands back into weapons and joined the other defenders at the wall.

Below, all of the campers who remained alive had managed to make it into the trade camp. However, a large knot of Purple Dragons smashed up against the closing doors like waves breaking against a reef. Hella fired blindly down into them and regretted the loss of the grenade launcher.

Gradually, though, the withering fire broke the line of armadillo bikers. They'd fought to get inside because they were afraid of retreating back across the no-man's-land that remained of the campsites. In the end, though, there was nowhere else for them to go. A few broke away at first; then they retreated en masse, like the tide going out.

Sharpshooters picked off all they could, but when she looked at all the dead strewn across the ravaged field that lay around the trade camp, Hella didn't have the heart for it. Silence flew after them for a short distance before gunners chased him back. He spit fire at the retreating bikers and succeeded in roasting several of them.

"Don't give up killing them." The guard to Hella's right glared at her as he reloaded his sniper rifle. "The ones we don't kill today, we'll have to kill tomorrow. They'll be back when they get desperate enough."

Hella ignored the man and returned to the ladder. She morphed her hands back, gripped the ladder, and slid to the ground. When she got there, Stampede was still holding Colleen in his arms. The woman lay still as death.

Hella couldn't see any wounds. "Is she okay?"

"Yeah. Passed out." Stampede rolled his head and grimaced. "You okay?"

"Bruised and banged up. You?"

"I'm fine."

"You took a risk diving off that wall, Red."

"Didn't stop to think. I just saw Colleen in trouble and knew I had to get to her."

"Your choice?"

Hella shook her head. "She didn't even know I was there. She had no control over me. She was so scared—or drug addled—that she couldn't save herself."

Stampede growled. "I'm going to have a word with Pardot. He's not going to continue to make her like this. In this state, she's a liability."

"Pardot's not big on listening."

"He'll listen now. I'm going to make him."

CHAPTER 11

As she walked through the dead, Hella turned off her emotions. She concentrated her attention on taking salvageable goods from the armadillo bikers, leaving the other corpses to family and friends who would claim them and take care of their burning. If she didn't touch the fallen campers, the sadness and the loss didn't linger, didn't become attached to her.

As part of the defenders, she and Stampede had salvage rights to the dead enemies. Anything—gear or weapons that could be saved—was theirs to claim when she found it, as much of it as she could carry back to the camp. Stampede was working out details with Pardot because they were leaving in the morning.

Despite the number of the dead lying around her and the number of salvagers working them, Hella moved slowly and carefully. She took her prizes methodically.

She was on her second trip back through the battleground, skirting a still-smoking crater, when she realized Riley had fallen into step with her. "What are you doing?"

"Came to check on you."

"I'm fine."

Riley looked tired and anxious. His restless gaze wandered around the dead and all the destruction. "About what you did to save Dr. Trammell—"

"I was just doing my job." Hella didn't want to talk about the woman. If she did, she was afraid that she would unload on Riley for helping keep the woman drugged. "Just part of the service."

"No, it wasn't. That was a brave thing." Riley shook his head. "I don't know if I would have dived over the wall and gone down into that bloodbath."

Pride and embarrassment warred within Hella. She was glad that Riley had noticed her helping rescue Colleen. She liked the idea that her actions had made an impression on the man. And she was at once irritated at feeling that way. She didn't like not being in control of how she felt or what she thought.

Hella knelt and fished a bandolier containing three magazines from under a file of dirt near a crater. The magazines held rounds that Stampede could use in his rifle. She hung the bandolier over her shoulder and stood again. "Stampede was the one that rescued Dr. Trammell and me. We wouldn't have made it out of there without him."

"If you hadn't reached Dr. Trammell, Stampede would never have gotten there in time. A handful of my men have told me that. I don't mean to take anything away from Stampede, and I've already thanked him. So has Dr. Pardot."

"I wish I hadn't missed that."

Riley grinned in the shadows of the open face shield. "Yeah, well it doesn't happen very often, I can promise you."

"Why are you working for Pardot?" Hella kept walking and Riley kept pace. "Isn't there someone else you can work for where you come from?"

"I'm a security guard, Hella. That's what I was tasked to do while I attended school. But I wanted to see more of the world."

"You went to school?"

"Sure. Didn't you?"

Hella smiled at him and shook her head. "You seen many schools while you've been out here?"

Riley sighed and shook his head. "No. They don't have schools here?"

"Not many in the Redblight, no." Hella pointed back at Blossom Heat. "Trade camp's got a school, but probably not like you're used to. You can't learn to be a security guard there, but you do learn how to defend yourself when you travel the trails or stand post inside the camp. If you don't learn, you die."

"Then what do you learn?"

"How to work at a trade camp. They teach you to read and write, some math, and maybe some kind of skill. Repair work mostly. Or maybe you get taught how to build buildings, furniture, stuff like that."

"How did you learn to be a scout?"

"On the trails. Same as every other scout. There's no other way to learn, and your marks come hard and quick. You fail, you get burned. If you were around long enough, your friends feel sorry you're gone. If not, they just burn you to prevent disease." Hella spotted a bit of shiny metal under an armadillo corpse, which didn't appear to have been moved yet. The body covered another magazine. She knelt again and slipped a small skinning knife from her boot.

With quick, deft movements, she sliced through the dead biker's pockets and emptied the contents, checking her haul before she slipped it into a leather bag that hung around her neck. The take wasn't much. A worn pocketknife, a couple of rings that didn't look silver and held glittering stones that looked artificial, a few ancient coins that really didn't have any worth anymore, and a green and white disk. She read the writing on the disk.

"Blue Skies Casino."

"That's a poker chip. From a gaming center that probably stopped existing shortly after the collider imploded. Where did you learn to read?"

Hella knew what a gaming center was. Gambling went on in trade camps and along the trails as well. She'd never been drawn to the games. Staying alive every day was gamble enough. She didn't know why other people didn't recognize that. "Stampede taught me."

"He knows how to read?" Riley couldn't hide his surprised look.

Hella shook her head and snorted. "He couldn't have taught me any other way, now could he?"

"Why did he teach you?"

"Because he thinks reading is important."

"Do you?"

Hella kept walking. Around her, other camp defenders raced from corpse to corpse. "You don't use reading for much while you're on the trail. Usually for identifying salvage. Occasionally Stampede and I share a book."

"Share a book?"

"Take turns reading out loud. We don't waste batteries on voxplayers." Hella hated that she was talking so much and wished she could find some way to shut up. She reminded herself that Stampede's comm link was on and he could be listening in. The whole situation was embarrassing—at both ends.

"Oh."

Hella studied Riley's reaction. She wanted to know if "oh" was a negative reaction and if Riley thought she was being an idiot. Then she told herself that worrying about what he thought proved she was an idiot . . . at least about that.

"You can learn a lot of things from books." She sounded more defensive than she wanted to.

"I suppose." Riley didn't look convinced.

"Do you read?"

"Manuals. But most of those are computer downloads."

Hella had seen computers only a few times. "I've never used a computer."

"Really? Because that surprises me. You've got nanobots in your body. That should give you some kind of affinity for computer hardware and software, I'd think." Riley seemed contemplative so Hella didn't know if he thought her nanobots were like a disease or not.

She also didn't like admitting that she didn't know much about the nanobots inside her system. "If I ever get curious about that, maybe I'll look into it." She pulled an M4A1 assault rifle from under the dead man. The weapon looked to be in good shape. With a little cleaning, she'd be able to barter it successfully.

"Is it all that important to rob the dead?"

Anger sparked inside Hella. "They're dead. They're not going to use any of this stuff again." She kept moving, forcing Riley to stay up with her. "Besides that, only a short time ago, one of these guys would have killed you. Or anybody else." She took a breath. "And it's not robbing them. It's salvage. It's also important. These are goods that Stampede and I can use to stay alive. Either we can use them with part of our kit, or we can trade them for stuff we can use. A meal. A room. Supplies."

"Sorry. I didn't mean to offend."

"You didn't." Hella didn't want to let him see that she felt defensive, and she was angry at herself for feeling that way because it meant she felt vulnerable.

"I'm just trying to understand. This world . . . is different from where I grew up." Riley looked around. "It's hard and it's dangerous and it doesn't care for you very much."

"Your world cares about you?" The idea was intriguing.

"I think so." Riley smiled. "We live in homes, Hella. With our families. We're safe. When we go to bed at night, we don't have to worry that someone will have a knife at our throats in the morning. There's always food on the table, and we don't have much sickness."

Hella remembered Colleen Trammell's concern about her daughter and almost asked about that, but she stopped herself. One thing that travelers on the trails learned quickly was to keep their curiosity to themselves. "Pardot is the leader there?"

Riley shook his head. "He's on the council, but he's not the leader. His voice is heard, and he gets a lot of respect."

"Then why is he out here?"

"Because our community is strong and we want to keep it that way. That means we have to find new things and adapt them if we can use them. Dr. Pardot is good with technology. He's reverse-engineered power sources, machines, and even"—Riley tapped the hardshell armor—"designed some of the microsystems inside these suits. The man is a genius."

"Sounds like a guy no one should be risking out here."

Riley nodded. "Everyone thinks that way, and they tried to stop Dr. Pardot from coming. But he doesn't trust anyone else to do the job."

That was something Pardot shared with Stampede. Except that Hella knew Stampede trusted her.

"When they found the first—" Riley stopped and grimaced. Then he shook his head. "Sometimes I talk too much."

"What did they find?"

"I can't tell you. When the time comes, Dr. Pardot will make sure you know."

If we're not dead first. Hella kept that thought to herself. One of the salvagers ran past her.

Riley smiled. "I guess he's in a hurry."

"He's young and stupid. That's a combination that doesn't last long. Sometimes, when an invading force has to retreat, they leave booby traps under the bodies of their dead."

"I didn't know that."

"Good thing you're not out looking for salvage."

"Did these bikers really think they could bring down the trade camp?"

Hella looked at the dozens of dead armadillo men and women spread across the ravaged earth. "They did. But Stampede thinks their leader got desperate."

"What do you mean?"

"Whoever put these gangs together, the group grew bigger than he expected. At first we thought maybe he was just stupid, believing that more was better."

"Isn't it?"

"Look at how many men you've got on this expedition. Think about how many supplies you've got to bring with you to survive. If you didn't have your own food, Stampede and I never would have agreed to sign on with you."

"Why?"

"Because we couldn't feed you off the land. All we would have been doing was hunting the whole time, and during that time, you people would have been sitting ducks. When people run out of food out in the Redblight, it doesn't take them long to decide to fit someone from among them in a pot."

Riley's face hardened in disgust. "Cannibals?"

"They don't see it that way. They think of themselves as survivors."

Riley hesitated.

Hella answered before he could ask the question that was on his mind. "No, I haven't ever eaten someone. Neither has Stampede. We know how to hunt and trap and fish, and there's only two of us to feed. We're sustainable on our own. Autonomous."

"I'm glad to hear that. Just so you know, we're buying more food here."

"Stampede and I know that, and we know you've got plenty left to trade with to get more food. Like I said, we weren't going to bring you out here and watch you starve." Hella kept walking. "But that's what the leader of these Purple Dragons was faced with."

"Watching his people turn into cannibals?"

"Yes. And if they did that, they'd have to have someone to blame."

"They'd blame him."

Hella nodded. "So he chose to attack Blossom Heat."

"Why?"

"If they were able to take the camp, their problems would be over. At least for a while. If they couldn't—which they weren't— he'd be able to cut the numbers of his gang down to a more manageable size."

"He knew they would die."

"If they believed long enough that they could sack the camp."

"So all of this was just for attrition?"

"To thin the herd, yeah."

Riley looked around at all the dead and the devastation; then he looked at Hella. "The world I come from isn't like this. We aren't staring down the barrels of guns all day. There's peace." He paused. "You should come back with me and let me show you."

For a moment Hella stood quietly, mesmerized by the idea of

seeing where Riley had come from. The idea of a city filled with people appalled her, but getting to see it even for a short time would be fascinating.

"Maybe." Her answer made Riley smile, but she knew he had too many secrets for her to completely trust him.

An explosion detonated only a short distance away. Riley's hardshell closed up automatically, covering his face as dirt and rock peppered them. Looking to the left, toward the sound of the explosion, Hella watched as the mutilated body of one of the scavengers dropped back to earth.

A woman, perhaps the dead man's mother, howled in anguish and rushed over to the smoldering corpse. Two younger children trailed after her. Then an older man joined them, and they collapsed in tears.

Hella felt sorry for them but knew there was nothing she could do. It was already too late, but the rest of the family had learned something that might save another's life later on.

Riley cursed softly. "Booby trap?"

"Yes."

"This isn't a good place to live, Hella. There is more to the world. Think about my offer."

■ ■ ■ ■ ■

Hella relaxed in the bathtub and thought about turning the hot water back on. The bathwater hadn't chilled, but it wasn't as hot as it had been. She didn't know if she wanted to listen to the water gurgle, though. At the moment the bath was quiet and the scent of the vanilla candles filled the room.

She kept trying to imagine the place Riley had described to her and couldn't. Even after reading magazines and books with Stampede, she couldn't wrap her mind around a place with streets and buildings and homes.

A heavy fist knocked on the door.

By the time Hella lifted her hand from the water, it was a weapon. "Who is it?"

"Me." Stampede's voice sounded tired.

"Do you need in?"

"No. Just wanted to make sure you were okay. I heard there were a couple people killed during the salvage."

"You don't think I'm foolish enough to get caught by a booby trap."

"No, but the thought crossed my mind that someone standing next to you might have been."

Hella smiled and dropped her hand back into the water. "Thanks for caring."

"I'll always care, Red. I also wanted to tell you that we're pulling out in the morning. I tried to talk Pardot into letting the Purple Dragons have more time to scatter or starve out, but we've already stayed here a day longer than he wanted to."

That meant she might be in the last bath. At least she could work in a shower in the morning.

"Look, I heard Riley talking to you about taking you back with them."

Hella closed her eyes and tried to relax. She really didn't want to have that conversation at that moment. "He offered. Doesn't mean I'm going."

"I know. I just want you to be careful. That's all."

Be careful? Hella wanted to argue that point. Their lives weren't about being careful or safe. They risked their lives every time they agreed to a guide job.

"I came back from the salvage in one piece, didn't I?" She knew her tone came out sharper than she'd intended.

"You did." Stampede paused. "Faust and I are having dinner in the big room below. Want to join us?"

"When?"

"How long do you want to soak?"

"Forever. I finally feel clean."

"You'll miss dinner if you do that, and what they're serving is better than stringy rabbit and a few wild onions and carrots."

"Give me twenty more minutes."

"Sure. It'll take that long to drink a beer." Stampede's footsteps retreated from the door.

Hella slipped back under the water and submerged completely, shutting off all sensory input except the beating of her heart. She wanted to stay a couple more days at Blossom Heat but only to stay in the bathtub and prune up till she couldn't stand herself.

That wasn't an option, though. However, as she lay there, she gave Riley's description of his world more thought. In his world she'd be able to bathe every night and she'd be in a home that wasn't filled with other people and noise and demands. She couldn't imagine why Riley—or any of the expedition for that matter—would leave such a place.

That made her think even more fervently about what Pardot had them searching for. Riley had mentioned they'd found one of something, but one of what?

Just as she was about to surface to take a breath and maybe turn on the hot water again, Colleen Trammell screamed inside her mind.

CHAPTER 12

The raw agony of the woman's scream reverberated inside Hella's skull. She thought her head would burst open; then she was afraid it wasn't going to burst because bursting was the only thing that could possibly alleviate the excruciating pain.

The visions knocked aside some of the throbbing, though. Images of Colleen standing in a laboratory, dressed all in white and wearing a white surgeon's mask, formed in Hella's mind. Colleen sat at a table and watched a group of small rodents inside a plastic cage.

Leprous contusions covered most of the rats, several running sores that wept thick, green pus. A number of the rats inside the cage lay dead. Two lay on their sides and kicked through what had to be their death throes.

Tears tracked down Colleen's face, but her features were devoid of expression. Calmly she shoved her hands into waldos, mechanical gloves built into the cage, and caught one of the rodents in one hand. The creature was so sick, it couldn't move much even though it was panicked. Its ears, nose, and paws were white as paper from improper blood circulation. "Give me the serum."

A lab-coated assistant standing nearby took a vial from a protective case. The contents were colorless, and the fluid looked like water.

"Load the injector." Colleen waited patiently but Hella sensed the impatience and fear inside the woman. Hella tried to break free of the experience, not wanting to observe whatever was coming, and couldn't. Colleen's hold on her mind was too strong.

The assistant attached the vial to a tube hooked into an apparatus that looked like a small, sleek pistol inside the plastic rodent cage. Colleen squeezed the trigger experimentally, and the apparatus cycled with a soft whir. Cautiously, she cupped the rodent in one gloved palm, slid the needle into the animal's hindquarters, and triggered the injector.

The apparatus whined as it cycled, and the rodent struggled to escape Colleen's grip. Tiny bubbles formed in the tubing as fluid drained. Colleen waited, her breath held and her chest tight with anxiety so strong that Hella felt it.

The rodent squirmed and squealed, barely audible because it was so weak and the plastic cage was so thick. Pink returned to the rodent's ears, nose, and extremities. More energy flowed through it, and it fought against the big, black glove that held it.

"Everything looks good, Dr. Trammell." The assistant's voice was thin and quiet. "The serum is working."

Colleen didn't say anything. Hella felt the woman's doubt and fear. Her breath rasped dryly against the back of her throat.

The rodent suddenly convulsed, and Hella thought the reaction was even more horrifying because she couldn't feel the movement. Blood suddenly streamed from the creature's eyes, nose, mouth, ears, and anus. Small, crimson bubbles popped over its nose as it panted. It managed one final, shuddering breath, then lay still.

"No." Colleen's voice broke as she moaned.

Hella didn't understand the woman's reaction. The rodent was just a creature, not even edible unless someone were desperate. And that was only if it had been healthy, which it obviously was not.

Then suddenly the rodent was gone, replaced by the body of a small girl with mouse-brown hair. She lay on her side, blood streaming from her eyes, nose, mouth, and ears.

"No! Alice!"

Sheer panic thrummed inside Hella, and she tried to look away from the dead girl in the cage. It wasn't real.

. . . . .

She had been dreaming.

Hella sat up in bed with someone holding her by the shoulders. Instinctively she fought against the hold and morphed her hands into weapons.

"Hella!" Stampede's voice rang out in the darkness of the room as he grabbed her wrists. Moonlight filtered in through the window and gave her just enough light to see him standing at the side of her bed. "Hella!"

"Okay. You can let me go." Irritably she pushed at his hands, knocking them from her wrists.

"What happened?"

"Bad dream."

Stampede studied her. "Not like you to have bad dreams."

"Plenty of reasons after this morning." Hella scooted up in bed and placed her back against the headboard mounted on the wall. She didn't want to talk to Stampede about what she'd seen. Giving voice to the horror in that lab seemed obscene. She wouldn't give the nightmare any more time than it had already demanded.

"Want to talk about it?"

"No." *Never.* Hella reached for the water bottle on the nightstand, uncapped it, and took a few sips. Her throat was so parched, it felt as though it would crack. For the first time, she realized she was covered in perspiration.

"You going to be able to go back to sleep?"

She looked at him, his shaggy face shadowed and barely revealed by the thin moonlight. "Sure." She shrugged. "If I don't, I'll just sleep in the saddle tomorrow."

"Until the Sheldons wake you up." Stampede examined her.

"I'm fine. Really. Go back to sleep."

Stampede looked as if he wanted to argue then decided against it. He lumbered over to his bed and lay down. He was calm, complete, and looked totally relaxed. In seconds, he was snoring.

Hella took a few more sips of water. She wanted to get up and start her day, try to shake the cobwebs of the nightmare from her head, but she knew she was too tired and there was too much night left. If she got up, she'd be almost useless during most of the next day. It wouldn't have been fair to Stampede.

She lay back down and closed her eyes, and she sent a mental message to Colleen Trammell to stay out of her mind.

・ ・ ・ ・ ・

After being cooped up in the barn the whole previous day, Daisy was restless. She tramped anxiously and strained at the reins in a manner that she seldom exhibited. Hella grew tired of fighting her and wished they could get through the gates and back into the forest. That was what Daisy wanted.

Riley had his men already suited up and on their vehicles. They had replenished their rolling larders with purchases at Blossom Heat. Stampede had told Hella to help examine the goods, and that had been the most boring hour Hella had spent in a long time.

Pardot checked over the expedition carefully, making certain everything was accounted for. As she watched, Hella felt sorry for Riley. The captain was put through his paces unmercifully.

Colleen Trammell came out of the main building last. Hella watched the woman with interest. Colleen didn't appear to be still in a drug-induced stupor, but she looked hard used and moved slowly. Before climbing into the sidecar assigned to her, Colleen looked back at Hella.

The woman's lips moved, but Hella heard the woman's voice in her mind.

I'm sorry about last night.

Shamefaced, Hella broke eye contact. She didn't want to deal with any more of the woman's misery.

Faust came over to see her off. A grin stretched his big lips as she slid down from Daisy and greeted him with a fierce hug.

"I wish you could have hung around a little longer, imp."

"Me too. We'll be back this way. Soon."

Faust thumped her on the back one more time then released her and stepped back. "You've grown up, imp. I'm proud of you. Stampede has done all right by you."

"He wasn't the only one."

The big gorilloid smiled broadly at that, and anyone who didn't know him would have been afraid for his life. "You take care of yourself, Hella. And you take care of Shaggy too."

"I will." Hella hugged him one more time then squealed in delight as he effortlessly tossed her up onto Daisy's broad back. Hella flipped once and came down in the saddle effortlessly, just the way she had when he'd tossed her onto a horse when she'd been younger.

Daisy swung her broad head over to Faust, and he patted her gently. Then Stampede gave the order to move out, and the expedition got under way.

Faust stood watching after them from the catwalk, but he finally disappeared as they entered the forest.

. . . . .

Hella and Stampede ate a walking lunch because Pardot wanted to stay moving. Thankfully the landscape stayed firm. After a day of drying out, the Redblight had crept back toward arid.

Taking a piece of jerky from the bag she'd packed on Daisy's saddlebags, Hella popped it into her mouth as she walked at Stampede's side. Salt taste exploded across her tongue, and more flavor came when she chewed. The growling engines trailed behind them.

"Pardot still hasn't told you where we're going?"

Stampede shook his head as he chewed a block of dried grass. He was an omnivore, able to eat meat and vegetables, but he still needed a high intake of fiber to meet his dietary needs. "He doesn't know."

"How can that be?"

"Finally got him to fess up to it this morning. He's got this expedition out here because of some vision Dr. Trammell had back wherever they came from."

"What did she see in the vision?"

"*That* he's not being so forthcoming with." Stampede looked at her. "I don't suppose you've learned anything over this connection you have with Dr. Trammell."

"No."

"That's just a bad break."

"Yeah." Hella wished she wasn't privy to the woman's nightmares either.

. . . . .

Early in the afternoon, they stopped at a clean creek to take on fresh water. Since the recent rains, there was plenty of water, and they didn't have to worry about getting sick from stagnant areas.

While walking upstream to water Daisy, Hella found a dead armadillo biker. The Sheldon lay half submerged in the creek. He'd suffered burns and two gunshot wounds, both of those through the chest. Hella was surprised that he'd lived as long as he had, given the severity of the wounds.

She called Stampede over to survey the body.

"Stripped." Stampede flipped the corpse over with his big toe. The body moved limply. "Since all his personal belongings are gone, that means one thing, Red."

"He wasn't out here alone." Hella didn't like the certainty that she felt.

Stampede smiled but the effort was devoid of mirth. "That's right. His buddies stole his stuff, but none of them thought well enough of him to burn him before they left him." He grabbed the dead biker by one foot. "Didn't care about him and didn't care if anyone else got sick when they found this guy later." Effortlessly he dragged the corpse over to a clearing and piled leaves and grass on him.

Hella helped.

"What are you doing?" Riley stood only a short distance away. He held his rifle canted with the butt resting against his hip.

"Gonna burn this body." Stampede didn't pause in his preparations.

"If you burn that, you're going to reveal our position."

"We're not staying here." Stampede piled more branches on the dead man. "We're moving on. If those Sheldons decide to double back and find out what's burning, we'll be long gone. And we can see if they're still in the area." He gestured to Hella.

Kneeling, Hella used flint and tinder to spread sparks across the dead leaves. She blew on the embers till they caught and flames leaped hungrily. By the time she was standing, fire had spread to the dead man's dry clothing and gray smoke clouded under the overhanging branches.

"Burning that body is risky."

Stampede glanced at the security captain. "Leaving it out here is just an open invitation to disease. The last thing anyone in the Redblight wants is to spread disease across the trails. Maybe you don't have disease where you come from, but it's an issue out here."

Hella thought about the rats Colleen had been working with in the nightmare. They knew what disease was.

For a moment Riley looked as if he would say something, but evidently he thought better of it. "We need to get moving."

Stampede hoisted his rifle over one broad shoulder and started back to the expedition. "Make sure you've taken on all the fresh water you can. In case we have to go up into the brush if we get unlucky enough to catch up with the Sheldons."

With a lithe leap, Hella sprang up onto Daisy's foreleg and vaulted into the saddle. The mountain boomer shifted restlessly and tossed her head. She didn't like being around dead things either, unless she was eating them, and Hella knew for a fact that Daisy would eat an armadillo biker. She'd seen Daisy do it before, and the experience had left her queasy for hours.

■ ■ ■ ■ ■

Hella took first watch that night. She bedded Daisy down then took her sniper rifle, her low-light binocs, and a bag of food with her when she walked down the hill to take up a position outside camp. Halfway through the night, Stampede intended to relieve her.

She wasn't as tired as she'd normally have been. Despite the battle at the trade camp and the nightmares, she'd gotten more sleep than she was used to. She already missed the bath. After hours of riding and walking the trails, she was covered in road dirt and had a few bites from insects that had refused to be scared off by the repellant Pardot insisted on being used around the expedition. She was back to situation normal.

The repellant was a bad idea too. Most creatures would get a nose full of it and head for somewhere else, which could make for bad hunting if they needed it. But the scent would draw human or humanoid creatures that knew what it was.

She unwrapped one of the journey cakes they'd purchased at the trade camp. Carnegie traded hams for corn and had the grain milled at a small town north of the camp. When the grain came back to Blossom Heat, they stored it and used it.

The journey cake was cornbread seasoned with wild honey and blackberries and sprinkled with sausage. It was one of Hella's favorites, but it tended to go bad quickly, so it had to be eaten quickly. In two, three days at most, the cakes would be gone and they'd have to stop at a trade camp again to get them. They were also expensive, and if she hadn't salvaged as much as she had from the dead biker gang, she knew Stampede wouldn't have purchased as many as he had.

She sat with her legs folded under herself, in the open under a spreading elm because she wanted to be able to hear the sounds of the night around her. Riley's men often tried to stand post up against a tree or a rock, doubtless thinking that they were getting shelter. Hella knew what they were also doing was blinding their senses because those shelters also blocked sight and sound.

After she'd pinched the journey cake to pieces and fed herself, she sipped from her canteen and gazed at the stars. With all the bad weather gone for the time being, the black sky appeared shot full of diamonds.

Except one of them was falling.

Hella focused on the falling star. She'd seen them before but not often. The one she looked at was strange. It had appeared out of nowhere. The trajectory seemed slow; then she realized it wasn't slow at all because it was getting bigger and bigger.

It took her only a moment longer to be certain that the falling star was streaking right for their position. She stood, knowing it was already too late to run.

CHAPTER 13

"Stampede!" Hella held on to her rifle and watched as the meteor—she was certain that was what she was looking at—rushed closer. It looked like a fireball as it rocketed across the sky.

Back at the camp, security lamps blazed to life and aimed at the sky. Tracking lasers from the security bots kicked on and strobed the night, finally intercepting the meteor.

"I see it!" Stampede sounded anxious. "It's gonna miss us!"

Hella saw that then, and she relaxed a little. In the next instant, the meteor hurtled by overhead, less than a hundred meters above them. Later she would have sworn she felt the heat of its passing, but she wasn't sure if that were just her imagination adding detail. Despite the fact that it zoomed past in an instant, time seemed frozen.

Then the meteor was gone, rocketing into the horizon to the east. The sonic booms caught up with her then, cracking and thundering all around her. The ground quivered or maybe she was just shaking all over. She wasn't sure.

The meteorite hit the ground in the distance. A huge eruption of flames lit up the night and stretched for the heavens. Then the fiery mass collapsed back to the ground. Less than a moment later, the horrendous *boom* of the meteorite striking the earth reached her ears.

An orange glow remained visible on the eastern horizon. Then Colleen screamed into the night.

●　●　●　●　●

At first Hella tried to remain out on guard duty. She didn't want anything to do with the madness taking part inside the camp. Riley's men rousted everyone from slumber and called a meeting together. All the voices, the yelling and the cursing, carried to Hella over Stampede's comm link.

"Pardot wants to break camp and get moving." Stampede clearly wasn't happy about the possibility.

"Why?"

"He says this is the event they've been waiting for. This is the ripple Colleen saw in a vision that they came here for."

"A hunk of fried space rock?"

"I don't know." Stampede sighed tiredly. "Pardot's not saying what it is."

"It could be anything, and whatever it *was*"—Hella emphasized the past tense of the word—"it's not that anymore. No way it could be anything after hitting the ground like that."

"Doesn't matter. Pardot's convinced that this is what they want. Either we're going to lead him there or he's going to set off on his way without us."

Hella stared at the burning glow in the distance. The meteorite wouldn't be impossible to find as long as it stayed on fire. And the longer it stayed on fire, Hella was certain, the less of whatever it was would be there to find.

She walked back up to camp, ready to follow Stampede's lead.

●　●　●　●　●

Less than twenty minutes later, Hella still couldn't believe how quickly Riley and his people could break camp or that the group was mobile. She sat astride Daisy and led the way along the trail to the east. They'd caught a break there: the way they wanted to travel and the trade route Stampede had elected to follow coincided with one another.

She took her readings from a compass and plotted the course through instinct and memory. Stampede stayed more toward the middle of the caravan, where he could provide some cover in case Hella had to retreat from the front.

• • • • •

Their path took them higher up into the Buckled Mountains. By the time morning tinted the eastern sky pink and gold, they'd gone into the highlands, out of the cover of the forest. Red-tailed hawks skated on the winds and watched over them. Carrion eaters, crows and vultures that had come up out of Texas, kept watch over the caravan as well.

At the top of the rise, a good hundred meters in the lead, Hella took up her canteen from the strap around the saddle horn and gazed back the way they'd come. Some of the expedition's land-crawling vehicles struggled with the incline and the soft ground as they forced themselves upward. Every now and again, a supply wagon lost traction, skidded, and became a danger to everyone below it. Several guards walked alongside the supply wagons, helping keep them in motion.

Although she looked for Colleen, Hella never spotted the woman. She assumed Pardot had Colleen locked down.

Curiosity nagged at Hella as she wiped sleep from her eyes. No one had mentioned what the falling star might have been. She suspected Riley and his men didn't know either because they were full of questions as well.

So far they'd been lucky with the Sheldons. The biker gang hadn't come around. She assumed the Purple Dragons had turned back to the south, maybe looking for action in the border towns where Mexico, Texas, and the Redblight crashed into each other along the Raider River.

She climbed down from Daisy, got a water bag, and tied it to the mountain boomer's face. Glugging with slow deliberation, Daisy drank her fill then whined for a handful of treats till Hella gave them up.

Then Hella remounted and they got under way again. She

couldn't tell for certain how far away the impact site was, and either the fires had dimmed or the morning had leached their color away. She kept her rifle naked across her pommel and watched the surrounding land. There were a lot of hiding places behind the large rocks and in the crevasses caused by the earthquakes that had ripped through the land after the collider had exploded.

She reached into a saddle and took out a crushable boonie hat that kept the sun off her head and neck. She pulled the hat on and kept going.

· · · · ·

An hour later they reached the main trade road that cut through the heart of the mountains. Little grass grew along the trail because it was constantly cut and shifted by horses' hooves and vehicles.

An old man and three small children sat in the shade of an unfurled canvas tarp that stuck out from the mountainside along the road. The man's black skin didn't show any signs of disease, and the three children looked healthy, but they quickly hid back up in the rocks behind the old man, moving as sure-footedly as goats.

"Hold up, Stampede." Hella glanced to her left and right and waved Riley's wingmen back.

"What's going on?"

"Looks like maybe we got someone stranded." Hella surveyed the mountainsides on either side of the trail. "Or he's bait in a trap."

At one time, before the collider had exploded, the area had been a road. Rusted remnants of metal guides and blocky stumps of the highway remained. The broken pavement made the going hard for wheeled, tracked, and hoofed mounts. Daisy negotiated the path easily, one of the benefits of being a lizard and not a traditional horse.

"I see him. Got my scope on him now."

"I'm not worried about him as much as I am the three kids."

"Did they have weps?"

"None that I could see. Of course, they could have plenty in those rocks. This doesn't even have to be all of them."

"Go slow."

Hella put her heels to Daisy's sides, and the big lizard went forward slowly, just as she'd been trained. After wrapping the reins around her saddle pommel, Hella morphed her hands into weapons.

Moving slowly, the old man slid out from under the canvas tarp and held his hands level with his shoulders to his sides. His clothing consisted of rags and red dust mixed in with the gray in his curly, black hair. He spoke in a hoarse voice. "If you intend mischief or murder, I'll tell you now that I've got nothing of value left to me. We've been robbed and all but killed these past few days. Them that took from us took all my weapons, everything worth anything. They left us just our lives, and I don't think that was done out of kindness." He touched a swollen spot over his right eye. "I only ask that you let these children be. They ain't harmed nobody and only had the bad luck of being practically born orphans."

"Neither mischief nor murder." Hella repeated the old trade road hail from habit. "Just travel. I'm Hella. A scout. Who are you?"

"DaBen. It's a simple name 'cause I'm a simple man."

"Where are you from?"

"Other side of the Buckled Mountains. Barely escaped with our lives, and we lost a lot of good people. Trade camp where me and these children lived done got burned out by a biker gang."

"The Purple Dragons?"

DaBen lifted an eyebrow in surprise. "That would be them. You know of 'em?"

"They attacked Blossom Heat a couple days ago."

"We were headed there." DaBen frowned. "Does it still stand?"

"It does but we burned a lot of Purple Dragons along the wall."

DaBen smiled. "Well, you done a good thing then, scout. Wish we could have made it there to be with you."

"Where's your vehicle?"

"Didn't have no vehicle. Had a mule, only he went lame nearly a week ago. We butchered him out as best we could then packed all the meat we were able to and came this way." DaBen pursed his lips, and dehydration showed in the cracks and blisters. "What meat we had went bad, and them little ones behind me ain't had any water in almost a day. The trade roads ain't been friendly to them that cain't take care of themselves."

"Your luck's about to change." Hella slid down off the mountain boomer and switched her hands back before the man could notice them. She pulled her rifle down with her. Stampede had taught her to be charitable when she could be but never to be foolish.

. . . . .

All of the children were younger than ten years. As she watched them stuffing their bellies with food she and Stampede had given them, Hella tried to remember what it was like to be that age and couldn't. Flashes of memory hit her, but all of them quickly faded.

Two of the children were girls, one white and one black, and the boy was white as well. All of them were dressed in clothing equally as hard used as DaBen's.

"Why are we stopping?" Pardot stood in front of Stampede while the bisonoid put together a kit of food and water.

Stampede wrapped the food in a tanned hide and tucked the ends in before he rolled it. When he had everything in place, he tied rawhide strips around the ends so it would remain closed.

Hella finished knotting a hide of her own. She felt guilty about the meager rations they were leaving the man and the children with, but Stampede had pointed out that the trio wouldn't be able to carry much in the way of supplies. DaBen was too weak, and the children were too small.

And if we give them too much, they'll just become a target for someone else on the trade road that's willing to take advantage of weaker travelers, Hella told herself.

"This man needs help with these kids." Stampede didn't stop his work.

"That's none of our concern."

"No, it's not. But I'm making it mine." Stampede stood and held the wrapped hide knobby with supplies.

"You're giving them food?"

"And water. Yes. It's mine and Hella's to give."

"We've got to get moving."

Stampede nodded. "We will."

"Every minute we lose is another minute that someone else could beat us to that meteorite."

"I know that but I also know that there's no reason to believe that someone hasn't already beaten us to it or that anything survived that impact."

"It's there." Pardot was adamant.

"What's there?"

The three kids sat on the rocks and watched the argument with interest. Their quick, little fingers pinched bites of the journey cakes Hella had given them. She was going to miss those cakes, but it was good to see the children enjoying them.

Colleen Trammell arrived, riding behind one of Riley's men on an ATV. For a moment she sat there and stared at the children. Then she slid off the vehicle a little unsteadily and reached into the travel carrier behind the ATV. She took out a medical bag and glanced at Hella. "Bring the children here. Let me see if they need anything."

Hella didn't like being designated as nurse, but she knew the children would come closer to trusting her than they would Riley's men or women. The hardshells made the guards look dangerous.

She crossed over to the children and to DaBen. "She's a doctor. She can check the little ones over for any kind of sickness."

DaBen nodded and spoke briefly to the children, explaining that they should see the doctor. The children backed away despite DaBen's calm voice and his firmer tone.

"Look." Hella fanned out flavored sugar sticks. The red, green, yellow, and blue colors shone in the morning sun. "If you see the lady, I'll let you have these."

One of the girls moved forward. "Sugar stick's okay but we want something else."

"What?"

"To pet your lizard."

Hella smiled. "All right. But not till after Colleen's checked you over."

One by one, Colleen examined the children. She bandaged a burn on the boy that was showing signs of infection then shot him up with antibiotics. She followed up with instructions to DaBen on how to continue to treat the wound.

"Begging your pardon, ma'am, but I know how to treat wounds." DaBen seemed more embarrassed than affronted. "We just haven't had any meds."

"Well, you do now." Colleen pressed a med kit into his hands.

The little black girl had a cut down one forearm that would have required stitches. Instead of sewing her up, though, Colleen used some kind of glue that left a hard, protective surface.

"Don't let her pick at that. As the wound heals, the glue will come off on its own." Colleen closed her medical bag and brushed a lock of hair back from her face. She looked pale and sickly, and she shook a little bit. Hella guessed that she was still recovering from the drugs she'd been given.

DaBen told her he would watch the children closely.

Hella stood by Daisy's side as the three kids wandered around her, touching her skin and oohing and ahhing. Frustrated with standing in one spot and wanting a treat, Daisy bellowed her displeasure. The kids jumped back at once then—realizing that the monstrous lizard wasn't coming after them—unleashed gales of laughter, enjoying the sensation of being scared over something that ultimately wasn't scary.

"Look at them." Colleen's whisper was full of amazement. "They're so innocent, even after all they've been through."

Though it was hard, Hella held her tongue and didn't point out that innocence generally got a person killed as sure and as fast as anything. She knew that Colleen wasn't seeing those children. The woman was seeing Alice, and Hella was seeing that dead rodent bleeding from all orifices.

. . . . .

"We can spare one pack animal." Stampede handed the reins of the small horse to DaBen. Most of the supplies the animal had carried had already been donated to the man and the children.

"And if we weren't heading into more danger than you're in now, I'd take you with us."

Pardot stomped up at that, but a glare from Stampede sent the man into clanking retreat.

"And there's this." Stampede handed DaBen an assault rifle, a pistol, and bandoliers of ammunition for both weapons. "I'm sorry we can't do more."

Tears glistened in the old man's eyes. "You done enough, scout. It'll be a long ride from here to Blossom Heat, but I'll get these children there."

Stampede smiled. "I know you will. When you get there, ask for Faust. Tell him Stampede and Hella sent you."

"I'll do that. If you don't mind me asking, where are you headed?"

"Wherever that rock that came down last night ended up."

A troubled expression appeared on DaBen's features. "You'll want to be careful over in that part of the mountains, then, my friend. I saw that rock come down. Looked like it landed in 'Chine territory."

"That's what I thought too. I hope we're both wrong." Stampede clapped the man on the shoulder. "Neither mischief nor murder, fellow traveler. May your ways only find mercy and mother's milk on the trade roads."

"I wish the same for you and yours, scout." DaBen called the children to him then got them situated on the pack animal amid the rolls of food and water. He talked to them, already telling them stories as he led them back toward Blossom Heat. The two little girls waved to Daisy.

Riley joined Hella. "What is the 'Chine territory?"

Hella pulled herself up onto Daisy back and took up the reins. "A bad place to be. Let's hope he's wrong."

CHAPTER 14

As they closed on the impact area, Hella surveyed the damage. The meteorite had come close enough to the ground on its trajectory to set the tops of trees on fire. Several of them had burned and blackened leaves and branches at the top.

She guided Daisy from the trade road and headed down toward the burn scar that ran in a straight line. The damage was only twenty meters across and grew steadily smaller.

"Whatever it was cooled as it went through the trees." Hella ducked under a low-hanging branch. "Not completely but the damage is lessening."

"Left plenty of sign for anyone that wanted to follow it." Stampede sounded grouchy.

Hella knew part of her partner's mood came from not being able to do more for DaBen and the three orphans the old man had taken on. If they reached Blossom Heat, Faust would take care of them. But Stampede and Hella wouldn't know how that turned out for a long time. That was part of life on the road. So many events and incidents remained unknowable.

"Don't tell me Pardot isn't the only one convinced that we're going to find this thing in one piece." Hella guided Daisy around a thick tree where embers spilled down from coals still burning in the upper branches. Once she was away from the spill area, she took off her boonie hat and knocked the embers off the brim.

"You seen any fragments yet, Red?"

Hella didn't think she had. "Might not know them if we did see them."

"Out here? With all this rain? With all that heat?" Stampede snorted irritably. "We'd have found something. Since we haven't found fragments, that means this thing has held together."

"Did you see it come out of a ripple?"

"No."

"Could be a satellite. Those things still fall now and again." Hella guided Daisy to a parallel position beside the burn trail. They were into the wilderness again, and the going was slower despite Pardot's wishes.

"Just got a head's up from Riley."

Two ATV motors revved behind Hella and briefly startled Daisy as two riders quickly caught up and passed them.

Hella grimaced in understanding and took a fresh grip on her rifle. "Pardot wanted to send his own scouts on ahead."

"Yeah."

"I guess he doesn't care much about his scouts."

"Riley wasn't happy about doing it."

Hella took a little comfort from that. At least Riley was getting trainable.

■ ■ ■ ■ ■

An hour farther on, the destruction got worse. The path narrowed to ten meters, and the trees were broken and burned to within five meters from the ground. A little later the burn area chopped the tree stumps down to a little more than two meters.

By that time, Hella could see the impact area over the tops of the ruined trees.

The meteorite had slammed into a hillside and scattered red dirt in all directions. The surrounding landscape appeared covered in a cayenne coating. The impact had blown over the trees in all directions. Some of them lay uprooted and scorched. Closer in to the impact site, black ash mixed in with the red dirt. The stink of wood smoke and charred flesh thickened the air. The breeze followed the burn scar and blew fast enough to raise dust devils and ruffle the leaves.

"Do you see it?" Hella took a fresh grip on her rifle.

"Yeah. You seen any sign of Riley's scouts?"

Hella glanced at the width of the burn scar. Less than a minute later, she spotted the thick tire treads from the ATVs. The vehicles had run in single-file formation, one set of tracks running right over the top of the first set of tracks.

Stupid. They should have stayed spread out. Less chance of being surprised by the same person or group.

"I found tracks but I don't see any of the guards."

"I wouldn't think they'd have left the impact area."

Hella didn't either.

. . . . .

Only a few minutes later, Hella reined in at ground zero. She stared into the deep crater in the hillside and wondered what had struck. She didn't know because whatever had hit was no longer there.

Four of Riley's security guards arrived on their ATVs. They stayed encased in the hardshells and kept weapons ready to hand.

"It's gone?" Stampede sounded a little irritated even though she knew he'd been expecting that.

"Yeah."

"Someone took it."

"Unless it got up and walked off on its own. Tell Riley to pull his men back while I take a look around. They're ruining whatever sign might be left. If someone took whatever it was that landed here, there has to be a trail." Hella slid down off Daisy and dropped the reins to the ground. She left the rifle in its scabbard on the saddle. She was in close quarters and would rather depend on her own weapons.

One of the security guards' face shields popped open. He looked tense. "Where is it?"

"You should ask Dr. Trammell. She's the precog. Now get back and let me look around."

"I'm not going to—" The man stopped talking, listened for a moment, then turned back to his teammates. Together, they all moved back.

Hella ignored them and concentrated on the area. Land told a story. It was like a blank page, and anything that happened there, whether from a person or animal or climate condition, left the story written on the landscape.

The crater was roughly three meters wide, an ellipse that lay almost horizontal on the axis. It was almost that deep as well. Under the thin layer of red dirt, the stones making up the Buckled Mountains had cracked and crumbled. Millions of years earlier, an ocean had formed over the Redblight and left behind a layer of limestone and sandstone. The ground held the footprints well because most of the recent rainfall had drained through the karst. The soluble bedrock was composed mostly of limestone and allowed quick drainage into the aquifer below. The natural spring water fed a nearby lake.

Closer inspection revealed metallic smears against the coarse rock. But it was a metal construct that was strong enough to keep from burning up as it hurtled across the atmosphere.

A lot of footprints crisscrossed the ground. Many of them showed bare feet, not shod ones. That immediately made Hella more tense when she thought about the 'Chine. It looked like them. The 'Chine weren't known for the stylish way they dressed.

Moving out from the empty ground zero site, Hella continued circling the area, picking up transient bits and pieces from recent travelers as well as older ones. She found a horseshoe nail, brass casings that she immediately picked up for salvage, and coals from fires where someone had camped there.

"Hella." Stampede didn't sound antsy, but Hella knew Pardot was probably giving him an earful.

"I've found a trail." Hella squatted and eyed the line of tracks under a layer of loose sand. "Whoever took the meteorite tried to cover their sign."

"But you have it."

"I have it." Hella stood and went back for Daisy. She tied the big lizard's reins to the saddle pommel and commanded her to follow. They weren't going to be invisible that way, but Daisy would alert her to other presences if she missed it while tracking the covered impressions.

"I'm coming to you."

Hella relaxed at that. Having Daisy to watch over her was helpful, and even Riley's people in hardshells would at least provide primary targets, but she was most comfortable with Stampede at her back.

■ ■ ■ ■ ■

The twin trails led down into the wilderness. After the first two hundred meters, the people who had taken the meteorite hadn't bothered to sweep their tracks. Trailing them became easier. Hella could almost jog and track at the same time.

"Some kind of sled?" Riley paced Stampede, both of them to the left of Daisy.

Stampede kept his head moving, tracking motion all around them. Shadows danced constantly across the ground, and the moving grasses made spotting anyone lying in wait along the impromptu trail difficult.

Hella pushed her fear aside and concentrated on her tracking skills. That was one area where her abilities transcended Stampede's.

"Yeah. A sled." Stampede kept his voice low.

"Why didn't they use a vehicle?"

"Because the 'Chine don't frequent trade camps and they're too mobile to set up stills to make their own fuel."

"They're primitives?"

Stampede snorted derisively. "Not like anything you've ever seen before."

"Then what are they?"

"Machine people. 'Chines."

Riley glanced at Hella. "You mean with nanobots?"

"No. I mean cyborgs. The way the story goes, there was a group of military survivors here or in Texas that tried to hide out after the collider self-destructed. They remained in lockdown for a few generations, till all their stockpiles were gone, before coming back out into the world. By that time they were inbred and physically deformed. They fixed what they could with military prosthetics. One of the military detachments was a medical unit working on next-gen bionics and neural mapping. So maybe things turned out better than they would have otherwise. But the way things turned out was pretty horrifying."

"How?"

"Intellectually the 'Chine aren't the brightest people these days. Worst case scenario, they're barely above animal intelligence. Every now and again, a genius shows up, a genetic joker in the deck, and keeps the 'Chine together. They've got baseline survival code hardwired into their nervous systems—kind of an auxiliary brain. They call it ApZero."

"Application Zero?"

"Don't know. You don't get much of a chance for discussion with the 'Chine. If they catch you, they eat you."

"Cannibals?" Riley's face inside the open face shield pinched.

"Not the way they see it. They don't eat anyone else who is a 'Chine. People that aren't one of them are fair game." Stampede shrugged and adjusted his rifle. "They're brutal and they're mean, and if they've got the meteorite, we're going to have a hard time getting it back." He looked at Riley. "My question is this: Why would the 'Chine want whatever landed back there? They only value salvage. Vehicles. Devices. Electronic as well as fuel powered. Your meteorite had to fit somewhere in that."

"Not *my* meteorite." Riley glanced away from Stampede and shook his head. "And I'm not the one you can be asking questions like that of."

"Pardot's not going to give us any straight answers."

Riley remained closemouthed.

"Then tell me this: Is what we're after dangerous?"

"It hasn't killed the 'Chine yet, has it?"

· · · · ·

The trail led over rocky ground and didn't follow a trade route or path. The going got tougher for the land vehicles. Riley had even given up on his ATV and let one of his security men shepherd it for him.

"We're getting ahead of the group." Riley paused at the top of a rise beside Hella and Stampede and pointed back behind them. The rest of the expedition was almost three hundred meters to the rear. Much of the time they were invisible, and only the continued grinding and groaning of the vehicles let Hella know they were there.

"The trail's getting more fresh." Hella pointed at the parallel tracks cut through the soft loam. They were close enough that the exposed earth hadn't had time to dry out. When she put her finger into the earth, black and red granules stuck to her skin. "We're gaining."

Stampede glanced around. "Because we're faster than they are? Or because we're getting close to where these things are currently calling home?"

Due to their nomadic nature, the 'Chine didn't stay in any one area long, but they haunted the trade routes to seize goods and machines. Thankfully their numbers were limited by the fact that everyone—traders as well as brigands—hunted them to extinction along the trade roads when they could. The 'Chine were dangerous.

Riley gazed down at the damp earth on Hella's finger. He didn't look happy. "We should wait."

"If we wait for the expedition to catch up, we're letting the 'Chine get ahead again." Stampede sipped water from his canteen and replaced the cap. He gazed around at the sky. "It'll be getting dark in another couple hours. If we don't catch them before then, they'll get away."

"Why? Won't they be stopping too?"

"Maybe. They don't have to. 'Chine can walk for days. It's what makes them so hard to kill. With their eyesight, it doesn't matter if it's night or day. And if you follow them too far into the wilderness, use up too much of your ammunition and reserves, they'll dog you all the way back to safety. If you don't have enough to make it back, or if they have time, they'll kill you and pick your bones clean."

"What do you think we should do?"

"Let the caravan keep rolling for now while we forge on ahead. That way when we make camp, we'll know if the 'Chine are around."

"All right."

While Riley radioed back to his people, Hella took the lead again.

. . . . .

Almost two hours later, when the sun was sinking into the west and had already gone into hiding behind the thick forest, the ground gave way under Hella's foot and she knew she'd stepped into a trap. She morphed her hands into weapons as she yanked her foot back. "Spider-hole!"

Before she'd had time to complete the warning, the ground erupted all around them and the 'Chine burst out of the hiding places. The half human–half cybernetic creatures attacked without a word. They kept in constant communication by their ApZeroes, and they functioned like a hive mind during joint operations. There was some speculation that the ApZero near-AI had hit an event horizon and become a functioning entity, but none of the 'Chine questioned had ever verified that.

Hella threw her hands out in front of her and fired at the 'Chine clawing out of the hole at her side. The thing had once been a man. Or at least, it had been most of a man. Both flesh and blood legs had either been too deformed to remain or they'd never been there at all. The 'Chine sat on a flat surface with three metal legs with knees that articulated a full three hundred sixty degrees. A prosthesis ending in a flamethrower took the place of its right arm. Its right eye was a targeting sensor that glowed red in the fading light.

Living in caves and a steady diet of human flesh had turned the 'Chine's skin color yellow. There was little muscle tone because the external servos that instantly reminded Hella of Pardot did most of the work. The cruel mouth, cupped by a metal brace under the jaw that tied into the one encircling its head, grinned. Saliva dripped down the malformed chin.

A line of fire jetted from the flamethrower straight at Hella.

CHAPTER 15

Hella dodged to one side while furnace heat blasted into her and left her feeling as though she'd been parboiled. Her burst of .50-caliber bullets smashed into the 'Chine's face, turning it into an instant ruin of blood, flesh, and cybernetic garbage. Incredibly the mechanical humanoid swayed unsteadily then balanced on its legs. The meat body above it was dead, though. Hella had no doubt about that. But she was astonished to see the flamethrower start tracking her again.

A woman, or at least something that had at one time been feminine, ran forward with two buzz saw arms extended. Before the creature covered half the distance to Hella, the thing exploded. Hella recognized the detonation of Stampede's rifle and knew he'd saved her. She stared at the monstrosity with the flamethrower, looking for the recognizable lump of its ApZero, finally spotting it on the dead thing's left shoulder. She fired again, taking more deliberate aim.

The bullets slammed through the thin flesh and ripped into the fist-sized cluster of cybernetic parts, scattering them in all directions in a spray of blood. To her left, Daisy reared back and brought both forepaws crashing down on another 'Chine. When she took her paws back, only bloody meat paste, mechanical parts, and hydraulic fluid remained. She reached down and caught another in her jaws then lifted it from its feet and slammed it against the nearest boulder. A leg and an arm fell off the lizard's opponent.

"They've formed a hive mind." Hella jumped and rolled away as one of the 'Chine leveled an autopistol at her and opened up. Rounds cut the air and ripped into the earth where she'd been only a moment before. She came up on one knee, hands in front of her, willing her rounds to go as big as she could make them.

The large-caliber bullets smashed into the face of a 'Chine armed, literally, with a rocket launcher and drove it four stuttering steps backward. The thing continued fighting against the damage until Hella's next round plowed through the ApZero and rendered it inert.

Two 'Chine clawed at Riley, overpowering him with their strength but unable to penetrate the hardshell with their projectile weapons. Riley buttstroked one of them in the face with his rifle, twisting the creature's head around at least one hundred eighty degrees. The 'Chine stood transfixed, its eyes blank. Then a green glow relit the pupils, and it twisted its head the rest of the way around to face Riley again. It raised its left arm, which opened and exposed a long drill.

Hella took aim and fired into the ApZero node that occupied a space to the right of its spine. The node shattered and the creature stumbled back before sinking down into a bloody heap.

Fighting panic, Riley thrust his rifle barrel into the next 'Chine's open mouth and pulled the trigger. The bullets instantly killed the flesh-and-blood body, but the hive mind kept all systems operational till the following burst destroyed the ApZero.

Daisy pounced on another prey, trapping it with one forepaw then grabbing its upper body in her jaws. She tore the creature in half with a spray of blood and amber hydraulic fluid. As she tossed the top half away, both mechanical arms struggled to bring the rifle in line to shoot her while flying through the air.

Hella pointed her left hand at the torso as it sailed by and hammered the ApZero with a flurry of shots. She scrambled to another position, staying constantly in motion while trying to keep Stampede, Riley, and Daisy all in sight.

The second wave of attackers took her by surprise. Low and lean, the mutated prairie dogs launched themselves into the fray with ear-splitting squeals. The animals probably weighed about twenty kilos and were all wiry strength and speed. Metal collars glinted at their necks. She'd heard that the 'Chine could slave some animals to them.

Hella fell back immediately and carved out space with her guns blazing. If she'd been a regular person with normal weapons, she would have gotten overrun during the time she'd have needed to reload. Instead the line of furry, dead bodies in front of her grew.

Light suddenly blossomed around her, turning the darkening world into a series of garish yellow, white, and black images that flickered movement. When the acrid stink filled the air, sharper even than the stench of burning meat, Hella guessed that Stampede had fired a phosphorus grenade into one of their attackers. She ran and vaulted to the top of a boulder during the brief respite and took stock of the battlefield.

Half of the 'Chine were down, sprawled out powerless or scattered in body parts or mechanical parts. Flames danced in the lower tree branches, leaping across the area as it sought out ropes of hydraulic fluid that had spread through the trees and brush. More fires pooled across the ground.

Hella morphed one of her hands back to normal, and she plucked an HE grenade from her belt. She pulled the pin with her teeth, slipped the spoon, and heaved the high-explosive sphere into the mass of 'Chine. "Grenade!"

Stampede threw an arm up over his eyes. Riley's face shield would automatically darken to protect him from the flash.

Turning, Hella dropped over the side of the boulder to take the protection it offered. She morphed her hand back into a weapon, closed her eyes tightly, and ducked her face into her right elbow.

The grenade detonated and filled the immediate vicinity with bits and pieces of 'Chine and roasted prairie dog. When she dropped her arm and blinked her eyes open, a slavering prairie dog with its back sheathed in flames lunged at her. Hella fell to the side, and the creature crashed into the boulder. Before the fear-enraged animal could recover, she shoved a hand to the base of its skull and fired a round that emptied its head.

She got to her feet and fired into the flaming mass of 'Chine at ground zero. Despite the flames clinging to them and the fact that many of them were burning down, the survivors continued the attack. Most of the prairie dogs lay in smoldering heaps.

"Ready, Red?" Stampede sounded calm, but his voice was hoarse with the smoke.

"Yeah." Hella knew her system was still processing firepower just fine, but the backpack she carried and siphoned raw materials from was running low. If she didn't get another backpack from Daisy, she'd have to rely on her rifle.

Stampede lifted his foot and stomped the ground. A quiver ran through the earth and buckled the ground where the surviving 'Chine stood. They flew in all directions as the ground betrayed them.

Blinded by the HE grenade, Daisy pressed back against the tree line with her forepaws raised in front of her. Anything that neared her would get crushed.

Hella took a breath and focused. Before the ground had completely stopped quivering, she ran forward. As she let the nanobots flood her mind with information, push away her human senses, and rewrite her reflexes and responses, she grew afraid. All her life, all of it she could remember at least, that programming lay on the fringes of her mind, ready, willing, and able to take over. Allowing the nanobots to interact with her on that level was easy. Pulling back from them seemed to get harder each time.

Fleet as a deer, she ran across the buckled earth and the dead bodies. Totally locked into the nanobots in her body, she was a flitting gun sight. Ranges and cross hairs burned into her vision, and she reacted with precision and speed that nothing human could ever equate. When she fired, 'Chine died or ApZeroes shattered.

A 'Chine caught her left foot. Before the dying thing could lock its hand, Hella threw herself into the air and flipped, arms thrown wide as the nanobots filled her head with target acquisitions. As soon as she fired, she flicked her wrists and found the next target, blasting away as soon as she'd locked on. When she landed on her feet on a bare patch of ground, she'd killed the 'Chine that had seized her and blasted three prairie dogs that closed in on her like heat-seeking missiles.

When she stood finally, shaky with the adrenaline that filled her and warred against the control demanded by the nanobots, Hella was the only thing left alive in the fire zone. The burning trees and grass lit up the gruesome scene. The stench of burned flesh and cooking hydraulic fluid filled her nose with acrid smoke that made her sneeze. She forced the nanobots' control back from her mind and body, and that was the hardest thing she could ever remember doing.

Pistols at the ready, the rifle slung over his back, Stampede walked forward slowly. He kicked one of the 'Chine, but the dead thing flopped over on its back without response.

Flames reflected from Riley's face shield when he stopped in front of her. "How did you do that?"

"It's what I do." Hella kept her voice level even though she wanted to scream. She felt the nanobots buzzing around her thoughts, demanding to have more control again. "All part of the service."

"I've never seen anything like that."

Ignoring the man, wanting to be away from the questions and the fears, Hella went to Daisy. She talked to the mountain boomer in a soothing tone and got past the panic the sudden blindness had caused in her. She morphed her hands back to human and stroked Daisy's hide, taking as much comfort from the lizard as she gave.

■ ■ ■ ■ ■

"You all right?" Stampede spoke low and gentle as he stood behind Hella.

"I'm fine." Outside the perimeter of the camp, in the privacy afforded by the darkness, Hella took off her blouse then unfastened the chain-mail shirt. She wet a towel from her pack with water and cleaned as much of the blood, smoke, and machine fluids as she could from the armor.

"You went pretty far into it, Red. Maybe Riley was really surprised by what he saw, but I've never seen you move like that." He paused and she dried the chain mail.

"I know. I was me but I was more than me."

"I shouldn't have asked you to do that."

"If you hadn't, I'd have told you I was going to do it."

Stampede growled angrily. "I was thinking."

"Bad things happen when you do that."

"These people are scientists. They know more about things than we've ever seen. Maybe they could—"

Hella pulled the cold chain mail back on and turned to face Stampede, interrupting him. "What? Lie to us some more? They've lied to us about everything so far. Or kept us in the dark. We're supposed to suddenly start trusting these people?"

Stampede looked at her with his liquid brown eyes. Tenderly he drew her to him and hugged her. His massive heart beat deeply within his body, and he felt warm and reassuring.

"I don't want to lose you, Red. Not to anything out here in the wilderness, and not to anything that's lurking around inside your mind."

"You won't." Hella curled her fingers in his fur and wished she were that little girl Stampede had found years before. Back then she hadn't known much about the nanobots, hadn't realized they had different thoughts than she did, and hadn't known that they wanted to control her. "It surprised me tonight."

"What?"

"How easy it was to let them slip into me. I was still in control. I was still me. But I felt like I was standing at the precipice of being someone else."

"Who?"

Hella didn't answer right away. "I don't know."

"You're going to be okay, Red. I promise."

"You can't make that promise."

"I just did."

"You can't keep it."

"Try me."

Hella pushed back from him and looked him in the eye. "I do want you to make me a promise."

"Sure."

"Remember how those 'Chine died? The way their flesh died but the hive mind kept their bodies running?"

Stampede's face hardened and from the sadness in his eyes, she knew he suspected what she was going to ask. "Don't." His whisper was almost lost in the darkness.

"If something happens to me." Hella could barely get the words out of her mouth, but she had let them go too long unsaid. "If something happens and I'm not me anymore . . . don't let the nanobots take what's left of me."

Stampede looked away from her. "That's never going to happen."

"You know it could. So did Faust. I think that's one of the reasons that Faust didn't stay with us."

"Faust was looking for an easy job. He was a slacker."

Hella managed a laugh, but her vision was blurry with tears. "Faust works hard. He's chief of security at Blossom Heat, and trade camps come with their own dangers. He just didn't want to be around to see me slip away." She knew that was true. "He made his decision to leave us only a few weeks after the first time I linked with the nanobots."

That time she'd managed to save their lives as well, and the merging had been necessary if they were going to live. At times when the nanobots felt threatened, it was even harder to stay out of the link.

"I need you to promise me that, Stampede. Tonight was harder to get back than it has been before. And I just can't stop thinking about the hive mind controlling those dead 'Chine. So promise me."

Instead Stampede wrapped her in his arms again, and she felt swallowed up in parental love. She didn't know who her parents were or if she'd even had them, but she knew who'd loved her and raised her.

"You got my promise, Red, but I promise you this too: there'll be a lot of dead people before I let that happen."

By the time Hella finished changing into fresh clothing and returned to the camp, Stampede stood bathed in firelight from the cook fire. Pardot paced angrily in front of him, shaking his head vociferously.

Hella had taken time to clean her other clothes as best as she was able, soaking the jeans, blouse, and underthings with cold water so the blood wouldn't set into the fabric, and finally washing them with hydrogen peroxide that she and Stampede carried for that purpose. There were too many things in the Redblight that could track potential prey even by the scent of old bloodstains.

"—and letting them get away with it is out of the question." Pardot stared at Riley as if everything were his fault.

"Dr. Pardot, those . . ." Riley's voice failed him. "Those 'Chine are incredibly dangerous. We were lucky to escape with our lives."

"They ambushed you, Captain Riley. I understand that. But I—we—didn't come all this way to lose that device now." Pardot swiveled his attention back to Stampede. "There were only three of you."

"And all of us lucky to be alive now." Stampede stood relaxed, one hand wrapped around the barrel of his rifle while the butt rested on the ground.

Colleen Trammell sat cross-legged on the ground. She wouldn't meet Hella's gaze and didn't respond to Hella's thinking about her. Not that Hella wanted any mental contact with the woman. Having the nanobots buzzing around inside her head earlier was enough.

"Surely we can catch those things and retrieve that device." With the firelight flickering over Pardot and the exo encasing him, Hella thought he looked a lot like one of the 'Chine. She wondered if they would think so as well.

Stampede shook his head. "They move fast and at night they see as well as we do in the day. Chasing after them in the dark would be suicidal."

"In the morning, then. If you think we can make up the lead they get tonight."

"Dr. Pardot." Stampede kept his voice polite with effort. "Even in the daylight, those things are dangerous."

"You say they communicate through a common radio frequency."

"Some kind of frequency."

"What if I said we have a low-yield EMP device that will knock that system off-line? At least for a time. Do you think we would have a chance then?"

That surprised Hella. She knew what electromagnetic pulse devices were from discussions at trade camps, but she'd never heard of one small enough to be used in a localized area.

Stampede shifted his attention to Riley. "You have something like that?"

Riley gave a tight nod. "We do."

That would definitely tilt the odds, but Hella still didn't relish the idea of clashing with the mechanical zombies again.

"Questioning what I tell you is disrespectful." Pardot clanked over in front of Stampede.

Snorting in disgust, Stampede pinned Pardot with his hot gaze. "Risking my partner and my neck is my business. Getting dead lasts a whole lot longer than getting disrespected. Are we clear on that?"

Pardot trembled with rage, and the body movement translated to the support exo, causing the servos to whine in distress as they tried to interpret the reaction. "We're clear." He paused. "I can offer a bonus at this point. A successful recovery of the device will net you twice what we'd agreed upon."

Stampede kept his broad face impassive, but Hella knew he was just as taken aback as she was. It was more money than they'd ever had at one time.

Please. Hella heard Colleen's desperate plea inside her head an instant before an image of the woman's daughter dead or dying in the lab formed in her mind's eye. *For Alice.*

"Take it." Hella spoke quietly but her voice caused every head at the cook fire to turn in her direction.

Stampede hesitated only for a moment, glancing from Hella to Colleen with dark suspicion, then nodded. "All right. We'll get your device back. But we'll do it on our terms."

CHAPTER 16

Pardot didn't like the terms. He fought tooth and nail, and he almost walked a rut into his side of the cook fire, but when Stampede pointed out that if he and Hella didn't get any rest, they couldn't ride out in the morning, Pardot finally gave up and angrily retreated to his tent.

Hella squatted on one side of their private cook fire and heated a ham. She could have just as easily eaten the meat cold, but after everything she'd been through and the chill of the semidry chain mail touching her skin after the washing, she wanted something hot. When the meat was warmed through its core, she sliced it, put it on bread, added cheese, sliced apples, and served all of the food on the tin plates they carried in their gear.

"What's the occasion?" Stampede sat across from her.

Since they were leaving in the morning, Riley had volunteered his men to stand watch. Neither Hella nor Stampede thought there would be any more trouble with the 'Chine. Usually the mechmen stuck with one action or another. They didn't tend to repeat things.

"I wanted a meal. Not just something to eat."

"Okay." Stampede picked up an apple wedge, gave it a test sniff, then popped it into his mouth. He chewed with relish. "So why did you want to take Pardot's money?"

"It was a lot of money. And if he has the EMPs like he says he has, it will make things easier."

"Easier but not easy."

"With the 'Chine, nothing is easy."

"Getting dead is." Stampede looked at her levelly.

"You can get dead anywhere in the Redblight." Hella picked up her sandwich and savored the taste of the grease and bread and meat.

"How much did the woman have to do with your decision?"

"Not as much as you did."

"You spoke before I said anything."

Hella smiled at him. "Let me play it out for you. In the morning, if not tonight, Pardot would chase the 'Chine anyway. The only way we weren't going was if we decided to quit the expedition. You're not ready to do that yet."

"I'm not? That's news to me."

"It's a challenge. Us against the 'Chine. Only now we have the EMPs, which we've never had before. In the past, we've always wiped out the 'Chine wherever we crossed paths with them."

Stampede scowled. "They're as bad as cockroaches. Multiply every time you turn around."

"They also feed on travelers coming through the trade routes, so any we leave behind we might have to encounter in the future. It's better to take them now, when there are fewer numbers."

A fierce grin lit Stampede's face in the darkness. "We did wipe out a lot of them tonight."

"So they're weaker. And you also get the chance to push Pardot back, remind him who's playing on whose field."

"Have to admit there's a certain satisfaction in that."

Hella licked ham grease from her fingers and took another bite. "Getting our fee doubled was just icing on the cake. It didn't really enter into what you had already decided, but you let Pardot think it did. That way he's underestimating you, letting him think he can buy you off."

"And why would I want to let him think that?"

"In case you decide that whatever he's after is too dangerous for him to have. Things that come through the ripples generally aren't a cause for celebration. If you think whatever we recover is a bad thing, we can *lose* it somewhere."

Stampede's grin was broad. "Sometimes, Red, I think maybe you know me too well."

· · · · ·

At first light, Riley joined them while they were breaking camp. The captain carried a Kevlar ordnance bag. "The limited-field EMPs." He handed them to Stampede.

Stampede took the bag, inspected the contents quickly, and passed it to Hella.

Squatting, Hella opened the bag and peered inside. Six gray-green egg shapes lay nestled in the bag. All of the spheres were stamped with some kind of scientific or military code. Two recessed buttons were on the sides. One was beside a digital timer, and another was alone.

"There are two ways of setting off the EMPs." Riley took one of the devices and held it gingerly. He pointed to the button alone. "This one is like a grenade. Depress it and it starts an internal three-second fuse. Get to cover because there's also an antipersonnel layer wrapped around it. Should help kill whatever's left that's human on those things."

Stampede nodded. "How big is the effective range?"

"For the antipersonnel contingent, about a five-meter radius. The same as a conventional grenade. The electromagnetic pulse travels about five times that before it loses effectiveness. If you're caught in the backwash of the EM flux, all your electronics will be fried. Including your comm links. You don't have to be close to use these. Stand clear."

Stampede grimaced. "I guess the hardshells are insulated against EMPs?"

"Have to be. Otherwise we'd be incapacitated if we used them."

Hella had already guessed that, and she was certain Stampede had assumed it as well. But it was good to know in case that kind of knowledge was ever necessary.

Riley reached into his hardshell and brought out two small cases about the size of the knuckle of Hella's thumb. "These are insulated cases you can use for you comm links if you're at a questionable distance. If you get the chance to store them."

Hella took both cases, gave one to Stampede, then split the grenades between them as well.

A hesitant expression filled Riley's open face shield as he looked at Hella. "I don't know what effect the EMP will have on your nanobots. They don't affect a human's normal electromagnetic field, but you could be something different."

That was something Hella hadn't thought of, but she didn't allow herself to swap looks with Stampede.

"I'm asking you again to reconsider going by yourselves." Riley returned his attention to Stampede. "If you use those EMP devices, you could seriously damage Hella. Especially since you don't know how integrated she truly is with the nanobots. If her body is in any way dependent on them, you could kill her. Or maybe just wipe out the person you know."

As she thought about the consequences Riley was talking about, of possibly having everything she thought of as herself erased by the EMP, Hella felt sickness twist through her stomach. She kept her face neutral through sheer willpower.

"We're going by ourselves because it'll be safer for you and for us." Stampede slid his rifle over his shoulder. "If anyone can get that device back from the 'Chine, we'll get it done. Having more people will just confuse everything, not make it more simple or safer. And we'll travel faster by ourselves than we would with any of you."

"All right." Riley frowned at that, though, clearly not happy with the answer.

"How am I supposed to know what it is we're looking for?"

"Dr. Pardot says you'll know. He also says it's in your best interests not to do anything with it other than transport it back. The best scenario, according to him, would be if you were to guide us to it."

Stampede glanced to the east where the sun was almost up and the darkness in the forest was at its thinnest. "You can find the rendezvous I marked?"

"I've got the coordinates locked into the map." Riley tapped a view screen embedded in his left forearm. "We stick to the trade route for a day. If you haven't caught up to us by the evening of the next day, we're on our own."

"Good luck." Stampede reached down for his huge backpack and pulled it on. He turned and walked away, heading in the same direction the sled tracks of the 'Chine had been traveling the previous night.

Riley looked at Hella. "Be careful out there. I'd like to see you come back safe, and I don't care if you find Pardot's lost cargo."

Hella smiled and felt strange inside. She didn't like the idea of leaving Riley in the Redblight on his own. There were too many things the security captain still didn't know about. "I'll be back."

"I'm going to hold you to that."

Turning away, Hella slapped Daisy on the shoulder then started out after Stampede on foot. The mountain boomer followed along, tossing her head into the air again and again to scent.

At the top of the farthest rise from the camp, just before she heading down into the valley and leaving the expedition behind, Hella stopped and looked back. Riley remained standing where she'd left him. He gave her a final wave, then his face shield snapped closed and he turned away.

Hella put her face into the wind, found Stampede already twenty meters ahead of her, and lengthened her stride to catch up. She tried to put Riley out of her thoughts and focus on what she was doing, but it was difficult.

• • • • •

Following the sled tracks became easy for a while then turned hard again as efforts had been made to disguise or cover them.

"Evidently they figured out their ambush team wasn't coming back somewhere in here." Stampede circled the last track they'd found, going farther and farther from the origin point.

"Think they'll have any more spider-holes waiting?" Hella walked along the back trail, acting on a niggling thought that wouldn't go away.

The spider-holes were the 'Chine's favorite ambush. Trade lore had it that a 'Chine could hole up for years, using just one fingertip to trickle charge his cybernetic systems through solar power and keep the meat part alive. Hella didn't know if that was possible. Living things, even barely living things like the 'Chine, needed water.

"No. I think they'll run for shelter now."

"I've been thinking about why the 'Chine took whatever it was that survived the impact."

. "That the 'Chine wouldn't take anything unless they could use it?"

"Maybe I'm not the only one that's been thinking." Hella knelt and brushed dust out of the sled tracks they'd found. She looked around for more 'Chine footprints.

"Had plenty of time for thinking on this little hike." Stampede was grumpy. They'd covered a lot of ground, probably traveling a lot faster than their quarry across the uneven terrain. Getting a sled through the trees couldn't have been easy so far off the trade routes. "The only thing I can come up with that they'd work this hard to get is something electronic."

"Remember when the satellite landed up in Little Sahara?" The area was in the northwest section of the territory. " 'Chine were all over that."

"According to legend."

"It was supposedly some sort of military satellite. When they downloaded it, people say the programming boosted the AI over that group. Made them smarter, harder to kill, and they figured out how to make laser arrays to use as weapons."

"Is this your morning for legends, Red?"

"I'm just saying. Whatever this thing is the 'Chine recovered, they've already had it long enough for it to change them."

"If it's uploadable. If it even has a program."

"I don't think they'd work this hard for something that was just raw materials. And if it was just raw materials, they'd have already divvied, not worked to keep it intact."

Stampede sighed in frustration at not knowing and went back

to his origin point. Then he looked up. "Maybe we should start looking through the trees."

" 'Chine don't climb trees. They think of the world as two-dimensional. You taught me that."

"Maybe these are some of those mil-sat Little Sahara 'Chine. Could be they've figured out the world isn't flat."

"They didn't use any lasers last night." Hella brushed away more loose earth and leaves.

"I know they didn't learn to fly." Stampede snorted. "That would be a nightmare."

Hella studied the tracks she'd found. "They know they're being followed, so maybe they're trying to trip us up. We must be getting close. And they had to have seen us." Hella moved along the tracks she'd found. "They doubled back here."

Stampede came back to join her. He dipped a finger into the sled tracks. "These are deeper than they've been."

"Yeah." Hella grinned at her own cleverness. "So unless someone hopped onto the sled to increase the weight, it's been over these tracks twice." She dragged a finger along the track. "The real giveaway is that the grain in this track is going the wrong way."

Stampede stood and looked around. "We'll need to be more careful. We're gaining on them and they know it. Good catch, Red." He shook his head. "Doubling back is something new. These 'Chine are smarter than any of the others we've come across."

"Probably because they downloaded that mil-sat programming." Hella was teasing but she didn't want to ignore the possibility either.

"Even if they did, that's not going to save them from an EMP." Stampede started circling then found the juncture where the sled had been turned off the trail to head in another direction. "This way."

. . . . .

The 'Chine continued doubling back every so often, but the ground at the base of the Buckled Mountains wasn't karst and hadn't shed the heavy rains that had come the past few days. The mechmen's attempts at disguising the sled tracks stood out as well. But since they were 'Chine, they didn't give up their efforts to throw trackers off their trail. Once a program started to run within a pack, it usually stayed until it was proven wrong or drew negative results. They weren't bright but they were adaptive. The longer they lived, the more they learned.

Hella and Stampede tracked on the run, settling into an easy lope that could cover several klicks a day. Their bodies, hardened from life on the trade routes, met the task easily. The pace was a lot more than Riley and his men would have been able to manage on the ATVs. Daisy thought they were just playing and chirped in bliss.

With dark starting to fog the eastern sky and the sun a dying spark to the west, they halted just long enough for a quiet bite to eat and to rehydrate.

Stampede screwed the lid back onto his canteen. "They're headed for the Coyle River."

"If they're not, they're going to find it anyway." Hella studied the tracks and saw that they ran south as far as she could see. "You can't go much farther before you find the Coyle. Unless they stop somewhere along the way."

"Not here. Maybe up around Coyle Point. Near the waterfall. There are a lot of caves in that direction. The ground's mostly limestone. That's a natural hiding place for them."

"How far to the river, do you think?"

"About an hour."

Hella nodded. That was what she had figured. "I'm thinking we're about an hour behind them. If we're both right—"

"We're going to catch them at the river."

A short distance away, Daisy had her head stuck in a feedbag and munched happily.

Reaching down, Hella fingered the tracks, felt the dampness of the earth. She was sure they were both right. "With the river swollen the way it will be from the rains, they'll have to cross at Wroth's Ferry. That's if the river's not too high for the ferry."

"I know. The question is, do we want to catch the 'Chine on this side of the river or the other?"

"If they're stranded there because the river's too high, that's where we'll find them. But if the ferry's not moving—" A chill raced through Hella as she considered that. "If we get caught on the other side of the river and things go badly—"

"You mean like the EMP grenades not quite living up to Pardot's description?" Stampede smiled.

"We'll end up getting run back into the river with nowhere to go."

"That's what I'm thinking too."

"You know what the good thing is?"

"What?"

"We swim better than the 'Chine."

If the river were navigable, that was; otherwise, they'd drown. Hella decided not to mention that because she knew Stampede was already aware of it.

They checked their gear and off-loaded everything that wasn't necessary. Water went into a small waterhole left from the rains that was deep enough to conceal them submerged, followed by their rations. Stampede marked the nearby tree with a small trail flag, a bit of off-green twine they could pick up easily because they were used to looking for it. The Coyle River provided plenty of fresh water, and they could go hungry for the night.

The hardest part was leaving Daisy. The mountain boomer fretted and bawled when Hella tied her to a small tree and told her to stay. Neither the leash nor the tree was strong enough to hold Daisy when she decided to leave, but she'd been trained well enough to be patient for a few hours. After that she'd get hungry and free herself as she'd done in the past.

Leaving the big lizard was hard. Hella didn't like leaving Daisy on her own. To everyone else in the Redblight who didn't know her, and to some who did, she was a monster . . . or a source of food.

Stampede clapped Hella on the shoulder. "The sooner we go, Red, the sooner we get back."

Hella nodded, ran her long gun across her back, and headed south at Stampede's side.

CHAPTER 17

Full dark was only minutes away when Hella and Stampede topped the final rise in front of the Coyle River. Occasional gunshots still echoed through the trees, but the pacing had slowed down a lot. When Hella had first heard them, they'd been fast, and they'd been silenced almost equally as fast.

The last remnants of sunset glinted off the hard, dark water that whooshed through the small valley at the bottom of the hill. Whitewater runs across the surface told how dangerous the current was. The river had swollen over the banks at least two or three feet. Through her binocs, Hella spotted the tops of trees and brush.

Wroth's Ferry sat on the north side of the river. Two stories tall, providing protection for passengers on the first floor and comfortable machine gun nests for the security guards, the armor-plated ferry jumped and jerked as the rushing water slammed against the sides. Four thick cables connected two poles on the south side and two poles on the north side. A fifth cable ran through the windlass that pulled the ferry back and forth across the river.

The Wroth family had built the ferry more than a hundred years before. Since then, they'd charged people for cargo carried across the river and made a decent profit. All of the charges were for convenience, not to cut a passenger's throat. There were other places to cross the Coyle River, east and west of the falls, but none as safe.

Only a few crossings could be made in shallow water, and the nearest one was seventeen klicks away. With the rainy season on the Redblight, that wouldn't be safe either. Travelers had to stay on one side of the Coyle River or the other, or they had to pay the Wroth family for passage.

Hella swept her binocs across the riverbank and spotted a half dozen men and women lying dead in the mud and the water. "The 'Chine killed the Wroths."

"The Wroths have been killed before." Stampede spoke matter-of-factly, but he kept his telescope trained on the ferry as well. Stampede used a telescope because they'd never found a pair of binocs that would fit him. He lost something on depth perception, but the telescope served him well enough. "Nobody's ever killed all of them, and I suspect that all of them weren't killed tonight."

Hella felt sorry for the family. She knew them well enough to greet a few of them by name. They were honest and hardworking men and women who had managed to find a way to thrive in the Redblight.

And Stampede was right. The Wroths had been murdered a few times, but the murderers had never gotten away with it. Scouts along the trade routes had killed the murderers when they knew who had done it. Or a few years passed and the next generation of Wroths came along and evened the score.

But the 'Chine weren't common murderers.

"This is our fault." The guilt over the carnage stung Hella. She tried not to see the dead faces and hoped that she didn't know all—or *any*—of the Wroths who had been killed. "We chased the 'Chine here."

"The 'Chine were coming here whether we chased them or not. Focus on what we need to do." Stampede counted softly to himself. "How many 'Chine do you see?"

Hella studied the figures trying to get the ferry into the water. "Thirty-two."

"I count thirty-four, but I might have counted a couple of them twice."

That was easy to do. Even though the mechmen tended to be somewhat unique in the way they were made, their sheer alienness made them look alike. With the water raging the way it was, the 'Chine struggled to get the ferry into the river. Normally the Coyle was only and one hundred twenty meters across, but with the river swollen, it was closer to one hundred fifty meters.

"Do you see Pardot's cargo?"

Hella shifted her binocs again, sweeping the ferry's deck. "No. They must have already put it inside. The sled is there by the high dock."

The ferry had three sets of docks for different levels of the river. The third one, the highest, sat back farthest from the river's edge. At least it was supposed to. The third dock stood in the water, and the floor was several centimeters below the raging current.

"Are we going to go down there and hope the EMPs knock out the 'Chine?" Hella sincerely hoped not, but she couldn't imagine another way of mounting the assault.

"I'd rather come up with a plan we can survive, Red."

"Me too but if we don't think of something quick, they're going to be across the river. We can follow in the ferry, but they can push us back to the Coyle if things go badly."

" 'Chine function best on level ground." Stampede put his telescope away. His voice was normal, as if he were discussing the weather.

Hella's stomach tightened because she knew that was when Stampede was at his most deadly and most risky. She also knew he wouldn't risk their lives for Pardot and the expedition or even for the promised bonus. He'd liked and respected the Wroths. Whatever he was coming up with, most of it was about vengeance.

"While they're on the ferry's deck, they're going to be out of their element, more vulnerable. That's when we'll take them."

"How?"

Stampede grinned and it wasn't a pleasant sight at all. "You're really not going to like this, Red."

. . . . .

Hella didn't like it. She liked it even less when she belly crawled down the hill to the two poles set deep in the earth to anchor the ferry to the north side of the river. During the last five meters, she got soaked as she climbed across muddy ground and through the shallows.

When she reached the first pole, the 'Chine were nearly all boarded. The ferry wrestled with the current, but it was holding steady enough. Hella still didn't think it would survive the rapids in the middle.

And you're about to put it through even worse than that. Hella shut down her mind and didn't think about that. She focused on looping plastic explosive around the anchor pole and inserting a remote-controlled detonator. Riley and his troops had a lot of firepower, and Stampede had borrowed liberally.

The 'Chine started turning the windlass aboard the ferry and the vessel slid out into deeper, rougher waters. Shudders ran through the ferry, and the mechmen on her second deck held on tight. Many of them shifted and knocked into each other. Stampede was right about them being more vulnerable on the ferry.

Hella hurried to the second pole and looped plastic explosive around it as well. At the same time, Stampede broke cover and ran for the first pole. "Take your comm link out, Red."

That was the part that Hella hated most. She was used to Stampede being in her head all the time, privy to everything but her most private thoughts. Not having him there, not being able to hear him and talk to him whenever she wanted, unnerved her. Still, she made herself pluck the comm link bud from her ear and place it into the special container Riley had provided. She just had time to snap the container closed and store it inside her pants pocket when the 'Chine spotted Stampede and opened fire.

"Throw!" Stampede drew back his arm.

Hella fisted one of the EMP grenades and readied herself to throw. She estimated the distance to the ferry as twenty meters. The Wroths had driven their anchor points deep into land that wasn't saturated with underground water from the river. She was within the effect radius. She threw and was dismayed to see that she'd overshot the ferry wide to the left.

The EMP plopped into the water and disappeared at once.

Stampede's grenade sailed prettily and landed on top of the ferry's open second deck. The 'Chine had hardly any time to react before the grenade blew up.

Hella barely remembered to look away from the blast so she wouldn't be night-blinded. After the initial explosion, she glanced back at the ferry in time to see a handful of mangled bodies blown free. They sank into the river without a trace.

Then the second grenade detonated, creating a flash underwater and shooting a spume of spray into the air. Metallic pings sounded as the antipersonnel shot peppered the hull from the underside.

Stunned, Hella ran her hands along her body, waiting to see if the electromagnetic pulse was going to do anything to her. She felt a momentary wave of dizziness, but that quickly passed. However, the buzz of the nanobots' voices in the back of her head sounded louder than ever. Evidently they hadn't liked what they'd been subjected to.

Stampede had already leaped up onto the first cable on his side then grabbed the second, higher cable. He wrapped a length of chain they'd gotten from their gear around the cable and gripped both ends in one massive hand. Instantly the chain slid along the cable as Stampede's weight fell forward along the downgrade of the support line. Sparks flew from the metal-on-metal contact. He gripped his rifle in his right fist and fired round after round as he shot forward.

Scared of moving but more terrified of the thought of leaving Stampede on his own aboard the ferry, Hella draped her own chain over her cable and kicked off her own slide. The cable jumped and popped as the ferry continued fighting the current.

Aboard the ferry, muzzle flashes on both decks revealed that the 'Chine hadn't been completely taken down by the EMP grenades. But they had been affected because they weren't moving very well and their aim was horrible. Still, with a fully automatic weapon, a gunner didn't have to be good, just determined.

Hella morphed her right hand into a weapon and fired, using red tracers for every third round to better target the 'Chine. Bullets cut the air around her, but the mechmen collapsed backward along the second deck as the withering fire took its toll.

Stampede reached the ferry first. He let go and dropped, landing on both big hooves on the lower deck outside the enclosed passenger area. He kicked one of the 'Chine over the side then grabbed another and hurled it over as well.

Hella came down beside him, greatly aware of the silence inside her head where Stampede's voice used to be. She fired into the 'Chine and noticed that their movements were loose and disjointed. The EMPs had definitely had an effect. In fact, some of the mechmen lay on the deck, completely inert. The telltale green glow in their eyes was missing.

Stampede pulled out another EMP, armed it, and shoved it through the window into the covered passenger area. He took up his rifle in both hands as bullets chopped into the ferry's metal hide. He looked at Hella. "Blow the anchors!"

Dizziness still swirled inside Hella's head, and her guts churned. The nanobots' frantic voices turned even more insistent, maybe even frantic. She grabbed for the detonator hanging around her neck, missed because her reflexes were off, and grabbed again. She wrapped her hand around the slim control rod, found the button, and slid a finger over it.

The EMP grenade went off inside the passenger compartment, and the unaccustomed whirling sensation trebled inside Hella's head. As a child, she'd never been sick. She'd been around people with fevers, some that had even killed a few of them, and they'd talked about the dizziness and nausea that had plagued them during those dangerous temperature spikes. She felt certain she was feeling what those people had been feeling.

Before she knew it, she was on her knees, but she retained enough presence of mind to press the detonator button.

■ ■ ■ ■ ■

On the north side of the river, two blinding flashes suddenly lit up around the anchor poles only a moment before the thunderous roar of the detonations reached Hella's ears. Immediately the poles tipped over and the cables went slack, trailing in the water as the ferry bucked and twisted sideways as the current took it.

A massive wave of cold water poured over the ferry's low wall and deluged Hella. The sickness twisting like a gutted pig inside her head barely spared her any attention for the freezing temperature. Her arms and legs failed her, and her hands morphed back into hands without her willing them to.

Off balance, she slid across the deck into a pile of partially functioning 'Chine. Her vision, something she'd always taken for granted, suddenly blurred. One of the 'Chine, Hella thought it was a young girl, which made the whole idea of the mechmen even more morbid, lashed out with a long knife attached to a third arm that sprang from her chest.

Hella blocked her attacker's wrist with her forearm and felt the blade slice her right jaw. Blood turned her skin warm, and she wondered how many nanobots were lost. Focusing, Hella turned her other hand into a weapon, shoved it into the knife wielder's pallid face, and fired.

Blood and brain bits blew out the back of the girl's head. Hella's next round destroyed the ApZero on her neck for good measure. After spasming for a second, the girl went slack.

Panting for breath, still dazed, Hella forced herself to her feet. "Stampede. *Stampede.*" She put her hand to her ear then remembered the comm link was in her pocket. Wildly she glanced around and saw Stampede throwing another 'Chine over the side.

The river ran unmercifully with the ferry like a dog with prey in its jaws. Caught in the current, the floating platform slid free of the cables. Hella watched the thick, metal strands whip through the air toward her, and she was barely able to go to ground an instant before one of them sliced the space where she'd been. It caught four of the 'Chine and ripped them into halves.

Panicked, Hella looked over to Stampede, expecting him to have suffered the same fate. Instead he was on his back on the deck and firing up at mechmen on the second deck. His bullets drove them back, and there was little return fire because his adversaries were disoriented from the EMPs and the pitching deck as the ferry rode the furious river.

Stampede rolled to his feet and changed magazines in the rifle. He thrust the muzzle into the passenger compartment and fired an incendiary rocket. A heartbeat later, smoke and flames belched from the interior of the ferry's lower level.

The ferry yawed again and nearly overturned. Hella barely had time to shift her hands back and grab hold of the railing. For a moment, as she watched a dozen of the 'Chine pour into the river, she thought the ferry would go on over. Miraculously it heeled back over and landed upright again. Hella's arms felt as though they'd been torn from their sockets.

As she gazed over the top of the railing surrounding the lower deck, she saw the world rushing by her. Trees and brush along the river banks became a blur then became a tangle as the ferry swapped ends again and again.

"Get up." Stampede growled in her ear and helped her to her feet.

Morphing her hands back into weapons, Hella looked around and saw that they were the only ones left on the lower deck. Fire still burned inside the passenger compartment. Stampede charged up the stairs leading to the second deck. Still feeling nauseated, Hella followed.

Only a few 'Chine remained topside. Evidently most of them had been lost overboard. A few lay inert on the deck, rolling in loose sprawls from one side of the deck to the other as the ferry rocked and rolled on the rushing river.

Hella fired at one of the 'Chine that tried to aim an assault rifle. The large-caliber bullets stitched the creature from the left hip to the right shoulder and blew her over the side into the dark water.

Stampede charged the remaining two 'Chine only to discover his weapon was empty. He swung the rifle like a club, catching one of his adversaries in the face and knocking it out of the ferry then grabbing the other one by its human arm and heaving it over the side.

"Downstairs."

Hella read Stampede's lips more than she heard him. The roar of the river drowned out all other sounds. She followed him, a little steadier on her feet but still struggling with her balance and the drenched metal deck.

CHAPTER 18

Three 'Chine popped out of the passenger compartment doorway at about the same time Stampede stepped from the stairs to the deck. He stomped his foot, and the deck quivered, causing the ferry to jerk like a fish at the end of a line in the river.

The three mechmen went down in a tangle of arms and legs, and Stampede shot them to pieces at close range. Growling, he kicked the remains away from the door, paused at the edge, and peered inside.

Falling into position on the other side of the door, Hella looked inside as well. She wondered if Pardot's cargo had survived the incendiary blast then reasoned that anything that could crash to earth as a meteorite couldn't be harmed by anything they could throw at it.

A handful of 'Chine remained active inside the compartment, and they shot wildly, obviously still in distress over the EMP grenades. The fire had all but gone out, but flames still clung to the wooden tables and chairs bolted to the floor. The garish light the flames provided rendered the burned and twisted mechmen even more horrible.

Bracing herself in the doorway, Hella fired into the surviving creatures and watched them go down, glad that they didn't have to use another EMP grenade. She didn't know if she could keep her senses about her if they did.

Satisfied that the opposition was all dead, Stampede took out his comm link and shoved it into his ear.

Hella did the same.

"All right, Red, let's see if we can save what's left of this tub." Stampede went back through the door, and Hella followed, grateful to have his voice back inside her head.

■ ■ ■ ■ ■

The river had gentled out some as they got farther from the falls. Hella gazed out at the turbulent water and couldn't believe they'd survived the assault. The ferry remained at risk, though. A sandbar or a riverboat sunk during the flooding or any time before, and they would be in the current themselves. Hella didn't think she had the strength to save herself if she ended up in the water.

Stampede led the way to the ferry's stern. Hella couldn't remember which stern had faced the north and which had faced the south bank. In fact, if it hadn't been for knowing that the river ran west, she'd never have known north from south. All along the banks, trees and brush grew rampant.

At the railing, Stampede opened a compartment built into the wall, ignoring the blood that stained most of it, and pulled out an anchor and chain.

"If you try to drop anchor in the river, the current will tear the ferry to pieces." Hella hung onto the railing and willed her stomach to be more settled.

"I know. But our luck isn't going to hold forever." Stampede let the metal, three-forked anchor drop to the deck and fed a length of chain out after it. When he was satisfied, he started swinging the anchor overhead. A moment later, he threw the anchor into the trees lining the north bank.

The chain jumped and juddered in Stampede's hands like a live thing, and in the forest it ripped through trees and brush. Just when Hella was certain the anchor was about to tear loose a final time and drop into the river and maybe become a hazard for them, one of the tines hooked something solidly.

Stampede grunted in pain and effort as he held on to the chain. He set himself and Hella knew he was using his power again to tie himself to the ferry's deck. Anyone who didn't have Stampede's power would have slipped. Anyone with less than his strength wouldn't have been able to hold on or would have had his arms torn from his sockets. Anyone less stubborn wouldn't have endured the agony that he went through.

Screaming in pain, Stampede held the chain in a death grip. The ferry stopped rushing forward and started slipping sideways in the current, edging closer and closer to the bank. Finally, after several minutes had passed and Hella didn't think that Stampede could hang on one second longer, the ferry's bottom touched the riverbed.

Then Stampede hauled on the chain, fighting the current till it finally bucked them to the side and the ferry rested wedged up against the bank.

"Tie the chain to the cleat."

Hella slid across the deck on her knees, grabbed the chain, and wrapped it several times around one of the mooring cleats passengers used to tie onto when they needed to float vehicles that wouldn't fit on the ferry across. "Okay." She scooted back as Stampede let go the chain. She half expected the links to slither free and whirl around in lethal arcs.

Instead the chain remained taut, and the ferry stayed in shallow water.

Stampede slumped to a sitting position on the deck and flexed his cramped hands.

For a long moment, Hella and Stampede just sat there and listened to the river race by them. She checked the magazine in her rifle to make sure nothing had jarred loose. "Do you think any of the 'Chine are still alive?"

"Not on this ferry." Stampede pulled his rifle around and slipped in a fresh magazine.

"What about the ones in the water?"

"Even if there were any that could swim, they either drowned by now or they're a long way from here. Even with the hive mind powering dead bodies, they're not getting out of the river any time soon." Stampede looked at her. "Those EMPs do anything to you?"

Only because Stampede would know that she was lying if she said no, Hella told him the truth. "They made me sick."

"You still sick?"

Hella sat quietly and took stock, but the weakness and nausea she'd felt were more memory at that point than anything noticeable. "No."

"Not like you to be sick."

"I know."

"Anything permanent?"

She shook her head because she didn't think that was the case.

Stampede forced himself to his feet. "Let's go see if Pardot's cargo survived the trip. I don't think he's going to be happy if we're the only ones that made it. And I wouldn't know where to start looking for it if we lost it overboard."

. . . . .

Inside the passenger compartment, a canvas-covered object lay in the middle of a group of dead 'Chine. The mechmen's cause of death was a mixture of things: antipersonnel flétchettes, bullets, and burns from the incendiary grenade. Stampede and Hella dragged the dead things away; then Stampede slipped his belt knife into the rope that held the canvas in place.

Gingerly they pulled the canvas back and found a metal man lying there.

Stampede cursed and stepped back. His hand slid around the grip of his rifle in smooth reflex, and he pointed the barrel at the metal man.

"Wait." Hella slid forward for a closer inspection. "This isn't 'Chine. Look at it. This thing looks more like a man than any 'Chine I've ever seen. There's nothing human about him."

In fact, the figure was beautiful. Every feature, every limb, everything about the man was perfect. His silver skin glistened in the glow of Stampede's flashlight. He was bald, his head perfectly shaped, and he was more handsome than any man Hella had ever seen. He was curled into a fetal position, as if he'd gotten afraid during the recent battle and had willed himself to go to sleep. He had no garments, and he wasn't immodest in spite of his nudity because there were no obvious genitalia, but Hella recognized him as male.

"Do you think it's some kind of statue?" Stampede sounded irritated.

"I don't know." Cautiously Hella prodded the metal man with her fingers. When she made contact, her whole hand buzzed, like she'd touched something carrying electrical current. She jerked back and Stampede dropped a big hand on her shoulder and yanked her back further.

"What happened?"

Hella gazed at her hand but couldn't discern any damage. "Shocked me."

"It's carrying voltage?"

"Yes. Not enough to hurt you, but it got my attention."

Stampede gazed around the bobbing ferry. "Nothing aboard this thing carries voltage."

"The Wroths use it back at their house. A waterwheel to turn a generator so they can use metal lathes and other tools."

The metal man remained inert.

Puzzled, Hella reached for the thing and touched it again. She was prepared for the shock and didn't immediately break contact.

"Current still there?" Stampede peered at her.

"Yes."

Stampede dropped a hand onto the metal man then frowned. "I don't feel anything, and I'm as soaked as you are."

Hella took her hand back and felt the residual tingle. She curled her fingers into a fist then morphed her hand into a gun. Everything worked perfectly. She looked at Stampede.

He shook his head. Drenched and covered in blood and 'Chine fluids, he looked bedraggled.

A beam of light suddenly blazed through the window.

Hella and Stampede slid into positions at the door and peered out into the night.

A line of figures huddled on the riverbank. Moonlight glistened from rifle barrels. None of them moved like 'Chine. One of them held a bull's-eye lantern and played it over the beached ferry.

Stampede raised his voice. "Are you Wroths?"

There was a hesitation; then a man's voice replied. "We are."

"My name's Stampede. I'm a trail scout."

"We've met. You knew my father."

"Is he out there?"

"No." The voice broke. "Those 'Chine killed him. We came down here hoping to kill the 'Chine."

"They're all dead." Slowly and carefully, Stampede stood up in the lantern light. He lifted a hand to shield his eyes.

"Krissa. Get that light out of his face." The speaker was a woman who was used to being obeyed. "I'm Twyla Wroth."

Hella remembered the woman as one of the elder Wroths.

"We've met, Mrs. Wroth." Stampede walked out onto the outer deck but kept his rifle ready.

"Those 'Chine killed my husband." The woman's thin shadow stepped forward, and the moonlight revealed the hard planes of her face. She wore her hair pulled back and carried a rifle.

"All of the ones on this ferry are dead."

"You blew up the anchor posts?"

"It was the only way to keep the 'Chine on the ferry."

One of the males grumbled loudly. "Gonna be a lot of work putting everything back to rights."

"Shut up." The second male voice was deeper and sounded older. "Those 'Chine taking the ferry out on the river with the current running like that, they'd have probably gotten all four anchor posts busted. They weren't going to cross the Coyle tonight. They were just too stupid to know that."

Twyla Wroth walked over to the river's edge in muddy boots. "How did you get to be here tonight?"

Stampede twitched his ears. "That's a long story."

"Do you want to stand out here in the cold and the wet? Or do you want to sit by a fire?"

"If a fire's offered, I'll take the fire."

"Then come on out of there."

Stampede hooked a thumb over his shoulder. "I've got cargo in here I need to pack out."

"Bring it and we'll get you settled."

• • • • •

Before they could join the Wroth family inside the house, Hella and Stampede helped the survivors gather their dead family members from the mud and the river. They'd lost seven, and two of the bodies had gotten washed downriver.

Packing the corpses back to the main house was sad work, and Hella watched as Twyla Wroth stoically tended to her dead husband, a teenage son, and a daughter. The rest were people the Wroths had brought into their clan as helpers and to keep the family gene pool fresh.

They laid the bodies to rest on a concrete pad, covered them in branches, and set them alight. When Hella started shivering while the family stood outside to watch their loved ones burn, Twyla Wroth walked over to her. "You go on inside, girl. Before you catch your own death." Tears streaked the older woman's face. "There's a fire, fresh-baked bread, and pot of venison stew we keep ready all day."

"I can wait."

Firelight played over the old woman's face. "These are dead, and we'll do right by them, but this isn't your family. You see to yourself and leave us with our grieving."

Hella glanced over at Stampede. He nodded and stepped off first. She followed and the wind turned her drenched clothing to ice.

• • • • •

"I've got clothes back here you can wear." The woman wasn't a blood relative of the Wroths, but she had the same hard look that living and working on the river brought to anyone who made a home there. "I don't know if we can save yours, but we can try."

"Thank you." Hella followed the woman to the back rooms of the Wroth house. Mechanically she stripped off her clothing in the bathroom and took a quick standing shower in hot water. The nanobots had already clotted the wound on her face. By morning she wouldn't have even a scar.

"Take as long as you need." The woman spoke from the other side of the door. "The hot water tank's powered by the generator, and it takes care of a large family."

Hella stood under the needle spray till the heat burned away the cold. Then she got out and found a dress hanging on the door. That stopped her. She'd never worn a dress. She pulled on the underthings then stuck her head out the door. "This dress?"

The woman waited in the hallway and looked at her. "Doesn't it fit? I thought it would."

"I don't . . . I don't wear dresses. I've never worn a dress."

"Oh. I'll be right back." The woman went into one of the other rooms and returned with a pair of jeans and a shirt. "Everything else fit?"

"It did. Thank you. I'm sorry."

"Ain't no reason to be sorry."

Gratefully Hella took the folded clothes and pulled them into the bathroom with her.

. . . . .

If the situation hadn't been so dire and so sad, Hella would have burst out laughing when she saw Stampede sitting near the stone fireplace with a blanket wrapped around his waist. He was so big that all his clothing had to be specially made or they had to find really large clothes. None of the Wroths came anywhere close to his size.

When he saw her, he evidently sensed what was going through her mind because he scowled deeply and his ears twitched. His hooves held fresh chips from the night's action. He drank stew from a wooden bowl and chased it with milk. The Wroths kept cows too and defended their small herd by keeping them inside the lower floor of the home.

The metal man sat on his side in a corner of the room near Stampede.

"Here." One of the younger Wroth children handed Hella a wooden bowl filled with stew and a slab of bread smeared with churned butter.

Despite all the violence and horror she'd seen, or maybe because of it, Hella was ravenous. Part of that was brought on by the energy depleted by the nanobots as they kept her weapons fed. She joined Stampede beside the fireplace and enjoyed the feel of the heat soaking up through the flagstones as well as from the fireplace.

Eight small children sat at the big table in the long room. The room was meant for family, made simple and roomy, with the table and bench seats. Flame-retardant board covered the walls, and pictures drawn by children occupied several places. All of the children watched Stampede expectantly.

"They've seen you before." Hella blew on a spoonful of stew.

"Not like this." Half naked, Stampede was a testimony to the hard and violent life he'd led. Scars crisscrossed his massive body and left pink and gray tracks in their wake. Fur no longer covered several areas where the cuts had been too numerous or he had been burned.

"They tried to put me in a dress."

Stampede grinned. "That would have been funny."

"Not to me." Hella pointed her spoon at the metal man. "Anybody ask about your cargo?"

"They thought it was 'Chine at first."

"So did you."

Stampede shrugged and wiped milk from his chin with a furry forearm. "I still don't know that it isn't."

Hella cocked her head and looked at the metal man. "A long fall like that, on fire and everything, you'd expect he would have taken some damage. Burned. Melted. Gotten bent and twisted. Something. And it's not like he went untouched when the EMPs and the incendiary went off in that passenger compartment."

Stampede cocked an eyebrow. " 'He'?"

"Yes. He's a he."

"It's a machine."

"A male machine."

"If you say so." Stampede scratched under his chin with a forefinger. "I don't know what Pardot expects to get out of the thing."

Hella shrugged and continued with her meal. She thought about Daisy, knowing the mountain boomer was doubtlessly off her leash. She hoped the big lizard wouldn't wander far.

After long minutes of silence and eating, her stomach full, Hella stretched out her legs and put her back to the fireplace wall. She didn't mean to, but she laid her head back and closed her eyes.

"Hey, mister." One of the children finally found his voice.

"What?" Stampede sounded half asleep.

"Make it stop."

"Make what stop?"

"The 'Chine."

That popped Hella's eyes open. Her hands instantly morphed into weapons, and Stampede pulled his rifle over to him. She scanned the windows, thinking maybe some of the mechmen had survived after all. But only darkness filled the windows.

She looked at the small boy. "What 'Chine?"

The boy pointed at the metal man.

When Hella turned to look at him, the metal man stared back at her with iridescent silver eyes. Then he opened up out of the fetal position and started to get to his feet.

The children cried out in alarm and scattered like field mice avoiding the sudden swoop of an owl.

CHAPTER 19

Effortlessly rising to his feet, Stampede pointed his rifle at the metal man. "Stop."

The metal man ignored Stampede. Moving slowly, the metal man reached his knees and started to push himself up further. His emotionless face revealed nothing of his intentions, but his head swiveled so his gaze took in the entire room. He opened his mouth, possibly to speak, but only a high-pitched grinding issued.

Mercilessly Stampede thrust the rifle butt into the side of the metal man's head. It connected with a loud clank. The metal man flew backward and bounced off the wall, but he looked more surprised than hurt when he caught himself on hands and knees.

Stampede towered over him. "Stay down."

The metal man looked up then tried to get to his feet once more.

Stampede lunged forward and put more effort into the second blow. Ready for it, the metal man evaporated into a million bright points of light. The rifle butt thudded into the wall and knocked a hole in the wallboard. Almost instantly, the cloud of bright lights flew behind Stampede and re-formed into the metal man. The bisonoid was still head and shoulders taller than the metal man, but the metal man didn't act afraid in the least.

Instead he opened his mouth, and the strange noise came out again. When Stampede tried to swing once more, the metal man caught the bisonoid's elbow and stopped the effort. Stampede wrenched free and swung the rifle. The metal man's head separated from his shoulders and allowed the rifle barrel to pass through without connecting. Before Stampede could pull the weapon back, the metal man closed his fist on the barrel.

Shifting, Stampede released the rifle and swung his left hand toward the metal man's face in a fierce backward thrust. The metal man evaporated, and when he solidified again, he stood beside Hella. Before she could move, he wrapped one hand around her upper body and covered the side of her face with his other hand.

Electricity shot through Hella's brain, mixing up her senses and making her sick. Just as she felt her knees go slack, the metal man released her. She fell forward onto the floor, barely able to raise her hands to keep from smashing her face. Panicked, barely able to move, she rolled sideways. Stampede stepped forward and over her with one foot to protect her.

The metal man held his hands up, palms out. His voice sounded like a rusty screech when he spoke, lacking the proper timbre for anything human. "No. Harm. No harm. No harm."

"Wait." Hella caught Stampede's leg and held him back.

"Don't know if I could hurt him anyway." Nervousness sounded in Stampede's voice. "I've heard of things like him." He paused. "Not *exactly* like him. But something like him. Made up of a lot of things. Faust swore he saw one in Dallas that was made out of rats."

The metal man spoke more slowly, more like a human. "No. Harm."

Despite her spinning senses, Hella got to her feet and stared at the metal man.

"Why'd he go for you, Red?"

"I think it's because of the nanobots. Somehow, he's able to connect with them." Hella's thoughts ran rampant. She'd never met anyone like her, and she'd lived in fear of the nanobots coursing through her. But the metal man seemed drawn to them.

"Don't go there." Stampede's voice was gruff. "Whatever he is, that's not where you came from. You're not like that. Not by a long shot."

"No harm." The metal man's eyes darted back and forth between Hella and Stampede. Even though his face didn't move, his body language, the upraised hands and the pensive glancing, spoke of desperation.

"No harm." Hella nodded. "We get it. No harm." She glanced at Stampede. "Do you think maybe it would help if you lowered the rifle?"

Hesitantly Stampede dropped the rifle barrel but held the weapon in the crook of his arm. "Sure. I can do that. Mainly because hitting him doesn't hurt him, and I'm not convinced that shooting him would either."

Without another word, the metal man walked over to a corner of the room. He flew into a million pieces again for an instant, and when he re-formed, he was sitting in the corner.

Stampede scratched his chin and twitched his ears in irritation. "You know, if he decides to leave, we can't stop him."

"I'm more interested in why he's deciding to stay." Hella crossed the room and sat cross-legged in front of the metal man.

He watched her, but he rested his hands on his thighs and didn't move. "No harm. No harm."

■　■　■　■　■

"He could be some new kind of 'Chine." Martin Wroth, the eldest of the family, stared at the metal man with black-eyed suspicion. "Just because he doesn't look like anything we've ever seen before doesn't mean he isn't one."

"Doesn't mean he is either." Even though the family had suffered terrible losses during the night, Hella was quickly tiring of the hard way they treated the metal man.

He sat there, as quiet and brightly alert as a small bird, with a calm face and watchful eyes. His metallic skin borrowed some of the brightness from the flames in the fireplace, and occasionally ripples ran through his body, as though his metallic flesh shifted into more comfortable space.

"I say he's trouble."

Hella shot Martin a warning glance.

Martin Wroth was in his late forties, only a few years younger than his deceased brother. He was thin faced and balding and had tan skin from constant exposure to the elements.

Hella knew the man was in shock and probably in touch with his own mortality. It could have just as easily been he who died earlier as it was his brother, niece, and nephew.

"He's not a 'Chine." Twyla Wroth sounded satisfied about that.

"What makes you so sure?"

"Because for one thing you keep referring to him as 'he.' You, and everybody I've ever talked to about those hellish things, refer to the 'Chine as 'it.' " She nodded at the metal man. "This is a man."

Martin sat forward like a hound on point. "I'd feel better if I knew who he was, where he came from."

Hella stared into the silver depths of the metal man's eyes. Every time she'd touched him, there had been some kind of connection. He had known it too. That was why he'd gone for her, used her to learn the words he'd needed to stop Stampede.

"Hey." She spoke softly then lifted a hand with her palm facing the metal man, and she leaned forward. "Can you talk to me?"

The metal man turned his head quizzically then lifted his hand as well. "No harm."

"No harm." Hella sighed and hoped she didn't regret what she planned to do. "Learn." She pushed her hand forward.

He pulled his hand back tentatively. "No harm."

"No harm." Gently Hella caught his hand and held on despite the electricity that shivered through her.

The metal man seemed to grow a little more shiny. "No harm." His fingers curled around hers. They felt warm and supple, no longer as hard and unrelenting.

Hella touched her free hand to her chest and thought of herself. "Hella."

Tilting his head, the metal man watched her.

"Hella."

The metal man's voice sounded scratchy again then leveled out in a more human monotone. "Hel. La."

In spite of the electricity that raced through her at just within tolerable levels, Hella grinned. She pointed at Stampede and said his name. "Stampede."

"Stam. Pede."

Some of the Wroth children clapped at the success. The death of their family members had stunned them, but that had happened before and would again. Everyone knew that. Death was accepted, but a metal man in their big room was something they didn't see every day.

Even though she had seen children react in similar manners before, Hella still marveled at the resiliency of their minds. It's survival. She knew that was true. As long as a person was alive, he or she concentrated on living. Death waited around every corner. She turned her attention back to the metal man.

"Right." Encouraged by the improvement, Hella smiled.

The metal man smiled back, but the expression was a mirroring reflex, not genuine at all. Then he closed his hand over hers in a viselike grip. "Learn."

Adrenaline spiked through Hella's system. The nanobots screamed. Her senses whirled and everything went black.

*   *   *   *   *

"Hey."

The fiercest headache Hella had ever known pounded at her temples. Tears slid down her face as she struggled to remember where she was and what had happened.

Someone nudged her again. "Hey."

She recognized Stampede's voice and opened her eyes. She lay on her side and stared into the Wroths' fireplace. When she tried to speak, her voice was dry as dust. "Did you kill him?"

"Who?"

"The metal man."

"No."

"Why not?"

"Can you sit up?"

"Don't want to."

Stampede wrapped his arms around her and helped her up to a sitting position.

The metal man sat in the same corner he'd been in the previous night. He appeared relaxed and well rested. Obviously he didn't have a headache that threatened to split his skull. He gazed at her speculatively but didn't move toward her. If he had, Hella was certain she would have shot him without hesitation.

She braced herself against the wall. "Give me a minute, and I'll kill him myself."

The metal man smiled.

For the first time, Hella realized she was squinting against the light streaming in through the windows. Several of the Wroth kids had bedded down in the big room, all snoozing in sleeping bags.

"Maybe killing Scatter isn't such a good idea. Here. Drink this." Stampede pressed a cup into her hands. He was dressed, his clothes worse for the wear but clean and dry again.

"Scatter?" Hella inspected the cup and found dark liquid. She sniffed at it and decided it was coffee.

"Scatter's what I call him. His other name—" Stampede waved at the metal man. "Name."

The metal man uttered a high-pitched squeaking squeal that sounded familiar and made Hella's teeth hurt.

"That's way too impossible to pronounce. Drink your coffee. You'll feel better."

Actually Hella was ready to believe she'd never feel good again. "What did he do to me?"

"May I speak?" The metal man's—Scatter's—dialogue sounded perfect and uninflected.

"You can now." Stampede grinned at that.

"I apologize for hurting you. I did not mean to."

"You did a pretty good job of it."

"It was unavoidable. Your world is strange to me. I needed to learn where I was. Since you were amenable, I learned from you."

Hella stared at him. "You didn't learn the word *amenable* from me. And unless it means 'stupid and naive,' I don't know what it means."

"It means 'willing.'" Stampede peered out the window. "We've read it in books we've shared, so I know you know the word."

Actually Hella did know the word. "It's not one I use."

"Scatter pretty much learned everything you knew then he read a few books the Wroths have." Stampede pointed toward the tall stack of books beside Scatter. Some were manuals; others were novels. "That's only part of it. While you were sleeping—"

"Didn't feel like sleeping to me."

"—the kids took turns lugging books up and down from the Wroth library."

"They have a library?"

"Yep. Surprised me too."

Twyla Wroth stepped into the room carrying a coffee pot and a plate. "Reading is important. It's all we really have to hang on to our pasts and have a chance at any kind of future. My husband knows—*knew*—that. Sometimes we write letters for people who are traveling that can't write those letters themselves." She looked at Hella. "I heard your voice. Knew you were awake. You need to eat and get your strength up."

Hella was surprised to discover she had an appetite. Carefully, head spinning, she eased up the wall. Stampede let her manage on her own, but he stood nearby in case she needed help.

At the table, she surveyed the bacon, eggs, and pancakes on the plate. She sat in the seat Twyla Wroth indicated. "Thank you. It's been a long time since I had pancakes." She looked at the older woman. "Have you slept?"

Twyla looked haggard. "Some."

"You should rest."

The older woman shook her head. "It's easier staying busy right now. Martin and the older boys are out at the river, getting ready to put in new anchor poles."

"You blew up the old ones." Scatter volunteered the information happily.

Hella grimaced. "Sorry about that."

Twyla waved the apology away. "This won't be the first time

that the ferry has been repaired. Or that the Wroths have died defending it." She sipped on her coffee.

"Your mind is amazing, Hella." Scatter sat in the corner and acted content. "If you had not been here, I might not have been able to learn what I needed to about this world. At least, not as quickly."

"This world?" Hella bit into a strip of bacon.

"I am not from this world. I am from another. I am certain of that."

"You came through one of the ripples the collider created when it exploded."

Scatter nodded and the movement was very small, very precise. "So Stampede informed me, though I found no mention of that event in the literature that I was given."

Stampede stood by the fire and took advantage of the warmth. "After the collider exploded and the world turned inside out, printing books wasn't exactly at the top of the list for survival."

"That is true. Still, the knowledge I have gleaned has been very useful." Scatter looked at Hella. "If I had not been able to link with you, I would have remained lost for a long time. Finding you was like rolling a perfect twenty."

"A perfect twenty?" Hella savored the salty taste of the bacon and dipped a finger into the molasses that covered the pancakes.

"On a twenty-sided die, yes." Reaching into the pile of books, Scatter plucked out a volume that had elf warriors and knights on the cover. "I also learned what to do when we're confronted by dragons, though Stampede tells me that will never happen."

"I didn't think robots fell out of other worlds into this one." Hella tasted the molasses, and the sweet flavor exploded in her mouth.

"I am not a robot. I am my own person. I am—" Scatter whistle-screeched another long series of notes.

"A fractoid." Stampede went back to the window.

"That is Stampede's interpretation of what I am." Scatter nodded. "Given the circumstances and your limited understanding of my nature, I will allow that assessment."

Hella winced as she chewed. The effort seemed to dislodge the pain that had taken root inside her skull.

"Do you still have discomfort, Hella?"

"Yes."

"Do you enjoy discomfort?"

"No."

"Then why do you tolerate it?"

Hella frowned at the metal man. "It's not like I can just turn it off."

"Of course you can." Scatter's body broke apart, and he flowed to his feet. When he was once more a single creature, he was already in midstride. "Let me show you." He reached for her head.

CHAPTER 20

Hella slapped away Scatter's hand and dodged back. "Stay away from me. Last night was plenty of showing."

Scatter cocked his head curiously and studied her. "Trust me."

"No."

"You would rather endure pain?" Somehow the fractoid managed to convey hurt feelings though his face didn't really express that emotion.

"Let me finish my breakfast before I pass out again." At least that would be a relief from the agony she was presently enduring, and she would have a full stomach, provided she kept the food down.

"You will not pass out. I promise. Once you are free of the pain, you can better enjoy your meal."

Reluctantly Hella submitted herself to Scatter's ministrations.

"From what Stampede has told me, you are different from most sentient beings in this world." Scatter traced his fingertips across her forehead. Only the gentlest of shocks trailed across her skin. "You have tiny robots within you. Nanobots."

"Yes. Other people have them." Hella knew that from reading some of the materials she and Stampede had found in their travels and had met a few people who had nanobots that helped mental abilities manifest or maintain their health.

"These give you a deeper control over your body than most humans have."

"Yes." Hella hadn't even heard of anyone else with nanobots inside their bodies who could morph their hands into guns or siphon raw materials through their bodies to make gunpowder propellant and bullets.

"Yet you only use it to make pistols of your hands."

"That's all I can do."

Scatter smiled slightly then. "No. You can do much more. You simply have to learn how to master the nanobots. Can you sense what I'm doing?"

Hella concentrated on the feelings outside her temples and forehead as well as inside. Scatter had set up some kind of pattern, and the nanobots were reacting to it. Within seconds, the headache vanished.

"I must apologize, Hella. There was damage to your cerebral cortex that I did not know about." Scatter removed his hand.

"I have brain damage?" The possibility scared Hella. She'd seen people who were brain damaged having seizures that eventually killed them. Most people didn't tolerate brain-damaged individuals and left them for the wilderness to prey on. She decided then and there that she wouldn't allow herself to become a threat to Stampede.

"You did have brain damage. Slight brain damage. But you have brain damage no more. You have healed yourself."

"I did that?"

"Yes."

"How?"

Scatter picked up one of her arms and indicated a long scratch that ran along her forearm. "You healed this."

The previous night the cut had been deep, had maybe even needed stitches or glue. "I heal quickly. It's just part of the nanobots."

"You can do more with them." Scatter traced his forefinger along her arm. As soon as his finger touched the scratch, creating a weird shock rhythm, and moved on, only unblemished skin was left behind. "You are limiting what the nanobots can do for you." He turned her arm over to reveal another scratch. "Here. You try to fix this one."

Hella concentrated, trying to recapture the rhythm Scatter had started with his touch. When she had the rhythm, she was astonished as the scratch instantly healed. "I didn't know that I could do that."

"That is because you have not totally embraced your nature at this point." Scatter looked at her with kind eyes. "You have pushed your heritage away and denied it."

"I don't even know what my heritage is." Hella looked at him hopefully.

"Nor do I." Scatter cocked his head to the side again. "But I do find that I am immensely intrigued. I hope this does not discomfort you."

At first, Hella didn't know what to say. "I hear them sometimes."

"Who?"

"The nanobots."

"What do they say?"

Hella shook her head, and the reflex was miraculously without pain. "I don't know. I can't hear them."

"Maybe you do not want to."

"Maybe."

"Do you fear them?"

"I don't want to lose myself to them."

"You do not have to."

"You don't know what it feels like when they take over."

Scatter regarded her. "They cannot take over your mind, Hella."

"They do. You just haven't seen it when they're strong inside me."

"Fascinating." Scatter smiled, and she could tell the effort was genuine. "Obviously this is a conundrum I would like to pursue at some point."

Hella took back her arm. "Not this morning." She didn't know if she would ever be ready to deal with that. "Where are you from?"

Scatter reflowed himself so he was suddenly turned one hundred eighty degrees—without turning around. It appeared as if he pulled himself inside out. Hella stared at him.

Stampede laughed at her astonishment. "Being around him is going to take some getting used to."

Glancing at Stampede, seeing how the bisonoid stood with his arms cross over his chest, Scatter stood and crossed his arms in an almost perfect imitation.

Scowling, Stampede unfolded his arms. His nostrils flared and his ears twitched. "Some things are going to take even more getting used to."

"I perceive that I have done something wrong." Scatter studied Stampede.

"It isn't polite to mock someone. And it's not very smart either."

"To mock." Scatter cocked his head. "To fake, to pretend, to simulate, bogus, ersatz." He paused. "I meant no disrespect. I am still learning your way of speaking, and body language appears to have a large amount to do with it. I thought if I stood like you, I might better understand what you were referring to as being difficult to get used to."

Stamped growled.

"Weapons and the intent to use or not use them also has a lot to do with the way you communicate. The implied threat of using them can be confusing."

"I'll take your word for it. I think I make myself very clear." Stampede waved a hand in a hurry-up motion. "Tell Hella about your world."

Scatter reflowed and faced Hella, looking was appearing to step through his own body as he dropped his arms and walked toward her. "My world is perfect. I would like to go back there now." He smiled hopefully and the innocence in his expression almost broke Hella's heart. "Well, it was almost perfect. Except for the sickness that almost killed everyone."

. . . . .

"On my world, we used to be flesh and blood. Like you." Scatter gestured to include Hella and the Wroths who had gotten up to listen to the story and have breakfast. "We were on the edge of star travel. Before we did that, though, we wanted to explore our own world. And our minds."

Hella sat at the table and worked on her second helping of

pancakes. Twyla Wroth was generous and appeared grateful for the diversion from the loss she was dealing with.

"We had developed several devices that helped us perfect our bodies." Scatter smiled a little. "That's how I knew about your nanotech, Hella, though I haven't seen anything quite like it. If we hadn't learned the things we did, we would have died when the sickness came."

"What kind of sickness?" Stampede's ears flicked to attention. Sickness of any kind was cause for concern.

"We didn't know." Scatter reflowed himself, turning inside out and walking back toward the window. He held his hands out to the sun, soaking up the solar power he claimed to run on. "Perhaps something escaped in a laboratory before our world became perfect, but not everyone was at peace. Divided into two camps, the groups struggled occasionally for supremacy."

Hella listened intently but the story was an old one that dated back to copies of the Bible and Koran and Torah she and Stampede had read. Large groups of people never learned to live in harmony—even when that was the professed goal.

"The disease spread in the form of a flesh-eating bacteria. It was virulent and unstoppable. The decision was made to transfer all survivors into these bodies." Reflowing, Scatter faced them again and tapped his chest.

One of the Wroth children poked her head up from her sleeping bag. "You had enough bodies for everybody?"

The sadness on Scatter's face looked hard and alien, but it also looked majestic in a way. "No. There were not enough bodies. The sickness spread too quickly anyway. Even as fast as they worked, the two governments could not transfer everyone in time. At the time of the last viable transfer, there were hundreds of these bodies left. Unused."

"You were lucky."

Scatter smiled at the little girl. "I was. I lived. But I lost a great number of friends and family." He reflowed and walked back to the window. "I cannot bear any more loss. I need to get back to my world."

Silence hung in the room, and it became a cold and uncomfortable environment to Hella.

Thankfully the little girl wasn't finished with her questions. "How did you fall into our world?"

"I do not know. The last I remember, I was at home. Then I was here. I fell and then I woke up on the ferry when Hella and Stampede came to my rescue."

Hella felt guilty about that too. They hadn't been there to rescue Scatter, and he still wasn't free to do as he pleased.

. . . . .

"You told him he can't go back to his world?" Hella repacked the small kit she'd brought with her when she and Stampede had decided to make the run to the Coyle River.

"Not exactly."

Fastening the leather strap that bound the kit, Hella raised her head and looked out the window of the borrowed bedroom. Scatter stood out in the yard in front of the house with the river rushing by at his feet. He looked like a lost child. Sunlight glinted off his metallic skin. "What did you tell him?"

"That I didn't know how to get him back to where he came from. I told him Pardot might be able to help him with that."

That was the truth, but it wasn't all of the truth. "No one has ever found any way to get anything back through the ripples."

"No one has yet." Stampede shifted uneasily.

"You should have told him. He needs to know. From what he says, he has family back there."

"I understand that." Stampede heaved a deep sigh. "I just don't need to be the one that tells him."

"Coward."

Stampede flattened his ears and wouldn't look at her. "Telling him would be like hurting a child's feelings. And it's not my place. I'm not responsible for him. The 'Chine would have probably chopped him up for salvage by now."

"Do you think Pardot has anything better in mind for him?"

Stampede shrugged. "I'll cross that river when I get to it, Red.

One thing at a time, you know that. First we get back to our expedition . . . if Pardot and Trammell and Riley haven't ended up dead somewhere, which wouldn't be good business for us.

"Do you believe everything Scatter told us?" Hella looked around the room to make certain she hadn't forgotten anything. She wore her old jeans, but her blouse was new, a pullover with a loose waist that would be problematic in the brush.

Stampede scratched under his chin and gazed out at the fractoid. "Yeah, I believe everything he told us. I also believe he hasn't told us everything."

· · · · ·

"I want to tell you again that I'm sorry for your losses, Mrs. Wroth." Hella held the older woman's hands briefly then had to stand her ground as Twyla Wroth leaned in for a quick hug. A lump rose in Hella's throat, and she had to struggle to swallow.

"I wish you safe travel, girl. Neither mischief nor murder." Twyla gripped Hella's hands tightly. "But whenever you find 'Chine near Wroth's Ferry, do your best to kill them."

"I will." The promise was easy to make. Hella would do that anyway.

Twyla released her hands and repeated the request with Stampede. She looked tiny against his bulk.

Minutes later, with food to tide them over during their walk back, Hella took the lead as they set out. Stampede walked slack and Scatter remained in the middle of them.

· · · · ·

At midday they stopped for a brief rest and to eat. The full heat of the day rolled over the forest, and the humidity even in the shade was atrocious. Hella's clothing was damp enough to stick to her, and she knew Stampede had to be miserable. He was happiest in the winter, when it was cold enough that he blew great jets of steam from his nostrils.

Scatter wandered around but didn't get out of their sight. He touched the leaves, ran his fingers through a small pool of water, and watched a hawk lazily circling overhead.

Hella finished the last of her chicken and drank her fill of water. She watched Scatter and thought about what he'd told her about the nanobots. She glanced again at her arm where the cut had been. Even in the bright light of day, no scar remained.

Checking the inside of her left elbow, she found a scar from a year past. When the wound had happened, she'd seen the inside of her arm, the ligaments and the blood vessels. At the time she thought she would bleed to death because she couldn't get the arterial flow to stop. Finally, though, it had, and it had healed in a short time. That was the first time she and Stampede had recognized she could heal so quickly.

She concentrated on the scar then traced the raised flesh with her forefinger and re-created the rhythm Scatter had pointed out to her. When her finger passed over her arm, only smooth skin remained. The scar was gone as if it had never been.

Glancing up, she saw Stampede watching her.

A hint of unease flashed in his dark eyes, but it quickly disappeared. "Neat trick, Red."

"Yeah." But she was uncomfortable with the newfound ability as well.

A dragonfly flitted in front of Scatter. His right hand moved so fast that Hella couldn't see it. When she could see it again, his hand was in front of him and he had the dragonfly trapped between his fingers.

Stampede shifted. "Fast. I've never seen anyone that fast."

Turning his hand over, Scatter inspected the insect. A moment later, he opened his fingers, and the dragonfly flew away unharmed.

"And I've never seen anything with that kind of control."

Scatter reflowed and stood facing them. He smiled. "I also have exceptionally good hearing. Thank you."

"Sure."

"Your world is not perfect, but it is fascinating."

"Don't let something fascinating kill you."

Hella grinned at Stampede's comment. "Didn't you have insects on your world?"

"Of course. But not in a long time. And not these insects."

"What happened to the insects?"

"They died. Everything organic on our world died." Scatter looked around. "There are no animals. No trees. No plants. Not even the oceans remain. The whole world is . . . fractal, to use Stampede's word. Of course, we can make landscapes the way we want them."

He held up a hand, and it flowed, quickly becoming a cattail similar to one in the nearby pond. Except that the cattail he made was silver, just like his skin. He frowned.

"Color is more difficult, and not everyone can agree on what color to make things." In the next instant, the silver cattail had perfect color and looked natural. "We can also shape the buildings we choose to have."

When the cattail became a hand again, tiny buildings rose up from his palm. One was an office building. Another was a pyramid. And a third was a log cabin.

Hella raised her hand and looked at it. She tried to morph it into a building, but it just became a weapon. "Will I be able to do that?"

"No." Scatter's hand flowed back into a hand, and he dropped it at his side.

"Why?"

"You were not made to do something like this." Scatter smiled. "But do not worry about that, Hella. You are perfect just as you are."

"Thanks." Hella morphed her hand back to normal.

"You are welcome."

Stampede snorted impatiently. "If you two are through playing games, we've got a lot of ground to cover."

Hella shouldered her kit and took the lead again, but she couldn't help watching Scatter take in the world around him and feeling sorry for him. She couldn't imagine a world like the one he described.

Of course, the good thing was that nothing on his world ever tried to kill him. And that got her to thinking, wondering what Pardot and Trammell intended to do with Scatter.

CHAPTER 21

Only a couple of hours later, Hella reached the spot where she and Stampede had left their discarded gear submerged in the small pond. Daisy's leash still hung from the tree, but the mountain boomer was gone. When she saw the rope pooled at the bottom of the tree, Hella grew instantly anxious.

Stampede put a hand on Hella's shoulder. "She won't have gone far, Red. Relax."

"I know." Hella reached into her pocket and took out the specially carved whistle she'd made. When she blew on it, the whistle produced a trill that sounded a lot like Daisy. Pausing, Hella looked around while Stampede hauled their gear out of the pond.

"You are looking for someone." Scatter stood beside Hella.

"Daisy."

"Vegetation?"

"No. A lizard." Hella examined the ground, reading the tracks Daisy had left. Judging from the way they crisscrossed, she'd spent considerable time in the area. Hella was going to have to venture wider to figure out what direction she'd gone in. She didn't plan on leaving the area till she had Daisy back.

A shrill bleat sounded to the west.

Hella had just enough time to glance up before Daisy crashed through the brush. She carried a freshly killed deer in her crimson-stained jaws. When she reached Hella, the mountain boomer laid her prey at Hella's feet and honked happily.

Scatter stared at the lizard. "Fascinating. It is yours?"

"Daisy doesn't belong to me. She's my friend. And she's a girl."

"I apologize."

Hella reached up and hugged Daisy around the neck. The lizard butted her head against Hella so hard, she almost knocked her over. "She missed me." She scratched the lizard under the chin, and Daisy licked her face with her rough tongue.

"Is she a dragon?"

"No, she's a lizard."

Stampede carried over gear from the pond. "She's just the biggest lizard you'll ever see."

Daisy swung her head over to bump up against Stampede.

Frowning, Stampede stood there and put up with the unwanted adoration. "Daisy's also one of the most obnoxious things you'll ever cross paths with." He glanced at the deer. "I guess we're having venison tonight?"

"We are." Hella took her saddle from hiding and threw it across Daisy's shoulders. She secured the straps then secured the deer as well, tying it behind the saddle with leather straps.

"We'll be having it in a few more hours, then." Stampede pushed Daisy's head away and squinted at the sun. "We still have some traveling time left. If we don't reach the expedition by tomorrow at noon, Riley may form up a unit to come after us. I don't want him getting anyone lost."

⬛ ⬛ ⬛ ⬛ ⬛

Shortly before they chose a campsite, Hella dismounted Daisy, strung the deer up from a tree branch, and field dressed the kill. The lizard gobbled the intestines eagerly then—after Hella had cut steaks for Stampede and herself—quickly disposed of the rest of the deer as well with smacking crunches.

Later, over a small campfire, Hella roasted the steaks on sticks and added spices from their kit. When the meat was cooked, she and Stampede ate and spread out their bedrolls close to the coals. Scatter simply watched them and talked.

Hella was fatigued from everything she'd been through in the past couple of days and the lack of easy sleep the previous night. Passing out didn't count as natural sleep. She struggled to stay awake.

Scatter sat by the fire and fed small sticks to the coals, watching with interest as the twigs caught fire and briefly blazed. From the way he was sitting and the way he stared into the fire, Hella knew his thoughts were somewhere else.

"You soak up solar power; I know that. Don't you sleep?"

Looking up, Scatter shook his head and smiled. "No. I am not fatigued."

"It's going to be a long night for you."

"The quiet will be good. I can think about all that I have experienced. I can review what I have learned. I can remember the books I read last night and reread them in my mind. There is much I can do. You should not worry. I will see you in the morning."

Hella thought she might talk to him a little longer, but she closed her eyes just to rest them, and the bottom of the world fell out from under her.

· · · · ·

The next morning, before the sun was up, Hella packed the leftover venison strips into pieces of bread and passed half of them off to Stampede. They ate while traveling.

Scatter rode behind Hella on Daisy. He'd asked and Daisy hadn't minded. It wasn't that Scatter was tired. From the relentless way he walked, Hella felt certain the fractoid could have walked them all into the ground. He liked being up high so he could see more and so he could ask her questions about things he didn't know.

The conversation seemed never ending because explaining one thing would lead to several other things. As she doled out the information, Hella felt even more guilty for not telling Scatter that he'd never be able to go home again.

· · · · ·

An hour before the sun hit its apex for the day, they reached the trade road. That started a whole new wave of questions from Scatter. Hella lunched in the saddle while Stampede kept pace behind them.

Less than two hours later, they reached the expedition.

The campsite was a half mile off the trade road, nestled under a copse of pecan trees around a small pond. Security guards in hardshells ringed the site, and a handful of travelers—most of them looking like peddlers—were held up at Riley's checkpoints. The security bots were active too.

Before Hella reached the campsite, word had reached Riley that they'd returned. He came out to meet them and ended up getting caught up in the small group of peddlers who smelled someone in charge of the campsite they could get to.

"Trade, sir. Neither malice nor murder. I've got trade goods. Maybe you need something?"

Ignoring the question, Riley brushed through the men and focused on Hella and Stampede.

"Trade, sir." One of the men remained adamant. "I've got goods. Carried them a long way. The least you could do is take time to take a look."

Riley turned to the man, and the face shield snapped closed. "Stand back or I will stand you back."

Hella recognized the man as Benjamin Thor, one of the more legitimate peddlers who traveled the trade roads. He could repair electronic things as well, and he was a fair gunsmith. He was a good cook and an even better storyteller.

Reluctantly Benjamin turned and headed away from the campsite. He glanced at Stampede as he passed him. "Not a friendly face in the bunch."

"I know." Stampede spoke in a low voice.

Riley's face shield popped open again, and he smiled at Hella. "It's good to see you. We were beginning to get worried."

Hella threw her leg over Daisy's head and slid off the lizard to the ground. "We had some trouble finding your meteorite."

Peering past her, Riley looked briefly then turned his attention back to her. "Where?"

Hella pointed at Scatter. "There."

Still sitting on Daisy, Scatter waved and smiled. "Greetings."

Hella watched Riley's face as he took that in. "Okay. Follow me to Dr. Pardot." He turned and walked back into the campsite.

Stampede twitched his ears and shook his head. "Don't know about you, Red, but I don't think he was expecting the cargo to be Scatter."

"Me neither."

"You've got to wonder if Pardot is expecting Scatter."

"We'll find out soon enough."

· · · · ·

Pardot stared at Scatter as the fractoid stood in the center of the camp. "Extraordinary."

"Thank you." Scatter smiled. "You are extraordinary as well." He looked at everyone around him. "We are all extraordinary."

Surprise drove Pardot back a step and his eyebrows raised. "You can talk?"

"Yes."

Pardot turned his gaze on Stampede. "You taught it to speak?"

Stampede shook his head. "No. He could already speak."

"Not our language."

Hella wondered how Pardot knew that.

Masking his perturbation, although his ears flicked, Stampede kept his voice level. "He taught himself."

"How?"

"I don't know."

Hella was glad Stampede didn't give away her part in Scatter's education. The last thing she needed was the man wanting to poke and prod her or yell at her because of her unwilling complicity.

Colleen Trammell stood beside Pardot, a genuine smile on her tired face. She didn't look any better rested than when Hella had last seen her. "It's more adaptive than we thought."

A stray thought from the woman bumped into Hella's mind: *Alice is going to be all right.* Hella felt the relief as well. She drew her thoughts back and tried to shield herself. "He's not an 'it.' He's a he. He has a name."

Scatter opened his mouth and that high-pitched screeching squawk that Hella remembered filled her ears.

"That's his name. We call him Scatter."

Servos on his exo suit whining, Pardot walked around Scatter. "Why would you call him such a thing?"

In order to follow the man, Scatter reflowed to continue facing Pardot. Stepping back quickly in surprise, Pardot's servos whined in protest at the sudden movement.

With effort, Hella kept from laughing. "That's why."

Pardot halted in his tracks. "Extraordinary."

Scatter nodded. "Thank you. It is nothing."

Ignoring the fractoid, Pardot looked back at Colleen. "Did you know it—*he*—could do this?"

"You know as much about the last one we saw as I do, Dr. Pardot."

The last one? Hella watched both of them carefully.

Pardot scowled. "I meant while you were in your precog state."

"No. I only saw it—*him*—falling to earth where we found him."

"Excuse me." Scatter folded his arms across his shiny chest. "You found another being such as me? Where did you find this being? Can you take me to this being?"

Pardot shot Colleen a withering glare.

Stampede cleared his throat and, to anyone who knew him, sounded testy. "If you knew we were looking for a metal man, you might have told us that. It would have made searching easier."

Impatiently, the first time Hella had seen that emotion in the fractoid, Scatter stepped in front of Pardot. "I want to know about the other being. I want to know—" He didn't get any farther.

Pardot raised a hand and placed it in the center of Scatter's chest. An azure energy blast arced from Pardot's hand and blew the fractoid back a dozen feet, taking two security guards down with him.

"What are you doing?" Hella's hands already formed weapons, and she took a step forward.

Shifting to her, Pardot lifted his hand, and his second blast slammed into her and lifted her off her feet. She never felt herself hit the ground.

. . . . .

Pain, way too familiar, jolted Hella back to wakefulness. She sat up in darkness, then realized she was under a tent. Her hands morphed into weapons before she drew her next breath.

"Easy, Red."

Focusing on Stampede's voice, Hella blinked and gave her vision a moment to adjust to the gloom. He sat cross-legged in the tent with his rifle across his knees.

"What happened?"

"Pardot shot you."

"I remember that." Hella morphed her hand and ran it across her chest, but all she felt was the familiar hardness of the chain-mail shirt. "With some kind of energy weapon."

"He calls it a disruptor. It's supposed to temporarily fry your synapses. Render you unconscious. He said it was nonlethal."

"I'm surprised you didn't kill him." Hella sat up. The disruptor had been nonlethal, but the experience felt only just.

"I might have but I knew you were still alive, and if I opened up on Pardot, Riley and his people would have killed us both."

Hella looked around the tent, but they were alone. "Where's Scatter?"

"They have him."

"What are they doing to him?"

"I don't know."

"Is he still alive?"

"I'm pretty sure that he is."

"Why?"

"They wouldn't have gone all this way to just kill him."

"What are we going to do?"

Stampede's ears twitched. "We haven't been fired. They still need us. At least that's what I was told. And Pardot is willing to overlook your bad behavior."

"What bad behavior?"

"Pulling weapons on him."

"Awfully generous, isn't he?"

"Not a bit. He's desperate. He still needs a guide, and we've got him this far."

Hella held her aching head. "Why did Pardot shoot Scatter?"

"Because he felt threatened."

"Scatter wasn't threatening Pardot. We saw Scatter catch a dragonfly on the wing. If he'd wanted to hurt Pardot, it would have been done before anyone could stop it."

Stampede sighed. "Pardot hasn't seen Scatter catch dragonflies. He said he felt threatened, and I've given that some thought while I've sat here and listened to you sleep."

"Thanks."

"If I'd been Pardot, out in the middle of unfamiliar territory the way he is, confronted with something he didn't know enough about that was suddenly up in his face, I'd have felt threatened too." Stampede fixed her with his gaze. "You would have too, and you'd probably have responded in the same fashion."

"Pardot shot me."

"You moved on him too quick, Red. He told me he just reacted and wasn't thinking clearly at the time."

Hella knew the explanation was logical, but she felt protective of Scatter. She also knew that her feelings compromised her. "You heard what Pardot said about having seen another metal man?"

Stampede nodded. "I did."

"I don't suppose he said anything more about that?"

"No, and I get the feeling that he's not going to be very forthcoming with any more information."

Taking another breath, Hella decided to try what she'd learned from Scatter. She put her hands on her head and rubbed her temples, trying to create the healing rhythm. After a moment the buzzing sensation kicked in, and her headache went away. She smiled.

"Better?" Stampede eyed her speculatively.

"Yeah." Hella peered through the open tent flap. "I know you're probably ready to leave Pardot and the rest, but I want to stay long enough to figure out what they're going to do with Scatter."

"I know, Red. So do I. But hanging around these people is going to be dangerous in a lot of ways."

"Scatter has taught me things about the nanobots. I'd like to see what else he knows. Maybe he can help me learn something about where I came from."

Stampede shifted his grip on his rifle. "I know, and I feel responsible for Scatter too. He's really . . ."

"Innocent."

Stampede nodded. "Yeah. That. You don't see that out here a lot. In fact, the last time I saw it was the day I found you."

CHAPTER 22

In the stream that ran near the camp, Hella scrubbed the tin plates she and Stampede had used for breakfast then rinsed them with sanitized water. Minnows and crawfish darted through the shallows and plucked tidbits of food that floated on the surface before swimming back into the depths with their prizes.

A shadow fell onto the ground beside Hella as she shook the water from the plates.

"You could have had breakfast with us."

Holding on to the plates and utensils, Hella stood up and faced Riley. "Thank you, but no. Stampede and I were fine."

"Look, about yesterday—"

"Scatter panicked Pardot and I overreacted. I understand that." She said that but she still didn't feel it was true.

"No hard feelings?"

"No."

Riley smiled and nodded. "Good. That's really good. I pointed out to Dr. Pardot that we couldn't have come as far as we have or found the fractoid without the help you and Stampede provided."

"I hope he understands that."

"He does."

"Are Scatter's people really called fractoids?"

Riley laughed and the sound was almost honest and easy. "No. I heard Stampede say that, and I liked it. Even Dr. Pardot has begun calling them fractoids."

"Scatter isn't the first one they've found?"

Face darkening, Riley was silent for a moment. "That's something I can't tell you."

"Can't or won't?" Hella kept her tone light, but she knew she wasn't fooling anyone.

"If Dr. Pardot told me not to tell you, I wouldn't. But he hasn't told me, and I don't know."

Back at the camp, everything was in full swing as the security team loaded up the ATVs and mini wagons. Stampede stood with Dr. Pardot and consulted a map.

Hella turned back to Riley. "Where's Scatter?"

"With Dr. Trammell."

"I haven't seen him this morning."

"Dr. Pardot and Dr. Trammell have had a lot of questions for him. As it turns out, he's had a lot of questions for them."

After her experience with Scatter over the past couple of days, Hella easily believed that.

"We should be ready to move out within the next thirty minutes."

Hella gazed at the eastern sky and saw the sun was up. She knew Stampede was antsy to get under way. "Do you know where we're heading?"

Riley shook his head. "East. That's all Dr. Pardot told me."

"How far?"

"I don't know. Why?"

"If we go very much farther, we're going to run into Amichi Mountain country."

A frown creased Riley's forehead creased. "That's a bad thing?"

"The eastern section of the Redblight is swampland. It's hard traveling and the area is filled with every kind of winged, walking, slithering, and swimming bloodsucker you can imagine."

"You don't paint a very appetizing scenario."

"Wait till you see the alligators. Some of them make Daisy look small." Hella headed back up the hill toward the camp.

Riley fell into step beside her. "That's a joke, right?"

"No."

. . . . .

"Where are we going?" Hella stood at Stampede's side, apart from the security people. She still hadn't seen Scatter and wasn't happy about that.

"East."

"That's what Riley said."

"Then you know as much as I do, Red."

"Why east?"

"Trammell."

"More visions?"

"That's what she says."

"She tell you that?"

"Pardot did."

Hella glanced around the camp and knew that Riley would have his people ready to go in a few more minutes. "Did you happen to tell Pardot about the Amichi Mountain range?"

"I did."

"He knows what he's getting into?"

"As best as I could explain it to him."

Taking a hard candy from her pocket, Hella popped it into her mouth. "Did Pardot tell you what we're looking for next?"

"No. He said we'll know it when we see it."

Hella sucked on the honey-flavored disk. "Have you talked to Scatter?"

"No. But I saw him." Stampede nodded his horned head.

Stepping around the bisonoid, Hella looked at the tent just behind Pardot's. Colleen Trammell stood outside her tent, talking to Scatter, who seemed to hang on her every word.

Alice is going to be all right. No matter what has to be done, Alice is going to be taken care of.

"Did you say something, Red?"

Startled, Hella glanced up at Stampede. "No." She went to saddle Daisy, but she didn't like the way the echoes of Colleen's desperate thoughts rattled through her mind.

• • • • •

Hella took point, but Riley flanked her with two wings to double up on security as they followed the trade road. Other travelers and merchants walked the road as well, and most of them approached the expedition. Several had goods they wanted to barter. A few had funds they wanted to invest in buying goods from the expedition.

The way was hot, humid, and hard. Daisy flowed effortlessly along the trail, but Hella started to feel fatigued as she rolled in the saddle. She missed having Scatter behind her asking questions. Every now and again she caught sight of the fractoid walking with Pardot. The two chatted constantly, and Pardot appeared to be matching Scatter question for question.

When they took a noonday break, Hella was disappointed to see that Scatter continued his dialogue with Pardot without approaching her.

"What's on your mind, Red?"

Hella glanced over at Stampede as he took a jar of peaches from the goods they'd purchased in Blossom Heat. "Scatter." She nodded at the fractoid still talking to Pardot.

"I suppose they have a lot to talk about." Stampede opened the jar of peaches and hooked out a slice with his fingers. He popped the peach into his mouth.

"I didn't figure he would stay away from us."

"We don't have the answers he's looking for."

"Do you think they've told him he doesn't have a way home again?"

"For all we know, Red, those people can get him there. But I've never heard about it."

"Why do you think that?"

Stampede shrugged and slipped another peach into his mouth. "Dr. Trammell seems capable of finding fractoids."

"Don't you think that's odd?"

"There's a lot of odd things out in the Redblight. You've seen them." Stampede cut his gaze to Daisy, who had her face happily inside a feedbag. "You ride one of the strangest anyone here has ever seen."

"You and I know how to follow tracks and sign. Do you think Colleen's precog is something like that?"

"Maybe." Stampede looked at her. "You and I learned to track by following things. We know track and sign because we've seen them before."

"Right. Colleen and Pardot have seen a fractoid before."

"That's what they said."

"I don't have any answers about it, though."

"You're right. But someone knows the answers."

Stampede screwed the lid back on the peach jar. "Maybe one of us should talk to Colleen Trammell."

"Sure."

"But do it carefully."

■ ■ ■ ■ ■

Although Pardot kept Colleen Trammell under his thumb most of the time, there were still occasions she was on her own. During the evening, after camp was made, Pardot took Scatter into the lab and performed tests by himself. Hella passed by without being seen. Through the tent flap, Scatter looked totally at ease as Pardot scanned him with instruments. Hella didn't understand how Scatter could act so relaxed after getting blasted by the disruptor.

Two guards stood watch over Colleen's tent. They stopped Hella at the doorway.

"I'd like to see Dr. Trammell." Hella remained polite with effort. The schism between the security guards and her and Stampede seemed to have grown wider and wider all day. Whatever secrets Pardot guarded were splitting the expedition.

"Dr. Trammell isn't seeing anyone." Broad and beefy, the guard bordered on the edge of rudeness.

"I have a wound that I think may be getting septic."

"Have your boss take a look at it."

"I'd rather have a woman look. Stampede doesn't embarrass easily, and I don't either, but he's not a medical doctor and he's not female."

"You could go see—"

Colleen stuck her head through the tent flaps and glared at the guards. "She can see me."

The guards didn't move.

"Now, if you please." Her words carried an edge to them.

Reluctantly the guards stepped back and allowed Hella through. Hella ignored both of them as she entered the tent. Colleen zipped the flap closed behind her then switched on a small device in the center of the dome roof.

"You're not really wounded, are you?" Colleen studied her. "I would have noticed it, and I don't think you would have waited all day to come see me."

Hella didn't speak.

Colleen pointed at the device. "That's a white-noise generator. It keeps anyone outside the tent from listening in. Even those men standing guard can't hear us speaking in here."

That also meant Stampede probably couldn't hear her over the comm link. "I'm out of touch with Stampede. He's going to come looking."

"Tell him you're with me." Colleen flicked a switch on the white noise device.

"Stampede?"

"Yeah. I lost you for a minute."

"I'm with Dr. Trammell. She's going to look at my wound. While I'm talking to her, you're not going to be able to hear me."

Stampede hesitated for a minute and Hella knew he was uneasy about the situation. The comm links were important in their line of work. "Okay, Red. If you get into trouble, you can always shoot your way out of the tent."

Hella smothered a smile since Colleen couldn't hear the exchange. She nodded and Colleen switched the white-noise generator back on.

The tent was small and neatly organized. A tiny desk and a computer occupied one corner, and an airbed took up about a third of the space. An energy-charged pad lay on the ground and kept the dust and allergens at bay. The air inside the tent smelled too clean, almost as if it were canned.

Colleen sat on the airbed and gestured at the desk. "Please. Sit."

"Thanks, but I'm all right." Hella sat cross-legged on the floor. "What did you want to talk to me about?"

"You came out here to find Scatter."

"Or something—*someone*—like him, yes."

"Why?"

Colleen composed her thoughts before speaking. She still looked worn out from the hard traveling they'd done that day. "Dr. Pardot believes he can reverse-engineer some of the technology that created Scatter."

Hella took a breath and considered how best to proceed in her questioning. She thought about simply asking the woman how they knew about Scatter or his people, but she decided that might spook Colleen. Hella didn't want to do that. "You told me this has something to do with your daughter, Alice."

"Yes."

"Is she dying?"

Colleen opened her mouth and looked shocked, as though she'd just been slapped. "I never told you that."

"Not in words but when you touched my mind, it opened up something that hasn't completely stopped."

Embarrassed, Colleen shook her head. "I never intended for that to happen."

"I didn't think so but it did." Hella hesitated. "When you were in Blossom Heat, still suffering from the drugs Pardot kept you on, you dreamed of Alice. I saw her. I saw you. In the lab where you were trying to find a cure for her."

Tears filled Colleen's eyes, and Hella almost panicked. She hadn't meant to make the woman cry. Hella had seen people cry before, but she'd never been the cause of it. She and Stampede lived apart from other people and didn't get involved on an emotional level or even get close to them. She didn't know whether to apologize or run.

"Alice has a disease." Colleen's words came hard and sounded hoarse. "A horrible, deadly disease. And if I don't save her, she's going to die."

Images of the dying rodents overlapped with those of the child in Hella's mind.

"There is nothing—*nothing*—as horrible as the death of a child."

Despite the gravity of Colleen's words, Hella almost objected. Any death was horrible. When they'd burned the Wroths back at the Coyle River, Hella would have been hard pressed to figure out whom she felt more sorry for. Age wasn't a distinction in her world. Death, when people weren't looking, took everyone.

"I will not allow my daughter to die." Colleen's voice shook with emotion.

"How did you know to look for Scatter out here?"

"I've dreamed about Alice for almost two years. I was desperate to find a way to save her. So I took drugs to amplify my precog abilities." Colleen took a breath, more under control. "I forced myself to *see* a way to save her. And I did. Even then, though, I almost killed myself before I found an answer. If Dr. Pardot hadn't found me and saved me when he did—" She shook her head. "Then no one would have been alive to save Alice."

"How do you know Scatter can help you?"

"I know he has told you how his people found a way to save themselves from the disease in his world."

"Yes."

"By putting their personalities into the machines."

Hella nodded.

"Alice is wasting away, Hella. Dying a little bit each day. If Dr. Pardot is successful in his endeavors, we'll be able to replicate the machine bodies in our labs. I can save my daughter."

The possibility didn't sound like salvation to Hella. It sounded too much like becoming a 'Chine. "You didn't just dream up Scatter, though. You already knew his people existed."

Colleen shook her head. "You're asking too many questions.

Dr. Pardot would be unhappy to learn that I've told you as much as I have."

"I'm not going to tell him. And what you know could help Stampede and me"—Hella was going to say, *save us,* but changed her mind.—"help you save your daughter."

For a time Colleen remained silent. Then she nodded. "We knew his people existed."

"How?"

"One of them came through a ripple in our city. Dr. Pardot and I got to examine it—*him*—but never managed to speak with him."

"Why?"

"There wasn't time. It—*he*—expired too soon after we made the acquisition."

"How?"

"Damage from coming through the ripple? From colliding with the ground? Or maybe he was damaged and dying before he appeared in our world. We don't know."

Hella thought about the entry Scatter had made into their world and figured it would be hard to destroy a fractoid. However, Dr. Pardot's disruptor had taken Scatter out pretty quickly.

"You've been an amazing help to us, Hella. You and Stampede. Dr. Pardot is aware that we're probably alive only because of the two of you and that we wouldn't have been able to recover Scatter without you. Please don't think any of us take that for granted."

Hella didn't, but she also didn't doubt that Pardot would still rather follow his agenda than give in to any sympathetic feelings of gratitude. Guides were worth time and money only if they were taking people where they wanted to go and getting them there safely. Even that didn't mean the client wouldn't bushwhack a guide to keep from paying him or to maintain secrets. Stampede had taught her that early.

"If you already have Scatter, why are you searching for another fractoid?"

"Because we have to have two of them."

"Why?"

"One of them doesn't survive alone."

"How do you know that?"

"Dr. Pardot's investigation into the fractoid we found months ago revealed that, and the tests he's conducted on Scatter bear that out." Colleen leaned forward and caught Hella's hands. Hella just barely kept from turning her hands into weapons. "Please, Hella. I know Dr. Pardot can be hard to get along with, impossible at times, really, but we need you and Stampede."

Hella sat quietly, looking into the woman's liquid gaze.

"Whether he's told you or not, Scatter needs to do this too. Otherwise he'll die just like the last fractoid did."

CHAPTER 23

After Hella finished relating her conversation with Colleen Trammell to Stampede, he sat back and scratched his chin. His ears flicked in irritation. Then he fixed his gaze on her. "Do you believe her?"

Hella thought about that for a moment then nodded. "Colleen has too many reasons to tell us the truth. At least *some* of the truth." She let out a disgusted breath. "The problem is trying to figure out what they're not telling us. Before it gets us killed."

"Remember the golden rule to scouting, Red."

"Try to save one life a day, especially if it's your own."

"Yeah. That's the one." Stampede lay back inside their shared tent and crossed his arms behind his head. "Also, take one day at a time. We'll follow this trail a little farther and see where it takes us. We're not any more invested than we want to be."

"I know. But I have to tell you, I don't want the death of that kid on my head. I don't want to dream about her or what I could have done if there was something I could do."

"That little girl isn't your problem. She isn't *our* problem. There are some things we can't do anything about."

"You say that, but it seems to me you and Faust went out of your way to help another kid not so long ago."

Stampede didn't say anything for a while. "Get some sleep. We're going to have a long day tomorrow, and when we head into the Amichi Mountains, we're going to have to be at our best."

Hella rolled over onto her side and closed her eyes. As wound up as she was, she expected sleep to come hard. Instead it came for her in a rush and carried her away almost at once.

■ ■ ■ ■ ■

For three days, Hella rode point on Daisy and almost grew bored. If it hadn't been for Riley's insistence that Colleen Trammell's precog visions were coming faster and stronger, she would have thought they were wasting their time. Usually she thought that anyway despite Riley's news.

She occupied some of her time hunting fresh meat for her and Stampede. Game was plentiful and she had a selection of deer, quail, squirrel, and rabbit. At least hunting gave her something to do that focused all of her attention for a time and she didn't have to think about anything else.

Since the night in the tent, Colleen hadn't gone out of her way to speak to Hella. The woman seemed happy to know that Stampede and Hella continued to guide them and didn't want to jinx the arrangement. Or maybe the precog visions were taking their toll. Or maybe Pardot was watching her more closely. Hella had had to admit it could have been any of those things.

Scatter also kept his distance. The fractoid remained talkative to Pardot for the most part, but not anyone else. Scatter's interest in the new world around him even seemed to wane.

On the next day, they cut an unmarked trail at the foothills of the Amichi Mountains.

■ ■ ■ ■ ■

When she saw the clearing snaking through the wilderness ahead of her in the early evening of the next day, Hella reined Daisy in. "Have Riley hold up his troops." She formed a weapon of her right hand as she stepped down out of the saddle and told the mountain boomer to stay.

"What's wrong?"

"I just cut a trail someone's been using a lot lately. I'm going to give it a look."

"I'm coming to you."

Hella eased through the brush and stayed low. Her passage didn't even disturb the foliage around her. Her rifle hung down her back, and she remained cognizant that a sniper up in the foothills could take her out in a heartbeat.

The narrow trail held tracks through the heart of it. Judging from the tread and wear, horses as well as motorcycles used the route regularly.

"Too far off the trade roads to be used by traders." Stampede suddenly stood in the trees only a short distance away. He surveyed the hillside covered with trees and brush ahead of them.

"Not too far for highwaymen. They like little bolt holes like this to run to after they take out a caravan." Hella tracked cardinals and bluebirds flying along the hillside in front of them. The birds were a good sign. They meant that no one lay in hiding in front of them. If someone were up there, all the birds would have left the immediate area.

"I know." Stampede scratched the underside of his chin, and his ears twitched. "We make an attractive target."

"Not to mention we're practically delivering ourselves to their doorsteps if this is a run for highwaymen."

"Riley says Colleen Trammel's precog is pulling her straight through this." Stampede scanned the surrounding countryside. "This is the easiest way of going. We know that."

Hella nodded. "Have you ever heard of a precog having a vision of something happening then not living long enough to see it come true?"

"No."

"Do you think it could happen?"

Stampede shifted his big rifle and kept it at the ready. "Anything can happen. We just need to make sure it doesn't happen to us."

"The trail goes up into the mountains along the same general route we're taking."

"I see that. Taking the trail would mean faster travel time."

"But we'd risk discovery by whoever uses this trail if they happen along."

"I know. We've got Riley and his hardshells with us. No matter who's running this trail, they're not expecting that. Let's roll with it for right now."

"Sure." Hella went back for Daisy, and they kept heading east. Stampede talked Pardot and Riley into bedding the expedition down early for the day so he and Hella could recon the area from higher up on the mountain.

■ ■ ■ ■ ■

An hour later Hella told Daisy to stay below the ridgeline of the mountain she and Stampede has chosen as their observation point. Working in tandem, they made their way to the top and hunkered down.

The Amichi Mountains had been shorter in the past, before the collider blew up. The resulting tectonic plate shifting out in California had manifested across the West. In the Redblight the mountains had grown taller, the swamplands more vast, and some of the fallout of mutations and strange creatures had taken up more frequent residence there.

The people who lived in the swamplands were hard and cruel. Strangers weren't tolerated as a general rule, and in many places were considered a delicacy. Legend held that the human stock that had once existed there had interbred till a number of genetic problems manifested. Still other legends held that some of the creatures that crossed over from other worlds had added to the gene pool in strange and deadly ways.

Whatever the truth was, the bottom line was that the Amichi Mountains were a bad place to be.

Hella scanned the surrounding terrain with her binocs, and Stampede did the same with his telescope. For an hour they ate jerked meat in silence and watched the landscape. Just as dark closed in, a silver mist swept in from the west and came to a stop in front of them.

A moment later Scatter formed out of the mist and stood before them. "Hello."

Stampede's ears twitched. "What are you doing here?"

"I came to see you." If Scatter noticed Stampede's irritable attitude, he gave no indication of it. "I thought it best that we should talk by ourselves. I do not trust Dr. Pardot or Dr. Trammell." He paused. "Actually I do not trust any of them. I trust you."

Hella couldn't help smiling at the bald-faced honesty.

Stampede's eyes narrowed and he looked grumpier. "Then why are you staying with them?"

"Colleen Trammell will guide us to the next ripple. Once there, I hope to find a way back to my world or to locate the other person from my world." Scatter looked from Stampede to Hella then back again, as if knowing he would be the one who needed the most convincing.

"You could have mentioned this earlier."

"When?" Stampede looked patient. "Dr. Pardot has never given me any time by myself." He smiled. "Plus, I did not know for certain that I could trust you till I discovered they do not trust you." He paused. "Does that surprise you?"

"That they don't trust us?"

"Yes."

Stampede shook his head. "They don't trust anyone outside of their own skin. That's the way most people are."

Frowning, Scatter shook his head. "The ways of your world are very confusing. In my world there are no subterfuges, no secondary agendas. Quite frankly, I do not like your world. I much prefer mine. Everything there is a known quantity."

"Your world wasn't always that way. Otherwise you wouldn't be in that body."

"True."

"Dr. Pardot gave you time to see us now?"

"No. Dr. Pardot has, for the moment at least, succumbed to his own excesses. In addition to being very frail, flesh-and-blood bodies exhaust easily. Dr. Pardot's exhausts more easily than most, it appears. I could not imagine living in such a vessel."

Hella smiled. "We don't think of our bodies as vessels."

"You should. That's what they are."

Stampede's ears twitched. "Pardot is asleep?"

"Or in a fatigue-induced coma, yes. At present he requires no medical attention."

"Has he told you about the other fractoid they found?" Hella continued scanning the countryside. Even with Scatter's ability to break into a collection of tiny robots and ride the wind, she didn't know if he'd escaped Riley's security equipment.

"No. But I knew about him anyway. Who told you?"

"Dr. Trammell. How did you know about the other fractoid if they didn't tell you?"

Scatter held his hand up level with his face then blew. Fine, silver dust blew off his hand for an instant. Then he made a fist and drew the nanobots back to him. "Dr. Pardot was marked by—"

The screech was so painful that Hella had to cover her ears. "I take it that's someone you know from your world."

"We had never met, but I know him, yes. I read his history. He was a very good man." Scatter paused. "Dr. Pardot is marked by warning nanobots that broadcast a constant stream of information about the deceased as well as the danger declaration. The other fractoid marked him at some point."

Stampede growled in the back of his throat. "Marker buoys."

Scatter thought briefly then nodded. "Yes, they serve the same purpose."

"If no one on your world is violent with anyone else, why would you have something like that?"

"We knew we were not alone in the universe. Even though we had not branched out into space, the people who designed these bodies knew we would need ways to defend ourselves. Knowledge of enemies is paramount. The marking system was simple and direct."

"And only other fractoids can read it?"

"As far as I am aware, yes." Scatter reflowed and suddenly stood looking back toward camp. "I should really return. Dr. Pardot sleeps fitfully at best. But I wanted to warn you that they may turn against you."

"We'd already figured that."

"I thought you might, but I wanted to let you know you were not alone."

"Thinking of leaving?" That surprised Hella to a degree.

"I fear I cannot at this juncture." Scatter hesitated. "There are a number of reasons that I must stay till the other fractoid is found. I still wish to return to my world. I have hopes that Dr. Pardot and Dr. Trammell will at least provide a path for me to follow that will allow me passage." He paused then stuck out his hand. "I bid you good luck and good hunting. Neither malice nor murder."

Stampede took the hand and shook it, and Hella did the same. Scatter's hand was cold and hard, and she felt the familiar tingle of her nanobots acknowledging him.

In the next instant, Scatter turned into a silvery cloud and floated rapidly back down the hill like fog.

• • • • •

"Hella. Wake up. We've got company."

Before she could shrug away from Stampede's grip on her shoulder and roll over to pull the blanket over her head, Hella heard the thrum of powerful engines rolling through the swamplands. The sound was distant but close enough it had to be investigated, especially since they'd heard nothing but the expedition since they'd entered the wilderness. She slid out from under the covers, grabbed her rifle and slung it over her shoulder, then pulled on her boots.

By that time Stampede was already through the tent flaps.

Hella followed him, taking two steps to every one of his to match his stride.

Riley and his hardshells shifted through the camp as well, taking up positions along the outer perimeters.

"Who is it?" Riley stood encased in his armor.

Stampede waved the handset radio that connected him to the security team at Riley. "Hella and I are going to take a look. We'll let you know when we know."

"I can come with—"

"No. You stay here. If I need you, I'll let you know." Stampede ran past the man. "Keep everything here locked down tight in case we have to hold a perimeter."

．．．．．

Ten minutes later Hella sat hunkered down on a bluff overlooking the trail that cut through the Amichi Mountains. The expedition had traveled hard the past two days to reach their present location. They'd also left the trail behind.

Early dawn lay over the land, cloaking the trees and brush in darkness that pooled over the ground and made most of the forest's features blend. A line of lights ran along the trail, though, winding around the morass of swampland that spotted the forest.

Hella focused her binocs on the riders, knowing from the engine sounds that they were motorcycles and ATVs. She wasn't surprised to spot the bikers riding in single file. Some of the ATVs pulled small trade wagons behind them. Closer inspection revealed them to be Sheldons. She couldn't tell if they were flying the Purple Dragons colors. If they were, they'd evidently lost more members.

"Must have taken down a trade caravan this morning or last night." Stampede hunkered down twenty meters away.

Hella silently agreed. "How close do you think their camp is?"

"Too close for us. From here on in, we're going to stay away from the trail. If they find our trail, they'll track us down."

Hella knew that was true. The expedition had too many wagons and wheeled vehicles for the highwaymen to pass up. Not only was there the physical evidence of everything they had, but stories flew along the trade routes. The biker gang could have heard of them.

Stampede took the radio from his chest pocket and spoke briefly. Then he put it away and glanced up at the sky. "Riley says Dr. Trammell says the ripple we've been looking for is about to open up any second."

"Bad timing."

Stampede growled in agreement.

Shifting, Hella found a spot where she could peer up at the sky through the trees. The rose-colored dawn pushed shards into the reluctant darkness giving up the night.

When the ripple arrived, it was only a minor tear in the fabric of reality that was much closer to the ground than the one that had delivered Scatter. Something streaked out of the ripple and left a white contrail behind it. For a short time, it was eerily silent. Then, just before she lost it in the trees, sonic booms hammered the forest around her.

Stampede cursed. "No way did that go unnoticed."

"No."

"Let's hope the Sheldons stay fat and happy with their score and stay out of our business. In the meantime, you and I need to see if we can find that meteorite."

"Fractoid, you mean."

"Yeah. Otherwise we're going to be out here for a while longer. Did you see where it landed?"

"No. But I know the direction."

"Let's go."

Hella took the lead and wished she'd thought to grab a bag of rations. Her stomach growled almost as loudly as Stampede.

CHAPTER 24

The object missed the Amichi Mountains and landed in the middle of one of the nameless swamps that filled the lowlands. Hella stopped eighty meters out and surveyed the surrounding wilderness. For a short time after the impact, the motorcycle and ATV engines had headed in their direction, but they stopped at least a klick away.

In a large area in the northwest corner of the swampland, a good seventy meters from the shoreline and in the boggy depths, the heated object caused the water to roil and bubble. The gasping, burping noise of it echoed across the flat waters of the swamp and around the shoreline. Birds flew from the treetops, abandoning the area. Chemical stink filled the air and burned Hella's eyes, nose, and throat. She took a piece of cloth from her kit and wound it around her face. Her sunglasses helped somewhat, and breathing the filtered air was better.

Stampede talked quietly and quickly over the radio that connected them to Riley and the expedition. Finally he dropped it inside his chest pack in frustration. "Riley won't hang back. He heard the bikers' engines too."

"He's an idiot if he comes this way."

"He's doing it, though."

"The Sheldons are going to be even more interested if they see him or his men."

Stampede nodded. "I pointed that out too."

"They don't trust us."

"I'd say that's about the size of it, Red." Stampede nodded toward the roiling water. "You or me?"

Thinking of entering the murky water gave Hella pause. She didn't like not being able to see everything around her. And the water slowed her down. She swallowed and slipped off her rifle, putting it by a tree so she'd remember where it was so she could get it on the run if she had to. Draping a coil of rope and a grappling hook from her kit over one shoulder, she stood. "Me."

"Okay." Stampede laid his rifle over a rocky outcrop and sighted on the swamp. "I've got your back."

At the shoreline, Hella hesitated a moment and thought about taking off her boots.

"You've got another pair back at the camp. You'll have to squish all the way back when you get those wet, but that's better than stepping on a spine-fin while you're wading through that swamp."

Hella knew that was true. Spine-fin were some kind of mutated cross between a catfish and lizard. Equally at home in the water and on land, they remained a constant threat to the uninitiated or the unwary. The spines were sometimes as long as twenty-five centimeters and pierced flesh like edged steel. They also carried enough toxin to cause a great deal of pain but no permanent injury. The larger ones were a meter long and weighed upward of forty kilos.

She morphed her hands into weapons, reminded herself that bullets tended to ricochet off the water surface, and waded in. Her throat grew tight with anticipation with each step she managed into the muddy bottom.

The swamp got deep quicker than she'd thought it would. Nearly twenty meters out, the water was up to her hips. Another ten meters and it had risen to her shoulders. Her stomach tightened and she thought she would be sick.

Throw up and you're just going to chum the water. Everything in here that feeds on everything else is going to show up for breakfast. She made herself breathe deeply and willed herself to remain calm, but she'd have rather been facing a dozen Sheldons than be out in the water.

"Easy does it, Red. You get water in your ear, and our comm link is going to get garbled."

"I know that." Hella didn't mean for the reply to come out so sharply, but it was gone before she knew it. "Sorry. I don't like this."

"I know. It doesn't feel any better from up here."

Hella visualized Stampede in her mind as she pushed forward and started swimming toward the bubbling spot in the swamp. He'd be behind his rifle, both eyes open, one trained through the scope, finger resting on the trigger guard.

"Gotta go under." Hella took a big breath of the stinking air, hoped she'd be able to hold it in her lungs, and dived. The water felt warmer as she swam down to the object resting on the swamp bed.

Only a few feet down, the object that had landed there glowed a dull red. The bubbling water muddied the image, but she felt confident that nothing that had a brain would be anywhere near the thing. With all the action, the outlines of the thing were blurred and indistinct.

She put out a hand and managed to get within a few meters before the heat made her pull her hand back. Nearly out of breath, she surfaced. When she blinked the murk from her eyes, she spotted the telltale triangular head floating barely out of the water as it arrowed toward her.

The muddy-green alligator was easily twice as long as she was tall, not the biggest she'd seen in the Amichi Mountains, but a lot bigger than she'd ever wanted to meet face-to-face. Treading water, knowing she'd never get away in time, she lifted her arms, turned her hands to weapons, and took quick aim.

"Stampede!" Her voice sounded odd in her ears, and she didn't think the communication got through.

The alligator opened its mouth, exposing the pink-white gums and throat and the curved, yellow teeth. Then its head evaporated in a bloody mist. Decapitated, the vicious creature slid past her, jostling her with its scaled torso and one leg.

"Thank you." Hella glanced up at the hillside and made out Stampede behind his rifle. She couldn't hear if he made a response. Sliding the rope from her shoulder, she took a few quick breaths and went down again.

Face almost scalding from the heat, Hella dragged the grappling hook over the orange blob till tension tightened the rope. She swam backward, shoved the alligator's corpse out of her way, and stopped when she could put her feet in the mud. Leaning back, she hauled on the rope.

The object stubbornly remained immobile, causing her to wonder if it buried itself too deeply in the mud. Then finally the suction gave way, and the object slid toward her. Despite her best efforts, the grappling hook slipped off twice before she got the thing into the shallows so she could see what she was working with.

Judging from the humanoid shape, Hella felt certain she was dealing with another fractoid. Making out specific details about the creature was hard. When it cleared the water, the heat baked the sludge caking it into a hard, dry crust.

As she walked off a few paces toward the rising shallows, she set herself to pull again. A second alligator exploded up from the depths where it had evidently been lying in wait for unsuspecting prey. It hurled itself from the water and lunged toward her.

Hella didn't try to run because the buoyancy of the water would lift her and the mud beneath her boots would betray her. Instead she shifted her weight to one side and twisted her shoulder away from the predator. Her left hand came up instinctively and formed a weapon. A line of bullets hammered the alligator's side as it twisted and thrashed.

A round from Stampede's rifle punched through its body and tore out its heart before it reached the shallows again.

Shaking, heart pounding, Hella took up slack on the rope and discovered that it had come free during the attack. It took her a moment to defeat the paralysis that gripped her and walk back into the deeper water to secure the fractoid again.

Trusting the heat-resistant rope, she coiled three loops around the fractoid's head and secured the grappling hook. She put her back into pulling, stretching out each stride she took to cover more ground more quickly. Even when she reached the saw grass that covered the shoreline, she didn't feel safe. The grass concealed predators as well as the water.

Even worse, the grass impeded her efforts to drag the fractoid across the open ground to the tree line. Stampede held his position to watch over her.

She looked up at him and took the comm link from her ear. Her breath blew hot and quick from the effort of dragging the fractoid. After shaking the water from the comm link, she slipped it back into her ear. "Can you hear me?"

"Yeah."

The connection sounded a little shaky and crackled every now and again, but Hella didn't feel cut off anymore.

"Is it still in one piece?"

"She." Gazing down at the recovered fractoid, Hella saw that the being was definitely female. She had breasts and rounded hips. Mud obscured her face. "I don't know. She's got mud and muck all over her. And she's heavy. Even after she cools down, she's going to be hard to move. We should have brought Daisy."

"Yeah, I know how that would have worked out. The first time Daisy saw one of those alligators going for you, we'd have had a battle royal in the middle of that swamp."

"Is Riley still on his way?" Hella knelt, slipped her knife free of her soaked boot, and picked at the hardened mud coating the fractoid.

"He's practically on top of us."

"The Sheldons?"

"So far there's no sight of them."

"At least Riley and his guys can do the heavy lifting." Hella examined the scorched metal revealed under the crust. The surface was burned black, but a silvery gleam remained beneath the flakes. However, the fractoid woman had melted down in several places. Sadness touched Hella's heart as she regarded the inanimate body. "I don't think this one made it."

As she stood up, Riley and his men arrived. She slipped her knife back into her boot as Riley fanned his men out to set up a protective perimeter.

"Hella?" Riley looked from the inert fractoid woman to the dead alligators then to Hella.

"I pulled her out of the swamp as soon as I could, but I think she was already gone before she got here." Hella started to stand up, but the fractoid woman reached out for her and locked partially melted fingers around Hella's wrist.

Pain surged up Hella's arm and tore a scream from her throat. She looked down as her wrist cooked in the heated grip of the metal woman. Hella yanked her arm and tried to get away, but the fractoid's hold was merciless.

Riley ran over to her, but even with the hardshell's amplified strength, he wasn't able to budge the woman's cruel grip. The stink of her own burning flesh filled Hella's nose.

Then a silvery mist poured in from above and instantly took Scatter's shape. He reached down and took the fractoid woman's hand, and the harsh grip finally opened.

Her mind wrapped in agony, Hella looked at her cooked wrist and tried to move her fingers. When she couldn't, when she realized that her hand no longer obeyed her, she grew even more afraid. Finally, thankfully, Riley grabbed an ampoule from his med kit and stabbed her in the leg with it. The pain, and her conscious mind, drained away. The last thing she remembered seeing was the fractoid woman's crazed, soot-blackened gaze as Scatter held her tenderly in his arms and broadcast that machine language.

* * * * *

Hella struggled through the cobwebs that wrapped her mind. She tried to open her eyes, but they felt as heavy as bricks. When she tried to take a deep breath, it felt as if someone were sitting on her chest.

"Easy." Stampede spoke softly. "You need to rest, Red."

Everything came back to Hella in a rush. Adrenaline spiked through her system when she thought about her ruined hand.

She opened her eyes and tried to sit up.

Moving gently, Stampede pushed her back into her bedroll. No, it wasn't her bedroll. She gazed around the unfamiliar tent.

"Pardot gave us access to one of the med tents." Stampede sat cross-legged beside her. His rifle rested across his knees.

"My hand?"

Stampede tried to speak and couldn't for a moment. "It's bad. Pardot was all for amputating it."

Hella drew her injured arm up to her chest. The pain still throbbed, but it felt a million klicks away.

"I wouldn't let him." Stampede's ears flattened. "I don't think he was as invested in the situation as he needed to be to make that kind of call."

"More interested in his new toy?"

"Yeah."

"Even though it's broken."

"Not entirely broken. Scatter has been able to talk to her a little. The fractoid woman isn't tracking very well."

"I know the feeling."

Stampede touched her shoulder lightly. "We'll get through this."

"I know." Hella closed her eyes for a second and realized she was parched. "Is there any water around here?"

Stampede picked up a nearby canteen and held it for her to drink.

Hella remained silent for a while, trying hard not to remember how bad her arm looked. Was the meat really so cooked that it was ready to fall off the bone?

"Scatter wanted to talk to you when you woke up, but Pardot won't let him." Stampede looked through the tent door. "Pardot put Scatter under lockdown. When he escaped and came to the swamp where we were, Pardot dropped all pretense of being friends." He paused. "If you hadn't been laid up, Red, we'd have bailed on them at that point." He heaved a sigh. "I really should have already made that decision. That way maybe you wouldn't be in the shape you're in."

"What did Scatter want?"

"When he found out Pardot wanted to amputate your hand, he got all worked up."

"Why?"

Stampede hesitated. "He thinks he can save it. Or you can."

"Because of the nanobots."

"Something like that."

Hella studied the thick gauze wrapped around her hand and wrist. Thinking of what she was about to do almost made her sick to her stomach. "Help me sit up."

"You should rest."

"According to Pardot, I should have my hand chopped off. And if we stay here, I don't see a good ending happening for us. Do you?"

After a brief pause, Stampede shook his head and twitched his ears. "No. I don't."

"Then help me sit up."

Stampede lifted her gently into a sitting position.

"I need this bandage removed."

"You don't want to do this. Trust me."

"I'm going to have to see it sooner or later, and it's going to have to be checked for infection." Hella pushed away all her fear and sickness, but she was afraid it would snap and rush back in on her if she wasn't strong enough to handle it. "I need to do this now."

"All right." Stampede pulled a small throwing knife from somewhere on his person and slit the white gauze that covered her wound. "You might lose some skin. Maybe more. Normally you don't cover a burn because there's a tendency for the wound to stick, but Pardot said the wound had to be covered to prevent infection."

Hella nudged the bandage free. Her head swam as her blackened flesh came into view. It was raw and red in places, like meat that had been burned on the outside but not cooked all the way through. Threads of blood dripped onto her jeans.

She tried to move her fingers and couldn't. She almost cried and gave up then. Everything was just too hard and too unfair. Blinking back tears, she concentrated on her arm and tried to re-create the rhythm Scatter had taught her.

At first nothing happened. The scarred, disfigured meat around her arm just sat there and nauseated her. Then almost imperceptibly, the rhythm grew stronger and more sure. Her flesh started to heal, tanned skin reclaiming the charred areas.

After a couple of minutes that left her dripping with perspiration, Hella could move her fingers. In spite of the new wave of pain that burned up her arm, she smiled at Stampede. "I don't think it's permanent. I think I'm going to be able to fix it."

Without a word, Stampede leaned into her and hugged her tightly, the way he had when she'd been a little girl. It felt good. But she briefly felt just as frightened as she had back then, and she didn't like that at all.

CHAPTER 25

Groggy the next morning, her arm still pulsing pain up into her skull, Hella woke when Stampede stepped into the tent. Through the flap, late-morning sunlight fought the shadows for ground space.

"We're not moving?" Hella sat up by herself, quietly groaning in pain when she inadvertently used her injured arm.

"Not yet." Stampede passed over a plate of food culled from their remaining supplies. Sausage links, boiled potatoes, and onions filled the tent with a pleasant odor.

"What are they waiting on?"

"Pardot isn't convinced the fractoid female is going to survive her landing here."

"If she doesn't?"

Stampede rolled his shoulders. "I guess we'll wait until Colleen Trammell has another vision."

Using her injured arm to hold the plate, Hella lifted food to her mouth with her fingers. "Has she been having other visions?"

"If she is, nobody's telling me." Stampede's ears twitched and his nostrils flared. "I think we're getting frozen out of the information."

"We were never inside the loop anyway."

Stampede smiled, but it was a cold expression that only served to bare his teeth. "I know." He scratched his chin. "Pardot is also keeping Scatter in a cage. Some kind of electromagnetic field that

Scatter can't pass through. I've seen him try a couple times. It's strange watching him melt away and end up flattening against an invisible field."

Hella lost her appetite at that bit of news, but she made herself keep eating. She needed to keep her strength up, and she'd been starving when she'd woken up. She suspected that had a lot to do with the energy the nanobots were using to heal her arm. "I don't like the idea of leaving Scatter behind."

Rolling an eye her way, Stampede looked at her. "Nobody said anything about leaving."

Hella shook her head. "I can't believe you'd think about staying after all this."

After a brief hesitation, Stampede growled and shook his head. "Right now we'd be out here alone too, Red. With the Sheldons around, maybe that isn't a good idea."

"We can take care of ourselves."

"You're not at your best."

"Getting better all the time." Hella set the plate aside and flexed her hand. Her forearm hurt, but the pain wasn't as bad as it had been the day before.

"Maybe. But what if that wound gets infected? Even with the healing you've done, maybe it's all on the outside and you've left a lot of damage on the inside." Stampede shook his head. "All this mojo you're doing, Red, it's all new to you. If you have problems with that wound and we don't have medical help . . . things could go badly."

Staring at her injured arm, Hella found the healing rhythm again and focused on it. More of the burned areas along her arm went away. After a while she'd gone as far as she could, and she just wanted to go back to sleep.

"For the time being, we're going to ride with the expedition." Stampede took her plate. "While they sit, you're healing. If we're running through the Amichi Mountains for our lives, you're not going to be able to do that." He stood and looked uncertain. "So you get some rest and heal up as fast as you're able."

Hella put her good arm across her eyes and sank back to sleep.

. . . . .

Minutes or hours later, a shadow hesitated at the front of the tent. The flickering shift of the person's presence outside the flaps woke Hella. From the short, slender build, she knew her visitor was neither Stampede nor Riley.

A moment later Colleen cleared her throat outside the tent. "Hella? It's Colleen Trammell. May I come in?"

"All right." Hella sat up effortlessly on her bedroll. She cradled her injured arm in her lap.

Colleen entered with a medical case in one hand. She gazed around the tent briefly.

"Stampede's not here."

"I know." Colleen sat beside Hella. "I thought maybe one of the fractoids might be in here."

"I thought Scatter was being held in a cage and the female fractoid was hovering on the edge."

"He is and she is." Colleen rummaged in the medical case and came out with a fistful of hypodermics. "Still, they've surprised us so far. Scatter's not like anything we expected, and the female has managed to survive in spite of everything she's suffered."

Hella nodded at the needles. "What's that?"

"Antibiotics. Steroids. Medicine that will help you get better."

"Nobody thought to give me these yesterday?"

Colleen eyed her levelly. "Yesterday no one thought you were going to survive your wounds. I think even Stampede believed you were going to die."

"I didn't."

Colleen smiled. "I know. Now we're going to see if we can keep you alive. Roll up your sleeve, please."

Hella didn't move.

"You don't trust me." Colleen didn't look surprised or offended.

"With all due respect, no."

"Why?"

"Stampede would say that we have different agendas. He's more polite than I am."

"I see." Colleen took another breath and let it out. "Is there anything I can do to change your mind?"

"Let me talk to Scatter."

Colleen shook her head sadly. "That's not going to happen. Dr. Pardot doesn't like the influence the two of you have over Scatter." She frowned. "Or the influence Scatter has over you two. Dr. Pardot isn't sure which way that works. And, frankly, neither am I."

"Then it looks like we don't have a lot to talk about."

Colleen sat for a moment longer. "I wish I could change that."

Hella wanted to tell her that she did too, but she couldn't lie to the woman like that because she kept remembering that Colleen was involved mostly because of her sick daughter.

Colleen stood and headed for the tent flaps. "I hope you get better. I do like you, Hella."

Without a word, Hella watched her leave. She felt tired and sad and empty. Focusing, Hella unwrapped her wounded arm and looked at her burns. For a short time, she drew on the strength she'd built up, triggered the rhythm again, and watched as unblemished skin gradually replaced the burned, oozing flesh. When her head thrummed with pain and she couldn't focus enough to maintain the healing effect, she rewrapped her arm and lay back down. After a few minutes, she slept.

. . . . .

Stampede returned after dark. He brought three rabbits on spits that were brazed almost to golden brown perfection and stuffed with vegetables and spices. The succulent smell filled Hella's mouth with saliva, and her stomach grumbled. She couldn't believe how hungry she was because she'd been eating jerky all day and had felt full until the rabbits appeared.

After handing her one of the rabbits, Stampede sat down with two of them. Dust covered him and dried mud clung to his hooves and lower legs.

"You've been exploring." Hella pinched meat from the rabbit and popped it into her mouth. The grease was filled with flavor.

She had been in only occasional contact with him over the comm link in between long naps that had taken up most of her day.

"Scouting the Sheldons."

"They're still in the area?"

Stampede nodded and rubbed a hand across one of his horns. "Yeah, but there's something going on."

Hella waited.

"They've started running patrols through the forest. I think they're looking for something."

"Us?"

"Don't know."

"If they were going to look around, you'd think they'd have looked around when the second fractoid came through the ripple."

"They did. You just weren't conscious when Riley and I had to hide you in the forest. We were lucky and got through them."

"Oh."

"The Sheldons weren't too dedicated to the effort yesterday, but they're spending more time at it now."

"Does Riley know?"

"Riley has his men out there keeping the perimeter, but he's not exploring much farther than that."

"You haven't told him about the Sheldon search parties?"

Stampede shook his head.

"Why?"

"Because we're going to let the Sheldons be our distraction so we can get away from Pardot. We can't wait any longer. We need to make our break while we're still in the wilderness, where Riley and his troops won't be able to run us down with their ATVs."

Hella nodded and thought about it. The plan was solid enough, and that was all they had. "How long do you think we have before the Sheldons get here?"

"From the way it looks, the Sheldon foot patrols will find this campsite tomorrow."

Hella thought about that, remembering how large the biker gang was and how well equipped Riley and his team were. "The Sheldons are going to get killed."

"I think so too. But Riley and his people are going to take some damage too. During the confusion, we're going to leave."

"Abandoning the expedition isn't exactly what we were hired to do."

Stampede snorted. "Red, at this point if we can get out of this with a whole skin, I'm going to count that as paid in full and a bonus."

Cold dread spread through Hella as she realized what Stampede was talking about. "You don't think they're going to let us leave."

"No, I don't. We know too much about their business. It's a long way back across the Redblight. If we get away from them and tell someone about the fractoids, they could end up chased all the way back home. Pardot has got to know that. The only reason they haven't locked us up is because you got injured and ended up being sidelined. I got to roam around today because you've been stuck here. If we were both able bodied, I think we'd be taking dirt naps or we'd be locked up the same as Scatter."

Hella thought she would be sick, and the need to be outside and gone was overpowering.

"Chill, Red. You need to eat. Heal up. Get rested."

"We're just going to let this happen to us?"

Stampede snorted. "It's already happened, Red. We're just trying to manage damage control."

• • • • •

A chill on Hella's face woke her; then she heard Scatter's hushed whisper. "Hella."

She blinked at the darkness that filled the tent and looked around for Stampede. She relaxed a little when she realized he slept in his bedroll. He held his massive pistols in his hands across his chest.

"Scatter?" Hella started to get up, but the chill on her face pressed her down again.

"Please. Do not move. They are watching."

"Riley?"

"His men, yes. They also have listening equipment planted near this tent. For the moment, I have nullified it so I can talk to you."

"Stampede?" Hella had detected the subtle shift in Stampede's breathing.

"I'm awake." Stampede spoke softly. "I'm listening."

The cold drew back from Hella. Nearly a meter from her face, Scatter's face materialized in thin air and hovered. The fractoid's features looked flat, like a two-dimensional curved mask.

"How did you get away?"

"I did not escape. I've managed to free this much of myself through the electromagnetic field, but maintaining control over this little of myself away from my body is difficult. I need your help, otherwise I am afraid Ocastya is going to die."

"Ocastya?"

"My mate. Ocastya is the name Pardot gave her when he could not pronounce her real name."

Hella figured her name was easily as impossible to pronounce as Scatter's. "She's your mate?"

"Yes."

"She's not recovering from her injuries?"

"Her body is repairing itself very well under the circumstances. I am referring to her self, that part of her that uniquely makes her Ocastya. She needs me with her to completely come back. I have endeavored to explain this to Pardot and Trammell, but neither of them will listen to me. They are only interested in keeping us both prisoner."

"We know that, but there's nothing we can do. Pardot isn't going to listen to us. He's got his own agenda."

"I know but you two remain our only hope." Scatter's face wavered in midair. "Ocastya is running out of time."

Stampede pushed out a short breath. "What's happening to her?"

"Our present bodies are nearly indestructible, meant to last forever, and they very probably will. However, the psychological mind is not meant to do something like that. Experiences are layered into our minds, and eventually the core self becomes dissipated and loses its frame. Without proper anchoring, a fractoid self can become irrational. In order to prevent this, we are paired forever, always true to each other because each of us is half of a greater whole."

Scatter's face flickered and lost cohesion, drifting into a small Milky Way inside the tent. When he spoke again, he sounded more strained. "Every seventy or eighty years, roughly approximating our original life spans, we have to—for lack of a better explanation and this one simplifies the process far too much—reboot."

"How do you do that?"

"We share our lives together. When the one of us that needs to reboot connects with the other, information, personality, memory, and *self* are exchanged. The core person gets rebuilt from the partner. But we have to be together, in physical contact, for that to take place. If Ocastya is not allowed to reboot soon, even if she survives her injuries and the remodeling of her body, she will never be herself again." Scatter paused. "I cannot bear to lose her."

Hella lay there quietly and didn't know what to say.

"I know I am asking a lot." Scatter sounded embarrassed and mournful all at the same time. "But there is no one else I can ask."

Quietly Hella tried to figure out what to say, but she never got the chance to decide on a course of action. Gunfire erupted around the camp, chattering in the automatic triple bursts that signaled they were being fired from the security bots.

Stampede pushed himself to a sitting position, his face grim in the muted yellow-white light from an exploding shell that momentarily lit his features. "The Sheldons aren't going to wait till morning."

Hella pushed herself up and formed her good hand into a gun. She got to her feet and was surprised by her strength as well as the residual pain in her injured arm.

"We are under attack." Scatter's hovering face spun quickly in the darkness, flickering silver again and again as explosions tore through the campsite. In the next instant, the face dissolved and floated through the tent flaps.

"Grab as much gear as you can carry." Stampede pulled on his backpack, holstered his pistols, and took up his rifle. "We're only going to get one shot at getting out of—"

The rest of what he intended to say was lost to the thundering assault of a nearby mortar round. The concussive force ripped and buckled the tent, and it knocked Stampede from his hooves. Hella got blasted off her feet as well and slammed into the hard ground.

CHAPTER 26

As she sucked air back into her lungs and struggled with the partial deafness brought on by the mortar explosion, Hella stared through the shredded tent walls and marveled that she was still alive. Muzzle flashes punched holes in the darkness all around her. She glanced around, searching desperately.

"Stampede!"

"Don't yell, Red. I'm deaf enough as it is." Stampede surged up from the ground like a mass of darkness come to life. Blood from a wound on his temple matted his fur. He raised his rifle and scanned the camp. His square teeth showed in a smile that held only lethal intention. "Let's get Daisy and get out of here. We can get lost easier in the night."

"Scatter." Hella looked around but couldn't find the fractoid anywhere.

Stampede shouldered his backpack. "What's the first life you save?"

"My own." After years of instruction, Hella's answer came automatically.

"Then let's get it done." Stampede nudged her with an elbow.

Hella's stumble turned into a full-blown run in a half dozen strides. Daisy bleated in fear, and that sound galvanized and focused Hella's resolve. There was nothing she could do for Scatter or his mate at that time. If she and Stampede were free and running, that could change. She hoped it would change.

The mortars continued to rain death throughout the camp, but the security bots quickly adjusted to the attack. Sizzling lasers leaped from the bots and exploded incoming mortar rounds in the air. Most of them never reached the campsite, but a few still did, and those created instant craters.

Around the camp perimeter, the Sheldons closed in and exchanged gunfire with Riley's hardshells. For the most part, the body armor turned away the biker's deadly assault, but one of the wounded security guards stuttered back with both armored gloves wrapped around her throat. Blood fountained down the black material. Hella didn't break stride, knowing there was no time to save the woman. By the time she could get through the armor safeguards, if the woman were even able to tell her the pass codes to get the suit open, she would be gone.

At the edge of the camp, Daisy fought her tether. She gentled at once when she discovered Hella was there then threw her head up and down in greeting.

Bullets chopped into the brush and trees. A security guard in a hardshell wheeled on them with his rifle to his shoulder. Stampede stamped his hoof, and the ground beneath the security guard erupted. The man flew backward several meters.

Three Sheldons surged forward with their weapons up and firing. They had their heads pulled down so their shells acted like collars and offered protection.

Bullets cut the air around Hella and Stampede. A least a pair of rounds hit the chain mail and drove Hella back, but she had her hand up and fired automatically. Two of the men went down, mortally wounded. Stampede removed the head of the first with a single rifle blast.

Breathing hard, pain arcing beneath the chain mail, Hella stopped at the equipment chest on the ground beside Daisy, clicked it open, and took out the saddle from inside. Stampede grabbed the chest and started lashing it into place on the mountain boomer's back while Hella fitted the saddle.

A rocket-propelled grenade slammed into a nearby security

bot and reduced it to a flaming pyre. The ammunition cooked off in rapid succession. One of the stray rounds hammered Hella between the shoulder blades hard enough to drive her forward and take her breath away. But the chain-mail armor held, though she knew she'd be covered in a massive bruise for days.

Once the saddle was cinched into place, Hella stepped into the stirrup, grabbed the pommel, and swung herself aboard. Daisy quivered in anticipation, already wanting to get out of the firefight. Hella hesitated, not knowing which direction to take.

"North." Stampede hauled his rifle to his shoulder, took brief aim, and fired. One of two of Sheldons nearest them went down with a massive bullet in his face.

Hella hesitated, staring at the skirmish confronting the camp. She didn't like the idea of running from the fight. Scatter and Ocastya might be all right, but she feared for Colleen Trammell.

Stampede stepped up beside her and spoke loud enough to be heard over the gunfire and explosions. "Riley and his people are establishing a line."

That was true. Riley and the hardshells repelled the ground attack, and the security bots had triangulated the mortar teams and were blasting them into the earth or into retreat.

"Colleen is back there."

"She's one of them, Red."

"Not entirely."

"Even so, if we go back there, we're either going to end up dead because of the Sheldons or because of Pardot. We've got to go."

Angry and frustrated, Hella reined Daisy over and pointed her toward the wilderness away from the camp. She put her heels to the mountain boomer's sides and rode, staying low in the saddle as Daisy scampered through the rough terrain.

With incredible speed, Stampede ran behind them, keeping up effortlessly.

Hella headed up into the nearest hill. Plunging through swampland or landing in a sinkhole in the darkness might have meant death. Three hundred meters away, safely behind a clutch of boulders, she reined Daisy in, grabbed her rifle, and dropped to the ground.

Stampede had already settled into a position among the rocks. "We help knock out the mortars; then we get clear and hope Pardot doesn't allow Riley to send people after us."

As she scanned the landscape, Hella dropped prone on a rock, shoved the rifle out ahead of her, and pulled the butt to her shoulder. "Even if he does, we can get away. The ground here is too rough for the ATVs."

Large flashes showed the positions of the mortar teams. Hella identified one of them then used her night scope to lock in on them. She squeezed off rounds and put down both Sheldons. Beside her, Stampede's huge rifle thundered again and again. When she couldn't find mortar teams, she picked off Sheldons attacking the camp.

Two or three minutes later, with dead sprawled on the ground, the Sheldons retreated. Some of the hardshells started out in pursuit, giving in to the bloodlust that filled them, but evidently got called back. Part of the group cycled through the campsite. Chemical firefighting grenades dropped into flaming tents threw out massive amounts of flame-retardant white foam.

Although he wasn't shooting anymore, Stampede lay still and surveyed the battle zone. "They're looking for us."

Searching through her scope and seeing the hardshells scrambling through the camp, Hella silently agreed. A few of the security guards were using binocs to search the surrounding wilderness. She wondered if they even knew she and Stampede had helped them.

"We need to get gone." Stampede pushed himself up but kept using the rocks as cover from anyone spotting them from the camp.

Reluctantly Hella used her elbows and backed away from the rock to keep a low profile. Pain filled her chest from the bruising left by the stopped rounds that had struck the chain mail. She took a moment to build the rhythm in her mind and banish the pain.

A silvery wisp formed in front of her. A moment later, the wisp wore Scatter's perfect features. "Hella, you are alive."

"Yes." Hella stayed hunkered down. She started to call out to Stampede, but she saw him turn around and knew that he had heard the fractoid.

"I am glad you lived."

"So are we."

Scatter looked around and it was strange watching the disembodied face twist and turn. Hella couldn't help wondering how far his range to control the small group of fractoids would extend. "You have left the camp."

"We had to."

"Ocastya and I are still prisoners. You cannot leave us. We cannot help ourselves at this juncture. Ocastya needs help. She needs to reboot."

"I know." Stampede walked over to join them. "It's a long way back to where they came from. A lot of things can happen. After tonight, Riley and his people are going to be hard pressed to continue to provide security for the expedition. If we can, if a chance presents itself, we'll help."

"I only hope that is soon enough." Scatter clearly wasn't happy. "I will send this much of myself with you, but I will need to focus my energies on helping Ocastya. That way I can keep you informed of our location."

"All right."

"Hella, may I ride with you? To conserve energy?"

"Of course."

"Please hold up your left hand."

Not knowing what to expect, Hella held out her left hand. As she watched, Scatter's face floated over and nested in her palm. Within seconds, his likeness had settled into a microthin layer over her palm. She flexed her hand and found the new coating didn't restrict her movements and wasn't noticeable.

"I will be in touch when I am able. Unfortunately I will have to initiate the connection. You will not be able to call to me."

"All right."

"Now I must go back to tend to Ocastya." Scatter sounded fatigued and worried. "I wish you good fortune." His likeness faded from Hella's palm and left only the shiny layer behind.

Hella flexed her hand then reloaded her rifle and clambered back aboard Daisy. Stampede fell into step with her as they jogged through the trees and crested the hill.

"Keeping up with the expedition isn't going to be a problem, Red."

"I know." Hella stayed focused, sweeping the surrounding landscape in case some of the Sheldons had scattered and gotten lost.

"We can travel faster than they can, but they're going to maintain the tactical advantage. More men. More guns."

"I know. But there has to be something we can use to shift that. This is our world. We know this place better than they do. And there's a whole lot of distance between here and where we got them. We've got days to think and plan."

. . . . .

The expedition moved out early the next morning.

From her position high in the mountains, Hella watched the ATVs grinding cross-country through her binocs. She reached down and shook Stampede awake. "They're on the go."

Stampede glanced at the eastern sky and saw the sun was barely up. "Got an early start."

"Probably didn't sleep after last night." Hella continued watching the line of hardshells and ATVs snaking through the forest. She caught only glimpses of them, but the overall movement of the expedition was plain. Disturbed birds took off from treetops as the noisy vehicles neared, creating a visual marker system to the trained eye.

"They're navigating by GPS, not maps." Stampede stood and stamped his hooves to work out kinks in his legs. "That'll slow them down too." He scratched his chin, and his ears twitched. "Why would Pardot do that?"

Hella didn't have an answer either. She and Stampede had created maps of the area and given them to Riley as they'd traveled. There were no real trade trails through there, but the expedition could get to one if they traveled north.

"Maybe they're staying off the trade routes, hoping to lose us."

Stampede shifted his gear. "Could be Pardot is thinking we might try to rob him."

"The two of us?"

"He could be worried that we could convince someone on the trade routes to throw in with us." Stampede rolled his head, and his massive neck cracked. "Let's get moving. We'll find out soon enough. With them moving on not enough sleep, they should break for camp early this evening. At the very least, they'll be fatigued tonight. That'll work to our advantage."

. . . . .

Hella rode Daisy and the forest around them became an endless sea of green leaves and gnarled bark. The mountain boomer's movements still caused twinges of pain to skyrocket through Hella. She undressed her wound and worked on it some more. She expected to have it healed completely in another two or three days.

That knowledge filled her with hope, but she knew the task she and Stampede had set for themselves was almost impossible. She wondered if it would be better if they just cut their losses and didn't try a rescue attempt.

Even trailing the expedition in a tandem fashion exposed them to danger they might not see coming. Another group, possibly the Sheldons from the previous night, might discover the group and try to close in on them. The first thing they would find would be Hella and Stampede.

If the new group found them, they'd try to kill them quietly to get them out of the way. Failing that, they'd just open fire and chase Hella and Stampede back into Riley's security team. The welcome there probably wouldn't be any less lethal.

A rock and a hard place pretty much summed up the potential situation.

. . . . .

Early that afternoon, a line of dust to the west drew Hella's attention. She pulled her binocs from her chest pack and studied the terrain.

"Something?"

"Dust to the west."

"How far out?"

"Maybe a couple klicks." As she watched the movement of the dust, the way it constantly hung in the air, Hella grew more confident and more afraid that the dust meant there was another group in the area.

Stampede clambered atop a nearby stand of rock and took out his telescope. "There's someone out there. Looks like a sizable group."

"A group that big, you'd think they were a trade caravan, but there aren't any trade routes there."

"Could be another highwayman team."

Hella tracked the potential forward progress of the group. Depending on the relative speeds of the unknown pack and of the expedition, one or the other would intersect. "One of them is going to cut the trail of the other. If the expedition gets there second, Riley will see someone else has been there and put his team on high alert. That's not a big deal."

"But if the new arrivals are highwaymen, they'll read the tracks as a possible target." Stampede growled in the back of his throat.

"That might work out for us. They won't be able to take the expedition all at once, so maybe we can use the distraction to get to the fractoids."

Stampede snorted. "You say that like that wouldn't also be an invitation to get shot dead by one side or the other."

Hella couldn't refute that.

■ ■ ■ ■ ■

Hours later, the unknown group, which had been making faster progress than the expedition, pulled up and settled in. The dust tattoo they'd left in the air vanished.

Hella studied the area through the binocs and grew frustrated with the thick forest that covered the group. She wasn't able to see the expedition either, but Pardot and Riley were known quantities.

"Do you think they're camping for the night?"

"Got an hour of sunlight left." Stampede stood beside her with his telescope to his eye. "Would you stop to camp?"

"Depends on whether I was where I wanted to be."

"How far do you think the expedition is from those people?"

Turning her binocs back to the expedition, which would come within a half klick of the unknown group's position, Hella estimated the distance, the rate of speed, then the travel time. "Half hour."

"Plenty of time for them to set up." Stampede snorted in disgust. "I'd say they're exactly where they want to be."

"Do you think Riley or his scouts know they're running into a trap?"

"They haven't altered course or slowed down. What do you think?"

Hella didn't bother to answer.

"Well, now. Who's ambushing who?"

"What?"

"Look to the west. Up in the clouds. You have to be careful looking into the setting sun."

Gingerly, Hella shifted the binocs and scoured the sky. She caught a couple of bright spots that made her eyes sting then she spotted what Stampede had seen.

Two zeppelins—no mistaking those cigar shapes—caught the sun and almost blended in as they sailed through the sky. Large fans on the tail assemblies and on the sides powered the aircraft.

CHAPTER 27

Hella stood frozen in wonderment. She'd read about the aircraft before and been fascinated, but she'd never before seen one. She'd heard they still existed, but no one in the Redblight used them, and no one had ever brought one there before that she knew about. Zeppelins were expensive to build and to operate, and unless whoever owned them had a secure place to keep them, they would have been primary targets for thieves.

The zeppelins glided through the air as effortlessly as a minnow through shallows and looked as graceful doing it. The sleek hulls bore no markings, no claim of ownership.

"You think those ships belong to Pardot?" Hella lowered her glasses. Once she'd fixed the locations of the zeppelins, they were large enough to be seen with the naked eye.

"Know anyone else that could call them out there?"

"They could be just sailing over."

"Yeah. Want to bet on it?"

Hella didn't. The cold realization that Scatter was going to be lost to them in a short time closed around her heart. She focused instead on the possibilities afforded by all the variables in play. "If Riley knew he was rolling into an attack, would he go there?"

"I wouldn't. You wouldn't." Stampede shook his head. "But Riley? I don't know, Red. He and Pardot concentrate on their own vision of the world and expect events to just line up behind it."

"The airships are probably armed."

"I would hope so. Maybe they'll even have some armor. But they also make a huge target for anyone who wants to bring them down. The question is whether the ambushers are after Pardot's expedition or the zeppelins. The real question is whether we want to take a chance and get involved."

Guiltily Hella gazed down into her left palm. She thought about Scatter and the pain and fear she'd heard in his voice when he thought about losing his mate. She couldn't imagine what it would be like to lose someone who had been that much a part of her life, but she knew how much she missed knowing who her parents had been.

And she knew how much she would miss Stampede if something happened to him. She closed her hand and hoped that would erase the guilt. It didn't.

"I know, Red." Stampede's voice was soft. "I don't know what Pardot has in mind for Scatter, but I'm sure it's not good." He took a breath and let it out. "So are we going to do this thing?"

■ ■ ■ ■ ■

Hella rode Daisy toward the intersection while Stampede loped behind her, using the mountain boomer's massive bulk to break the path for him. Branches lashed Hella's head and shoulders repeatedly. She lowered her head and peered under the uncertain protection of her arm, though occasional branches made it through her defense. Thankfully she kept everything out of her eyes, but her cheeks stung, and she'd gotten a bloody lip.

Even moving as quickly as they could, they arrived too late. The ambushers rushed their trap, moving down to intercept the expedition ahead of the tall hill where the zeppelin pilots had chosen to approach from. The aircraft moved slowly. With darkness gathering, lights flared to life around the gondolas. The expedition had set up some of the camp, mainly the medical tents and food supplies. Evidently they intended to leave some of their equipment behind and had wanted to make sure everyone was taken care of and fed before the rendezvous.

"The hill." Stampede raced ahead of Daisy then scrambled up a rocky promontory that overlooked the ambush area and sat adjacent to the zeppelins.

Hella guided Daisy up the incline. The mountain boomer's long claws dislodged small avalanches of rocks and uprooted young trees and brush. Hella pulled the lizard up short, stopping her twenty meters from the site she knew Stampede would choose as their stand. Daisy snorted in protest, certain she was in a race with Stampede.

"Not now, girl. Down. Lie down." When the mountain boomer did as she instructed, Hella patted Daisy on the neck then slid her rifle free and threw on an extra ammo rack from their supplies. She leaned into the incline and ran up the hill to join Stampede.

He already lay prone, rifle aimed at the ambush area where muzzle flashes and lasers winked like fireflies. The harsh reports of the weapons were muted and indistinct. He took up trigger slack and fired. "First we help out; then we try to scare the aircraft off. Leave the expedition stranded here. If they get Scatter into the air, we'll never see him again."

Hella didn't respond. She found a good area for her rifle and sighted in. The range finder revealed that the distance to the targets was five hundred eighty-three meters. Her rifle was calibrated out to eight hundred meters. Stampede could shoot and kill at more than twelve hundred meters.

His rifle banged loudly again.

Sighting in, Hella dialed the night scope into play and watched as the world turned into myriad shadings of green. The hardshells stood out against the ragtag armor worn by the ambushers. She sighted on the head and shoulders of one man and squeezed the trigger. Not waiting to see the results of her shot, she moved to the next target.

Before she could squeeze the trigger, the new man suddenly leaped into the air, and flames jetted from his feet. His hair caught on fire, and flames blazed in his hands. He opened his mouth and spit a conflagration over the hardshell in front of him.

Wreathed in flames, the hardshell jerked back and tried to beat the fire from his body. He managed only a few stumbling steps before the heat, burns, or the lack of oxygen claimed him.

"That's Silence." Hella struggled to pull the pyrokinetic into her sights, recognizing the profile. "Trazall is behind the ambush."

"Find the roach if you can." Stampede slammed a fresh magazine into his weapon. "Kill him when you do."

Hella squeezed the trigger and rode out the recoil. She kept the scope on her target. She spotted a brief flare only a few centimeters from Silence's body and knew that his fiery aura was hot enough to act as armor. Her bullet had vaporized before touching him.

In the next instant, several other bullets vaporized as well. A hardshell narrowly missed Silence with a laser, and that instantly drew the pyrokinetic's attention. Shifting in midair, Silence spit another stream of incendiary death. The hardshell with the laser rifle spun away, covered in fire.

The green-haired man, Jack Hart, gestured toward a four-man squad of hardshells. Wavy, purple-black force, almost invisible, spread outward from his hand movement. In the next instant, the hardshells jerked sideways as if their servos had suddenly gotten corrupted. Then the men fell, arms and legs splayed helplessly as increased gravity pinned them to the ground.

Hella put her sights over Hart's chest and squeezed the trigger. At first she thought she'd missed. Then after three more shots, she knew she couldn't have missed every time. She noticed one of the purple-black blossoms around Hart and realized that his power was pulling bullets to the ground before they reached him.

She shifted her attention to the normal thieves among Trazall's crew and punched bullets through them as quickly as she could. When she exhausted one magazine, she plugged in another.

"The zeppelins are closing in." Stampede rolled to one side, and a bullet cored through rock where he'd been. "And one of Trazall's snipers has a bead on our position. It won't be long before others do too."

Glancing back toward the airships, Hella saw they were moving toward the quagmire of fighting men. She rolled to a fresh position as well just ahead of a shot that notched the rock she'd been using as a rifle stand. "Did you see Trazall?"

"No. You?"

"No."

"That scans. Trazall is usually the one behind the scene. He's not there when things head south."

A moment later, Hella peered back down her rifle. Movement through the brush drew her attention. She used her peripheral vision against the darkness and spotted two men racing toward their position. "We've got company incoming."

"Where?"

"Three o'clock. Do we hold or move out?"

"Pull back. Take up a new defensive line. And keep Daisy out of the fire lines. We go to your right to intercept those gunners. We need to keep this hill clear as we can."

Hella checked her rifle. "Ready."

"Go."

Turning, Hella rose to a half crouch and ran to the right. She used her right hand to vault over a large boulder then hunkered down low as the brush again. Tracer-equipped bullets sliced through the brush after her. "They see me."

"Go to ground. I've got one of them."

Hella dived to the earth. Rock kissed her cheek hard enough to break the skin. She stayed flat, her heart beating frantically, as bullets combed the brush for her.

The familiar basso bark of Stampede's rifle rolled over her. Thirty meters away, a shadow jerked suddenly sideways and fell in a loose sprawl. The shadow didn't get up again, and the second rifleman quit firing and faded into hiding.

"Flush him, Red."

Shoving her right arm out, Hella blasted the trees where she'd seen the first man fall, gambling that the two hadn't wanted to get separated in all the confusion. Her bullets scored white scars on the tree trunks and chopped down branches and bushes.

The second man broke cover, heading back the way he'd come

and managed two steps before Stampede fired. The heavy-caliber bullet caught the man from behind and pitched him forward. He didn't move again.

Stampede pushed himself up from the ground. "Let's go."

"Where?"

"Get closer if we can. If we can't, we hold back and hope we can pick up the pieces."

Hella gazed at the two approaching zeppelins. "If Pardot manages to get aboard the airships, we're going to lose Scatter."

"If we get killed, we're going to lose Scatter anyway. We do what we can, Red. That's how we've always worked it."

In the dark sky, the zeppelins suddenly opened fire. Machine guns and small cannons pounded the earth and the ambush party. The devastating onslaught created a line between the ambushers and the expedition. The no-man's-land created by corpses and pieces of corpses widened from a few meters to nearly twenty in as many heartbeats.

Scatter's face lifted from Hella's palm to the air. "Hella."

"We're here." Hella ran to cover behind a tree and knew it would be poor cover against one of the zeppelins' cannons.

Sadness pulled Scatter's face down heavily. His face shook. "This is too much. I do not want you and Stampede to die."

"We're not dead yet." Blood trickled down Hella's cheek as she peered around the tree.

"The two of you should go somewhere else. Be safe."

"If we have to, we will. Dead heroes don't do anybody any good." That was another one of the sayings Stampede had first taught her, but it sounded really dumb saying it to Scatter. She just didn't know what else to say.

The zeppelins cruised closer then hovered over the battleground a couple hundred meters up.

"They're idiots getting that close." Stampede shook his head. "If Trazall brought any—"

A rocket streaked into the sky atop a chemical burn tail. When the rocket first crashed into the zeppelin, Hella thought nothing was going to happen. Then a secondary round exploded inside the bag and ignited whatever gas had been used to fill it. A series of successive detonations ripped through the bag.

Almost instantly, a pool of fire hung in the night sky then began the long fall to earth. The gunners aboard the second craft fell silent, obviously overcome by what had happened to the other ship.

Hella wondered if the zeppelin crews had ever before been in battle, and she thought again of the perfect world Riley had taken pains to describe to her. They weren't living in peaceful times. Stampede had taught her that. He'd trained her to be a warrior because that was the only way she would survive. He'd trained her to be a scout because being on her own was safer than trying to exist within the shifting allegiances of towns and trading posts.

The wreckage of the first zeppelin hit the ground ahead of flaming bodies as survivors of the explosions tried to escape. The mass indiscriminately killed Trazall's people as well as the expedition members while they fought. Another rocket launched and narrowly missed the second zeppelin, though Hella had no idea how a target that big could be missed.

Evidently the commander of the surviving vessel had decided on discretion as the better part of valor because the airship started pulling away. Before it got more than fifty meters away, a third rocket slammed into it amidships and burst it open in a fiery gush. As the zeppelin fell, ammo cooked off in a hail of bullets and rockets. Fiery debris lay spread across the treetops.

Eyes stinging from all the smoke and smarting from the bright explosions, Hella looked around for Stampede. He stood behind a copse of trees with the big rifle held before him. Flames wreathed the trees behind him.

He nodded. "I'm fine."

"I'm going to look for Scatter." His visage had disappeared again, and the silver film covered her left palm.

"*We'll* go."

"No. You'll stand out." As far as Hella had seen, there wasn't another bisonoid in either of the two groups. "I'm depending on you to cover me."

Stampede hesitated. "In and out. Don't try to get cute with this."

Hella plunged through the trees and brush before he could change his mind.

. . . . .

Chaos spread out as far as Hella could see. Fire cast uncertain light and weirdly twisting shadows. Smoke poured in all directions and stayed low in the brush rather than rising above the trees. She ran and even after only a short distance felt her lungs, throat, and nasal passages burning from the smoke-laced chemicals. She hoped she wasn't breathing anything lethal.

Skirmish groups still battled. Gunshots rang out singly or in rapid-fire bursts as she vaulted over dead bodies. She thought of Colleen Trammell and hoped the woman was still alive. Of everyone in the expedition, Colleen had seemed the most kind.

One of Trazall's warriors strode out from behind a flaming tent. He was barely visible in all the smoke. Hella raised her left hand and fired into his face. The body was still falling when she sprinted past him. She knew time worked against her. Eventually one side or the other would claim supremacy on the battlefield and she'd stick out.

Scatter's face suddenly formed in front of her. "Ocastya is only a short distance from you."

Hella dived and took brief shelter beside an overturned ATV. She covered her head as bullets smacked into the vehicle. The sharp tang of fuel filled the air. "Where are you?"

"I am still locked in the electromagnetic field. Dr. Pardot has the key."

"Where's he?"

"A security team has taken him into hiding to protect him."

Hella pushed herself up and ran. The ATV exploded just behind her. The heat washed over her, and the concussion almost knocked her from her feet.

"You cannot shut down the field without Dr. Pardot's key. Please, Hella, take Ocastya. She is under guard, but she is not locked up."

"Show me."

Scatter's face darted ahead of her and cut left around a burning tent. Hella followed. Before she turned the corner, one of the hardshells lunged out of the smoke and brought up his rifle.

The face shield looked alien and unforgiving. The amplified voice sounded mechanical and cold. "Stop where you—

CHAPTER 28

The hardshell suddenly lifted as a large-caliber round smashed into his chest and knocked him backward.

Hella never broke stride, following the shimmery silver gleam that floated in the air in front of her. She knew that Stampede had taken out the hardshell. No one else was around.

"Here." Scatter hovered over the entrance to one of the medical tents. Flames engulfed the back half of the tent and were already twisting inside.

"Careful, Red. You're going to have chemicals all throughout that tent."

Knowing Stampede had his eye on her made Hella almost feel protected, but she knew that was false. Until both of them got clear, they were at risk. Still, it was good hearing his rifle boom almost constantly. Two of Trazall's men went down around her as they spotted her.

She ducked into the tent and discovered she could barely see through all the thick smoke. On one of the tables, chemical vials exploded in quick succession, unleashing bright colors, different-colored smoke, and detonations loud enough to hurt her ears.

Ocastya lay on one of the collapsible examination tables the expedition had packed in.

Scatter hovered fretfully over her. "Here. She is here."

"I see her." Hella hurried to the fractoid's side. Ocastya looked a lot better than she had the day Hella had pulled her from the swamp. Nearly all of the blackened metal had turned pristine silver again. Evidently the fractoid was healing even better than Hella. Memory of the burns she'd suffered and the horrid thing her arm had been turned into kept Hella back. "Can she move?"

"Not yet. Soon."

"She moved back at the swamp."

"That was reflex. A conditioned response from the near-death experience." Scatter's floating face turned to Hella. "Please help her."

Reluctantly Hella approached the table and the strange being lying on it. An explosion outside the tent hurled shrapnel through the material, shredding it instantly.

"Hella?" Stampede sounded tense.

"I'm fine."

"Get out of there. I don't have eyes on you, and I'm starting to attract attention."

Knowing she didn't have time for indecision anymore, Hella slipped her knife from her boot and sliced through the restraints holding Ocastya to the table. The fractoid's head turned smoothly toward Hella, and she lifted a hand. Blades sprang free of her fingers.

Hella lifted her knife and morphed her other hand into a weapon.

Scatter's face slid between Hella and Ocastya. The harsh, screeching machine language filled the smoke-laced air. The chemicals burned Hella's eyes strongly enough to bring tears.

Ocastya's knife blades disappeared. She swiveled her attention to Hella. "I am to go with you."

"Yes." Hella let out a breath, but her newfound calm was shredded when another rocket struck the earth outside. "You can't move?"

Ocastya bent at the waist effortlessly and looked at her legs. "I am still damaged. I am unable to walk."

Great. I'm not exactly the one to sling her over my shoulder and take off with her.

Scatter turned to her. "One of the ATVs is nearby."

"Won't help." Hella shook her head and felt helpless. "I've never driven one." Opportunities to drive something like the ATV hadn't come along, and she'd always preferred traveling on Daisy.

"Easily remedied." Scatter hovered close to her then wrapped his face over hers with a suddenness that startled her into stepping back.

Hella thought her brain was overheating. She felt as if she had a fever. Then, in the time it took to blink, she knew how to drive an ATV.

Scatter peeled off her and hovered in the air again. "Hurry, Hella."

Pushing her curiosity to the back of her mind and focusing on survival, Hella sprinted through the tent flap and turned left, automatically knowing the ATV's location as well. She clambered onto the vehicle as though she'd been doing it all her life. The engine caught when she pressed the start button. She put it in gear as one of Trazall's warriors spotted her and brought up his weapon. Before he could shoot, his head exploded in a geyser of blood.

"Move." Stampede's voice cut through all the chaos.

Hella drove the ATV into the medical tent, ripping through the opening. She got off only long enough to slide Ocastya from the table onto the rear of the vehicle. The cargo space on the four-wheeler was limited, but Ocastya folded up a lot easier than a human being would have. Hella used the cargo straps to tie the fractoid into place. "It'll help if you can hang on."

Ocastya gripped the rear roll bar with her two hands. "I will."

Clambering back aboard the ATV, Hella revved the engine and drove forward. There wasn't enough room in the medical tent to try turning around. Putting her arm across her face, she drove the ATV through the flaming back wall. The weakened canvas gave way at once. The flames clung to her only momentarily; then she was speeding through the campsite.

A pair of hardshells vectored in on an intercept course. Hella heard Stampede's rifle roar, and one of them went down as he brought his weapon up. She drove over a dead Sheldon, probably one of the men Trazall had brought with him, and the ATV's front wheel pulled up as the vehicle vaulted into the air over the armadilloid's body.

The hardshell managed a short burst from his weapon. At least one of the rounds struck the underside of the vehicle, and Hella hoped it didn't do any lasting damage. The man tried to duck away, but he got slammed by a hail of bullets from an approaching insectoid. The ATV hit him in the chest and knocked him backward.

Hella drove with desperation, amazed that she wasn't already dead. Stampede laid down covering fire all around her, knocking down gunners and driving others to shelter. Most of them had their own problems staying alive without giving her chase. Hella took advantage of that.

Amazed at her dexterity and familiarity with the vehicle, Hella tried not to think too much about her actions and just let them flow. She blew through the campsite and roared up the hill toward Stampede. She was surprised at how little attention she drew once she was out of the camp, but most of Pardot and Riley's people were in full retreat. Trazall's crew was more interested in claiming what they could of the expedition's goods.

When she reached the promontory where she'd left Daisy, Stampede was at her heels. She unstrapped Ocastya, and Stampede threw her up onto Daisy's back. The mountain boomer pawed the ground in protest.

"Easy, girl." Hella patted the lizard on the side of the neck, but she stood on one side of Daisy and secured Ocastya while Stampede did so on the other side. "Where do we go?"

"North." Stampede didn't hesitate. "We can lose ourselves in the mountains. At least have a chance of escaping."

Hella vaulted into the saddle and took a last look at the campsite. Smoke hovered over the area, but occasional gunfire announced the fact that the confrontation still continued. Flames burned patches of nearby forest.

"Let's go." Stampede slapped Daisy on the rump, and the mountain boomer dug her claws in, muscles bunching as she raced forward.

Hella stayed low over the creature, riding her effortlessly, becoming one with her mount as Daisy careened through the wilderness. She gazed down at her left palm. Scatter had dropped back into place there, but she couldn't help thinking of the fractoid being held captive somewhere.

· · · · ·

Hours later, hurting from the action and the hard riding, Hella tended the small fire in the cave she and Stampede had been fortunate enough to find an hour or so before dawn. The pot of stew hung that over the fire smelled almost ready. She lifted the lid and poked her knife in to skewer a chunk of squirrel. She tasted the meat and decided it was cooked enough.

Stampede sat over to one side of the cave and cleaned their rifles with respect and care. Ocastya sat beside him, still paralyzed from the waist down. So far, Scatter hadn't put in an appearance.

"Stew's ready." Hella poured most of the pot's contents into one of their tin plates and handed it to Stampede along with a spoon.

"Thanks." He set the rifle aside and took the plate.

Hella poured the rest of the stew into her plate took her spoon. She leaned back against Daisy, who had stretched out on the other side of the cave and gone to sleep. The ride had been long and hard, and the lizard wasn't a nocturnal creature by nature. She lived for warmth and the sun.

For a time they ate in silence while Ocastya watched them. The fractoid had talked with them some, but her language skills weren't as good as Scatter's. Hella was also fairly certain there was something wrong with her. She would trail off in the middle of sentences and be unable to return to her train of thought, and she sometimes looked afraid of them.

She asked about Scatter a lot.

Stampede had gotten tired of answering the same questions over and over again. It was like being around a mentally deficient child, annoying and sad and unsettling at the same time. Some of those children had carried weapons, but none of them could spring blades out of their fingers the way Ocastya could.

"We're running low on ammunition." Stampede spooned stew up and ate it with obvious relish.

"Considering how we've been burning through it, that's not surprising."

"So are you." Stampede gestured to her special backpack. "I've loaded up the last of your supplies."

That stopped Hella for a moment. With the way her body processed raw materials and turned them into bullets, she sometimes tended to take ammunition for granted. "There's a trade camp a day from here."

"That's traveling by day. By night it will take even longer. And I don't want to try to travel by day because Trazall knows as much about this area as we do. If he's looking for us—and we still don't know that he isn't—he'll know where to find us."

"If we go to another trade camp, we run the same risk. Even if we get through, we're too far out. By the time we get back, Trazall, Pardot, and Scatter will all be gone."

Ocastya looked at them and said something in the machine language.

Hella looked at her. "I can't understand you if you don't speak like this."

The fractoid waited a moment then nodded. "Where is my mate?"

"I don't know." That was the truth. Hella didn't know if Pardot still had Scatter, or if Trazall had him. There were no guarantees Scatter had survived the attack. The thought of the fractoid's possible death depressed her, and she worked hard not to think of that.

"Will he be here soon?"

"I don't know."

Ocastya looked troubled. "If he does not come soon, I may forget myself." She'd said that a lot too.

"He'll be here as soon as he can."

"All right. May I sit in the sun?"

"Sure." Hella put her bowl down and crossed over to the fractoid. She picked Ocastya up and carried her into the sunlight. The fractoid's useless legs dragged.

"Thank you." Ocastya stared out at the world as sunlight beamed down on her.

"You're welcome." Hella returned to her meal and watched the fractoid.

Stampede watched as well. "We don't have a lot of choices, Red."

"Do you think we can lie low and keep out of sight long enough for Trazall to pass on by?"

"Maybe."

Down in the valley below them, sporadic gunfire echoed. The erratic, staccato noise made the bright day seem frightful. Death walked the hills.

Stampede grinned coldly. "We wait long enough, maybe Trazall and Pardot will kill each other off."

· · · · ·

High-pitched piercing woke Hella from a dreamless sleep. Her left hand was a weapon before she opened her eyes.

Stampede hovered over Ocastya. His size dwarfed the fractoid. Ocastya shook and shivered. She fought against Stampede, slapping at him and trying to escape. His nose and mouth were already bleeding.

Hella rolled to her feet and grabbed a stun baton from Stampede's pack. With the baton in hand, Hella trotted over to them just as Ocastya broke free of Stampede and hit him hard enough to drive him back. Her legs still didn't function, and that was the only thing that kept her from getting away quickly. Even without the use of her legs, she started hauling herself out of the cave with her arms.

"Ocastya." Hella stood behind the fractoid.

"She can't hear you." Dizzily Stampede pushed himself to his feet and wiped at his bloody snout.

The high-pitched keening continued echoing through the cave. Hella started to feel certain that her eardrums were about to explode.

Scatter suddenly manifested in the air in front of her. "Stop her, Hella. Pardot and Trazall must not find her."

Hella thought either of the others might be in more danger from Ocastya. The injured fractoid had hurt Stampede, and that wasn't an easily done thing.

"How do I stop her?"

Scatter hesitated but Ocastya was already at the cave mouth. "Use the baton. It is the only way."

"Will it hurt her?"

"I do not know. I hope not."

Unable to wait any longer, Hella darted forward, touched the baton to Ocastya's back, and pressed the firing stud. Electricity crackled and flickered along the baton's length before spreading out across the fractoid's body. She froze, straining forward, and when the charge finally exhausted, Hella was afraid Ocastya would resume her escape.

Instead the fractoid slumped forward. Her face clanged against the rock floor of the cave.

Hella rushed to her, afraid to touch her in case the electricity was running through her. She wanted to check to see if she was still alive, but she didn't know how to do that either. Ocastya didn't have a pulse, didn't require respiration.

"She lives." Scatter's face floated in front of her. He looked tired and sad.

"Where are you?" Hella gazed at him and tried to get a clue to his location.

"I do not know."

"Are you with Pardot?"

"No. I am with Trazall."

"Do you know where he's taking you?"

"No. Not for certain. I have heard some of the men talk about an encampment that is not too far away. They say there is a laboratory there with a working generator and that Dr. Trammell is happy about that."

"Trammell?" Stampede growled. "She's there?"

"Yes."

"Why?"

"She is in league with Trazall. From what I have gathered, she is the one that told Trazall where Pardot planned to meet the zeppelins."

Stampede shook his shaggy head, and his ears twitched. "Why would she join forces with Trazall?"

"I have not heard." Scatter's floating face turned to regard Stampede. "I am sorry."

"It's not your fault." Stampede wiped blood from his mouth. "We're in a bad situation." He glanced at the unconscious fractoid. "She's getting worse and she's more than Hella and I can handle. Even if Ocastya was behaving, she's paralyzed from the waist down. Hella and I can't pack her out of here while dodging Trazall and Pardot."

"The only answer, then, is to repair her." Scatter shifted his attention back to Hella. "In order to do that, I need your help."

Hella shook her head. "I don't know anything about fixing her."

"Together, Hella. Together you and I can save my mate. I cannot do it without you, but it will be hard and possibly dangerous."

Hella knew what he was going to ask of her, and that made her afraid. The experiences she'd had with Scatter being inside her mind, even when he'd given her the skills to ride the ATV, hadn't been good. Whatever Scatter planned to do to his mate, it would probably be horrifying. She tried to think of the best way to say no.

"If you do not let me help her, then it would be better if you put her out of her misery quickly." Scatter's face hovered in front of Hella. "I cannot bear to think of all the suffering she is going through now. She is scared and alone, and she has never before been those things."

"Red." Stampede's voice was soft and hesitant. "You don't have to do this. Probably you *shouldn't*."

"I know." Hella swallowed then nodded. "Okay. Just tell me what I need to do."

CHAPTER 29

Cross-legged, Hella sat on the hard rock floor of the cave and steeled herself as Scatter's thin, metallic face floated close to her then touched her and wrapped itself over her features. She closed her eyes and sucked in her breath at the chill that pricked her flesh.

"Everything will be all right." Scatter spoke calmly.

"When did you learn to lie?" Hella tried to make light of the situation, but the fear that knotted her belly wouldn't go away.

"Only since I have been among your people. I have found that it is a most useful tool. Does it help?"

"No."

On the other side of the cave, Stampede stood at the ready but looked lost. He didn't know what he was supposed to do, and he was clearly unhappy about that judging from the frown and the twitching ears.

Daisy sat in the back of the cave with her snout in a feedbag.

Ocastya lay on the floor in front of Hella. The fractoid's face was relaxed, but her eyes stared up at the cave roof, clearly not seeing anything.

"We will begin."

Before Hella could respond, Scatter lifted her arms and placed one of her hands on Ocastya's forehead and the other on the fractoid's stomach. Hella felt the buzz of the connection immediately. She felt as if she were rubbing her hands over electrified knife blades.

"You will have to go deep into her mind." Scatter spoke calmly, almost hypnotically. "Although you think maintaining the contact with her as you are now is the hardest part, the most difficult task lies ahead of you."

"What?"

"Keeping the skeins of yourself from getting tangled up in the skeins of Ocastya. You will have to pay attention to your individuality as well as hers. If you are not careful, you will lose your memories to her and find her memories lodged inside your head."

"I don't want that to happen."

"No. Both of you have to remain whole."

For the first time, Hella realized that Scatter was speaking through her as well. She heard her voice in her ears even though she knew it was him talking. He had already slid into her thoughts and into her mind.

"Are you ready?"

"No."

"It is time."

"I'm afraid."

"I know. I will be with you. Just concentrate on remaining yourself."

Not in control of her own body, Hella leaned forward and increased the pressure and contact with Ocastya. The cold, metallic body beneath her palms suddenly heated up. Scatter tried to draw her inside his mate. Hella felt the pull and instinctively resisted. She didn't know if she held back or if Ocastya—even in her unconscious state—was keeping them at bay.

Then, without warning, the world around Hella opened up, and she fell through the cave floor. She screamed but she didn't know if the sound ever made it past her lips.

* * * * *

When Hella opened her eyes again, she wasn't in the cave, the Redblight, or even her world anymore. Around her, a room filled with squared, metallic furniture rendered in pastel purples and greens stood out against a gold flake floor.

Hella reached down to touch a metallic chair and caught sight of her reflection. She wasn't herself and she wasn't Ocastya. At least, she wasn't the Ocastya lying in the cave. The woman reflected in the bright surface had dark hair and pale skin. Hella wished she could see herself.

Almost instantly the chair covered over in a mirror surface. The woman had black hair, alabaster skin, and pale lavender eyes. She was beautiful.

"No. That is not what I wanted."

Hella knew she spoke the words, but she also knew they were the woman's words, not hers. She was looking through the woman's eyes.

Ocastya touched the chair again, and it turned a light green and burned with light from within. "There. Much better." She turned, walked over to one of the walls, and touched it.

Immediately a vid feed pumped through the surface. The images were of a city like nothing Hella had ever seen. Tall spires reached for the sky, and small aircraft flitted between the metallic canyons. All of the buildings looked as if they'd been made from seamless metallic glass. As she watched, a few of them changed colors, and the transition briefly turned them into prisms. Beyond them, in a golden sky, two suns—one nearer and one farther—shone down.

"Ocastya."

Hella recognized the name even though the nuance of it was different. She turned to face a doorway that suddenly came into being.

Scatter stepped into the room. He didn't look human. He looked exactly as Hella had first seen him. He smiled but Ocastya pulled away. She blinked and Scatter was suddenly human in appearance. He was tall and thin and blond, handsome.

"Hella? Are you there?" The Scatter in front of her didn't speak, but she heard him inside her head.

"Yes." Panic welled up in Hella, and she tried to control it. She closed her eyes, and it was strange to realize she didn't know if

Ocastya closed hers as well. When she opened her eyes again, Scatter was metallic.

"You will have to control Ocastya at this point. We are in her subconscious mind, in her memories. She will fight against you and your perception of me. She sees me now as you see me, and that . . . is not easy. This is from a time before we had to give up our flesh-and-blood bodies. She is every bit as frightened as you are. Do you feel her fear?"

"Yes."

Regret flashed across Scatter's face. "I would not wish this for either of you."

"I understand." Hella made Ocastya stand when all she wanted was to run. "It's hard to keep her here."

"I know but you have to do it." Scatter placed a hand against Ocastya/Hella's head. The metal palm felt cold and hard. "Together we have to remember all that we can in order to save her."

And to save you. Scatter had stated that his continued existence depended on Ocastya's.

The world opened up again, and Hella fell through, going deeper than before.

. . . . .

When she opened her eyes again, Hella thought the perspective was all wrong. The world looked huge. Then she caught a glimpse of herself/Ocastya reflected in a nearby window and realized she was just a little girl of six or seven.

Scatter's face formed in the window reflection. "I did not meet Ocastya as a child, but I got to know her as a child through her memories when we shared them."

Hella stared at the stranger in the mirror, at the metallic dress she wore, and knew that Ocastya was younger in the memory than Hella could remember from her own life. How could Ocastya remember those things so well when Hella didn't have the first clue?

"You must be patient, Hella. Your memories of your parents will come back to you when they are ready. They are there waiting for you. When the time is right, you will have them again."

Hella swiftly quelled the tremor of hope that quivered inside her, focusing instead on the task she had ahead of her. When danger was around, you paid attention to that first. Stampede had drilled that into her.

"Ocastya?" A male voice called from behind Hella. She turned toward it and saw a tall man with a generous face and a smile looking at her.

"This is her father."

Hella could have guessed that. She wanted to fight as the big man reached down and took her up into his arms, but Ocastya embraced him instead. The man's scent and his cologne filled Hella's nose and made one of them sneeze.

"He was a good man, a good father." Scatter sounded sad. "Ocastya lost him when we made the transitions to our new bodies. She lost her mother too. She also lost two brothers and a sister."

A wave of sadness—whether from Ocastya or just from a sympathetic reaction, Hella didn't know—pierced her. She started to relax and share the feeling of protection Ocastya was experiencing.

Then the bottom dropped out of the world again.

■ ■ ■ ■ ■

Afterward Hella couldn't even guess at how many memories she had gone through. The emotions had been the roughest part up until the time when Scatter separated her from Ocastya. That separation was the hardest thing of all. By the time she'd finished spending years in Ocastya's memories, Hella felt as if she were being ripped out of her own body.

She blinked her eyes and discovered she was still in the same position, leaning over Ocastya's body. Sweat dripped from her, and her arms and back were knots of agony. Her legs were numb, and for one insane moment, she thought the paralysis that held Ocastya had somehow spread to her.

"Red?" Stampede sat across the cave. The cook fire flickered between them, the foot-high flames licking the breeze and caressing the pot that hung to one side.

"Yeah." Hella felt tears on her face and grew embarrassed. She wiped them away with trembling hands.

"Are you okay?"

"Sure." Hella was parched and her voice came out as a croak.

Stampede stood and crossed the cave to give her a canteen.

Uncapping the canteen, Hella drank thirstily. After a moment, Stampede gently pulled the canteen away. "Go slow. You'll make yourself sick. You probably don't want that."

"No." Hella wiped her lips with the back of her hand. She looked around then down at her unmarred palm. "Where's Scatter?"

"I don't know." Stampede shrugged his broad shoulders. "I haven't seen him since he wrapped around your face and put you in that trance."

Hella felt for the fractoid but couldn't sense him. She glanced down at her palm and saw his face there. Despite her efforts, she couldn't elicit a response.

For the first time, she noticed that it was dark outside the cave mouth. Stampede had evidently dragged brush over the opening to hide the mouth to mask the presence of the fire. He'd left bare centimeters at the top for the smoke to stream out. "How long was I gone?"

"Hours." Stampede's ears twitched. "I was getting worried, but the last thing Scatter told me was to leave you alone and let you come out of it on your own. Otherwise you might not make it back." He smiled. "I'm glad you did."

"Yeah. Me too."

"Want something to eat?"

Hella nodded. "I'm starving."

"Figured you would be." Returning to the fire, Stampede spooned up a plate of stew and handed it over. "Go slow."

As she ate, Hella told Stampede everything she could remember about the worlds she'd just visited. She had to share it. She couldn't keep something like that to herself. If she did, she felt certain she'd explode.

Only a few meters away, Ocastya lay inert. But the burned and twisted parts of her body glowed and shifted.

. . . . .

By morning, Scatter still hadn't returned. Hella's worry grew. She'd slept a little in the wee hours of the morning, and her dreams had been a constant, uncoiling and blending of her memories with Ocastya's. She'd been gone hours from the cave, but she'd traipsed through years, decades, of Ocastya's life. She believed she remembered less of those times than she had the day before, but there was still enough to be confusing. She had to concentrate to remember her own history, which had already been cored with holes.

Without a word, Stampede handed her a venison steak wrapped inside fried bread he'd made in a pan over the open fire.

"Thank you."

"Eat all you want. I took a deer this morning." Stampede waved to the silver, insulated bag in the back of the cave. "We can eat well for two or three days. Even feeding that black hole." He jerked a thumb at Daisy, who slept on her side. Miraculously a small pile of deer carcass remained beside her. The blood on the rock was dark brown with age.

The meat was warm and tender, seasoned with some of the herbs they'd packed. Hella ate hungrily and stared out at the cotton white morning fog lying over the lowlands. "Did you see Pardot or Trazall while you were taking the deer?"

"No."

"There can't be many places around here that would have the laboratory Scatter said he was taken to."

"I know. I've been thinking." Scatter took out a map. "We haven't strayed too far off the trade roads here in the mountains."

"There are no raw materials or salvage areas out here worth having, and it's dangerous because of the land as well as the creatures that live here. And that's not mentioning the two-legged predators."

Stampede nodded and tapped a section of the map to the northeast. "Before the collider exploded and the world changed, there was a large city up here."

"Tulsa. I know." Tulsa had been one of the largest cities in Oklahoma before the collider destroyed everything. Hella had never heard what happened to the city, but when the physical world had ruptured and changed, *something* had destroyed the city.

Some of the local legends talked about a massive star cruiser that got pulled out of orbit in one of the alternate worlds and crashed into Tulsa. The resulting series of detonations had ripped through the city and rendered it into a toxic wasteland. Seriously twisted and mutated things were pretty much all that remained of the populace.

"The city has a lot of research and development places there." Stampede tapped the map. "If Scatter is correct, that Colleen Trammell is looking for facilities like that, she might head here."

"Doesn't mean she's going to be there."

"True. But if she has joined up with Trazall for the moment, I don't see that as a long-lasting arrangement."

Hella snorted derisively. "When Trazall is sure he's milked Colleen for everything that he can, he'll either sell her or kill her. And the profit he can get isn't going to be worth much aggravation or effort on his part."

"Yeah. I know. But if he's going to play along with her to get all the information she has, he'll have to deal with her a while longer. That gives us time."

Hella's palm with Scatter's face on it itched. She scratched the flesh but couldn't satisfy the irritation.

"You can't reach Scatter?"

"No. I've tried." Hella stood and approached Ocastya.

New metallic flesh had replaced the burned areas, and the twisted lines had straightened out.

"She looks new, like she should just open her eyes and wake up." Hella knelt and hesitantly reached out toward the fractoid.

"You sure you should do that?"

"No. But you can't feel a pulse in her."

"I already tried. If she's alive, in any form or fashion, I can't tell it."

"And if she's dead, we need to know. If she's dead, Scatter is too.

Doesn't matter if he's already dead; he will be. Then we don't have any involvement in what Pardot and Trammell do to each other."

"Trazall's still got some pain coming for jacking our expedition."

"He didn't exactly jack it if Trammell approached him."

"He could have turned away." Stampede's ears twitched and he snorted. "Any self-respecting scout would have."

Working through the vibrating fear that filled her, Hella placed her hand on Ocastya's forehead. All she felt was the cool metal.

Then Ocastya's eyes opened. "We need to go. My mate is dying."

CHAPTER 30

Hella drew back her hand and watched in astonishment as Ocastya "flowed" to her feet, shifting from a prone position to a standing one. The fractoid peered around the cave anxiously.

Stampede took a wary step back. "Can you speak to Scatter?"

"Scatter?"

Gingerly, moving slowly, aware that Ocastya flowed to face her more directly, Hella got to her feet. "Scatter is what we call your mate. We can't say his name."

"I see. And how am I to call myself?"

"Ocastya."

"All right."

Stampede shifted impatiently. Hella knew the past day or so had been hard on him. Stampede wasn't used to taking an inactive role. His voice when he spoke sounded almost surly, though she knew he took care not to have it sound like that. "Can you speak to your mate?"

"No." Ocastya frowned and shook her head. "He's very . . . far from me right now."

"How far?"

In the back of the cave, Daisy snorted and woke, obviously alerted by the new voice.

"Not so much distance. Perhaps twenty kilometers, if I understand the measurement conversion correctly." Ocastya held a hand up in front of her, flowed it from open to a fist to a mallet then back to hand. "But he *feels* far. I can't sense his thoughts, only that he is there."

"That's good, right?"

"It means he still yet lives. But only just." Ocastya shifted her gaze to Hella. "My mate shifted most of his energy to me through you. I did not know such a thing was possible. Normally, if we were together, that energy would reciprocate. One of us would never drain the other. Things are not what they were in our world."

"No." Hella saw the metallic woman standing before her, but she remembered the child Ocastya had been. That same innocence resonated in her.

Ocastya surveyed her body. "I have never been injured like that before." She paused. "In fact, I have never been injured before. Not in this body."

"I'm sorry."

Ocastya glanced at Hella curiously. "My arrival here had nothing to do with you, did it?"

"No."

"I did not think so. My mate—Scatter—told me many things while I convalesced, but most of what he told me did not make sense. I have no reference." Ocastya looked at Hella's damaged wrist. Most of the burn scarring was gone there, and she finally had full range of movement. "I damaged you."

"You did."

"I am sorry. I did not wish to."

"I know." Hella put out a hand. "I can help you with information about our world. I helped Scatter."

Ocastya made no move to accept Hella's offer. "You were inside my mind. I remember that."

"Scatter asked me to help. He said if I didn't, that you would die."

Ocastya's lips firmed. "My mate knows more about these bodies than I do. I trust his judgment." She frowned. "However, the idea of you there—among my personal remembrances—is *distasteful*."

"I know. I agree." Hella took back her hand.

"But I need knowledge if I am to help my mate. If you are willing, I will accept your offer." Ocastya held out her hand.

Hella put out her hand and pressed her palm to the fractoid's. Almost immediately, dizziness swept through her, and her knees almost buckled as fire blazed through her skull.

"I beg your pardon. That was my mistake."

Thankfully the pain subsided. Hella stood and controlled the sour nausea that sloshed inside her stomach. She managed to stay focused and caught occasional glimpses of the information Ocastya acquired from her.

· · · · ·

"You sure you're up to traveling?" Stampede stared at Hella with his liquid brown eyes.

Hella didn't pause as she threw her saddle across Daisy. "I'm fine."

"You didn't look fine when Ocastya finally let you go."

Self-consciously, Hella nodded at the fractoid, who stood in the cave mouth. "She can hear you."

"I don't care. I'll hurt her feelings every time if it means protecting you."

"I'm fine." Hella reached for one of the saddle straps and missed.

Stampede snorted and twitched his ears.

"I'll be fine." Hella shot a glare at Stampede. "We don't have a lot of time."

"We don't have *any* time to get this wrong. If we end up dead, there's not going to be anybody riding to Scatter's rescue. There's no guarantee we can get him out of the situation he's in now."

Hella secured the strap, positioned the saddle, and cinched it tight. "Somebody once told me that sometimes you have to ride a trail through before you make any decisions about it. Better to go see for yourself than to blindly guess. Sound familiar?"

"Yeah, but I recall something about always making sure your risk didn't outweigh the gain."

"Pardot is menace enough. There's no telling what he can do with any technology he can learn about from Scatter and possibly use. He's already learned enough to track the fractoids when they came into our world. And someone like Pardot?" Hella shook her head. "We can't allow that."

"Who told you we were supposed to save the world?"

"Nobody. But somebody did tell me a scout travels through the land, respects it, and tries to leave it as unchanged and better for others as possible."

Stampede sighed and nodded. He clapped Daisy on the side, startling the mountain boomer into a honked protest. "All right. Let's go see what we can see. But if it looks back, we cut our losses and save ourselves." He walked away before Hella could reply.

. . . . .

Mounted on Daisy, Hella took point and rode in the direction Ocastya indicated. Riding helped sort her thoughts, but she still caught a stray memory every now and then that belonged in Ocastya's head, not hers.

They moved on through the day, stopping only to water Daisy, eating on the go, and paying attention to the wilderness around them. The unforgiving sun burned down, and the humidity from the swamplands and the plant life made the air thick and fragrant. Down in the bottoms where they were, everything smelled of death. The occasional traces of a mineral spring tainted with sulfur reminded Hella of the stories she'd heard about the Christian hell.

And they traveled, going as fast as they dared.

. . . . .

As soon as the sun rose the next morning, they were on the move again. Daisy was recalcitrant at first, objecting to the hard ride only because it was boring and she wasn't getting to explore as much as she wanted to or to hunt, but she finally settled into the distance-eating gait that made her a smooth ride.

At midmorning, they cut a fresh trail.

Senses alert to everything around her, Hella reined Daisy in and dropped down to the ground. The mountain boomer nuzzled

Hella, seeking a treat or a scratching session, doubtless bored again. "Watch."

Daisy instantly abandoned her attempts and focused on the world around them. She snorted, stomped her feet, and set herself in the ready position.

Stampede spoke over the comm link. "You've stopped."

"I've cut sign." Hella knelt, brushed loose dirt and grass from the tire impression cut into the ground, then stuck her fingers into it. The dirt was still moist enough to stick to her fingertips.

"Who?"

"Looks like one of the ATVs. Must be Pardot's group, so some of them survived."

"Could be Trazall."

"His group didn't have any vehicles."

"None that we saw."

"He doesn't like vehicles any more than you do."

"Trazall doesn't like them because they cut into his bottom line. Too expensive to operate and maintain. I don't like them because you become too dependent."

Hella brushed the wet earth from her fingertips onto her jeans and stood. "Ground's still damp and the impression is sharp, not worn down. They didn't pass this way too long ago."

"Headed in the same direction we are?"

"Yeah."

"Break off the trail. Find a new path that's just ours."

Hella didn't like that. "We're going to lose time doing that."

"Better to find our own way than to get too close to Riley's hardshells and get discovered."

"I know." Hella peered up into the mountains. "We still have forest up to the ridgeline. I'd rather go up than down into the swamps."

"Agreed."

Hella remounted Daisy then cut off the trail and climbed the incline. Soft ground peeled away under the mountain boomer's claws, but she gained purchase and smoothly headed up.

While she waited for the rabbits to cook in the coals of the fire they'd burned till sundown then allowed to burn down so the flames wouldn't be seen at night, Hella stared at Scatter's image on her palm. It seemed as though he were right there, just out of her reach.

"You're thinking too much."

Hella closed her hand and looked up at Stampede. She hadn't even heard him come up to her. "I guess so."

Stampede knelt with his rifle across his thighs and warmed his hands above the coals. "We'll know more tomorrow."

"Yeah." According to Ocastya, they were within only a few klicks of wherever Scatter was being held.

"I spotted Pardot's expedition. Thought maybe you and I would go take a look at them tonight. See what we're dealing with." Stampede grinned. "Gonna have to be sneaky, though. Out here in the woods, away from everything they know, they're gonna be extra paranoid."

"We're really sneaky when we want to be, though."

"I know." Stampede gestured at the coals. "Are those rabbits about done?"

"You can always eat grass."

"I have been eating grass. Not very much of it around here is good, and it's not gonna fill me up."

Hella used her knife to fish the mud-encrusted coneys from the coals. She'd left the fur on and caked the whole animal in mud. The heat from the coals had baked the mud hard and, she hoped, cooked the meat inside. Rapping the egg-shaped chunk with her knife hilt, she broke open the mud crust to reveal the coney. The fur peeled easily away with the dried mud and left the cooked meat intact. She handed that one to Stampede then fished out another for herself.

She cracked open the second rabbit, peeled away the mud and fur, then slit the creature's belly with her knife. She poured the guts onto the pile Stampede had made with his then told Daisy she could eat. The mountain boomer lapped the bloody mess up with her long tongue and chomped happily. Hella pinched the cooked flesh from the rabbit and popped it into her mouth. The meat needed seasoning, but it was succulent enough.

"When do you want to go see the expedition?"

"As soon as we finish these rabbits." Stampede gnawed industriously. "We'll give them time to settle in good for the night."

. . . . .

Swaddled in the shadows on the mountainside a half klick from the expedition, Hella lay prone on the ground and peered through her binocs. She'd switched the lenses to low-light properties so she could see almost as plainly as day.

Less than half of the defense bots remained from the initial number, but Riley—assuming he was still alive—had them assigned to the perimeter.

"Not exactly on stealth mode there." Stampede's whispered comment carried over the comm link. Ocastya hadn't been happy about staying behind at the cold camp, but she had.

"Riley isn't big on stealth."

"He likes having a presence, getting noticed."

One of the nocturnal creatures only partially kept at bay by the light from the encampment got too close to the perimeter. A defense bot's gun roared to life a moment later and threw a hail of bullets into the transgressor. Even with the binocs, Hella never saw what it was. Whatever it was, it writhed in agony for just a few seconds then lay still.

Two hardshells left the camp to confirm the kill. They moved cautiously but quickly. Once they'd finished, they returned to their posts.

"Riley still has a lot of firepower."

"Gotta be going through it fast, though." Hella tracked her lenses through the camp and finally found a hardshell she recognized as Riley. The knot in her stomach loosened a little; then she felt ashamed almost immediately. Riley was the enemy. She couldn't lose sight of that. Riley would have killed her and Stampede if he'd gotten the chance. Still, part of her was glad he was alive.

Another burst from a defense bot ripped through the trees. A severed branch and a small cloud of leaves fell to the ground as a furry mass flailed in spastic reflex.

"That was a slayer?"

Hella watched two hardshells duck through the trees and check the mutated raccoon's mangled body. "Yeah."

"Riley wants to be careful and not pull a colony of them down on the camp."

Mutated raccoons could be fierce and were often called masked slayers by the locals. The largest were a meter and a half tall and weighed eighty pounds, though still svelte enough to hurl themselves through the trees. They also possessed near-human intelligence and tool-making abilities and could be total terrors when they took up the revenge trail.

Self-consciously Hella glanced up in the trees around her, making sure none of the masked slayers lurked nearby. Once they got it into their heads that humans were targets, they didn't care which humans they attacked.

Stampede chuckled in her ear. "Nervous?"

"I hate those things. When you're in the middle of them, you never know where they are until it's too late." They'd had a few encounters with the mutated raccoons and had always been good enough—or lucky enough—to escape with their lives. "They don't know when to stop until you bring out fire."

"Riley and his people are following an old road, right?"

Hella trained her binocs on the area before and after the camp. She felt bad because she hadn't noticed the unnatural straightness in the tree line around the camp. The forest hadn't yet broken through the line created by the old highway. "Yeah."

"They're going to miss the area where Ocastya says Trammell and Trazall are holding Scatter."

"Yeah."

"That means they haven't sniffed out Trazall's true trail. He's probably got a small group staying out in front of the expedition, putting down false sign. Since Trazall can't just overpower and kill

Pardot's little hunting party, he's going to lose them in the swamp and let nature take its course." Stampede was silent for a moment. "Not a bad plan, actually."

Although she wouldn't say it, Hella didn't like the idea of Riley's getting killed out in the wilderness. She couldn't explain that reluctance even to herself.

"That's probably what would happen. If we let it."

Hella stared at Riley through the binocs. "You're not going to try to join up with them again."

"No. They'd probably shoot us on sight. But we're not going to lose them either. We're seriously outmanned here, Red. We're going to create advantages and use them. Pardot and Trazall are enemies. We all want the same thing, but we can't afford to take Trazall on head-to-head. We're going to let them engage each other. If that helps us."

"We're going to guide Riley back to the lab where Trammell is?"

"If it suits us. C'mon. Let's head back. We need to get up early and find this lab then figure out if having Riley and Pardot on hand there is going to help us."

Hella put her binocs away then faded back into the darkness with Stampede.

CHAPTER 31

"That was a mil-site that was off the grid even back before the collider blew up the world."

Hella trained her binocs on the installation, taking in all the straight lines of it that were revealed through the overlapping brush and trees. At first glance, the building blended into the surroundings, but upon further study, she saw how it had pushed up from the ground like bones breaking through a decaying corpse. The engineers had built it to outlast the stone around it, to weather attacks and breaches, and the steel-reinforced concrete still stood. One day, when the earth around it ground down into dust, the building would stand fully revealed.

Someone had put considerable effort into keeping the complex disguised. If Ocastya hadn't led her and Stampede to the area, Hella doubted she would have seen it.

She lay among the rocks of an adjacent mountain and studied the complex through her binocs. Morning hadn't yet burned away, and long shadows lay over the ground from the nearby trees and the tall mountains.

Ocastya sat beside her and regarded Hella curiously. "Why do you use that device?"

"Because I can't see the building from this distance."

"Of course you can."

"I think I would know."

"You simply have to alter your eyes to compensate for the distance. It is an easy adjustment. Let me show you."

Hella waved the fractoid's hand away before she made contact with her head. "No. Don't."

Ocastya withdrew her hand and looked hurt. "I apologize."

"You don't have to apologize."

"I offended you. It is only logical that I apologize."

"You tried to help. I appreciate that. But I can't adapt to many changes like what you're suggesting."

"I do not understand."

"The things you and Scatter do, they're not normal for me."

"Of course they are. Your nanobot assembly is capable of many things."

"Let me rephrase that. Those things you do aren't normal *to* me." Hella took a moment to assemble her thoughts. "When I first discovered I could morph my hands into guns and process metal and chemicals through my body, I went into total swampmelt."

" 'Swampmelt'? That term is unknown to me."

"It's when something unusual happens. It's like your brain locks up. Like when a section of the swamp suddenly bubbles up and sucks down whatever is above it."

"You mean you were surprised."

Hella glanced at her. "How did you feel when you discovered you were in freefall in this world and one second away from becoming a comet?"

"Oh. I see."

"Yeah. Like that."

"But appearing in another world, falling to earth from a high altitude, those are very unusual things from anyone's standard, I would think."

"Changing my body is very unusual to me."

"I understand. This is a skill that could save your life, though."

"The fewer changes I have to adjust to now would be great."

Stampede shifted a couple of meters away and snorted in disgust. "Maybe we could leave off the chatter and concentrate on studying the complex."

"What would you like to know about the complex?"

Stampede looked at Ocastya. "What do you know?"

"The construct buried in that mountainside is three hundred forty-one point seven meters above sea level. It measures one point nine klicks from north to south, two point three klicks from east to west. It is five stories deep."

"How do you know that?"

"I have hacked into the computer security that monitors the systems throughout the complex. Not all of them are working, nor are they all working at peak efficiency, but there is enough information in the data files that I can tell you that. I can also tell you the average ambient temperature inside the structure is sixty-eight degrees."

"You did that from out here?"

"Of course. My mate aided me."

Hope leaped inside Hella. They hadn't discussed Scatter in hours. "He's still alive?"

"Yes, but he is dwindling." Ocastya pursed her lips and stared at the building. "I am afraid there is not much time left to him. If we are going to do something, it will need to be soon."

Stampede turned his attention back to the building. "Can you get us inside?"

"I can get us through the cybernetic safeguards monitoring the building, but I cannot keep the guards from seeing us."

"Getting us in will be enough." Stampede focused his telescope. "I've got a plan for the flesh-and-blood contingent of the security system. Can Scatter hold out till tonight?"

Ocastya was silent for a moment. "I believe so. He says he can."

" 'He says'?" Hella glanced at her palm. The image of Scatter there wasn't saying anything.

"Yes. He is hard to understand because the machines Colleen Trammell has him hooked to are attacking his personality core."

"Why is she doing that?"

"I do not know. My mate does not know."

Stampede rolled over onto his back and put his telescope away.

"We've got a few hours before we need to make a move. Until then, we need to rest. Ocastya?"

The fractoid looked at him.

"Do you know where Scatter is inside that building?"

"Counting the topmost floor as the first, my mate is on the fourth floor down."

Stampede rummaged in his pack and took out paper and a pen. "Can you draw a map of those floors? Show us what we're headed into?"

Ocastya took the paper but ignored the pen. She held her palm over the paper, and Hella watched in amazement as lines burned onto the page. "I am using thermal energy." The fractoid smiled at Hella. "If you were trained properly, I believe you could do this as well."

"If you can do all of this, why can't you or Scatter turn your hands into weapons?"

"We are no longer organically based. Your ability to process materials and chemicals is something that is uniquely yours, Hella. You are very special. I do not know why, though I am curious." After Ocastya burned each page, she handed it over to Stampede.

Hella took jerky from her chest pouch and started eating. She lay back, grateful for the shade that covered them, and closed her eyes. Stampede would wake her when he had something she needed to know. Until then, she'd rest. The previous night's excursions had left precious little time for sleep, and she was still tired from helping repair Ocastya.

She didn't sleep well, though. In her dreams she was helping restore the fractoid, but she got sucked into Ocastya's memories like a fly on a spiderweb and couldn't free herself.

· · · · ·

Three hours before sundown, Hella and Ocastya rode Daisy through the wilderness in the direction Pardot's expedition had gone. Stampede easily loped alongside the mountain boomer, and it became difficult to keep Daisy from breaking out into a full-fledged run.

As expected, the expedition had gone right by the hidden military complex. They were hunting blind.

Nearly two klicks from the expedition, Stampede pointed to a tall outcrop. "There." He took off toward it.

Hella reined Daisy over and charged up the mountainside after him. By the time she reached him, Stampede was already setting his long rifle up on its fold-out legs to get a steady shot.

"We're one point seven klicks from the expedition." Stampede lay behind his weapon and squinted through the sniper scope. "How far do you think we are from the mil-plex?"

Hella lay beside Stampede and peered through the spotter scope he'd unpacked as well. "Seven point five, eight." She'd kept track through her spotter scope, ticking off landmarks and mapping the distance, because he'd told her to in order to backstop his own efforts.

"That's what I figure. With the broken terrain and the thickness of the brush, I'm guessing it'll take us about an hour at almost a dead run to make it back to the mil-plex."

"At least." Covering that distance while dodging pursuers was the part that worried Hella. Well, that and being pinned between two enemy forces.

"We do this right, we'll arrive at sundown. Things will be confusing for both sides. We play our cards close to the vest, we can lose ourselves in the confusion."

Ocastya flowed into a puddle on the ground then straightened out into a prone position. She watched them with interest.

"All we have to do is stay ahead of them."

Stampede spoke calmly, but Hella sensed the tension resonating through him. "And not get shot by Riley's people or Trazall's."

Stampede laughed. "Yeah. I didn't think I'd have to remind you about that part." He took deliberate aim. "Once we start this, things are going to happen pretty fast."

"I know." Hella's stomach churned, but she knew most of that was from having to wait. Once everything started . . .

Stampede fired. The recoil blasted back against him and the harsh *crack* rolled over them.

Peering through the spotter scope, Hella watched. For a moment she believed that Stampede had missed. Everyone in the line of travelers continued what they were doing.

Stampede fired again. Before he fired the third time, the first bullet punched into one of the hardshells and knocked him from his feet. The second round tore through an ATV and exploded the gas tank, turning it into a flaming deathtrap for the man aboard it. The third round missed its intended target because the group went to ground.

A few of the hardshells fired back, but their aim was nowhere near where Stampede, Hella, and Ocastya took cover. Stampede managed four more shots before the defense bots vectored in on their position. A barrage of twenty-millimeter cannon rounds slapped into the ground around them and left smoking craters.

"Pull back." Stampede withdrew just as a fresh onslaught ripped through the trees only a few meters from where he'd been. He slung the large rifle over his shoulder as a hail of broken rock rained down over them. "Let's go."

Staying low, using the discrepancy between the lower area and the protective ridges, Hella sprinted back to the small copse of boulders where she'd left Daisy ground tethered. Ocastya matched her stride for stride.

When she reached the mountain boomer, Hella vaulted into the saddle, took up the reins, and kicked Daisy softly in the sides as Ocastya flowed up behind her.

Panicked by the hail of gunfire and mortars knocking holes in the wilderness around them, Daisy dug in and launched herself into a careening sprint. Hella let the lizard have her head and concentrated on staying on top of her. The creature's muscles bunched and released in great explosions of movement that echoed through Hella.

"We've only got to be fast over a short haul." Stampede breathed rhythmically over the comm link. He kept pace with the lizard, running faster than anything human could match. "Riley will allow the ATVs out for a brief run, but he'll call them back. He won't chance getting his forces divided and picked apart if he's being ambushed."

Hella hoped that was true. She stayed low in the saddle, becoming another layer on top of Daisy as the lizard stretched her legs and got up to speed. The mountain boomer plunged through the forest, knocking down small trees and plowing through brush as if it were paper.

. . . . .

Almost an hour later, Hella reined Daisy up as she spotted the hidden mil-plex ahead of her. Sporadic gunfire pursued them, but none of it had come close enough to hurt them.

As Hella peered back at the advancing line of hardshells, a bullet slammed into her chain mail and drove the breath from her lungs. She would have slid from the saddle except that Ocastya caught her by the belt and prevented that.

Stampede took up a brief position beside a thick-boled elm tree, raised the rifle to his shoulder, and took aim. Before Hella could take a breath, Stampede fired. She didn't know if he hit anything at the mil-plex, but the round triggered an instant response from Trazall's guards manning security.

Riley's hardshells kept coming, and the gunfire increased, accompanied by rockets launched by both sides. Within a couple of minutes, the sun dipped in the west and the shadows swelled out of the forest to fill the night.

"Time to go. Before anybody from either of those two groups takes our scent." Stampede stayed low and followed a line of trees to the mountain ridge they'd climbed earlier that day. Hella followed on Daisy, and they left the two groups at war behind them. Rockets, mortars, and small cannons lit up the deepening night. Tracer fire streaked the darkness, identifying the positions of both groups.

. . . . .

Her face streaked with mud to lessen the chance of reflection, Hella trailed after Stampede on foot. They'd left Daisy up in the mountain range while they'd set up to invade the mil-plex. Quiet and withdrawn, Ocastya followed.

Stampede was barely visible in the darkness. Occasional flashes of light from exploding rockets and mortars highlighted his shaggy fur, horns, and eyes. He gripped his rifle in both hands as he fell into position beside one of the exposed walls of the mil-plex. He focused on Ocastya. "Can you still feel Scatter?"

"Yes." Ocastya's voice was tight. "But we must hurry. He is weakening. Soon Colleen Trammell's devices will conquer his resistance; then my mate will be gone from us."

Placing one shaggy hand on the concrete wall, Stampede ran his palm over the surface. His eyes were half closed. His fingers drummed rapidly against the concrete, and Hella knew he was listening to the vibrations given back. He could sense weak spots. That was part of his gift.

"Okay." Stampede stepped away from the wall, took the rifle in both hands, and lifted his right hoof. After a moment of concentration, Stampede drove his hoof against the wall.

The contact shivered across the concrete and peeled earth back from the mil-plex. Cracks showed on the surface, but the wall held. Then Stampede raised his hoof and slammed again.

On the fourth try, the wall dissolved into a hail of flying shards and collapsed inward. Bright, electric light fell out onto the ground. Stampede drew back. "Hella."

Moving forward, Hella leaned in through the opening, morphed her left hand into a small-caliber weapon that cycled suppressed fire, and quickly shot out all the lights throwing illumination through the hole. The breach went dark. Hella went on inside then waited till Stampede joined her.

Without a word, his path already mentally mapped from all the drawings Ocastya had provided, Stampede went forward down the hallway. Hella pulled her night-vision goggles up from her neck and fitted them over her eyes. Almost instantly her vision was incredibly clearer.

The hallway was clean for the most part, except for stray bits and pieces of debris. Farther down the hallway in both directions, electric lights mounted on the walls removed the majority of the gloom. Echoes of shots revealed the battle still raged through the hole in the wall.

Stampede passed through the halls quickly, without hesitation and without a false step. Hella followed, a shadow at his side.

CHAPTER 32

"Sensor!" Stampede shoved back against a wall.

Falling into place beside him, Hella glanced up and spotted the bubble-shielded sensor mounted on the ceiling sweeping the hallway. The wicked snout of a machine gun hung beneath it. A red dot glowed within the smoky gray, bullet-resistant material.

"It is all right. I have hacked the sensors in our area." Ocastya stood in the middle of the hallway. "They will not see us."

When the machine gun didn't fire and the sensor continued its sweep without pause, Hella let out a sigh of relief.

"Well, that's handy." Stampede took the lead again. "You didn't mention anything about the security systems."

"I did not think I had to."

Stampede held up only a moment at the door leading to a stairwell. "Was that a joke?"

"I believe so." Ocastya looked confused. "My mate indicated that you and Hella prefer levity when situations appear grim."

"It's not exactly something we look for."

"Oh. I have erred?"

"No. It's fine. I just didn't expect it."

"Does humor still work if you expect it? That does not seem possible or logical."

Stampede growled. "Not a time for a discussion about rhetoric."

Despite the situation, Hella couldn't help grinning at Stampede's discomfiture. "We can talk about this at another time."

"I look forward to that."

Stampede's ears twitched. "Can you do the same thing to the sensors in the stairwell?"

"It is already done. The building's security will not know we are here."

Hella hoped that was true. In the meantime, Trazall and the building's security had their hands full dealing with Riley and his forces mounting a full-scale attack along the perimeter. Explosions echoed through the great halls, and the shrill warning klaxons pierced them like surgical steel.

They went down the stairwells in rapid fashion. Stampede went first and Hella kept him covered till he reached the landing; then she hurried to catch up and repeated the process. When the mil-plex had first been constructed, there would have been more guards. And they would have had the sensor array intact.

In less than a minute, they reached the fourth-floor landing. A wide, steel door barred the way. Bullet-resistant glass filled a small window that offered a view of a narrow, lit hallway lined with doors. Plaques beside the door indicated the presence of medical equipment and operating rooms.

Ocastya held a hand out, and a trid presentation took shape above her palm. Although the image was less than half a meter wide and tall, the details stood out sharply edged. The view evidently was from one of the sensors at the front of the mil-plex. "Pardot's team has breached the outer wall."

In the image the hardshells waded through Trazall's mercenaries. Bombs and rockets knocked down walls and splintered furniture. Bodies and pieces of bodies spun through the air. Out in the wilderness, Trazall's mercenaries stood a better chance, but in the urban combat arena, Riley's forces ripped through them.

Jack Hart gestured at a group of hardshells, and purple-black spots clustered on them. In the next instant, they plummeted to the floor under their increased weight. Bullets caught in the gravity shield around Hart dropped at his feet.

Then Riley, his hardshell distinctive enough for Hella to recognize it, sprang out of the shadows. Riley launched himself into the air a moment before purple-black spots started swarming over him. As he fell, he thrust his right fist forward in a savage punch toward Jack Hart's head. An instant before the fist ripped through the gravity shield, a long blade snapped out of the forearm armor.

Hart tried to evade the knife strike, but there wasn't time. Even as he dodged, Riley's blade pierced his right eye and broke through the back of his skull. In the same instant, bullets hammered past the gravity shield, and Hart's body jerked with the impacts.

On his knees, Riley yanked his blade free and snapped it back into his forearm. He picked up his rifle and stood then got hit with a twisting mass of flames as Silence breathed on him. Riley staggered back under the onslaught, and the image winked out of existence.

The suit will protect him. Even as she thought that, though, Hella knew that would only allow Riley to potentially threaten her and Stampede.

Ocastya shifted her hand. "We don't have much time."

Another image shimmered into view above her palm. It showed a medical lab. Computers filled the walls, and lights flashed in syncopation. Scatter lay strapped to a chair with a dozen computer leads attached to him. A skullcap covered the top of his head.

Colleen Trammell stood next to a hospital bed, where a small girl lay on the starched white sheets. The girl looked pained and drugged at the same time.

Stampede's ears twitched. "Who is the kid?"

"Alice." Hella gave the name instantly.

"Who is she?"

"Colleen's daughter. She has a disease. She's dying."

A hurt look pulled at Ocastya's silver eyes. "She's only a child. That is horrible."

Hella silently agreed.

Stampede shook his head. "There's nothing we can do about that. What's she doing here?"

"I don't know."

Colleen held her daughter's unresponsive hand for a moment then settled another skullcap onto her head. The wires led to a computer bank that shared the leads from Scatter.

"But it has something to do with Scatter."

The image winked out of sight as Ocastya closed her hand. "We must go."

Stampede tried the door. A palm print scanner lit on the wall next to the door, and a retina scanner slid out. He glared at the technological security. "Well, that's not gonna happen." He raised a leg and smashed a hoof into the door.

Pummeled by the energy he commanded, the door shrieked as it tore free of its hinges and flew into the hallway beyond. Before the door hit the floor, a half dozen gunners from Trazall's group stepped into the hallway from nearby rooms and lifted their assault rifles.

Stampede ducked behind the door frame just before a fusillade of bullets struck the wall and ripped through the open doorway. His ears flattened as he hunkered down. "Could have done without that." He drew his pistols.

Hella gauged the hallway. To her there was plenty of room to maneuver, but Stampede was so large that he'd have a hard time moving or finding cover. He'd become an instant target. She morphed her hands into weapons.

"I need a quake."

Stampede snorted and the ring in his nose stood out briefly. "You step out there, they're gonna put holes in you."

"We stay here, somebody's going to think of lobbing a grenade in after us, or Riley and his people will shoot us from above. Or maybe Trazall's retreating crew will do it when they hit the stairwell." Hella sucked in a quick breath. "Make it a big quake."

"Stay to the sides. I'm gonna fill the hallway with lead so they don't forget about me."

Hella nodded and held her hands up at her sides.

Stampede swiveled around the door and stomped a hoof on the floor. The metal floor quivered, lifting and falling a few centimeters, but it didn't shatter.

In motion at once, Hella whipped around the doorway with her hands before her. She fired, filling the air with a buzz saw of lethal projectiles that skittered from the walls.

True to his word, Stampede filled the open doorway with his bulk and fired his massive revolvers. They sounded like cannons in the enclosed space, and Hella went temporarily deaf before the comm link could compensate.

One man peeled away from a doorway and sprawled, hit by her bullets or Stampede's, Hella wasn't certain. She ran two steps up the wall, finding just enough purchase to manage that, knowing that Stampede's revolvers would empty quickly.

Two more men spilled into the hallway by the time gravity started to take over. She kicked against the wall hard and hoped that Stampede's weapons were empty. She flipped through the air, burning through bullets to knock down a fourth man then a fifth. Landing on her feet, she stayed low and took deliberate aim at the sixth man.

"Reloading!" Even with the comm link, Stampede sounded a million klicks away because of all the noise filling the hallway.

Surging up, Hella opened fire on the sixth man. Bullets burned by her head, and she felt a sharp nip at her right earlobe. As the last gunman fell to the floor, she felt warm blood running down the side of her neck.

"Hella!"

"I'm fine." Walking in profile, always keeping her left foot in front of her right so there was no chance of crossing them up and tripping, Hella closed on the lab doors. She whirled around the door frames and swept the rooms with her weapons.

Stampede covered her back and filled the hallway behind her. She felt his presence, massive and unrelenting. She went to the next door then the next.

When she entered the fifth doorway on the left, she discovered the lab where Scatter, Colleen, and Alice were.

Colleen wheeled away from a sensor monitor to face them. On the monitor, the view out in the hallway showed the dead mercenaries, Hella, Stampede, and Ocastya. Colleen aimed a pistol at them and fired.

Hella ducked back into Stampede just before the bullet ricocheted from the door frame. "Colleen, listen to me."

"Go away! I can save her! You have to give me more time!" Colleen fired again and the bullet ricocheted inside the room. One of the computer banks suddenly sprayed a cloud of sparks.

"If you keep shooting, you're going to kill Alice." Hella held her position beside the doorway. When a moment passed and Colleen didn't fire again, Hella stuck her head around the door frame.

Colleen swarmed over the computer equipment, frantically tapping a keyboard. "Stay out! I'm warning you!"

Seated in the chair, Scatter suddenly strained against his shackles. His mouth opened and his high-pitched screams reverberated inside the lab.

Hella whipped around the door and lunged forward with her weapons raised before her.

Colleen picked up her pistol again and wheeled back around. "Stay back! I said, *stay back!*"

Ducking, Hella dodged below the line of fire, but she couldn't shoot Colleen. She felt sorry for the woman and for the small child lying on the hospital bed, but she also knew that whatever had been done to Scatter might be undone by only Colleen. So close in, Hella didn't want to lose him.

Two bullets streaked over Hella's head. Before Colleen could fire a third time, Hella morphed her hands back and threw herself at the woman. Grabbing the weapon, Hella wrested it away with one hand and wrapped a fist in Colleen's lab coat.

"No!" The woman screamed and struggled, but Hella didn't release her. "I brought Alice here, I betrayed Pardot, to save my daughter. You're not going to stop me. Let me finish what I started."

Ocastya ran to Scatter and hesitated before wrapping her arms around him. Scatter didn't respond; he did not even look at her.

Stampede stood guard over the door. "Can you get Scatter free?"

Picking at the leads, Ocastya shook her head. "I do not understand what has been done to him. He is trapped in some sort of limbo." She glanced up and looked around the room desperately. "Maybe in one of these computers. Maybe somewhere else."

"He's in that chair."

"His physical self is. Not the part of him that makes him who he is." Ocastya turned to Colleen. "What have you done with my mate?"

Colleen struggled to get away, but Hella held her fast. "The two of you have lived *hundreds* of years. Several lifetimes. You don't deserve to do that." Tears ran down the woman's face. Mucus dripped from her nose, and her lip trembled in fear, but Hella didn't think the fear was fueled by a survival instinct. "My little Alice has barely lived nine years. It's not fair. She deserves more out of her life. I will not watch her die when I can do something about it."

"I understand your pain. I have lost people—loved ones—in my life. I would feel pain again if my mate is lost to me." Ocastya stepped toward Colleen. One of the fractoid's hands flowed into a long, sharp blade. "I will not permit you to take him from me. You need to understand this."

Hella glanced at the sensor monitor array on the wall in front of her. Through the shifting images, she saw that Trazall's mercenaries had broken and were now fleeing for their lives, trying to stay out of the kill zone created by Riley's hardshells. Although they had taken considerable losses, the hardshells were definitely a threat that was closing fast. "Stampede."

At the doorway, looking massive against the enclosed space of the room, Stampede nodded. "I see them. They'll be on us in minutes."

"We have an exit strategy."

"Not if we get caught in this room."

Ocastya stopped in front of Colleen and raised her weapon. "Tell me what I need to do to save my mate. Otherwise, I will kill you and risk finding an answer on my own."

"No." Colleen slapped Hella's face and almost succeeded in getting away. "I have almost saved Alice. I can transfer her mind to that body. She doesn't have to die. I can overwrite all the programming that's there."

Despite the stinging pain from the woman's slap, a cold chill crept through Hella. Was it so simple? Could Scatter just be *erased*? Overwritten?

"Mommy?" The child's plaintive cry barely reached them even so short a distance away. The gunfire and explosions from the confrontations on the floors above carried into the lab with ease. "Mommy?"

Colleen tried to go to her daughter. Hella didn't release her. Colleen closed her hands over Hella's and looked at her desperately. She smiled and the effort looked sick and twisted.

"Please, Hella. Let me got to her. Alice is scared. She needs me."

Hella stood frozen, uncertain about what to do, thinking that if she released Colleen, Ocastya would kill her. Images of the dead rat in the dream kept haunting her, changing from rat to child.

"Mommy!" A coughing fit racked the child on the bed. She convulsed and got sick, throwing up a bit.

"Please. My daughter *needs* me." Colleen pushed back from Hella. "She's dying. I don't want her to die alone."

Numbly Hella released the woman and stepped in front of Ocastya, wondering if the fractoid would simply try to kill her first to get her out of the way.

On the walls, the computers continued flashing.

Ocastya regarded the hardware then Scatter's body seated in the chair. "She's stealing him away from me." She focused on Hella. "You know I cannot permit this. Even if she succeeds in overwriting my mate's self with her daughter's, her daughter will not survive. My mate and I are twinned to one another. Both of us must survive. We cannot survive on our own."

At the child's bed, Colleen took Alice's hands and held them tightly. "Everything's going to be all right. Mommy's here. Just close your eyes, and you'll wake up feeling much better. Listen to Mommy." She leaned over her daughter and kissed her. "You're going to get better."

Hella crossed to her. "Colleen."

The woman ignored her.

"Colleen, you can't do this. It's not going to work."

"It will work."

"No. It won't. The fractoids are joined. They're two parts of a whole. If one of them dies, the other will too."

Still holding her daughter's hands, Colleen glared at Hella. "You're lying."

"I'm not. You've been inside my mind. Take a look for yourself."

"I won't trust you. You'll lie."

"Look." Slowly Hella gripped the woman's elbow. "See if I'm lying to you. I would help you if I could, but this way you're only going to watch your daughter die and kill Scatter in the process. Both of them don't have to die."

Ocastya stood beside Colleen for a moment, and Hella thought the fractoid was going to stab the woman. Instead Ocastya's gaze rested on the feverish girl. "My mate and I wanted to have children. We never had the opportunity." She shifted her attention to Colleen. "I am sorry for your loss, but I will not lose my mate. If you do not free him, you will soon join your daughter in death."

CHAPTER 33

"Colleen." Hella pulled on the woman, turning her attention from her child and Ocastya. "Trust me. I'm sorry but we're telling you the truth. This isn't going to work. You can't save your daughter by using Scatter that way."

Colleen wrapped her hand around one of Hella's. Immediately a bright, hot pain slashed through Hella's mind. At first she thought Colleen was mentally attacking her; then she realized that the woman had just blown through her defenses in an effort to get to the truth. The pain subsided slightly, and Hella felt Colleen rifling through her thoughts.

A moment later Colleen pulled away. "No. *No.* I was supposed to be able to save Alice. That's why I dreamed about the fractoids. I used my precog power to find a way to *save* Alice. That's why I saw them entering our world. I *saw* myself saving her. This can't be true."

Ocastya grabbed the woman's arm and shook her. "Save my mate. Do it now, and you can still be with your daughter in her final moments."

The declaration was cold and vicious, but Hella couldn't fault Ocastya. If Stampede's life had hung in the balance, Hella knew she would have been just as focused and driven.

Angrily Ocastya shook Colleen and pushed her toward the computer. "Do it now."

Trembling, overcome with pain and sorrow, Colleen tapped commands on the keyboard. Ocastya stood at her side, watching the scrolling numbers, letters, and symbols on the computer monitors.

Grimly, Hella split her attention among the computer screen, the security monitors, and Scatter. She didn't know how any of it would end. Alice's breathing thickened and became more troubled. Hella hated standing there, knowing she was listening to the little girl's last moments. She'd heard people die before, had held some of them in her arms, but Alice would leave her marked forever.

"There." Colleen tried to speak more but she couldn't. She pulled away from Ocastya's grip and returned to the hospital bed. She took her daughter's limp hand in hers.

In the security images, Riley led the hardshells down the stairwell. Others took a nearby elevator that was still working.

Scatter moved suddenly then reached up and took the wires in one hand to rip them free. He stood and embraced Ocastya.

Ocastya looked at him. The high-pitched machine language filled the air.

Scatter wound his fingers in those of his mate. The machine language passed back and forth between them so loud and so piercing that Hella wanted to plug her ears. She concentrated on the security images.

Riley and his team had reached the fourth-floor landing.

Hella looked at Stampede as she morphed her hands into weapons. "They're here."

Stampede's ears twitched as he snorted angrily. "We played this one too close, Red. My fault." He readied his rifle.

"You can apologize after we get out of here." Hella took a deep breath. "We're still getting out of here, right?"

An evil grin spread across Stampede's face. "Yeah." He held up the remote control for the satchel charges they'd left in the fourth-floor landing. "Button up."

Hella pulled a face mask from her chest pouch and put it on. The mask filtered out the smoke and pepper gas in the satchel charges.

"Do you know where Pardot is?"

A quick check of the security images showed Pardot's location on the third-floor landing. "One floor above. He's in the stairwell."

Stampede looked at her. "Don't hesitate, Red. Those guys would have killed us if they had the chance."

"I know."

"No mercy."

"I know."

"And don't make me come after you."

Hella blew out a breath.

"Go!" Stampede pressed the remote control. The satchel charges blew immediately, filling the hallway with thunder, screams, and flying body parts.

Hella whipped around the doorway and ran into the maelstrom of death. The satchels had been packed with flash-bangs that disrupted the hardshells' vid and aud feeds as well. A small EMP explosive detonated on the second wave, flashing a system-killing pulse that threw the hardshells' musculature off.

The hardshells struggled to stay on their feet, fighting against systems that no longer supported them or moved the way they wanted to. That was the primary reason Stampede didn't embrace technology. In a heartbeat cybernetic infrastructures and smart programs could be disrupted.

Hella's nanobots shivered, and she feared that she would be affected as well.

"Concentrate, Hella." Scatter's voice echoed inside her skull. "Your nanobots are not like those systems in the hardshells. Yours are part of you; they are tied to you in ways those men in those suits will never know. You are stronger, faster, and better than any of them. You know what your body is supposed to be like. This is just like the burn scarring you recovered from."

Pistols blazing in front of her, bullets punching into and throwing the hardshells, Hella concentrated on the rhythm Scatter had taught her. With every rapid step, even at the speed she was moving, her body grew more controlled. She was a blur, getting faster, getting more sure-footed. And she was death for every hardshell in the hallway who lifted a weapon in her direction.

The armor-piercing rounds she created for the assault took longer to form, but they were there when she needed them. They ripped through the hardshells.

In the stairwell, operating at a speed she'd never before reached, she planted her left weapon in the face of a man who managed to intercept her by design or by accident. The bullets ripped him away, and blood misted her vision.

She leaped over a dead man lying at the bottom of the steps, avoided another man who reached for her, and brought her knee up into the man's crotch. Right before impact, she imagined a protective layer of armor over her knee, and it was there. Instead of injuring herself on the hardshell, her knee caved in the armor and knocked the man away.

Morphing her left weapon back into a hand, she grabbed another man as she went up the stairs and levered him across her hip into freefall between the stairwells. He fell another floor and lay still. By then she had continued advancing, and her hand was a weapon again.

She head-butted another man and bulled him back with her speed. Then she whirled out of his embrace, weapons flared out and tracking targets on the stairwell. She ran toward the wall, stepped onto a fallen man, and ran up onto the wall. Hurling herself into the air, she flipped and fired ceaselessly. When she landed on her feet, she was behind Pardot.

Wrapping her left arm under Pardot's chin and pressing hard against his neck, Hella held the muzzles of her right weapon against Pardot's head.

In front of and around her, hardshells struggled to get to their feet and level their weapons at her.

Hella pulled Pardot backward with her till she reached the wall. She shook the small man viciously. "Tell them to put their weapons down, or I'm going to kill you."

Dazed, shaking in fright, Pardot raised his hands. "Put down your weapons! Put them down!"

The blank faceplates on the hardshells didn't show any emotions, but Hella read the anger and fear in the men's body language. They wanted her dead, and her life briefly swayed on the shifting emotions. She and Stampede knew if they couldn't get Scatter and get gone without a confrontation, the stairwell was the best hope they had of gaining the upper hand. It had been an all-or-nothing risk, but it was something they had used before. Against a group controlled by someone, it would work, not against a disorganized gang.

But a group was an animal, every bit as wild and unpredictable as any creature living in the forest. The only law an animal obeyed was one for survival.

"Put your weapons down! I order you to do as she says!"

From below, leaking blood down his right side, Riley climbed the stairs and forced his way to the front of the group. He held his rifle in both hands, taking aim at Hella.

"Are we okay out there?" Stampede's voice was loud enough to carry into the stairwell from the laboratory.

"Not sure yet." Hella held her fright in check. She wished she had a faceplate like those on the hardshells. Her face grew itchy, and she felt the nanobots stirring beneath her skin. Her reflection showed in Riley's face shield. As she watched, metal plates formed around her face and created a shield the color of her hair. She didn't know if it was bulletproof, but it looked thick enough. Her astonishment numbed her for just an instant; then she focused on survival. "Got a few guys up here who seem to be determined to hang on to their weps."

"Riley."

Riley ignored Stampede.

"*Riley.*"

"Yeah?"

"I know you care about Hella. Maybe that's enough for you. If it's not, it's gonna play out like this: if you kill her, I've got a secondary charge in that stairwell that will kill everyone."

Riley never flickered. His rifle remained unwavering.

"Did you hear me?"

"Yeah."

"That's the deal. The next move is yours."

Pardot swallowed hard and Hella felt the effort against the inside of her arm. "I told you to put your weapon down."

"You got my men killed, you pompous little rat." Riley's voice was thick with emotion. He waved one hand at the dead lying around him. Only four hardshells seemed capable of standing. A few others moved on the floor. "I told you not to play with these people. I told you I wanted to take this insertion slowly. But you were in a hurry."

"Put your weapon down, Captain. You have your instructions." Pardot almost had that commanding sneer back, as if he were the one calling the shots.

"Yeah. I guess I do." Slowly Riley lowered his rifle to the floor. Then he stepped forward. "Stampede, if we let you go—"

"You're not letting us go; we're letting you go."

"Sure. Do you care if Pardot comes out of this in one piece?"

"No."

"Okay." Riley popped the blade from his forearm and punched it through Pardot's skull. The exo whirred out of control. Pardot managed one shrill scream. "Hella's fine."

"Hella?"

Stepping away from Pardot, Hella let the man fall, not believing what had just happened. "I'm fine." She trained her weapons on Riley, aware of the blood that dripped across her face shield and her blouse.

"Bring them down."

The hardshells lined up at her command. They managed to pick up three men who were still alive in the tangle of dead. Then she escorted them down to the lab.

■　■　■　■　■

Riley and the other guards sat against one wall in the lab. The only sounds in the room were the cries of the wounded and the plaintive mewling of Alice Trammell as she succumbed to her disease. Colleen watched helplessly, crying silently as her daughter lost her battle.

Scatter and Ocastya talked in their language, and Hella sensed they were emotionally affected. They never looked away from Alice. Finally Scatter broke off and approached Colleen. "There is something we might be able to do."

Colleen looked up at them, her eyes hollow and empty. "What?"

"Possibly we can save her. Will you allow us to try?"

"Yes. Whatever you need."

Scatter stood on one side of the bed. Ocastya stood on the other. Each of them put one hand on Alice's head, and they held hands. "Saving her body is impossible. The disease has taken that from her. But we may be able to save that part of your daughter that makes her the person you know."

Colleen's tears rolled down her face.

A lump formed in the back of Hella's throat, and she couldn't swallow it down. Tears slid down her face as well.

Scatter and Ocastya stood still as statues, their bodies gleaming. Then golden light pulsed along their skins. Alice's pain-filled cries silenced, and she seemed to settle into a deeper sleep. For a moment Hella thought the little girl had perished. Then she saw a pulse beating at the hollow of her throat.

Ocastya and Scatter raised their joined hands over the little girl, and a stream of silver metal gleamed as it spun down and poured over Alice. In the space of a drawn breath, the liquid metal formed a shell over the girl. Then the medical machines screamed alerts as her heart stopped and her struggling respiration ceased.

"No!" Colleen stepped forward.

At the same time, Scatter took his hand from Alice's head and held it out. "Alice?"

Incredibly the girl's hand lifted. Only it wasn't her hand. It was the silver metal shell. She gripped Scatter's hand in her two-dimensional hand and sat up. The silver replica of the girl was perfect in every way, but she rose off her dead body.

Alice looked down at her torso and ran her free hand along her body. She looked up at Colleen. "Mommy?"

"Alice." Colleen took her daughter's hand. "Alice? Can you hear me?"

"I can." Alice smiled and the silvery expression was childlike and innocent. "My stomach doesn't hurt anymore."

As Hella watched, the girl's body thickened and filled in as the fragments replicated themselves. Ocastya and Scatter kept her hands on the girl's shoulders, and Hella was certain they were adding to Alice's body, giving to her from themselves. Hella wept unashamedly.

EPILOGUE

"I guess Trazall lit a shuck." Stampede stood outside the mil-plex and glared down over the forest farther down the mountain.

"You keep standing there, maybe he'll spot you and have one of his snipers take you out."

Stampede shifted his glare over to Hella. "If they were out here, I'd know it."

Hella wanted to be away from the place. Death clung to it. Corpses lay everywhere. She'd already stripped as much gear and supplies as she dared. Daisy was packed heavy and shifted under the burden. She wouldn't have to carry it far, though. They could trade along the nearest road or unload it at a trade post.

Only a few meters away, Alice took joy in her new mobility. She'd been bedridden for more than a year with her illness. Except for the silver coloration, she looked like a little girl.

"Has Scatter told Trammell that her daughter is going to have to stay with them?"

Hella nodded. "Yeah. She didn't sound too surprised. I think she had that figured after learning about the bond between Scatter and Ocastya."

Stampede shifted his rifle over his shoulder. "What's Trammell going to do?"

"Go with them."

"And where are they going to go?"

"I was going to talk to you about that."

Stampede grimaced. "We travel faster alone, Red. You know that."

"I do. I was thinking they could come with us till they find a place of their own."

"Might be hard for them to trust Trammell."

"None of them have a choice, not if they want to keep Alice happy."

"They didn't have to take on that burden or risk losing themselves saving her."

Hella looked over at Stampede and smiled. "I've known a few people that didn't turn away from that burden when it came up. We risked a lot coming here to help Scatter and Ocastya."

Stampede's ears twitched. "We got lucky."

"Only people who put it all out there on the line get lucky. I seem to recall somebody telling me that."

"Just means stupidity rubs off." Stampede nodded at Riley, who was approaching them. "Looks like you got company." He hesitated. "Whatever you decide, Red, you know I love you." Before Hella could ask him what he meant, Stampede walked away.

Hella started to go after him, but Riley called out to her. He stopped in front of her, and his faceplate popped open. Bruises showed on his face, proving he'd gotten pretty rattled inside the hardshell when the explosions had gone off in the stairwell.

"Dr. Trammell says you're about to leave."

Hella nodded. "We are."

"About that." Riley cleared his throat. "Look, I know we've been through a lot getting here, but I may never be this way again."

Thinking about that possibility made Hella's heart ache more than she thought it would.

"I wanted to ask you, before you left and before the zeppelin we've sent for arrives, if you wanted to come with me."

Excitement flared through Hella. Over the past several days, her imagination had toyed with that idea.

"I mean, it's probably strange after everything that's happened, but I want you to know that I wouldn't have allowed Pardot to kill you. There was a line there, and I wouldn't have crossed it. I hope you know that."

Looking at Riley's handsome face, Hella believed that was the truth. But she knew the decision could just as easily have gone the other way.

"You should see our world, Hella." Riley spoke low and excited. "It's a real civilization. We have roads, homes, plenty to eat. I would love to show it to you." Before she knew what he was going to do, he leaned in and kissed her. His lips felt hot and demanding against hers. She didn't break contact for a while. She'd never been kissed before and wanted to know what it was like.

And for just a moment, she was certain she knew what it was like to be in love.

Then she pulled away and knew she had a stupid smile on her face.

Riley smiled back hopefully.

"No." Her voice was a croak that she had to force out. "Your world and mine, they're not so different. Your world has predators in it too. If I stay in my world, I know the predators here. Most of them at least." She shook her head. "And I don't trust you. Not now and not ever. You can't just fix trust when it's been broken. I can do a lot of things, but I can't do that." She turned and walked away from him, knowing her answer had hurt him but that it had been true.

Stampede stood beside Daisy and waited.

"What?" Hella grinned at him. "Did you really think you'd be rid of me that easily?"

"I wasn't sure."

"You didn't like Riley from the beginning."

"Not when I saw he was interested in you."

"If I decide to spend time with a guy, it'll be one you approve of."

"We'll see."

Hella vaulted onto Daisy's back. "I'm ready to shake the dust of this place off me."

"Me too." Stampede called out to the rest of their group. Scatter and Ocastya walked hand in hand, but Colleen and Alice—very excited by the prospect of riding the mountain boomer—joined Hella on Daisy.

Together they headed west down the mountain. Hella looked back at Riley standing apart from the rest of the team, but she had no regrets.

THE END

THE ABYSSAL PLAGUE

From the molten core of a dead universe

Hunger
Spills a seed of evil

Fury
So pure, so concentrated, so infectious

Hate
Its corruption will span worlds

The Temple of Yellow Skulls
Don Bassingthwaite
March 2011

Sword of the Gods
Bruce Cordell
April 2011

Under the Crimson Sun
Keith R.A. DeCandido
June 2011

Oath of Vigilance
James Wyatt
August 2011

Shadowbane
Erik Scott de Bie
September 2011

Find these novels at your favorite bookseller.
Also available as ebooks.

DungeonsandDragons.com

LEWIS, the master of all video games

PAUL, the sports star

SARA, the straight-A class president

JAKE, the juvenile delinquent

They'd played at being heroes—casting magic missiles, fighting back dragons and goblins, conquering terrible villains. And then one afternoon, this unlikely group stumbles on a secret door and slips into the world they'd only imagined. Ready or not, the Nentir Vale desperately needs them.

It's Time for Them to Learn It's More Than a Game

DUNGEONS & DRAGONS
Nentir Warriors

The Lost Portal
A.M. Jenkins
September 2011

The Hidden Shrine
Ree Soesbee
November 2011

Find these great novels at your local bookseller.
Also available as ebooks.

DungeonsandDragons.com

BOOKS FOR
YOUNG READERS

Get More Out of Your D&D® Experience.

Add more to your characters and campaigns with a constantly growing source of new and exclusive tools and online applications like:

D&D CHARACTER BUILDER
D&D COMPENDIUM
D&D ADVENTURE TOOLS

Plus articles, art, maps, galleries, and other exclusive content.

Level up your game at
DungeonsandDragons.com

3 1901 04968 4022